Heart of the Patriot

by

Stuart W. Reid

**Grosvenor House
Publishing Limited**

Stuart W. Reid is hereby identified as author of this
work in accordance with Section 77 of the Copyright, Designs
and Patents Act 1988

The book cover picture is copyright to Stuart W. Reid

This book is published by
Grosvenor House Publishing Ltd
28-30 High Street, Guildford, Surrey, GU1 3HY.
www.grosvenorhousepublishing.co.uk

A CIP record for this book
is available from the British Library

ISBN 978-1-906645-45-8

For Matt and Gareth,
the best friends a man could have

Prologue

He kept running. It was pitch-black, total darkness all around, and it took all his concentration to find his way between the pine trees. The sound of his laboured breathing filled his ears. His heart pounded furiously. Sticks cracked beneath his feet, piercing the still night air like gunfire. The mist was settling over the forest now, reducing visibility to just a few metres; looking over his shoulder he saw nothing but the impenetrable cloak of night. He had no idea if they were still behind him but he couldn't risk stopping to find out. The thought of what they would do to him was too much to bear.

The choice was made for him. As he moved between two trees, he caught his foot on something and fell to the ground heavily. Rolling over on to his back he sat up, looking back in the direction from which he had come. Nothing. Feeling a sharp pain in his lip he instinctively reached a hand up. His fingertips were tinged with blood, the barrel of his weapon bloodied where it had hit him in the face.

He heard a dog bark somewhere out in the fog. A voice called out and the dog barked again, closer this time. He pulled himself up on to his feet and stood still, listening for a moment. Another voice called out nearby. He turned around and starting running again. It began to rain, softly at first but as he reached a clearing in the woods it was getting heavier. The ground that had been firm underfoot was softer here; the going became more and more arduous.

Without warning his legs collapsed from under him and he dropped to the ground. He tried to move, to get away from the spot where he had fallen, but he couldn't; his arms and legs did not respond to his commands. Looking up and finding himself lying in the undergrowth beneath a giant oak tree rather than in the open, he breathed a sigh of relief. The rain was driving hard by this time and he hoped that might put the dogs off his scent. It was a lot to hope for. He put his head down and passed out.

CHAPTER ONE

London, June 1944

The clock continued to tick. The room was silent except for the incessant sound as the seconds ticked by slowly, piercing the consciousness like a needle. The sun was trying to get in through the window but was denied by the heavy dark curtains that were drawn across. A single thin shaft of light was all that made it through, stretching across the worn and tired carpet, curling up the back wall to the ceiling. The sheets on the bed were sprawled over the mattress where they had been tucked in lazily. The room was bare; white walls, sparingly furnished with an old tattered wardrobe and dresser, a small wooden table and the armchair where he sat.

The bottle of cheap whisky on the table was almost empty but still the alcohol was having no effect. Johannes Sneijder had not slept properly in months. He was like a ghost, a soulless spectre that occupied no real place in the physical world. His senses were numbed; his mind felt like it had been in an ice bucket. Each day he was merely existing, holding a marker until the day he would be ready to step back into his life; a day far ahead.

He could barely see the glass in his hand in the half-light but he got it to his lips and felt the warm scotch wash down him. As he leaned over to put the glass on the table, his hand started shaking. The glass slipped from his fingers and dropped to the floor.

Sneijder watched it roll to the wall and stop. He sat for a few moments, and then reached down the side of the chair for the bottle of barbiturates which was also nearly empty. He took a couple of pills out and swallowed them, washing them down with a swig from the whisky bottle. He closed his eyes, but his mind would not switch off. And that clock! That damned clock! Sneijder rubbed his eyes and stood up slowly, staggering to the wall and putting a hand out to steady himself. He picked the alarm clock up off the dresser and put it under the bed-sheets, then moved to the window and peeled back the curtain.

It was a warm summer afternoon, the sun high in the cloudless sky. In the street below, people were going about their business. It could have been a day like any other; it was hard to imagine that there was a war on. It was almost three weeks since the Allied invasion of Normandy and Eisenhower's forces were blazing a trail through France with remarkable speed. The final assault on Cherbourg was underway after the German forces had declined the chance to surrender, under express orders from the *Führer* to fight to the end. The British XXX Corps would launch their offensive at Rauray, ten miles west of Caen, in the next couple of days. In Italy, British troops had entered Perugia with little resistance, and American forces would soon take Piombino Harbour in Tuscany. The Germans were collapsing on all fronts and for the first time in years there were whispers about victory, but they would surely not surrender their homeland easily.

Sneijder could still hear ticking. He ripped the sheets off the bed in frustration and picked up the alarm clock, wrestling with it for a moment in an attempt to get it open. It was useless. He threw the clock violently at the wall to stop the interminable racket; it bounced off and settled in the middle of the floor. It stopped ticking.

Sneijder breathed a sigh of relief and sat down on the end of the bed. He stared straight ahead, a blank expression on his face, his mind somewhere between awake and asleep. He couldn't understand it; all the nights in occupied territory, from his escape in Austria until he reached England, he'd slept perfectly well but as soon as he was safe, the memory of what he'd done had come back to him. Now it wouldn't leave him alone. Sneijder lay back on to the bed and closed his eyes, and finally felt himself drifting into sleep.

There was a knock at the door and Sneijder woke with a start. He'd been having that dream again, the one where he was back in that damned prison. He'd spent sixteen months in that God-forsaken place; and for sixteen of them he'd been trying to escape. The memories flooded back to him on the few occasions he slept. 'Yes?' he called out groggily.

The muffled voice of the hotel proprietor came in reply from the other side of the door. 'Mr Sneijder, there is a telephone call for you.'

Sneijder went downstairs to the telephone booth in the reception area and answered the phone weakly. 'It's me. Go ahead.'

'Confirm codename,' the voice on the other end of the line said.

'Polo,' said Sneijder.

'Confirmed. We need you to come in, Polo.'

'When?'

'Tomorrow morning, nine o'clock. N3's office. And bring the report with you.'

The line went dead and Sneijder replaced the receiver. He made his way back upstairs and went into the small bathroom across the hall to splash some cold water on his face. His mind turned to the report he was yet to complete. It was ridiculous; after everything he'd been through to get back to England, they'd arrested him on his return and accused him of being a German spy. Three months later they still weren't convinced of his story.

Sneijder looked up and saw his reflection in the mirror. He was looking at a stranger, a tired shadow of a man. He was only twenty-four years old, but the man staring back at him looked more like forty-four, with skin pulled taut over his cheekbones, wrinkles which creased his forehead and light brown hair which was long and unkempt. The stubble that covered his chin was growing into a full beard and Sneijder remembered that he hadn't shaved in a fortnight. His bare chest, though toned and muscular, was covered in scratches and bruises.

Sneijder hadn't been taking care of himself; he'd just sat in his hotel room and tried to sleep while his thoughts pounded in his head. He had no reason to feel guilty; he'd done what he'd had to. But he had still done it, and it reverberated in his mind like a perpetual echo.

'Look at yourself,' Sneijder said aloud in English, then he repeated in his native Dutch: 'Just look at yourself! What are you doing?' The frustrated desperation in his own voice was a surprise to him. 'They're dead, Johannes. They're all dead and you know it.'

The gravity of his words hit him like an express train and he exploded, swinging his hand fiercely across the top of the sink, scattering everything that was placed there. A bottle of aftershave shattered on the tiled floor. Sneijder slumped down on the floor, put his head in his hands and was still.

An hour later he was still sitting in the same position with a concentrated look on his face as he thought. It was time to let go of the past before it consumed him completely. It was a war, and everybody was forced to do things they didn't want to do in a war. It may have felt like cold-blooded murder, but all he had done was eliminate an enemy, and an animal of a man at that.

Sneijder stood up slowly. '*Right, it's time to get a grip.*' When he returned to his room he found it almost in darkness. He opened the curtains and leant out of the window, feeling the warm summer breeze on his face. It was approaching sunset and the sky was orange and gold as the sun dropped behind the city. The narrow side street below was deserted now and the only sound was that of the evening traffic.

Sneijder pinned the curtains back and moved back to the bed, switching on the small lamp on the bed-side table. He opened the leather-bound writing pad that lay next to it, took out the silver fountain pen which was inside and set about examining what he had written so far in his account of the last twenty months.

Sneijder had been dropped by parachute into occupied Holland in October of '42 with the intention of moving to Amsterdam, his home city. His mission had been to make contact with members of the Council of Resistance, the RvV, who were rumoured to be active in the area, and to co-ordinate sabotage on occupying German forces. However, the reception committee that awaited him when he landed was somewhat different to what he anticipated. The Abwehr, German military intelligence, had arrested him at the drop zone.

For the following year and a half Sneijder had been imprisoned in an old Catholic seminary along with one hundred and fifty other political prisoners. The regime at the prison was hard and Sneijder had made several escape attempts. One of these break-outs had very nearly succeeded and the commandant had acted swiftly to prevent a similar occurrence in the future; the next day Sneijder was shipped off to the concentration camp at Mauthausen in Austria.

Sneijder was not proud of what had happened there, and had omitted much of it from the report. The man in question had been Nazi scum and had been responsible for the deaths of thousands of people, but still Sneijder was ashamed and he wanted to keep the matter to himself. He'd escaped – that was all anybody needed to know.

The report was highly detailed as both MI5 and Sneijder's own superiors demanded. They were obsessed with minute details; the heights of fences, the colours of wooden posts, the brand of cigarettes that the guards carried. Every time he misremembered something and described it differently to previous inmates' accounts, it was put to him as evidence that proved he was lying. There was widespread paranoia about infiltration by German double-agents, the result of which was that Sneijder had received harder treatment at the hands of the British than at those of the Germans.

Sneijder spent an hour completing the report. When he finished he realised it was now dark outside and he had better draw the blackout curtains before one of

those Home Guard types came up to admonish or eve
arrest him. As he went to close the window a sudden feeling of fatigue came over him. Within minutes of lying
down he was out cold.

The alarm clock rang, the bell loud and shrill. For a
few seconds, Sneijder regretted spending half-an-hour
the previous night trying to fix the damned thing but he
needed to get up. In reality he welcomed the opportunity
to do something other than just sit around with his
thoughts to bother him. He reached out an arm with his
eyes closed and fumbled around for the clock, eventually
silencing it.

It was seven a.m. but Sneijder had not had much
sleep. Unable to open his eyes after a minute of trying he
stumbled blindly across the room, through the hallway
and into the bathroom. He took a bath and shaved, then
found a pair of scissors in his bag which he used to cut
his hair. Though he did not make a good job of it, it was
at least short and fairly presentable. Afterwards he found
a white shirt and a black tie in the bottom of his suitcase
and then opened the wardrobe to find the one thing he
hung up; a dark grey two-piece linen suit.

When he stood in front of the bathroom mirror
moments later, the difference from the previous day was
remarkable. Sneijder looked like a young man again, and
more importantly he looked and felt alive. His head
throbbed slightly from all the alcohol he'd drank the
previous day and he needed something to eat, but apart
from that, he felt good.

Sneijder took a breakfast of porridge and a cup of tea
in the small dining room, and left the hotel just after
eight-thirty. It was a dull and overcast morning as Sneijder made his way south along Baker Street, cool with a

...lly breeze, and he was glad that he was wearing a long overcoat. He stopped to buy a newspaper outside the Underground station; a train must have pulled in because a large crowd swelled in the doorway. A red London double-decker bus stopped nearby and scooped up some pedestrians.

Sneijder crossed Marylebone Road and continued south. The buildings became taller and more claustrophobic either side of the narrow street, six- and seven-storey Victorian designs, and much of the street was in shadow. The crowds thinned out as Sneijder passed Paddington Street and approached his destination. He soon came upon it, 82 Baker Street, a beautiful building made of grey stone with flashes of Victorian embellishment. The upper two floors were separated off from the rest of the building by a wide ledge and it looked like they had been added to the building at a later date. Gabled windows lined the roof.

Sneijder went in, nodding to the doorman whose eyes conveyed recognition. He passed without incident and registered his arrival with the pretty girl at the reception. On the desk there was a notice with the words 'Ministry of Economic Warfare'. She lifted the telephone receiver, turned her back and covered her mouth as she spoke. After a few moments, she replaced the phone and instructed, 'Okay, go on up. You know where to go?'

Sneijder smiled, replied, 'Top floor but one,' and took to the staircase. At the top he found himself in a darkened corridor, and at the end turned into an outer office. Bright light poured in from the large windows. At a desk there was a middle-aged woman on a typewriter, and a man of a similar age was standing behind her peering over her shoulder. A pair of reading glasses rested on his nose.

He turned when he saw Sneijder. 'Ah, Polo. Thank you for coming in.' He nodded towards the file tucked under Sneijder's arm. 'Is that the report?'

Sneijder nodded.

'Good. Let's hope MI5 have the good sense to drop the matter now.' The man smiled warmly. 'Right, mustn't keep you. N3's waiting.' As Sneijder walked towards the door the man added, 'I ought to warn you, he's got company. Some chap from the BBO, name of De Beer.'

Sneijder knocked on the door and was told to enter. It was a large office with dark wood-panelled walls and a light brown carpet, tastefully furnished with comfortable leather chairs, a small table and well-stocked bookcases. There were two men sitting at opposite sides of the large mahogany desk and they stood as he went in, removed his coat and hung it up.

The man standing directly in front of the large floor-to-ceiling window leaned across and offered a hand which Sneijder shook. 'Sneijder. It's good to see you,' he said in a clipped public school accent. His name was Harry Wilkinson and he was over six feet tall with grey hair and a moustache, both of which seemed to contradict the freshness of his face and made it difficult to guess his age. His clothing gave no clues as he wore dark green military uniform which sported a cluster of medal ribbons. 'This is Major de Beer from the BBO.'

The man he indicated was short, chubby rather than fat, balding, with round silver spectacles. The BBO was the *Bureau voor Bijzondere Opdrachten*, the Office of Special Operations. It was an organisation of the Dutch government-in-exile in London, who usually liked to keep their activities separate from those of the British government. These were troubled times in the world, and trust was at a premium.

'Here's the report you asked for, sir,' Sneijder said. 'I believe it is as complete as I can make it, bearing in mind how long ago some of it was.' He handed his report to Wilkinson, whose assigned codename of N3 indicated that he was third in command in N section, the department which dealt with subversive operations in the Netherlands. The overall head of this section was code-named simply N but for reasons of security he was never risked in the field and rarely met agents personally.

'Oh, good,' replied Wilkinson. 'I'll read through it and pass it on to MI5. Hopefully that will be the end of this nonsense. You must understand, we have never doubted you here.'

'It's okay, sir. MI5 are just doing their job.'

Wilkinson was taken aback. 'That's very gracious of you, Sneijder. You're right of course; they are just doing their job.' He put the file to one side without looking at it. 'But on to more pressing matters.'

Sneijder took a seat next to De Beer, who up until now had not spoken. Sneijder wondered what the other Dutchman was doing there.

Wilkinson continued, 'As you know, the Dutch organisations are not in the practice of working with us here at the Special Operations Executive. However, this is a matter of some........ sensitivity. I shall let Major de Beer explain further.'

De Beer pulled a couple of brown files from the leather satchel at his feet and tossed them on the table in front of Sneijder, then began speaking in heavily-accented English. 'I've been reading through these; your personnel and operational files. Very impressive, I must say. Good reports from all your instructors, a commendation from Arisaig for your marksmanship, and you completed the training course in record time.' He turned to Wilkinson. 'A very capable man.'

Wilkinson smiled. 'Yes, he's done well.' He turned to face Sneijder. 'I should explain something to you before we go any further. As you are aware, it is SOE policy not to return to the field any agent that has been captured and interrogated by the enemy. I have to abide by these rules; it's out of my hands. However, it seems a waste to have a man like you sitting around doing nothing when you could be serving your country. Major de Beer has a job that needs doing and I thought you might be interested.'

De Beer stood and moved across the room to the projector which sat on a table. He switched it on and a fuzzy image appeared on the white screen that hung opposite. 'Harry, the blinds please.' Wilkinson pulled the heavy blackout blinds across the window and the room was plunged into darkness, the only light that which was coming from the projector. Sneijder turned around in his chair so that he could see the screen. He now observed that the image was a photograph of a group of men in SS uniform.

'A regiment of the SS,' said De Beer. 'A regiment like any other except every man you see in front of you is Dutch. I'm sure you must have run into a few of these guys while you were imprisoned.'

'There were one or two, yes.'

'They call themselves the Germanic SS. We're not exactly sure about the number of Dutch citizens who have joined up but it runs into the thousands. Some have remained in the Netherlands but a large number have served in the Waffen-SS on the eastern front, fighting our Russian allies.'

Sneijder grimaced. 'Eastern front? I'll bet they weren't told they were going there when they joined up.'

De Beer continued, 'A large proportion of the people in the Germanic SS are members of the NSB. As for the others, I suppose they were either promised some kind of reward for joining up, or were forced into it with the threat of violence.'

The *Nationaal-Socialistische Beweging,* or NSB, was the prominent right-wing political party in the Netherlands, and the only party not banned under the German occupation. They had largely fallen under Nazi control and their members filled many positions of power in Holland.

'Whatever the reason, this treason is unacceptable and will not be tolerated,' De Beer went on. 'It is extremely damaging to morale back home to see your own men not only oppressing Dutch civilians, but actively fighting for the Germans against the Allies. Our government is hugely embarrassed by the whole thing and is concerned that it will adversely affect our standing with other countries.'

De Beer moved the projector on to the next slide. It was a photograph of a wall riddled with bullet holes, several bodies lying in the road in front of it. 'This was in Rotterdam. The work of Dutch members of the SS in response to a Resistance attack on a power station. The Germanic SS have already been a part of many atrocities, and will be a part of more. They have personally carried out countless reprisals for Resistance activities against the Germans and killed many innocent people.'

'How many have died?' Sneijder inquired.

'To be honest, we just don't know,' De Beer replied gravely. 'All the reports we've had are sketchy and we don't know which of our operatives have been compromised. As you yourself have experienced, it is so easy to be duped by German intelligence.

'The point is that it is time we did something about it. Our information suggests the Germans plan to step up recruitment of Dutch civilians into the SS following the Normandy invasion. The Germans already have native Waffen-SS units to defend the Netherlands against Allied forces. Just think about it; when the fighting gets there, we could end up with Dutchmen fighting against the force that has come to liberate the country.'

'Surely they'd all desert as soon as the Allies arrived?' Sneijder commented.

'Not necessarily. They are specifically targeting fascists from the NSB movement for recruitment to prevent just that scenario. These men feel more loyalty to the Nazis than to their own country.'

'I see,' Sneijder mused. 'So what are you proposing to do about it?'

'The Dutch SS are led by a Dutchman named Johannes Hendrikus Feldmeijer.' De Beer moved to the projector and the image changed to a photograph of a young man in black SS uniform. 'A pretty despicable individual I can tell you, and a committed Nazi. Being an important officer and a Dutchman, he has always been our number one target but our intelligence has found that getting to him would be almost impossible. So we've started to look further down the chain of command to see where we could inflict some damage on SS operations. We came up with this man.'

The projector moved on to a photograph of an older man also dressed in black SS uniform. On his hat was the Nazi military insignia - the eagle clasping the swastika - and below that the chilling skull symbol, the *totenkopf* or 'death's head.' The man's face was large and fat with a double chin, and his eyes were clear behind the thin-rimmed spectacles. Instantly, for a reason he could not explain – perhaps the blankness of the stare or the slightly down-turned lips - Sneijder was struck with the impression of a man resigned to who he was, a man who did not enjoy the position in which he had found himself as a member of the infamous SS.

'This is SS Obersturmbannführer Albrecht Koestler,' De Beer announced. 'A veteran of the Great War, with a distinguished military career behind him. He is now a high-ranking member of the SS in Holland, with links to Feldmeijer, and a personal favourite of the High Commissioner, Reichskommisar Seyss-Inquart. He is heavily involved in the recruitment of civilians into the Germanic SS. Over the years he has cultivated an excel-lent relationship with the NSB and gets plenty of volun-teers. He has one of the highest success rates in the SS.'

'Where is he based?' Sneijder questioned.

'Arnhem,' De Beer said. 'Amongst his other duties he is in charge of SS recruitment in Gelderland province, although his NSB contacts in the major cities send a lot of people his way from other parts of the country. That's why he enjoys so much success. He's not a man who likes to be in danger so he stays as far from the front and as close to Germany as he can manage. The good thing from our point of view is that there are fewer German soldiers around to get in the way.'

'In the way of what?' Sneijder asked.

De Beer raised his eyebrows, glancing quickly at Wilkinson. 'Come now, Mr Sneijder, you know exactly what I'm talking about. Liquidation of a target.'

'You want me to go to Arnhem and kill this Koestler?'

'Precisely. Getting rid of this man will close down one of the SS's most productive sources of manpower.'

Sneijder thought for a moment. 'I don't understand why you've come to me and not given this task to one of your own agents? From what I've been told the Dutch government get the pick of suitable people; you must have someone.'

De Beer explained that he had been running an operation to assassinate SS officers, both German and Dutch, who were involved in the recruitment of civilians. It had gone well, and several officials in key positions had been removed. However, SS reprisals had become more and more brutal until it had got to the point where the Dutch government-in-exile had forbidden any more assassinations. De Beer had been ordered not to send any more agents into Holland, but it was his opinion that continuing the liquidation operation against the SS was essential. 'If we stop now because of their reprisals, it just reinforces their belief that they can do what they like. I want the SS to know that nobody is safe from us. They will not turn our own people against us without a fight.'

Wilkinson spoke up. 'So you see the problem the Major has, Sneijder - the problems we all have? The Major needs to continue his mission but cannot without disobeying the orders of Queen Wilhelmina. I have a potentially fine agent sitting here in London who I am not permitted to use, and you are left kicking your heels in England while your countrymen suffer under Nazi occupation. Taking this mission will solve all of our problems. You can go in unnoticed and raise hell, as you will not officially be working for either SOE or the BBO, and Major de Beer and I can go to our superiors and assure them that we are following orders.'

'And I suppose as an inactive agent, the theory is that if I get killed nobody will miss me? I am expendable?'

Wilkinson laughed. 'My dear boy, all of our agents are expendable. That's just the point.'

By this time De Beer had switched off the projector, opened up the blinds and taken his seat with the morning light now flooding in again through the picture windows.

Sneijder sat back and looked at his feet, frowning.

'Is something troubling you, Sneijder?' Wilkinson asked.

'Sorry, sir, but this whole thing – taking out this Koestler – it just seems like......well, like cold-blooded murder to me. Parachuting in behind the lines, getting close to the man, creeping up and popping him; that's not war - it's just killing. There is a difference.'

De Beer began to get irritated. 'Let me tell you something about war, young man. War is all about killing, whoever kills the most men wins. Sometimes it is necessary to do unpleasant things in the service of your country. Killing an enemy is killing an enemy, however it comes about. If Hitler himself was standing in this room and you had a pistol, would you shoot him?'

Sneijder hesitated. 'Er...'

'Would you like to see Koestler's work?' De Beer continued, angry now. He stood up, grabbed a pile of photographs from a file in front of him and spread them out across the desk, thumping each one down emphatically. 'Here.'

Sneijder was horrified by what he saw. Each picture was a close-up of a dead body; men, women, children. Most had bullet wounds to the head, but some had been stabbed or had their throats cut.

De Beer went on, 'Innocent people murdered, all by men put in the SS uniform by officers like Koestler. Fellow Dutchmen, your people, cut down by vicious, remorseless traitors. We must not let them get away with this.'

'Were these people not murdered as reprisals for just the type of assassination you're talking about?' replied Sneijder, riled by De Beer's attitude. 'Is killing another German not just going to make things worse? If I do this and more civilians die, it will be on my head.'

De Beer opened his mouth to say something but Wilkinson raised a hand and he fell silent. The Englishman nodded and said, 'Sneijder is right, Guido. Killing this man will lead to further reprisals and your government will want to know who authorised it. No, I think we'll need to be cleverer than that. Arrange a convenient accident for our Herr Koestler that stands up to investigation. That way no reprisals can be carried out, and it spares our boy here from having to actually pull the trigger.'

A knowing expression spread across Wilkinson's face and De Beer enquired, 'What do you have in mind?'

Wilkinson laid out a general idea. It appeared that Koestler lived in a commandeered house to the north of the city of Arnhem and travelled by car every day to his office, with an escort of a single motorcyclist. This appeared to be almost an invitation for somebody to make an attempt on his life. According to the information that De Beer produced, Koestler was very casual about his security and believed he was safe from attack.

Fortunately for him the majority of Dutch civilians were too afraid of the SS to contemplate taking out one of their officers. However his regular and therefore predictable use of a car opened up other possibilities.

Sneijder nodded when Wilkinson had finished. 'You know, sir, that might just work.'

Wilkinson winked at him. 'I didn't get to the rank of Brigadier for nothing, you know.'

De Beer turned to Sneijder. 'So, young man, in those circumstances, with the plan that the Brigadier has just described, would you do it? Would you be prepared to do what needs to be done in order to serve your country?'

Sneijder did not answer immediately and Wilkinson cut across him, 'I can't make you do this; that wouldn't be right. If you'd rather I can have you sent over to the Dutch government - I should imagine they could use an able young man like yourself - but it will be a great service to your country and the Allied war effort in general if you can take care of this man Koestler and stop the flow of traitors. Take the rest of the day to think about it and come back with your answer tomorrow. Does that suit you, Guido?'

De Beer looked unhappy but nodded.

Wilkinson leaned forward, as if to emphasise his next sentence. 'But Sneijder, if you can't decide by tomorrow, you will never be able to. And indecisive people are no good to us.'

Sneijder got out of there fast.

CHAPTER TWO

Arnhem, Holland

Across the North Sea from London the weather wasn't much better. It was a dull morning with a brisk wind and thick cloud covered eastern Holland and the German border. An air of apprehension hung over the soldiers that lined the parade yard as they awaited the arrival of their commanding officer. The uniform they wore was the standard black dress uniform of the SS, but for the shield on the helmet that carried the Dutch flag. Some men did not wear the traditional sig-runes – the archaic Germanic characters which formed the SS emblem, instead sporting the *wolfsangel* logo of the NSB.

The yard was located at the rear of a large country house the SS had commandeered on the outskirts of Arnhem, a grand old place set in extensive grounds, with wide stone stairways leading up from the gardens. The ground floor had been kept in its original condition, with a dramatic entrance hall and long dining room, but the top two floors were used for administration. Huge swastikas hung everywhere, the constant reminder of Nazi occupation.

There was the roar of an engine, a motorcycle, and then the sound of an approaching Mercedes staff car. A young soldier came out of the rear entrance and whispered something to the supervising officer who was standing at the top of the stairs. He turned to the men below and shouted an order in German. '*Achtung*! Obersturmbannführer Koestler has arrived.'

At the front of the house, the motorcycle outrider moved past the entrance and stopped. The Mercedes halted at the front door. A guard immediately came down the stairs and opened the rear door of the car. Koestler stepped out in a long, flowing brown leather overcoat and replaced his military cap. His adjutant, a captain named Klimitz followed him. As he climbed the steps a lieutenant rushed out of the door to meet him, clicked his heels together and gave a Nazi salute. 'My respects, sir.'

Koestler scowled and brushed past him, sweeping through the door. He walked straight through the house and out of the rear entrance, down the stairs to the yard. The men were lined up in formation in three rows; around two hundred of them, all fresh-faced youngsters who had no idea what they were doing. Young Dutchmen with little concept of what collaboration with the enemy would mean. That was just the way Koestler liked it; it saved a lot of trouble. Koestler walked along all three rows of men, inspecting the uniforms of the troops. As he passed, they all looked straight ahead, avoiding eye contact with their superior.

Koestler returned to stand in front of them. He whispered something to the lieutenant and was answered, then addressed the assembled ranks loudly in Dutch. 'This is it, gentlemen. Today you join the ranks of a sacred brotherhood, one that is steeped in the glorious tradition of the great Germanic people. None of you are German, but the pure Aryan blood that runs in your veins makes you all worthy to serve the Greater

Germanic Reich, and the Führer, Adolf Hitler. The oath you have taken is a vow to give everything you have to ensure final victory and the glory of the Fatherland.

'The Dutch people are close cousins of the Germans; fine, strong, well-bred members of the master race. It is your duty to protect the Germanic people from all enemies; communists, Jews, and those who would try to destroy us. Do not fail in this duty and we cannot be defeated.'

The soldiers looked on in silence, motionless.

Koestler gave a dramatic straight-arm Nazi salute and shouted at the top of his voice. '*Sieg heil!*'

The soldiers returned the salute instantly. Koestler turned and walked back into the house with his adjutant, leaving the lieutenant to organise the new recruits. The two men climbed the staircase to the first floor and went to the office of a major who was in charge of the induction procedure. Koestler knocked on the door and entered.

The man behind the desk was a young man in his mid-twenties, who had been a bomber pilot flying Dorniers until he had lost an arm in a direct flak hit over London. He was writing with his one hand, but looked up when Koestler came in. 'Sir?'

'Baumgartner, give me some good news.' Koestler sat down in the leather chair opposite the younger man. He looked at his attire. Baumgartner wore a field-grey SS tunic with Luftwaffe wings pinned on the right breast, the Knight's Cross at his neck. His trousers were army issue and he had flying boots on his feet. 'I do wish you would wear full SS uniform,' Koestler added. 'It would have made your father proud. You look like you can't decide which service you want to be in.'

'I want to be in the Luftwaffe, sir, but I can't very well pilot a plane with one arm. What sort of good news are you looking for?'

Koestler sighed. 'I don't know, something that makes what we're doing seem worthwhile. I just had to make a division of new recruits swear allegiance to the Führer. The fool is dragging Germany down with him and I'm standing out there praising him.' He laughed. 'I even mentioned victory. Perhaps I'm a bigger fool than Hitler.'

Baumgartner put down his pen and picked up a red file from the pile on his desk. He opened it, found the page he was looking for, and ran his finger down it. His hand stopped and he read from the file. 'Last month we inducted four hundred and sixty-three men. That's up from April. Most of them are already serving on the eastern front.'

'Four hundred and sixty-three?' Koestler raised his eyebrows. 'We're losing a thousand men a day to the Bolsheviks. Four hundred and sixty-three of these Dutch traitors a month are hardly going to stop the Red Army. We're treading water, Hans, waiting to be crushed. If the Allied advance keeps up pace, Germany is finished.'

Baumgartner shrugged his shoulders. 'We do what we can. This war was only ever going to end one way, from the moment we invaded Poland. It was just a question of time.'

Koestler shook his head. 'No, we had a chance of victory at the beginning. If it had all been handled differently, who knows where we would be now? If Hitler hadn't got so fixated on his personal squabble with Stalin...' He left the sentence hanging. 'Anyway, here we are, recruiting treasonous foreigners to fight our battles for us. It's going to get harder too now that I've lost another man.'

'Oh?'

'Yes – Gilbert Krol, probably my most important contact within the NSB, killed by communists in Amsterdam. He was responsible for a large number of my recruits. I will find it difficult to replace him.' Koestler stood. 'And that, in fact, is what I must be getting on with. I'll leave you to it.'

Sneijder had left the office at Baker Street as soon as he'd finished the meeting, and decided to take a walk. He'd taken away a couple of files to look over but he was determined that he would not take on the mission they were proposing. It was totally different to killing an enemy in battle, surely, he thought. He had never fought in combat himself - the Netherlands had been overrun far too quickly for that - but in the heat of war, when you had no choice but to take a life, when it was him or you, you would do what you had to. Going out after an individual on the other hand, knowing from the very first moment you saw him that you were going to kill him, that it would never be over until he lay dead; that just seemed wrong, evil even. No matter whom he was, to know that he would be alive until you took his life from him; that would be too much to bear. Sneijder was no assassin.

He had walked in no particular direction, just letting the world go by and allowing his thoughts to drift through his mind. The busy streets soon gave way to the leafy calm of Hyde Park, where the trees were full and green, the flowers bright. The cool breeze from the morning had disappeared and the sun had made its way through the clouds. As Sneijder passed Buckingham Palace and moved down the Mall, it was turning into a typical English summer's day, with the odd bit of cloud threatening to spoil a glorious afternoon. By one o'clock he had made it across the river and began to walk along the south bank. He stopped at a bench not far from Lambeth Bridge and sat looking out over the Thames towards the Houses of Parliament.

It was a good place to be, London – one of the few cities in the world not under any sort of occupation, where people were free. Except they weren't of course – the fear of what might happen to their loved ones fighting abroad gripped them tightly. Those who had not already experienced the torture of losing someone had to spend every day wondering if they would finally hear the same news that had devastated innumerable British families over the last four-and-a-half years of war. There was every reason for Sneijder to want to remain in London – it was safe, with food to go around, drink in the bars and plenty of willing female company. It could offer everything a young man could want, but that was just the problem.

Back home in Holland, young men were being rounded up and sent to Germany for forced labour. In France, Italy and South East Asia, millions of men were laying down their lives for their countries, facing the unimaginable hell of war because it was their duty, none of them knowing if they would ever see their home again. Sneijder looked around his surroundings, the fine old city in the summertime, and was immediately ashamed. He had been through a lot in this war, but what was he doing now? Men were dying in horrific circumstances to stop Hitler while Sneijder lay around a hotel room feeling sorry for himself, getting drunk to try to forget.

A dark green army truck swept across the bridge in front of him, the large red cross of the medical corps clearly visible painted on the side. In the back of the truck Sneijder could see around fifteen men, all with bandages, some missing limbs. A stretcher bearing a soldier lay in the centre. At the rear an injured man with his head wrapped in a bandage stared straight ahead, his clear blue eyes vacant. As the truck disappeared from view the sight of these broken men was etched in Sneijder's mind and when he closed his eyes, there was the piercing look of the man with the clear blue eyes. Sneijder's feelings of guilt deepened.

The files lying on the bench next to him fluttered in the wind and caught his attention. He looked down at them with a sense of compulsion. He couldn't really turn down an opportunity to do something for the war effort, could he? To refuse the mission purely for the sake of his own conscience would be an insult to the men serving on the front line and to the injured men in the back of that truck. They were facing up to their duty; it was time he did too.

He picked up the first file and leafed through it. It was written in a mixture of English and Dutch and contained intelligence reports that estimated the extent of SS recruitment in Holland, plus evidence of terrible reprisals carried out by German authorities. Sneijder had always believed in the Dutch will to resist, and the numbers of men that had been drafted into the SS surprised him.

The other file was Obersturmbannführer Koestler's personnel record. It read much like the record of many a top official in the SS; a devoted military officer who served his country well and immediately fell for Hitler's brand of national pride, his declaration that Germany was a nation above all others. The positions he had occupied in the early years of the Nazi government stood him out as a rising star in the SS. When the war had broken out he had been posted to Poland, and then to Holland. At some point his path had crossed that of Reichskommisar Arthur Seyss-Inquart, the highest Nazi authority in the Netherlands, and the senior officer had taken him under his wing. Since then Koestler had taken on a succession of safe positions, ones unlikely to lead to much contact with the enemy.

The rest of the file was filled with reports of incidents that were alleged to have taken place all across Holland under Koestler's authority. Few of these incidents could be confirmed, but they ranged from the theft of civilian property to murder in response to minor misdemeanours. As Sneijder read on, the events seemed to get worse and worse and he realised his perception of the man he was meant to kill could swiftly change. Taking a life was hard, but if these things were true? It made killing seem less of a big deal.

An image flashed suddenly through Sneijder's mind; the camp, the feeling of the pistol in his hand, the man on his knees begging for his life. In his mind he always walked away but in reality, back in that place, when he saw what he had seen, it hadn't been that hard to squeeze the trigger. He heard the loud crack of the gun going off and suddenly the man's face was in front of him, wide-eyed and lifeless, blood pouring from the hole in his forehead.

Sneijder leapt up from the bench, terrified. And then it was over, the image gone. He breathed deeply, trying to regain his composure. 'I need a drink,' he uttered to himself, then he gathered together the files and walked away to find a bar. The clock at Big Ben told him that it was approaching four o'clock when he crossed the river and began moving back towards Baker Street.

It was about fifteen minutes later that Sneijder reached Victoria Station. It was starting to get busy as the early evening rush approached and the newspaper men were out in force with the early editions. A man rushed forward through a crowd clutching a copy of the *Evening Standard*, almost barging Sneijder to the ground. He stepped over to the edge of the kerb and tried to go around the outside of a group of people who were standing on the pavement. There was a black car parked at the side of the road which Sneijder had to squeeze past, and just as he reached the rear of the vehicle, the front passenger door swung open and a thick-set man got out. He moved straight towards Sneijder, blocking his path, and pulled the rear door open. 'Get in, sir,' he urged.

'Wait a minute. What is -,' Sneijder was manhandled forcefully into the back of the car. He went down face first to the floor, the door was closed firmly behind him, and the car was already moving when the big man jumped back in. Sneijder looked up to be greeted by a pair of shiny brown shoes.

'Get up off the floor, Polo, there's a good chap,' said Harry Wilkinson.

A short while later, Sneijder and Wilkinson sat alone in the back of the car which was parked in a narrow alley between two tall buildings. The two men who had been in the front seats stood at the entrance to the main road, keeping watch and smoking cigarettes.

'Sorry about all that cloak-and-dagger stuff,' said Wilkinson. 'I'm ordered to remain in the shadows – security. You never know where Jerry might be.'

Sneijder nodded.

Wilkinson looked at him. 'What's up, Sneijder? You look like hell.'

Sneijder ignored the comment and said what was on his mind. 'How did you know where I would be?' His eyes widened. 'Did you have me followed?'

The older man replied, 'Not my doing. The Secret Intelligence Service has been watching you since you returned from Europe. They tell me it's standard procedure. Seems like a waste of resources if you ask me, but thanks to an advantageous family connection within their ranks I was able to track you down.'

Sneijder was furious. 'For Christ's sake, when will this end? Our own side spying on me! I went back into occupied territory voluntarily and this is what I get in return. I get treated like a German spy. They should be out there finding the real spies.'

'I know, Sneijder, I know. I don't agree with it – I just used the situation on this occasion because I needed to talk to you. Our meeting this morning didn't exactly go as planned. I'm sorry about the Major – he tends to get a little belligerent when he has an opinion.'

'You're telling me,' Sneijder said.

Wilkinson's response was incisive. 'Ignore him. Guido de Beer is an office boy, a pen pusher. He's never been out from behind a desk in his life. Don't let him lecture you on killing; until you've been there you've no idea.' A look of recognition filled the Brigadier's eyes, as if he was remembering some distant past event. 'What he is right about is that in a fight like this there are many necessary evils, assassination among them.'

'As long as someone else does the dirty work,' Sneijder remarked.

Wilkinson sighed. 'I don't like working with him any more than you do but I'm getting pressure to at least make it look like I'm co-operating with the Dutch organisations, on an intelligence level anyway. Besides, I owe him one after a job he did for me a while back. He saved the life of one of my finest agents.'

'I see.' Sneijder pondered for a moment. 'May I ask you something, sir?'

'Certainly.'

'Will killing this man really make that much difference?'

Wilkinson turned and looked out of the window. 'When Churchill formed this organisation, his order was to 'set Europe ablaze.' It's a terrible cliché but he wanted us to do everything we could to hurt the Germans. There is no question that killing Koestler will damage their operations so that's what we shall do. It won't make a big difference; the nature of a subversive war is that no one action causes significant damage. Each time we attack it is a mere pin-prick in the side of the enemy. The hope is that with a sustained campaign of strike and counter-strike we can make an impact.'

Sneijder was silent.

'Of course all this is irrelevant if you don't want to do it,' Wilkinson said. 'As I said, it's your decision. De Beer wants to see this man dead and I promised I'd help him, but you did your job and got eighteen months' imprisonment for your trouble. I can't order you back into occupied territory. It would be a great service to your country however, and you would be suitably rewarded, in secret of course.'

'I have been thinking about this, sir,' Sneijder replied. 'I want to do the right thing for my country but it's just the killing. I'm not a murderer, and that's what this will be - murder.'

'Ah, the moral question,' said Wilkinson. 'Is a man right to do wrong in order to defend what is right? Can it be wrong for a man to always do the right thing?' He shrugged. 'That I cannot answer. My advice to you as a field agent is to take your morals, put them in a box, and leave them alone. They will cause you nothing but trouble.

'You know, before the war, I was a journalist for the Financial Times.' The Brigadier almost broke into a chuckle. 'I used to spend my days writing about share prices and interest rates. The most I could do to people was reduce their bank balance a little - I could never have imagined that one day I'd be sending people into war zones to carry out assassinations. You see, if you kill this Koestler I'll be just as guilty as you. If it helps, put the blame on me. I'm the one sending you to do this.'

'I don't know,' said Sneijder in frustration. 'I just don't know.'

Wilkinson paused for a moment, then reached down to a briefcase at his feet and pulled out a thin file coloured bright blue. He took a sheet of paper from inside and began to read a list of names from it. 'Arjan Cornelius Sneijder, aged fifty-four, Edith Heike Sneijder, aged fifty-five. Names I believe you know.'

Sneijder was as white as snow as he looked open-mouthed at Wilkinson. 'My parents,' he blurted out.

'Piet Sneijder, aged twenty-nine, Liesbeth and Helena Sneijder, both aged twenty-six, Janna Sneijder, aged twenty-one. Your siblings.'

Sneijder noted with horror that Wilkinson had specified every member of his family's age as of two years ago. 'How did you.....' his voice tailed off. 'What happened?'

'How I came by this information is my concern,' the Brigadier said tersely. 'You told your conducting officer you had no family.'

Sneijder regained his composure. 'Yes.'

Wilkinson scanned the file, then looked up. 'I may have done the same in the circumstances. Your family were last seen in Amsterdam on 11 August 1942. The Gestapo cleared out a whole stretch of your neighbourhood, burned your father's shop. That's all I know.'

Sneijder looked at his feet, tears forming in his eyes.

Wilkinson went on. 'However, I am a firm believer in repaying a good turn with another. I am prepared to look into the situation further, see if I can't find out what happened and where they are. If you go into Holland –'

Sneijder looked up. He knew exactly what his superior officer meant. He wasn't sure if he should be pleased or angry, but he needed to know about his family. He'd expected them to join him in Switzerland nearly three years ago, but things hadn't turned out that way.

Wilkinson almost appeared apologetic. 'I'm sorry – it's the best I can do.'

Sneijder was dubious. 'You can find out? I don't see....'

'SOE Dutch Section has many contacts, even within the German administration,' Wilkinson declared. 'That's all you need to know.'

Sneijder hesitated.

Wilkinson's tone became firmer. 'Go to Holland, Sneijder, find a suitable time to eliminate Koestler and do it. I will find out about your family, you have my word.'

Sneijder raised his eyebrows. 'Is that an order?'

Wilkinson's reply gave nothing away. 'Do you need it to be?'

The two men focused their gaze on one another, each trying to figure out what the other was thinking. Wilkinson had consistently pointed out that taking on the assignment was optional, but now his position seemed to be changing. Sneijder wasn't sure what to make of the shifting scenario.

Wilkinson obviously sensed that agreement was close. 'This is the right thing to do. De Beer has given me his personal assurance that you can expect a decoration if you are successful. Your countrymen need you, Sneijder.'

Sneijder raised his hands. 'All right, all right, I'll do it. I'll go to Arnhem and I'll do it. If my country needs rid of Obersturmbannführer Koestler so much, it may as well be me that does it.' He opened the door to climb out of the car.

Wilkinson caught Sneijder's elbow. 'We meet again tomorrow, my office, nine o'clock sharp. I'll let you know the details then.'

Sneijder exited the vehicle, then turned and leaned back in. 'Whatever happens from now on, sir, I'm not a murderer. I'll do my duty, but I'm not a murderer.' He shut the door before the Brigadier could reply and walked away down the alley, passing Wilkinson's men and disappearing into the evening throng.

CHAPTER THREE

The death of Gilbert Krol was a setback that Koestler could have done without. The man had almost uniquely been held in high regard by both the SS and the NSB, a situation that had made him an extremely useful ally for a man charged with bringing the two organisations together. The NSB's meetings in bars, cafes and social clubs across the country were the starting point in the chain that brought Dutch civilians into Germany's much-reviled security force. Many of the recruits came directly from the pool of right-wing young men available to the NSB, while others were persuaded by the party that resistance was futile and they should make the best of the situation.

None of the other NSB members that Koestler had encountered possessed the intelligence and organisational skills necessary to fulfil Krol's position. Indeed it was probably somebody's indiscretion when organising anti-Resistance operations that had got him killed. No, they would be no good. Koestler would need to look outside his circle of contacts to replace Krol.

It was a bright summer evening, the sun still shining across the fields. The roads that ran north from Arnhem to Koestler's residence at the northern end of Kemperbergsweg passed through thick woodland, and dappled shadows strafed the car as it moved toward its destination. The driver in the front was a young Dutchman who looked barely old enough to drive and seemed to be in fear of his German passenger. He avoided his gaze and concentrated intently on the job in hand.

Koestler was alone in the back, having left his adjutant Klimitz at the SS headquarters in the centre of Arnhem. The captain was conscientious and an excellent soldier who had been with Koestler since his days in Poland. As well as organising his affairs, Koestler looked upon Klimitz as something of a confidant, and rewarded his loyalty with extra time off.

Koestler had refused a motorcycle escort for this short trip home. Despite warnings from colleagues that he was putting himself at risk he had never felt in danger in Arnhem. Nobody had ever tried to attack him in two years, no doubt put off by the draconian German reprisals that had followed assassinations in other parts of the Netherlands. Besides that, Koestler sometimes felt that travelling with a motorcycle outrider made it obvious to onlookers that he was an officer of importance, and could actually put him in more danger.

He was sure he could handle himself in a pistol fight anyway. He'd once held off three marauding Frenchmen with his service revolver when they had invaded his trench at the Battle of Verdun. True, he had taken two bullets for his trouble but he had received the Iron Cross second class. He was no longer the young man he had been then, but he was a German, and that would always give him an edge.

The woods became more and more impenetrable as the car approached the group of houses that clung to the edge of the forest. The young driver turned off the main road onto a narrow track which was muddy and rather bumpy, and he was forced to slow to a crawl to navigate a safe passage. The thick forest canopy obscured much of the daylight and the driver switched on the headlights to cut through the gloom. About a quarter of a mile along there was a side turning that led to three houses, the first about twenty metres down. The car swung into the small driveway at the front of the house and stopped.

Koestler opened the rear door of the car and stepped out, picking up his overcoat and military cap from the seat next to him. He closed the door behind him and moved to the front window to address the driver. 'Eight-thirty tomorrow morning.'

'Yes, sir,' the young man replied nervously.

'Don't be late.' Koestler walked away towards the house and behind him the car moved quickly out of the drive and back along the track. The young Dutchman couldn't get out of there fast enough, and Koestler felt momentarily empowered by the fear he could instil in another man. The thought was buzzing around his head as he reached the door of the house.

It was a modest place that had been owned by an old couple until the SS had commandeered it for its own purposes. Koestler's predecessor had wanted to live in a quieter area away from the city, and Koestler had been more than happy to take the same accommodation. The house was constructed in the classical Dutch style with large windows and elaborate brickwork, the roof line embellished with delicate carvings. It was surrounded by trees on all sides, screening it from the other houses and making it an ideal base for an official of an unpopular occupying administration.

Either side of the entrance there was an attractive flowerbed filled with brightly coloured fuchsias. A guard in Waffen-SS uniform sat on the low wall that ran along the front of them, a Schmeisser MG-38 machine pistol strapped across his chest. He had been a front line soldier until he had been wounded in the stomach at Stalingrad, and was now declared unfit for active service. He guarded the house regularly, although Koestler was sceptical about the injured man's ability to defend himself if it came to a battle.

The guard rose quickly as he spotted his superior, and seemed embarrassed to have been found sitting down. 'Sir......I'm sorry – I –'

Koestler was not in the mood for a confrontation. 'At ease, Sterchler. Any problems today?'

'No, sir. Very quiet.'

'And Frauke?'

Sterchler shook his head. Koestler went into the house and closed the door behind him, finding himself in the long narrow hallway that led to the other rooms. The kitchen lay directly ahead, and from his position Koestler could see out of the window to the back garden. The staircase to the upper floor was to the right, snaking up the wall to a large window which provided natural illumination for the otherwise dark house.

Koestler hung his leather overcoat on one of the wall hooks and dropped his cap on the side table. It landed with the *totenkopf* 'death's head' emblem facing towards him, and he looked at it for a moment. He wouldn't let anyone know it, but there were times he really disliked what he had become. He had never been a good man by any stretch of the imagination, had always looked out for himself, but some of the things he had done crossed the line by a long way. Even when he hadn't given the orders himself, Koestler had done nothing to stop the torture and murder and he had the blood of many on his hands. It was too late now for him to make a difference; the die had been cast and the play would run until the curtain fall. Koestler would just have to follow the script that had been written for him.

In the sitting room, he moved straight to the old-fashioned mahogany sideboard in the corner and took out a half-filled bottle of brandy. He poured some into a glass and knocked it back quickly, then poured some more and replaced the bottle. Koestler walked over to the fireplace, glass in hand, and looked along the dusty mantelpiece. There were a couple of inexpensive-looking ceramic ornaments left behind by the previous owners and a photograph of an attractive middle-aged woman in a silver frame. Koestler picked it up and admired the image of his late wife, Elsa.

Cancer had taken her from him in the summer of 1938, almost exactly six years ago, but the years had passed so quickly. How the world had changed since then, particularly for a German. The young Albrecht Koestler had fallen in love with his future wife the moment he had met her – two o'clock in the afternoon on the 11th of November 1918, a day of desperation for the German nation. Armistice Day had finished the world's first global conflict, but on it had begun a whirlwind romance and they were married in 1919.

However the young Koestler had grown up and become involved with the National Socialist movement. His feelings for the beautiful woman he had found had softened the initial blow of his country's capitulation, but over time his resentment grew. The way the nation for which he had risked his life had surrendered and the terms to which it had agreed had angered him. He had remained in the army, and seen first-hand the results of the restrictions on the military imposed by the ludicrous Treaty of Versailles. As far as Koestler was concerned as a young man of twenty-five, Adolf Hitler spoke the truth and his words inspired him.

As the Nazi party had grown in strength and power, Koestler devoted more and more time to it and had spurned his wife. He had never stopped loving her; it was just that the idea of a glorious German victory had consumed him completely. Carried along on the wave of hysteria generated by the *Führer*'s extraordinary rhetoric, he had begun to see his work for the party and the fledgling SS as the purpose for which he had been born. It seemed ridiculous now, with bombs falling on Berlin, but in the early thirties the idea that Nazism had some divine blessing seemed altogether possible.

Koestler's expression changed as he studied the photograph. The wistful smile that creased his face faded away to an agonised grimace as he thought of the final months of his wife's life. By then he was spending nights sleeping in his Munich office so that he could get more work done. His administrative skills and attention to detail had always been noteworthy, but it was his desire to work harder and go further to please his superiors that was both his greatest strength and weakness. He was not a brilliant man, and his current rank was purely down to his ability to impress senior officers, but in 1938 his work ethic had left him devastated.

The cancer had been diagnosed in early March but had attacked her savagely, stripping a proud woman of her vitality. Her husband and she had not sat down and talked properly for years, and it had been two weeks after the diagnosis before she had told him. It should have been the wake-up call that focused his mind back on the broken relationship, but Koestler was too busy to take in the fact that Elsa was going to die. She lasted less than three months, and it was only after her death that Koestler realised how much he had pushed her away. The day she died he had been absent – in his office, doing paperwork.

The memory made him sick. Koestler drank his brandy in a large gulp and went back to the sideboard for the bottle. He settled in the armchair by the fireplace, the bottle and glass in his hands, and placed the picture frame on a small table in front of him. He could be with Elsa for a few moments now. He wished he had done the same when she was alive.

Sneijder had walked straight back to the hotel after his encounter with Harry Wilkinson, events spinning in his tangled psyche. The truth about the fate of his family seemed as elusive as ever, but somehow he was sure that if news ever reached him it would not be positive. Sneijder had personal experience of the camps in the east where enemies of the Third Reich were held, but while the majority of the inmates at Mauthausen were there to work, albeit in horrifying conditions, there were rumours that in other camps the Germans were carrying out mass exterminations. This seemed preposterous – what could they possibly hope to gain by disposing of valuable resources of slave labour? Sneijder didn't know what to believe; he just prayed that his family had found themselves in no such places.

Sitting in his room that night, old family photographs spread out on the bed before him, Sneijder's mind flashed back to a cold November evening in 1941. The

German administration in Holland had begun to clamp down on anything it saw as threatening and Johannes' father Arjan, a man devoted to his wife and five children, had decided it was no longer safe for them to remain in Amsterdam.

A friend of his from the jewel trade was a Swiss diamond merchant named Rainer who travelled widely and dealt regularly with the Sneijder business. Being a citizen of a neutral country that was particularly valued by the Nazis, Rainer was able to drive his truck freely around occupied central Europe. If a German patrol stopped him, he simply pointed out his Swiss licence plates and was promptly allowed on his way. Arjan Sneijder realised that this might offer his family an escape route from Holland into Switzerland. It was decided that it was too risky for more than one of them to go at a time; Johannes was chosen to go first as it was felt that he could take care of himself if anything went wrong.

Arjan Sneijder had agreed to pay Rainer four hundred Swiss francs to take his son to Geneva. The truck that was parked in the alley behind the jewellery house that dark and chilly night was a battered old Opel goods vehicle, the cab painted red, the rear enclosed with a black canvas canopy. It carried a cargo of large wooden crates filled with precious stones that were bound for expensive boutiques in Zurich and Montreux.

Rainer was a small man with a gentle face and a toothy grin. He seemed like a trustworthy soul and met Johannes Sneijder with a firm handshake. '*Bon soir.*'

Sneijder was thrown by the man's French, and he was relieved when his father stepped in and answered the man in the same language.

Arjan Sneijder addressed his son, 'He only speaks French. Mine's not the best, but I think we understand one another.'

It was raining in a torrent and the only shelter in the alleyway was beneath the protruding rooflines of the buildings. The three men were gathered there against the wall, doing their best to stay dry. Sneijder was apprehensive, preparing himself for the gauntlet that was a dash across enemy territory, knowing that if he was caught the consequences would be dire.

Arjan Sneijder turned to his son and embraced him warmly. 'Take care, my boy,' he said. 'Now listen carefully. Mr Rainer will take you as far as his warehouse in Geneva. From there you need to make your way to Nyon, to the address I gave you. You'll be safe there.'

'Yes, father,' Sneijder replied. 'We've been through it all. I understand what I need to do. It'll be fine, everything will work out.'

His father tried to force a smile without success. 'I wish I had your confidence. For goodness sake just be careful. If they find you...'

Sneijder cut him off. 'They won't. You said yourself; the Germans will not touch anything with Swiss plates. It'll be all right.' He tried to look relaxed and confident, hoping to put his father's mind at rest. It was a futile exercise of course; no parent could send their child into such danger and not feel intolerable anxiety.

The door at the rear of the shop flew open and Sneijder's mother charged out, tears running down her face. She threw her arms around her son's neck and kissed him on the forehead. 'Johannes, oh my boy Johannes!' she exclaimed. 'I was afraid I'd missed you! I thought you'd gone already and I wouldn't see you and I wouldn't be able to say goodbye and...'

She was gushing and Sneijder put his arms around her. Holding his mother for a few moments, her head resting on his shoulder, he could feel his heavy woollen sweater becoming damp with her tears. 'Don't worry, mother,' he attempted to reassure her. 'Please. I'll be all right. A couple of months and we'll all be together in Switzerland.'

Sneijder's mother was not to be calmed easily. 'But it's so dangerous! I might never see you again.' She continued to cry, becoming ever more hysterical.

Arjan Sneijder stepped forward and put a hand on his wife's shoulder. 'Edith, my dear, he needs to go. We all need to go; Amsterdam is getting too dangerous.'

Edith turned and looked at her husband angrily. 'It's your fault if anything happens to him. You're the one making him go.' Tears streamed from her eyes. 'We should keep the family together, not send our boy away. I won't forgive you...'

Johannes Sneijder cut in. 'Mother, please. It is not Father's fault. It's not safe here, especially not for you and the girls. We all need to get out, and we will. It won't be long until we are all together again.'

Edith Sneijder said despairingly, 'How do you know? The Germans are everywhere!' With that she broke down completely. Her husband took her shoulders in his hands and pulled her away from her son.

Sneijder looked at his father and received a cautionary glance. If he was to go it would have to be now, before his mother could make him stay by encouraging his feelings of guilt. Rainer, obviously embarrassed to have witnessed such a private outpouring of emotion from a relative stranger, had already made his way around to the cab of the truck and started the engine. Sneijder picked up his knapsack and slung it over his shoulder, bade a brief farewell and clambered up into the back of the vehicle. He reached a hand up to get some leverage as he climbed over boxes, trying to find a suitable place to hide. A proper search by a German patrol would locate him in seconds but ducking down behind the crates would probably be enough to survive a quick inspection with a flashlight. With that in mind he dropped his belongings in an open crate and settled down on the floor, his back against the wall of the cab.

Outside the truck, Sneijder's mother was inconsolable. The sounds of her sobbing could be easily heard even over the noise of the lashing rain. Her husband had her in a firm embrace and was trying to reassure her. Sneijder knew that any attempt to pacify his mother was futile but he couldn't just leave with her in this state. He began to get to his feet, still in two minds over what to do, but at just that moment his father moved forward and banged a hand on the side of the vehicle.

Rainer took that as the signal intended and with Sneijder still paralysed in uncertainty, the truck began to move. He lost his balance and fell back, struggling to his knees as the vehicle turned out of the alley into the street. Edith Sneijder let out a cry of distress as the truck moved away, and the last thing Johannes saw was her face, her tortured expression and the tears pouring from her eyes. His father, standing behind her, raised an arm in the air to wave him off and then he was gone.

The sound of the rain faded away and Sneijder was back in the hotel room with the photographs. He picked up a picture of his mother that had been taken at a family wedding and looked at it carefully. It seemed like a totally different person to the one in Johannes' memory, a vibrant woman living in happier times. Sneijder fought back the tears that were welling up in his eyes and smiled gently.

In that moment he knew that he had to see the job through to the end. He simply had to know where his family was, even if the search led to places he did not want to go. But to drop into occupied territory with hostile intent and come out alive he would have to be at his best, and that meant cutting down the alcohol.

Sneijder gathered up the photographs and put them away in a leather satchel he had stashed under the desk. He collected all the bottles of scotch that were lying around - some empty, some still filled with drink - and took them out to the dustbins at the rear of the hotel to dispose of them. Sneijder was sure his dependence on alcohol was psychological rather than physical, a way of coping with the extreme conditions a war created, and that simply getting rid of all the bottles would solve the problem. He returned to the room, fully intending to do the same with the sleeping pills that had been maintaining him for the past few months. With the bottle of pills over the sink, however, he had a change of heart. Perhaps giving it all up at once would be a bad idea.

Instead he took a couple of the pills with a glass of water and decided to get an early night. As he settled down to sleep Sneijder was aware of the most unexpected of feelings. Despite his misgivings about the task he had been given, the trepidation with which he looked ahead to travelling to Holland and the fear he felt for his family, he could feel a tingle of excitement. After months of hanging around London with only his thoughts to occupy him, he was going to work.

It was a couple of minutes before nine the following morning when Sneijder arrived once more at 83 Baker Street. He was taken straight through to Wilkinson's office, expecting to find his superior officer behind the huge mahogany desk. Instead he was confronted by the humourless face of Guido de Beer.

'Good morning, Mr Sneijder,' De Beer said in Dutch. 'I believe you have come to a decision.'

Sneijder paused, not knowing how much Wilkinson had said to the older Dutchman. 'Yes,' he said cautiously. 'I decided it was time I did something for my country.'

De Beer almost managed a smile. 'Good. I'm glad you came to your senses.' His tone was patronising and immediately put Sneijder on the defensive. 'The Brigadier will be joining us a little later. He was called to a meeting but we can go through the formalities without him.'

Sneijder nodded in agreement. 'We should get started then.' Despite only having encountered De Beer briefly, Sneijder did not much care for him and was keen to spend as little time with him as possible.

'Indeed. The first thing I should tell you is that you will be going in very shortly, next week if not sooner. One of my agents in Holland has a contact close to Koestler who should be able to assist you, but this contact is getting jumpy and might not be in place for much longer. We need to get you on the ground before the opportunity is lost.'

Sneijder exhaled apprehensively. 'A nervous contact. Terrific. The surest way to get yourself killed.'

'We have to work with what we've got, 'De Beer replied. 'Either that or we just abandon our land to the Germans.' The jibe was far from subtle.

Sneijder was not one for confrontations and he remained calm despite his growing anger. 'With respect, it is easy to take that position when it is not your life on the line. I spent over a year in a German prison camp as a result of defending my country. How many of the enemy have you killed from behind your desk?'

De Beer rose to his feet. 'Listen to me, young man. The Brigadier tells me you are the best man for this job and I trust his judgement but I don't like your attitude. All I have heard from you are reasons why you can't do a thing. Now it's up to you whether you do this but if you do, you do it my way.'

'Actually Guido, he'll be doing it my way.' The door to Sneijder's left opened and Harry Wilkinson entered. He removed his hat and placed it on the stand, then did the same with his coat. Having cut into the conversation in Dutch, he now continued in English with a pointed observation. 'I see you've made yourself at home.'

De Beer immediately edged away from Wilkinson's chair. 'Harry, I wasn't expecting you....'

'No. I went the whole way to Whitehall only to be told I didn't have the required security clearance. The bloody Secret Intelligence Service and their stupid suspicions. No matter how much SOE does, the silly bastards still don't trust us.'

Neither De Beer nor Sneijder said a word.

Wilkinson moved across the room towards the desk. 'I hope I didn't interrupt anything. How far have you got?'

De Beer regained his composure. 'I was just saying that we need to get his mission started quickly. I was explaining about our contact that we might lose if we don't move soon. Your man here doesn't seem too happy about it.'

Wilkinson nodded. 'Yes, I heard that. You were putting him straight in that unique way of yours.' The Brigadier's face showed nothing, a real poker expression, and it was not clear if he was being serious. De Beer seemed to have trouble responding.

Sneijder spoke up. 'I was just a little nervous, that's all. It's nothing.'

Wilkinson moved behind the desk as De Beer went to stand next to Sneijder. The older Dutchman moved awkwardly and left an uncomfortable distance between himself and Sneijder, emphasising the hostility between them.

The Brigadier said, 'I should hope so. We are all on the same side after all. Now let's continue.

'As the Major has mentioned, we need to get you on the ground in Arnhem pretty swiftly. It all depends on when we can get a Special Duties flight arranged. RAF Bomber Command are not always the most co-operative of people but we'll see what we can do. In the meantime we shall have to get you out of that awful hotel where you've been staying and in to one of our safe houses. STS 43 should be suitable. We'll get a car to take you out there. I'm afraid it's then just a question of waiting for the order to go.'

'Suits me,' replied Sneijder.

'I'll have it arranged,' Wilkinson said. He turned to De Beer. 'Guido, can you sort out some kind of reception committee to greet Sneijder when he lands in Holland? We don't have any other agent in the area and many of our contacts are compromised.'

'It is already in place,' the Dutch Major said. 'I will make sure you are given all the necessary details in due course. All that will be required to set events in motion will be a message from your home radio station. I assume this is appropriate.' He looked at Wilkinson, and then fixed his gaze on Sneijder.

'Perfectly,' said Wilkinson.

'Yes,' Sneijder agreed. 'And when I get in position, how do I alert home base? Will I be going in with a wireless operator?'

Brigadier Wilkinson flashed him an apologetic look. 'No can do I'm afraid. We just don't have anybody available. We are hoping we can get somebody up to you from Eindhoven in a couple of weeks but I'm afraid there are no guarantees.'

Sneijder shrugged. 'Well, it might make things a little more difficult but at least I won't be slowed down.'

'Of course we will need to know when you're there,' Wilkinson explained. 'What you'll need to do on your arrival is send a postcard to our address in Stockholm with an innocuous message - something that won't arouse the Germans' suspicions.'

The telephone on the desk rang and Wilkinson picked up the receiver. He spoke for a couple of seconds in English, then switched to Dutch for the next minute or so. The nature of the call must have been unexpectedly urgent because the Brigadier's tone changed quickly. At first he was cordial and relaxed, but by the end of the conversation he seemed tense.

When he put down the phone he looked up and said, 'Gentlemen, as you may have noticed I have a rather urgent matter to attend to. We will need to leave matters as they are. Sneijder, I shall get a car to take you to your hotel to collect your things and then on to the safe house. I think it may be a good idea to visit Margaret Street to get you some suitable clothes. If that all sounds fair, I would appreciate it if you'll excuse me.'

CHAPTER FOUR

The car that arrived to take Sneijder on his way was driven by a young woman in green uniform. The badges she wore indicated that she was from the First Aid Nursing Yeomanry, or FANY, an organisation that supplied many women to SOE as drivers or signals clerks. She gave no hint of a smile and seemed totally focused on the job she was undertaking, speaking only to confirm the visit to Margaret Street. Sneijder was not in the mood to push her into conversation and they made the rest of the journey in silence.

SOE's camouflage section based in Margaret Street was a vital part of the organisation and was staffed by people with expertise in various fields, from dressmakers and costume designers to film industry prop makers. They employed a range of techniques to help agents blend in to the environment to which they were introduced. British-style clothing would be out of place in occupied Europe, so professional clothes makers produced items for both men and women that were designed and cut in the continental style. Small details such as British names on labels and zips were also taken care of. Due to the material shortages brought about by the war, brand new clothing and accessories would immediately raise suspicions, so items were subjected to processes to roughen them up and age them.

Sneijder was provided with a set of white cotton shirts, a dark woollen double-breasted suit with pleated trousers, a light woollen sweater, and a few other casual shirts and pairs of trousers. He was also given a small leather suitcase which had been suitably treated and a pair of dark brown leather gloves that appeared to be about twenty years old by the time the camouflage section had finished with them. Sneijder noticed with amazement that the label inside the gloves carried the name of a well-known Dutch clothing manufacturer, a detail which could ensure that an agent could pass inspection by German officials.

The car took Sneijder past his hotel, waiting just long enough for him to collect his belongings. The place was nothing special, in fact it was positively dreary, but it had been home to him for three months now and he had become used to the safety of the four walls he inhabited. After the misery of imprisonment at the hands of the enemy, the kindness of the hotel's owner had been greatly appreciated by Sneijder. The old man bade him a warm farewell and sent him on his way.

The car drove northwards out of London, passing through the northern suburbs and the towns that clung to the edge of the capital. Gradually the urban throng gave way to the pleasant green landscape of the English countryside, and the natural beauty of Epping Forest. On the other side of the forest, the scenery changed to that of wide open fields and cultivated farmland. Sneijder had always liked the countryside of England, and how different it was to the hugely irrigated flat plains of the Netherlands.

They had been driving for just over an hour when they turned into a long driveway nestled in the beautiful surroundings of rural Essex. A low stone wall flanked the entrance and a car painted in army green was parked in front of it, the distinctive figure of a military policeman at the wheel. He was reading a newspaper, his helmet and Lee Enfield rifle up on the dashboard in front of him. At the sound of the approaching car he looked up, but he straight away noticed the uniform of the girl behind the wheel and waved them on. The road opened up into a wide avenue lined with trees which in the midday sun was truly spectacular. In the distance Sneijder could see the outline of a large house, and as they moved closer he realised what a magnificent building it was.

'What is this place?' Sneijder asked the driver. 'I heard I was going to a safe house.'

The girl in the front smiled at him in the mirror. 'Yes, this is it. Audley End. There are miles of gardens around the house, and just wait until you see the inside.'

Sneijder had expected to be going to a country house hidden away from view, like Lord Montague's estate at Beaulieu where he had spent time training, but there the agents had been stationed in lodges well away from the main house. Here he was staying in a proper English stately home, a mansion of three floors constructed from grey stone, its façade sporting huge windows and dark oak doors.

Audley End had been built in the mid-seventeenth century on the site of a former Benedictine monastery by the first Earl of Suffolk, Lord Treasurer to James I, and became a royal palace when it was bought by Charles II in 1668. Upon being returned to the Suffolks in 1701, large parts of the house had been demolished but it had remained one of the finest Jacobean houses in England.

The successive owners of the estate had each left their mark but it was the third Baron Braybrooke who had had the biggest impact on the building's interior after he inherited it in 1825. He had introduced the furnishings and historic picture collection that now adorned the house, and returned it to something approaching its former glory.

The car drew up towards the front of the house, the road curving around a large lake upon whose mirrored surface ducks and swans drifted serenely. There was the crunch of tyres on gravel as the car came to a halt in front of the huge oak doors at the house's main entrance. A military policeman stood outside, his finger tapping on the trigger of the rifle which hung loosely from a shoulder strap. Sneijder's driver got out of the car and came around to his door, but he already had it open and was stepping out of the vehicle. That just seemed improper, expecting a woman to get the door for him, even if the war had blurred the lines of gender and what was considered acceptable.

The girl moved quickly to the rear of the car and opened the boot to allow her passenger to reach his luggage. Sneijder pulled out a large suitcase, another smaller suitcase, a small leather satchel and a canvas knapsack. He threw the knapsack over his shoulder, and used his two hands to carry the other three bags the best he could. The driver closed the boot lid and ran ahead. She gave a yellow slip of paper to the military policeman, and after glancing at it he nodded and allowed her through. The front door of the house was opened by a very young MP, and Sneijder squeezed through with his luggage. He moved along a corridor, eventually finding himself in a huge grandiose hall.

The driver followed him in. 'Just wait here. Someone will be down to see you soon. I have to get back to London.'

'Thank you,' Sneijder replied. 'I didn't get your name.'

She seemed to hesitate, unsure whether to answer, but then she smiled. 'It's Mary.' She turned and walked away towards the door. Just as she was leaving, she turned back. 'Good luck.'

Sneijder was left alone and he had a chance to look around the room he was in. It was a huge room perhaps twenty-five feet high, with wooden panelling on the walls from the floor up to about halfway, enormous nineteenth-century oil paintings suspended above. At the end of the hall there was a stone screen with three open archways, two of which led onto stairs beyond while the central arch led onto a narrow corridor.

A man appeared on one of the staircases, an older gentleman with dark hair that was thinning on top. He had a friendly face and wore a smile as he introduced himself. 'Ah, you must be agent Polo. My name is Chapman, Teddy Chapman. I am pleased to make your acquaintance. Mr Sneijder, isn't it?'

Sneijder shook the hand that was offered. 'Please, call me Johannes.'

Chapman smiled. 'Well I suppose that is the name your father gave you, so it seems only right that I use it.' He continued, 'I am in charge here at Audley End. It's quite a place, wouldn't you agree?'

Sneijder nodded, noticing a dramatic Flemish carving hanging on one wall.

'Exquisite, isn't it?' Chapman commented. 'Sixteenth century, I believe. So Harry Wilkinson sent you, I hear.

How is the old dog?' Sneijder detected a lot of affection in Teddy Chapman's comment.

'He's well, I believe,' Sneijder replied. 'To be honest I don't see him much.'

Chapman stepped forward and picked up Sneijder's small suitcase and the leather satchel, leaving him with the knapsack and the larger suitcase. He motioned for Sneijder to follow him and moved off down the hall, continuing to talk as he went. 'Yes, Harry and I were at Cambridge together, many years ago, Queens' College. Those were good times, until the Germans marched into Belgium carrying machine guns and we had to go and put a stop to it.'

'You served in the first war?' Sneijder asked.

'Oh yes,' Chapman replied. '2nd Battalion The Royal Warwickshire Regiment. A terrible business; you'd have thought we'd have known better than to go through it all again.'

Chapman led Sneijder down a long corridor, through a set of heavy doors and onto a large staircase. The stairs wound up to the next floor, past more huge oil paintings and brightly coloured Victorian pennants, and came out into an open landing. Sneijder dragged his large suitcase behind him, struggling to get it up the steps.

The older man chuckled light-heartedly. 'I trust you're not planning to jump out of a plane with all of these bags. The Germans may just notice a man who falls out of the sky with a full set of luggage.'

Sneijder smiled. He already liked this man. 'No, I wasn't planning on taking all of it.'

'Just the essentials, that's the best way to play it,' Chapman advised. He took Sneijder down a darkened hallway, moving towards the front of the house. The scale of the building and the complicated system of halls were disorienting but they eventually arrived at a door at the end of a corridor. Chapman led Sneijder into a small room with a view over the lake. It was lavishly decorated but the furniture, though old and probably Victorian had not been looked after and seemed to be falling apart. There was a rickety four-post double bed in dark mahogany jutting out from one wall, a large wardrobe in the corner. An antique dressing table ran along under the window and a large full-length mirror stood at one end.

Sneijder put the bags down next to the bed and walked over to the window, peeled back the net curtain and looked out. The front lawn of the house ran for around fifty metres down to the edge of the lake, and the water stretched back for quite a distance beyond. Behind that, the grass started again and reached back almost as far as the eye could see, disappearing into a copse several miles away. One or two trees were dotted around in the middle ground. It was a serene composition, very different to the sprawl of the city. Sneijder was pleased to be here.

'It is a very peaceful place,' Chapman said. 'The last refuge of sanity before you go into the madness of occupied Europe. I'd make the most of it.'

Sneijder was distracted by the tableau in front of him and did not turn around but managed a reply. 'Yes. I will.'

'We are not that busy by our usual standards,' Chapman replied. 'As you may be aware, although its size allows for the housing of many agents, this station is requisitioned primarily for Polish section so it's almost all Poles that we have here. They're friendly enough, although not many of them speak English as well as you do. As for meals, breakfast is at eight until nine, lunch is served at one o'clock and dinner is at seven.

'For security reasons, I am not informed about any agent's mission. You will be here for a few days until it is decided that you are to be sent out. Your conducting officer will come to see you to give you the details.'

Sneijder smiled. 'Thank you, Mr Chapman. You have been most kind.'

Chapman walked to the door. 'If there is anything you need, come downstairs and somebody will be able to assist you. Good afternoon.'

For the next few days, time passed slowly for Sneijder and he was aware of every hour that ticked by as he amused himself the best he could. He read books in the house's library and walked in the extensive grounds, which had been landscaped by Lancelot 'Capability' Brown at the behest of the first Baron Braybrooke in the late eighteenth century. The weather was fine and a man could easily lose himself in the gardens or in the woodlands that surrounded the magnificent stately home. Sneijder found enjoyment in wandering in the outdoors, thinking through everything that was happening to him. If he was honest with himself, he was not really sure what to expect when he arrived in Holland. He had left three years ago and had been arrested and incarcerated within minutes of his return. From there he had been taken to Austria and since escaping from there, despite crossing many occupied territories, he had not returned to his homeland. He really had no idea how badly the Dutch were being treated by the Germans at this stage of the war, and he was apprehensive about the conditions to which he was about to subject himself.

As Chapman had explained, most of the residents of Audley End were Polish. Some of them liked to keep themselves to themselves, and the more sociable ones tended to stick together. There always seemed to be a card game going on somewhere, and it seemed to be the same men that were always playing. It was odd how different people had different ways of coping with a situation; some seemed to be very withdrawn before a dangerous mission whereas others were laughing and joking as if they had not a care in the world. Sneijder was not really in the mood to be sociable, and the Poles did not seem all that interested in speaking to a foreigner.

It was two days later when Sneijder received a message that the conducting officer who had supervised him through his training was due to visit him. Taking into account the unofficial nature of his deployment, it surprised Sneijder that the usual lines of communication were being followed. He had assumed that the details of his task would be given to as few people as possible. The conducting officer who had been assigned to Sneijder was a discreet man, however it seemed strange.

Sneijder had been an excellent student at both of the Special Operations Executive's training centres, at Arisaig in the Scottish Highlands and at Beaulieu in the New Forest, and had got on very well with his conducting officer, a Scotsman by the name of McIntyre whose father had been a diplomat in the Dutch East Indies and who had picked up fluent Dutch in his childhood. Being a young man in his early thirties, McIntyre was able to join in the games of football played by the agents in their spare time and had struck up a good rapport with many of the men, Sneijder included.

Sneijder was reading a newspaper in one of the public rooms when McIntyre arrived. The Scotsman's white-blonde hair immediately caught his attention and Sneijder stood to be confronted with his piercing blue eyes. The two men shook hands and embraced one another informally.

'Johannes, it's good to see you,' McIntyre said in his unusual Scottish-accented Dutch. 'How long has it been?'

Sneijder replied in English, 'Nearly two years.' Sneijder and McIntyre had always had fun when speaking to each other, using each other's native language as much as possible.

McIntyre smiled. 'Let's take a walk.'

The two men went out into the grounds and strolled towards the stables. The day was overcast and dark clouds drifted across the sky, threatening rain. Sneijder was dressed casually in a shirt and woollen sweater, and he hoped he would stay dry. McIntyre was immaculate as he always was in a smart dark suit.

McIntyre offered Sneijder a cigarette. 'Here, take one.'

Sneijder shook his head. 'No, I don't smoke. When the Germans had me prisoner, cigarettes were hard to come by. It was easier to give up.'

McIntyre grimaced. 'Yes, that whole situation was absolutely ridiculous. We lost so many good agents because of laziness and stupidity.' He was visibly angry.

'There were a lot of us in that prison camp, all arrested at the drop zone. The Germans seemed to know we were coming.'

'They didn't just know you were coming, they were arranging it!' McIntyre said. 'The Abwehr were calling our home stations claiming to be agents of ours and asking for more people to be sent. We were obliging and for nearly two years we were dropping agents into their hands every month.'

Sneijder gasped. 'Nobody told me that. I've been interrogated for months and nobody would tell me what happened. They were talking to me like I was a bloody traitor! Did they find out who was responsible?'

'Sure; one of the wireless operators we sent in early was captured and broke under Gestapo torture. They made him send messages back to us, which of course he was strongly opposed to. As you know, each message sent via wireless is supposed to carry certain security checks which identify that message as genuine. The captured operator deliberately left out the security checks, assuming that the signals clerks back in England would notice and realise that something was wrong.'

'And nobody did?' Sneijder ventured.

'No, nobody at all,' replied McIntyre. 'N section was totally taken in, and immediately started sending agents into Holland. As far as we know, every single agent that went in from the end of 1941 until the middle of last year was dropped to a reception committee of SS and Abwehr agents. It is total madness; how can it take two years for anybody to notice that there is something wrong?'

Sneijder sighed. 'No one told me any of this, not even Wilkinson. It was obvious that something went wrong when I was dropped right into the Germans' hands, but it was never explained to me.' He shook his head. 'I find this difficult to understand. I risk my life for these people and they never tell me what is going on.'

A smile appeared on McIntyre's face and he laughed gently. 'Well, Johannes, it's hardly been N section's finest hour. I should think they are pretty embarrassed about the whole thing. Wilkinson probably wants to keep it as quiet as possible.'

The pair walked in silence for a couple of minutes, leaving the edge of the woods and crossing a wide expanse of grass. The morning rain had left the lawns soft and muddy underfoot, and neither Sneijder nor McIntyre was wearing suitable shoes. The conducting officer looked down at his shiny black brogues which were now thick with mud and frowned. Sneijder chuckled softly, and eventually McIntyre did too.

'So how do you feel about going back in, to Holland I mean?' McIntyre asked.

Sneijder thought for a moment. 'I think it's probably time I got back to helping the war effort. I went through a lot, and of course London is safe, but men are risking their lives to fight the Germans. How can I sit around and do nothing?'

'And the mission?'

'I don't like getting involved in killing,' replied Sneijder. 'You know that, but I'm prepared to kill if it really can't be avoided, and I accept that if Holland is to be freed from the Germans then we are going to have to do some pretty unpleasant things. If killing this man is the task I have been set, then I will carry it out.'

McIntyre turned to face Sneijder. 'Are you sure that's how you really feel?'

'What do you mean?' Sneijder said defensively.

'You are happy to assassinate Koestler?' the Scotsman replied.

'I never said that I was happy about it. It goes against all my morals, but he is responsible for the deaths of innocent people. It would seem he should be stopped, and I have been chosen to do it. That's all there is to it.'

McIntyre did not pursue it further. 'Okay, Johannes, I suppose you want to know the details. You will be going in tomorrow evening. There is a special duties flight arranged for you, assuming all is well as far as the weather is concerned.'

Sneijder gulped. 'Tomorrow?'

'Yes. De Beer wants to get you in before he loses his contact on the ground. Speaking of which, there are a few things you need to know. Let's go back inside and finalise matters.'

Later, Sneijder and McIntyre sat around a desk in an upstairs study, a map of Western Europe spread out before them. Several aerial routes from England across the North Sea to Holland were marked out on the map in red ink. McIntyre pointed to an airfield just south of Cambridge, and Sneijder nodded in recognition.

'You will fly from Tempsford along the northernmost route to Holland, in the usual way over the Afsluitsdijk and the Zuyder Zee,' said McIntyre, indicating the dyke that ran along the northern coast of the Netherlands. 'We hope to drop you just south of Arnhem, assuming there are no problems with anti-aircraft fire.'

RAF Bomber Command had never been happy flying special duties missions into Holland due to the number of planes they would lose to flak. The Kammhuber Line of anti-aircraft defences was the second most formidable in the world after the line that defended Berlin and losses could often be high.

McIntyre continued, 'A reception committee of Dutch Resistance will be there to meet you and help you get into the city. We've left it to them to sort you out a place to stay and some work to cover your subversive activities.'

'Are they reliable?' asked Sneijder.

'Of course. Here, read that and remember it. I need that file back before you leave this room.' McIntyre tossed a manila envelope across the table. 'It's important.'

'Yes, I know,' Sneijder replied defensively. 'I have done this before.' He opened the file and began reading through it. It was a thoroughly comprehensive false identity and cover story, with a detailed life history. For the foreseeable future, Sneijder was to be a market worker from Amsterdam by the name of Johannes Voorman returning from forced labour in Germany. It was essential for Sneijder to take in all the information before him, as his new identity would have to stand up to German questioning.

McIntyre passed Sneijder a bunch of papers. 'You need these as well.'

There was a perfectly forged Dutch identity card complete with fingerprint, a letter informing the fictional identity that he had been called for work in Germany - signed and stamped with official German ministry of work emblems - and a German pass that Sneijder did not recognise. 'What's this one?'

McIntyre smiled. 'They call that a *Rücktehrschelme*. It's a pass that says you have already worked in a German labour camp, and were discharged on grounds of ill-health. It will stop you from being rounded up and sent to Germany. The Germans are pulling out all the stops to try to increase production now it looks like they are losing the war, so it is a real danger.'

Once Sneijder had spent a few minutes getting to know the person he was to become, McIntyre filled him in on exactly what he was to do once he was on the ground. De Beer had identified a contact in Koestler's entourage who had agreed to assist in his assassination, but he was beginning to waver. Sneijder was to make contact with this man at the earliest opportunity and ensure that his support could still be relied upon. As with any operation behind enemy lines, securing the cooperation of local Resistance groups was essential. This often meant earning their trust through involvement in their operations, and McIntyre explained that Sneijder would have to help them in order to get their help in return.

Sneijder knew that one of the hardest aspects of the job was knowing who to trust. His own experience early in the occupation had told him that many people were prepared to collude with the enemy in return for preferential treatment. It required good judgement of character and continual vigilance if one was to avoid betrayal.

It was about an hour later when McIntyre concluded the briefing. Sneijder took a final look at the file and, satisfied that he had taken in as much information as he could, passed it back over to the conducting officer. He put the identity card and German pass into the pocket of his trousers.

'Is everything clear?' asked McIntyre. 'I believe I have given you all the information you will require.'

Sneijder nodded.

'Good,' McIntyre said. 'I shall leave you until tomorrow then. A car will be here to collect you in the evening around seven-thirty. Make sure you are ready.' McIntyre stood and took his wide-brimmed hat from the hat-stand behind him. 'Have a good evening, Johannes.'

Sneijder rose and shook the hand that was offered. 'Thank you, Alan. It's good to see you again.'

'And you,' McIntyre replied. 'Just like old times. Now if you'll excuse me, I'm afraid I will have to go.'

Sneijder had managed perfectly well without alcohol for several days but now, with his infiltration into occupied Holland fast approaching, all he wanted was a drink. He had known that this time was coming and it had never bothered him before, but it was suddenly very real. He was apprehensive both about taking a life and possibly losing his own, and a feeling of fear was growing in his stomach.

After dinner, Sneijder went to one of the public rooms which had a small bar. A young girl was pouring drinks for some of the agents while at one of the tables four Polish officers were playing poker for cigarettes. Sneijder took a large glass of scotch and sat alone by the window. By nine o'clock he had lost count of the number of drinks he had consumed and was hopelessly drunk.

When he slept later that night, his demons returned. Past events that were fluttering around inside his mind merged and were entwined with things that were yet to happen. It was all there; the pistol in Sneijder's hand, the crack of the gun going off and blood pouring down the German uniform. A vision of the Sneijder family jewel store in flames flashed through his mind like a firecracker. In his dream, Sneijder turned away from his burning home in horror to find himself facing six faceless soldiers in black SS uniform, their rifles trained on him. They opened fire in unison, shattering his body.

Sneijder could hear himself screaming before he was awake. His eyes popped open and he was bolt upright in an instant. For a few seconds his brain was unable to grasp where he was or why. He thought of his family, and was suddenly taken over by the crushing emotion of unimaginable grief. It was unstoppable. He buried his head in his hands and let his tears flow.

Chapter Five

Koestler was sitting in his office at the SS headquarters in Arnhem when Klimitz knocked at the door and entered. Koestler was reading through intelligence reports from various parts of the country, some of it garnered by the appropriate sections of the SS, some based on information from Dutch collaborators. It was part of an as yet unsuccessful attempt to identify a possible replacement for Gilbert Krol. The captain's entrance gave him a welcome distraction.

Koestler dropped his pen and looked up. 'Yes, what is it, Klimitz?'

'A message just arrived for you, sir,' the adjutant replied. 'Hand delivered. I assumed it was important.' He handed Koestler a sealed envelope.

Koestler raised his eyebrows. 'Yes. Thank you.' He lifted a small gold-plated letter opener from his desk and slid the blade through the paper, slicing the envelope open. He removed a small folded slip of paper from inside, opened it out and examined it. After a couple of minutes he dropped the letter onto the desk, sat back in his chair and sighed.

Klimitz stood in front of Koestler, waiting for his next order. 'Trouble, sir?'

'Klimitz, you will be pleased to know that while many Germans are fighting for their existence on the front line, we are going to a drinks party. It seems that it is the birthday of the Commisioner-General for Justice and the great and good of the German administration want to celebrate. Worse than that, they have seen fit to invite me.' He laughed softly to himself. 'A bloody drinks party.'

'May I ask where, sir?' Klimitz ventured.

'The Hague,' replied Koestler. 'Reichskommisar Seyss-Inquart will be there along with Rauter so I must attend. At least Naumann is gone, but I hear the new commander of security is even worse.' The lieutenant-colonel stared into space for a moment, then turned to his adjutant and forced a smile. 'Still, I had nothing else planned for tomorrow evening.'

Klimitz was dismissed and left the room. Koestler screwed up the invitation and threw it into the waste paper basket. The decadence of the German forces was totally ridiculous at times. The German army was in full retreat across central Europe, the air force was now non-existent, German cities were being bombed night and day and here was the SS organising a social occasion. It was this self-pampering that had destroyed the Fatherland, twisting an admirable ideal into a disaster. The hard work of millions of Germans had been squandered by men who had grown too accustomed to the trappings of power. It was now inevitable that the war would be lost and Germany would once again lie humiliated, at the mercy of other nations. It made him so angry.

Koestler arrived outside the International Hotel in The Hague around seven-thirty the following evening. It had been a beautiful summer's day and the sun was still visible above the rooftops of the Dutch administrative capital. Koestler's motorcycle escort cleared a path to the front of the hotel building and his large open-top Mercedes staff car stopped at the bottom of the grand staircase that led to the entrance. He exited the vehicle, followed as usual by Klimitz. Koestler had taken great care over his uniform, making sure it was in immaculate condition and that he had remembered to attach all the appropriate badges and emblems. He took great pride in serving his country, even if he did not always approve of what that represented.

The lobby of the hotel was Romanesque in its architecture, with large whitewashed pillars supporting the high vaulted ceiling. The walls were festooned with huge Nazi party flags and pictures of the Führer. The swastika was on display throughout the building, on its own or clutched in the talons of an eagle. There was certainly no mistaking that this was an event of Holland's ruling German elite. Beyond the lobby a large set of doors led to a huge ballroom which was also decorated in Nazi paraphernalia. The dance floor was surrounded on all sides by tables and chairs; at the back of the room was a band playing jazz and ragtime tunes.

The ballroom was starting to become busy as Koestler made his way in but most of the important guests were yet to arrive. He moved to the bar and ordered himself a whisky.

'Have yourself a drink, Klimitz,' he said to his adjutant. 'It's been a long day.'

'Thank you, sir.' He took a whisky as well.

'Enjoy yourself tonight. You deserve it.'

'With respect, sir, I think I'd better be on my best behaviour. From what some of the men say I need to stay on the right side of Rauter.'

Over the next half an hour the room began to fill up as more and more guests filtered in from the lobby and onto the dance floor. Koestler moved around the room greeting the people he knew and being introduced to the ones he did not. He was standing with a military intelligence attaché named Beck when there was a commotion in the doorway and two men entered followed by several junior officers. One of them was SS Obergruppenführer Hans Albin Rauter, the chief of all police matters in the Netherlands. He was a tall man, almost two metres in height, and was known as an obsessive workaholic. The other man Koestler did not recognise.

'That's Schöngarth, the new commander of security,' Beck said in Koestler's ear. 'He is apparently a real monster, more brutal than any of his predecessors. He knew Heydrich personally, they say.'

Schöngarth was a small man unremarkable in appearance but for peculiar eyes that seemed to look right through everyone he encountered as he moved across the room.

'He looks the part,' Koestler commented. 'Where did they get him from?'

'I believe he has been the police commander of security in Poland until recently,' Beck replied. 'They have almost completely cleared it of Jews now so I guess they're going to do the same with Holland.'

'That should please Rauter.'

'Isn't that the truth,' Beck said.

Rauter was a devoted Nazi who had made the removal of the Jews from the Netherlands his personal goal. His idolisation of Hitler went beyond that which was displayed by even the most adoring of Germans and he served Himmler without question. Despite being technically subordinate to Reichskommisar Seyss-Inquart he was in charge of all SS troops in Holland and was one of the most powerful men in the country. Upon entering the ballroom he walked straight over to the bar to order a drink. He greeted Beck and Koestler with a Nazi salute. 'Heil Hitler.'

Koestler returned the salute. Beck did not.

Rauter addressed Beck first. 'Good evening, Herr Beck. You are well?'

'Yes, I am.' Beck shuffled uncomfortably for a few seconds, then hastily made an excuse and walked away. Koestler eyed him enviously, wanting to do the same but not having the strength of character to shun a senior officer.

Rauter watched the attaché go and laughed. 'A strange one, don't you think, Koestler? I don't think he likes me.'

Koestler laughed as well. 'A strange one, yes sir,' he replied.

'And how are things going for you, Obersturmbann-führer?' Rauter asked.

'As well as can be expected, sir,' Koestler replied. 'It is becoming more difficult to find volunteers for the Germanic SS as most of the young men suitable have been taken to Germany for labour, but we try our best.'

Rauter frowned. 'You find our labour policy a problem? It is necessary to sustain the Reich. Production must be increased if we are to achieve total victory.'

'No, sir, I do not find it a problem. It makes things a little more difficult, that's all.'

'Nothing that is worthwhile is ever easy, Koestler,' said Rauter. 'Just remember that you are carrying out an important task for your Führer. How are civil matters in Gelderland?'

'Everything is very quiet. Our reprisals seem to have quietened down the Resistance.'

'And the Jews?'

Koestler grimaced. He believed that the Jews had corrupted German society, but sometimes he found the treatment of them unpalatable, particularly when those involved were women and children. It was wise not to show this feeling publicly, especially not to the hardliners like Hans Albin Rauter. 'As you are no doubt aware, removal of all Jews to transit camps was completed at the end of last year, but for those with exemptions. Transportation to the East from these camps is going well as far as I know. That is not my area; you would need to ask the commandant at Westerbork.'

'Of course,' replied Rauter. 'Himmler has ordered the complete removal of the Jews from Europe. I intend to make that happen, hence my particular interest.' He picked up the glass of vodka that had appeared before him and turned to Klimitz who was standing behind Koestler. 'Captain, will you join me in a toast to the Führer?'

Klimitz stood to attention at once. 'Of course, sir. It would be an honour.'

Rauter raised a glass, followed by Klimitz, Koestler and one or two others standing around them. 'Adolf Hitler! Der Führer!' He swallowed his drink in one, put the glass down on the table and walked away.

Bad weather over England put Sneijder's flight back by twenty-four hours, and so it was around the same time that Koestler was arriving in The Hague that a car arrived at Audley End to take Sneijder the short distance to Tempsford airfield. He dressed in a casual shirt and trousers, a dark woollen sweater and leather flying jacket. He packed some other clothes in his knapsack along with a few items of equipment; a small flashlight, a three inch knife and a compass in case he was dropped deep in the countryside. After collecting together his personal items and taking one long final look at the photographs he had of his family, he put everything into the large suitcase and left his bags with Chapman.

Sneijder was deep in thought from the moment he entered the back of the car. McIntyre, who was accompanying him to the airfield, evidently sensed this and was silent, instead concentrating on reading through a file. Tempsford Airfield was situated between Bedford and Cambridge, near the main London to Edinburgh railway line. It was well camouflaged beside the Great North Road and seemed to avoid German bombing.

Darkness was beginning to fall when the car turned off the main road and moved through the gates. A military policeman raised the barrier that blocked the path into the aerodrome and waved them through. Sneijder looked out of the window, making out the control tower and enormous hangars in the gloom. A couple of planes sat on the grass on one side of the tarmac, bombers of some variety. The car made a turn to the right and its headlights flashed across the main runway. A Stirling bomber was suddenly illuminated, its large square body squatted in front of a couple of corrugated iron sheds. An engineer stood beneath one of the wings with a flashlight examining one of the aircraft's four Bristol engines.

The girl driving the car opened up the engine and accelerated down the runway. About a quarter of a mile down she turned to the left and pulled up in front of a small stone building. Sneijder and McIntyre got out of the vehicle and the Scotsman led the way in.

The house was very small inside with low ceilings throughout. They moved into a room just beyond the staircase to be confronted with a long wooden table covered with firearms of all types and ammunition. A small man in a military cap stood at the end of the table.

'Johannes, this is Captain Quinn, our quartermaster,' McIntyre said. 'He's got every kind of weapon you can imagine.'

Sneijder eyed the collection of pistols, rifles and sub-machine guns in front of him. 'Yes, so I see. It's very impressive.'

'Captain?'

The small man responded to McIntyre's prompt. When he spoke it was with a strong Cornish accent that Sneijder found difficult to understand. 'Yes, of course. Obviously you have been trained in the use of all the weapons that I have here. For subversive operations you will not be needing a rifle so we'll get you something a little more discreet.' He lifted a Browning 9 mm handgun and ejected the cartridge. 'A fine gun, a favourite of the Special Air Service. A British-issue weapon may stand out behind enemy lines however.'

'Something that could realistically be obtained from the enemy would be more suitable,' suggested McIntyre.

Quinn nodded in agreement. 'Oh yes, not a problem.' He replaced the Browning and picked up a very distinctive looking pistol with a wide body and narrow barrel. 'The German standard issue Luger, carried by all of their soldiers. There are thousands of them knocking around Europe so it wouldn't be that unusual for a Dutchman to have one.' He passed it to Sneijder who felt its weight in his hand. Quinn picked up another similar looking pistol. 'This is their latest 9 mm, the Walther P-38. They reckon it is much more reliable.'

Sneijder took the Walther in his other hand and tried to assess the weights of the two weapons. He aimed them in front of his eye one by one. 'You can never be too careful. I'll take both.'

Quinn gave a mischievous smile. 'Whatever Sir desires. We'll get you some ammo too. You may need a small calibre assault weapon so I'll put a Sten in your kitbag.'

'A Sten won't raise suspicions?' McIntyre asked.

Quinn shook his head. 'I shouldn't think so. We've dropped so many of them to partisans that Europe must be awash with them.' The quartermaster picked up the three sections of the gun and assembled them swiftly. It did not look the way Sneijder remembered it. 'This is the Mark V,' Quinn explained. 'It's still a bloody awful weapon but it's cheap and easy to put together, and it'll take the same ammunition as the Luger and the Walther.'

Despite his ruffled appearance, Captain Quinn was meticulous in his preparations. He took a large canvas bag from under the table and began to fill it with items. Sneijder's knapsack went in first, the clothes placed at the bottom to cushion any more fragile objects. Quinn checked Sneijder's compass and flashlight to ensure they were working satisfactorily and put these in next along with the Sten, a collection of cartridges, and a small box of hand grenades. He tucked the Walther in the top of the bag and tied up the drawstring to close it.

'This bag will be attached to your knee with the strap,' he explained. 'That way your kit will not land too far away from you. You've got about fifteen feet on the line so it'll give you a bit of warning when you are about to hit the ground. When you feel the bag strike you'll have about two seconds.'

It was ten minutes later that Sneijder stood before them, his parachute strapped to his back. He felt bulky in the three layers of clothing plus the restraints that held the parachute over his leather jacket. The Luger was tucked lazily in his jacket pocket, secured by the zip. Sneijder felt the rising sensation of nausea in his stomach. He had always hated jumping out of planes from the first time he had ever done it, and now he was going to do it in the dark, into an incredibly dangerous situation.

Quinn shook his hand warmly. 'Good luck, agent Polo. I hope all goes well.'

Sneijder turned to McIntyre. 'I guess this is it. Thank you.'

McIntyre shook Sneijder's hand. 'Good luck.'

Sneijder was driven back along the runway to the waiting Stirling bomber. The interior of the aircraft was filled with light and the flight crew were in the cockpit carrying out their pre-flight checks. Sneijder barely had time to scramble up the ladder into the belly of the plane before the pilot readied for takeoff. He settled into a position on the floor of the aircraft just forward of the dorsal gun. He fidgeted nervously and checked his equipment again and again, more to take his mind off the situation than because he thought he had overlooked anything.

The sound of footsteps clattered along the fuselage and the dorsal gunner appeared. He was a man older than most serving at this stage of the war, with a bright, friendly face. 'Are you all right, son?' he asked Sneijder. 'You don't look too good.'

Sneijder smiled weakly. 'I don't like flying, to tell you the truth.'

'Particularly when you're doing it without the aid of a plane,' the man joked. 'I'm not too keen on parachuting myself. Fortunately I've only had to bail out the once.'

Sneijder took the Luger from his pocket and checked the mechanism.

The gunner began to move away but stopped to give one last piece of advice. 'Don't worry too much about the flight. It shouldn't be too bad. It may get a bit bumpy clearing the Dutch coast because of the damned flak but we'll get you there no problem.' He clambered up into the gun turret and vanished from view.

Shortly afterwards the plane's four engines burst into life and the Stirling taxied to the end of the runway. There was a loud roar next to Sneijder as the pilot engaged full throttle and the aircraft began its takeoff, starting slowly but rapidly picking up speed, hurtling itself down the tarmac. With the perimeter of the airfield in sight, the fence glinting in the moonlight, the Stirling lifted off the ground and rose into a clear sky.

The flight was smooth and uneventful, much to the relief of Sneijder who tried to get some sleep, knowing that the night could be long and he would need to be as alert as possible when he got on the ground. He was beginning to drift off when he was disturbed by a low booming sound in the distance. He lifted his head and listened hard, hearing the sound getting gradually louder.

The flight crew's navigator, sitting in his chair behind the cockpit, noticed Sneijder's concerned expression and shouted to him. 'We'll have a bit of flak for about twenty minutes. We'd try to fly under the radar if we could but the bloody searchlights would get us.'

The booming sounds continued to get louder but the Stirling was untroubled by anti-aircraft fire. The Luftwaffe fighter cover that was often the scourge of Allied aircraft travelling into Dutch airspace was also absent, instead being deployed to protect the beleaguered German forces in Belgium. The sounds of the flak were beginning to drift away when the navigator came back and crouched opposite Sneijder.

'It's time, sir,' he said. 'We're about six miles south of Arnhem. The pilot's just going to reduce our altitude, give the Germans less time to shoot you on your way down.'

'You English have a hell of a sense of humour,' Sneijder grunted.

The navigator took a flashlight from his pocket and shone it on the floor. He fumbled around on the bare metal with his other hand, located a handle and twisted it, then pulled the lever upwards. A hatch opened in the floor exposing a metre-square hole in the bottom of the plane. Instantly the cabin was filled with the deafening cacophony of four engines at full power. A stream of cool air blasted in from outside, scattering paper across the aircraft. It caught Sneijder full in the face and took his breath away, sucking the oxygen from his lungs. He leaned back, out of the fierce wind, and composed himself.

The navigator clung on to a steel cable hanging from the ceiling of the plane and yelled to Sneijder. It was almost entirely unintelligible over the roar of the engines but as he spoke he pointed to a set of lights mounted next to the open hatch. At the top a red light was illuminated while the green one at the bottom was dark. Sneijder got the message; jump when the green light came on. He made a quick final check of his equipment and shuffled across the floor towards the hatch. With a deep breath he swung his legs into the void.

Immediately his legs were buffeted by the strong rush of air. Sneijder looked down into the darkness. Far, far below he could make out patches of light and dark where fields met woods, and the shimmering reflection in the moonlight of the many waterways which traversed the landscape. The canals and drainage ditches appeared like threads of silver on a patchwork of black, giving some form to the abyss. The navigator reached across for Sneijder's kitbag and handed it to him, tugging at the line to ensure it was securely strapped to his leg.

The red light was extinguished and the green light flashed on. It was time. Sneijder said a quick prayer to himself, desperate for some divine force to help him on his way. The navigator gave him a dramatic military salute and smiled. Clutching the kitbag to his chest with both hands, Sneijder threw his weight forward, hurling his body through the open hatch.

The entire world went upside down as Sneijder was propelled into darkness. His head pounded with the wail of the screaming engines for just a second and then the sound seemed to disappear. He was aware of the Stirling close by but then it was suddenly high above, tearing away at great speed. Sneijder picked up velocity as he fell to earth. Air rushed past him and his clothes billowed in the wind. He found himself spinning around in all directions, turning upside down. He located the cord dangling from the parachute and pulled it hard, hearing the clunking of metal and a whoosh as the fabric began to unfold. The straps holding the para-chute on to his body yanked painfully under his arms and around his chest as he slowed down immeasurably in a tenth of a second.

And that was it. The madness was over. The para-chute open, Sneijder floated downwards at a compara-tively leisurely pace. He was at a thousand feet and for the first time he could begin to make out objects on the ground. To his right there was a large wood and to his left an expanse of open country. Sneijder yanked at the parachute cords, trying to get the limited control that was possible with a round military chute. He aimed for a patch of flat ground near a thick hedgerow as he figured it would give him somewhere to hide if it be-came necessary.

As he got near to the ground a gust of wind picked up behind Sneijder and carried him forward. He came over a ridge, and suddenly realised that there was a high dyke directly below him and a ditch beyond it which was full of water. It was far too late to do anything about it. The kitbag struck the ground hard and came to rest on top of the dyke. Sneijder was not so lucky. A second later he landed very hard and very painfully. He cried out in agony as he felt a shooting pain in his spine and his legs crumpled under him. It was obvious straight away that he had also hit the dyke but instead of coming to rest he rolled over several times and slipped down the bank. He was still travelling at speed when he plunged into the water.

The ditch was several feet deep and Sneijder went in headfirst. He squirmed around, managing to get him-self facing upwards but he was immediately engulfed by the parachute. Summoning all his strength he forced himself up in the water, trying desperately to get some air into his burning lungs. It was no good; everywhere he moved the parachute was there to block his escape. Sneijder thrashed around violently, flinging his arms in every possible direction. Finally he found the buckle on his chest which secured the parachute to his body. He wrenched it open. It came off with little resistance and Sneijder was able to release himself from the parachute's grasp.

He could breathe no more and was still tangled in the sodden silk material, but suddenly he was aware of a gap. The parachute moved to one side and Sneijder realised he could reach the surface. With his final reserve of energy, he pushed himself up and broke through into the open air. Coughing and spluttering, he dragged himself up the bank. Water poured out of his lungs as he gasped in oxygen from the night air. Terror and panic had gripped his body and it was several minutes before those feelings abated. He closed his eyes and rested.

The party in The Hague had been going for a couple of hours before the High Commissioner arrived with his entourage. The band which had been entertaining the assembled guests fell silent and an announcement was made.

'Ladies and gentlemen, the High Commissioner of the Netherlands, Herr Arthur Seyss-Inquart.'

There was a ripple of applause as Reichskommisar Seyss-Inquart descended the stairs gingerly. He was a tall man, balding, and wore thick horn-rimmed spectacles. He walked with a pronounced limp and sported the dove-grey SS uniform of Gruppenführer rank. A junior officer rushed across the ballroom to assist him but

Seyss-Inquart waved him away and moved straight towards a large round table next to the dance floor where a group of men and their wives sat. One of these men was the Commissioner-General for Justice in whose honour the party was being held.

From the other side of the room Koestler watched the two men greet each other with the obligatory straight-arm salute and a handshake. The band struck up another tune as Seyss-Inquart began to speak and his words were drowned out.

Koestler extinguished his cigarette in the ashtray in front of him and finished off his fifth large whisky of the evening. He turned to Klimitz and said, 'I'll go and put in an appearance before he settles down with Rauter and I'm stuck talking to that bastard all night.' He stood up from his chair unsteadily and began to walk, but stumbled clumsily.

Klimitz rose quickly, put his cigarette between his lips and used his free hands to grab his superior officer as he fell. He held Koestler until he got his balance. 'Sir, are you sure you should....'

'Of course, I am perfectly fine,' Koestler snapped. He brushed his adjutant off and headed across the crowded floor. He struggled to walk in a straight line and only narrowly avoided the dancing couples who were performing an upbeat waltz. Koestler paused to accept a glass of champagne from a waiter and continued on his way. As he neared the busy table several of the men looked up, amused by his display of intoxication. Koestler swayed slightly and grasped the table to steady himself; one of the men's wives glared at him in disapproval.

Seyss-Inquart turned to face him upon finishing his conversation with the commandant.

'Good evening, sir,' said Koestler.

Seyss-Inquart's face brightened when he saw his former protégé. 'Albrecht! How good it is to see you. Where have you been hiding, it's been months?' Seyss-Inquart shook Koestler's hand, hesitated for a moment, and then embraced him warmly. The High Commissioner turned to the crowd around the table. 'For those who do not know him, this is Obersturmbannführer Albrecht Koestler – a good man, a very good man.' He turned back to Koestler. 'Come, let us talk.'

The two men moved away from the group towards the bar, skirting around the edge of the dance floor. Koestler wobbled slightly as he walked, and Seyss-Inquart laughed. 'You have been enjoying the hospitality of the Reich, I see. Perhaps another drink is the last thing you need.'

'No, if anything is going to get us through this war it will be drink,' replied Koestler. 'There are not very many pleasures for a German these days.'

Seyss-Inquart nodded. 'It is not a great time to be an Austrian either, as I am sure the Führer would agree. However he is confident that we will soon launch a counter-offensive against the British and Americans. He tells me our technology is advancing at great pace.'

Koestler did not wish to upset matters by voicing his own opinion. 'Then that is good news,' he said diplomatically. 'Now - a drink.'

Koestler took another whisky, Seyss-Inquart a large schnapps.

'So, Albrecht,' the Reichskommisar began, 'to what shall we drink?'

'How about 'the great days of Germany'? Days I fear may be behind us.' This seemed to trouble Seyss-Inquart so Koestler added, 'and to Krakow, where we showed the enemies of the Reich no mercy.'

The mention of the Polish city where the High Commissioner had mentored Koestler had the desired effect and Seyss-Inquart raised his glass. 'To Krakow.'

The two men emptied their glasses. Koestler put his down on the table and took a deep breath. His face was pale, his eyes red and swollen.

'Are you okay?' Seyss-Inquart asked. Koestler hesitated, so the older man rephrased his question. 'Is everything all right, Albrecht?'

Koestler laughed, a terrible ironic grin breaking across his face. 'All right? We have failed, Arthur. The Führer has failed us. Look at what is happening; Germany is on the brink of collapse. We are about to be humiliated once again.'

Seyss-Inquart's face dropped. 'You are drunk. You don't know what you're saying. This is not you. The fight shall continue; the Führer knows what he is doing.'

'Open your eyes!' Koestler exclaimed. 'It is not going to happen. Everything we have done, all that we have sacrificed has been for nothing! How much longer can we go on believing it will be okay? It will end in the worst possible way and we will be called to account. We will all be called to account for the things we have done.'

Seyss-Inquart was astonished. For a moment there was fury on his face, but he looked Koestler in the eye and his expression softened. When he spoke, his voice was firm but understanding. 'Albrecht, I shall excuse this only because it is you and we are friends. If it was anybody else they would find things become rather unpleasant. However, I will only tolerate it once. Now I don't know what this is about and in the state you are in tonight I don't suppose we'll find out, but you cannot talk like this in front of the men. It could be catastrophic for morale.'

Koestler had fallen silent. He had said too much and was ashamed of himself. He wanted to offer up a defence for his inappropriate outburst but none was forthcoming.

Seyss-Inquart reached into his pocket and took out a notebook. He scrawled on a page, ripped it out and gave it to Koestler. 'I want to help you, Albrecht. Here is my private telephone number. If there is anything I can do for you, please call. Now, please excuse me. I have many people to speak to.' He stood up and walked away.

Koestler watched him go. Long after the Reichskommisar had disappeared from view he was still sitting in the same position, staring blankly into the crowd. He spotted Rauter at a nearby table, laughing with a couple of Wehrmacht officers in that harsh way of his. It filled Koestler with rage. Here was a man who dared to lecture him on his duty, and here he was cracking jokes at a drinks party while his nation faced ruin.

Koestler rose from his chair and went over to challenge him. He was nearing the table when Klimitz appeared in front of him and blocked his path.

'What is it, Sebastien?' Koestler asked irritably, trying to get around his adjutant.

'There's a telephone call for you, sir,' Klimitz replied. 'It's urgent.'

Koestler raised his eyebrows. 'A telephone call for me here? At ten o'clock at night?'

'I'm afraid so. Whoever it is will only speak to you, he was most insistent.'

Koestler scowled. 'Well, all right then. Where is the telephone?'

'In the reception office, through the lobby. I'll take you there.'

The two men made their way across the ballroom, and up the flight of stairs that led to the lobby. The hotel's entrance hall was totally deserted. Koestler looked around at the various doors which branched off it. 'Which is the room with the phone?'

'There isn't one,' Klimitz replied gingerly.

'Sorry?'

'There isn't a phone. Well, there probably is but there isn't a call for you. I made it up to get you out of there.'

Koestler turned, his anger growing. 'What the hell for?'

'May I speak frankly, sir?'

'It had better be good.'

'I thought I should stop you embarrassing yourself,' Klimitz said bluntly. 'You're drunk, and when I saw you heading for Rauter I thought I'd better stop you. With respect, sir, what were you thinking? You might get away with it with the High Commissioner but Rauter is a different story. He'd savage you.'

Koestler glared at him in fury. 'Embarrass myself? How dare you? I will act in whichever manner I like.'

'If you want them to know you have an alcohol problem then carry on,' the captain replied. 'I don't care if they find out but you will when they post you to the front line. There are plenty of people waiting for an excuse to take your position.'

Koestler moved his face close to that of his adjutant and spoke aggressively. 'You will reveal nothing of this to anybody. Is that understood? Otherwise you may find yourself fighting on the Russian front.'

Klimitz's reply was devastatingly disarming. 'Sir, I have been your adjutant for over three years and I have always done what is in your best interests, have I not? It is my strong advice that we leave before you do something you regret. Believe me, you will thank me tomorrow.'

The lieutenant-colonel was going to protest, but Klimitz was right. He should leave now, before he repeated his outburst at Reichskommisar Seyss-Inquart. 'Okay, very well.'

Klimitz smiled. 'I took the liberty of arranging your car. I hope you don't mind.'

CHAPTER SIX

Sneijder had been lying on his back at the top of the bank for almost fifteen minutes. The struggle to escape from the water-filled ditch had sapped his energy and he was just beginning to regain his breath. He heard a noise in the distance and his head snapped to one side. He surveyed the landscape quickly, taking note of his surroundings.

The dyke on which he had landed ran parallel to a small country lane, with about six metres and a thick hedgerow between them. On the other side of the ditch, where Sneijder currently lay, there was a large area of open ground covered in long grass and surrounded on three sides by thick woodland, the trees beginning about a hundred and fifty metres from Sneijder's position.

For a moment he saw and heard nothing. There was absolute silence but for the sound of his own breath. He caught a glimpse of a light in the distance, somewhere in the forest. It was there for barely a second before it vanished again but it was enough to shake Sneijder out of his slumber. Alert again, he continued to watch. The light was there once more, a brief flicker, and then it returned permanently.

Sneijder moved, scrambling down the bank towards the ditch to give himself some cover. He crawled forward so he could look over the parapet and drew the Luger from his jacket pocket, cocking it in a single movement. As he watched, another light appeared not far from the first. Seconds later there was a third. Sneijder pressed his body flat against the grass, raising his head as little as was necessary. The three lights in the distance swung from side to side and bobbed up and down. Sneijder knew straight away that he was looking at flashlights carried by men who were approaching rapidly. Still there was silence.

Sneijder put his head down for a moment and tried to collect his thoughts. This could be the reception committee arranged for him, but after being snared so easily by the Abwehr after his previous parachute drop he was determined not to make any mistake. Whoever they were, they were going to be on top of him within a minute or so. Looking behind him to assess his options, he caught the sight of his reflection in the glistening water. The fear he saw on his own face shocked him.

'What are you doing here, Johannes?' he muttered to himself. 'Trying to be a hero?' He would never have the time to reach the road without being seen so he elected to stay where he was. His fingers tightened around the butt of the Luger. Instinctively he fumbled in his pocket for a spare clip but there was nothing there. He remembered he had watched Captain Quinn putting all the ammunition into the leg bag earlier in the evening; the bag which was still tied to his knee. His eyes moved along the length of the line until it disappeared into the water. The bag lay at the bottom of the ditch, totally immersed.

Sneijder's attention returned to the scene in front of him. It was very dark but as the lights began to get nearer, the shadowy figures behind them started to take shape. There were figures between the lights as well, making it five men altogether. As they moved out of the trees and into the open ground, Sneijder analysed their body shapes. None of them wore military helmets or headgear of any kind, which meant it was a good bet they were not German soldiers or officials. They continued to bear down on Sneijder and he could now tell that one of them was a woman, which seemed to confirm they were civilians. They covered the ground in less than half a minute and soon Sneijder could hear their conversation. He decided to take charge of the situation, but for somebody who was usually so careful his actions were extremely foolish.

Sneijder leapt to the top of the bank and pointed the gun straight ahead. He gave a loud cry as he went and addressed the astonished group in Dutch. 'Don't come any closer! Put down your weapons!'

The nearest member of the group was no more than two metres from Sneijder. He was a tall well-built man who appeared to be in his early thirties, dressed in dark clothing, his face smeared with boot polish. He shone his flashlight into Sneijder's face. 'I don't think so. It's a bit of a mismatch in terms of firepower.'

Sneijder looked behind the man and saw a teenage boy and the woman, both pointing Sten submachine guns at him. He kept his Luger aimed at the man with the flashlight. 'Who are you?' he asked firmly.

'We were told to come and meet you at the rendezvous point but we saw you come down over here,' the man replied. 'It's a tough walk through the woods to get here.' The two other figures with torches remained back in the shadows.

Sneijder needed to be sure. 'How is the health of my aunt?'

The response was instant and correct. 'Your uncle Bertrand sends word that she is well.'

Sneijder smiled. 'He is a wise old man.' He lowered the Luger. As soon as the boy and the woman lowered their guns he retrained the pistol on the man wearing the boot polish.

'Hey, what is this?' the man said angrily.

'I was told to expect three of you,' Sneijder explained. 'I don't like plans to change.'

'My nephew and his friend wanted to join us. They are good boys and useful to have around. Can you please now put the gun away?'

After a moment, Sneijder lowered the gun and put it back into his jacket pocket. 'I am sorry. I have had some nasty surprises in the past.'

'I understand,' the man said. 'My name is Kees van Rijn. This is my wife Klara and my nephew Jelle.' They moved forward so that Sneijder could see them. The woman was around the same age as her husband and had long dark hair. She was quite big, not fat but obviously had a healthy appetite which she satisfied despite the rationing. The boy could only have been seventeen and seemed extremely nervous.

Sneijder held out his hand. 'Johannes......Voorman. Pleased to meet you.'

Van Rijn shook his hand. 'Yes, the same to you. Oh, at the back there are Arnold – Jelle's friend – and Max Bruggink. Max and I have been giving the Germans hell for quite some time.'

Sneijder pointed to Van Rijn's darkened face. 'That's how you know all the tricks of the trade.'

For the first time Klara spoke. 'Your clothes are wet, Mr Voorman. Did you have trouble with your landing?'

Sneijder grinned through his embarrassment. 'I hit the dyke and very nearly drowned myself in the ditch. My kit is still in there.' He turned and picked up the line in both hands, running it through his fingers until it went taut. Following the thin cable he made his way slowly down the bank, taking care not to slip, and tried to drag the kitbag out of the water. The sodden canvas bag was heavy and Sneijder had trouble shifting it. Suddenly it moved and popped out of the ditch onto the grass. Sneijder turned to find the other youngster Arnold holding the line, having used his impressive physique to assist in retrieving the equipment.

'Thank you,' Sneijder said.

Arnold responded with a wide toothy grin. 'No problem.'

The pair of them turned to find the other four standing along the top of the bank. Van Rijn said, 'We had better get going. There have been a lot of German patrols in this area since one of the LKP action groups raided the prison in Arnhem last week. If we want to avoid them we shouldn't stay out long.'

'Where are we going?' Sneijder asked.

'We'll go to my grandfather's farm tonight. It's not far from here. He's an old man and the Germans would never suspect him of helping the Resistance, but he's tough. We'll move you into the city tomorrow when the curfew is lifted.'

Sneijder nodded and picked up the kitbag, swinging it over his shoulder. Cold water dripped out of the material and ran down his back, soaking the areas of his body that had begun to dry. 'After you,' he said.

Before they left Klara van Rijn clambered down to the water's edge and grabbed hold of Sneijder's parachute which was still floating in the ditch. She took a small knife from her pocket and sliced through the cables one by one until the silk material of the chute was free, leaving the rest of it to sink beneath the surface. She motioned to her husband who reluctantly went to help her fold up the expanse of fabric, then turned to Sneijder and explained, 'I'm not going to let good material go to waste.'

The group left the dyke and crossed the forest clearing quickly. They were soon swallowed up by the woods which grew thicker in no time at all, and without the moonlight it was total pitch-darkness. The man who Van Rijn had identified as Max Bruggink, a small forty-something man with grey receding hair, led the way. He had been silent up to this point and concentrated on following the beam of light generated by the torch in his left hand. Behind him were the two boys, Jelle with his Sten and Arnold carrying a flashlight. Sneijder walked next to them with the Van Rijns bringing up the rear.

After about twenty minutes the group emerged from the trees onto a road.

They followed it for a few hundred metres until they reached a van which was parked just out of sight beyond a small stream. Kees van Rijn and his wife climbed into the front of the van and shared the bench seat with their nephew. Sneijder and the other two men clambered into the back of the vehicle, which was littered with thousands of grains of wheat and maize. Three large sacks sat in the corner, filled right up with the same grains.

Van Rijn shouted over his shoulder. 'Don't worry if we meet any patrols – Max here was in the army. He'll sort them out.' He started the engine, crunched the gears and moved off, bouncing the van across the stream and on to the road. He switched on the headlights, keeping them dimmed. Van Rijn picked up speed until it seemed he was travelling much too fast considering the visibility, but he evidently knew the road. The narrow lane took them through woodland for several miles before opening out into wide corn fields and arable land. The moonlight illuminated the road in front of them, but still nobody noticed the vehicle coming the other way until it was too late. As the van rounded a bend, a German kubelwagen flashed past in the opposite direction.

'Aww, shit,' said Van Rijn in frustration. 'Time to hold on.'

Sneijder peered out of the rear window. The kubelwagen veered to one side, swung around and came after them. 'He's on our tail.'

For the first time Bruggink spoke. 'I can't make out who they are, Kees. Probably SD or Green Police.'

'You'll have to take them out,' Van Rijn shouted in reply. 'We can't run the risk of them following us to the farm, and we won't outrun them in this.' He stepped on the accelerator and gave it as much power as he had, and hit full beam on the headlights. The engine growled menacingly but delivered little.

Behind them the kubelwagen closed the distance. Bruggink swung open one of the van's rear doors and pulled out an antique-looking revolver. He fired twice at the pursuing vehicle. The first bullet thudded into the spare tyre mounted on the bonnet; the second shattered the windscreen. The German car swerved and dropped back. Sneijder saw the uniformed man in the passenger seat stand up and take aim at them with his Schmeisser machine pistol. He loosed off a burst of automatic fire, clipping the edge of the door that remained closed and narrowly missing Bruggink. Sneijder fired a series of shots with his Luger but the two vehicles were bouncing around violently and all the bullets flew wide.

Van Rijn braked hard, throwing both Sneijder and Bruggink off balance, and took a turn to the right. The kubelwagen missed the turning but the driver was extremely skilful and managed to spin around rapidly. The heavily-laden van took time to build up speed again after Van Rijn's ferocious deceleration and as it reached an acceptable level the German car was already back with them.

Sneijder dragged himself off the floor and moved over to the doors which had slammed shut when Van Rijn hit the brakes. He grabbed his kitbag and fumbled around in it for a spare ammunition clip. Arnold had his entire right arm in one of the sacks of grain and seemed to be rummaging around for something. Bruggink moved forward and swung the door wide open.

Sneijder emptied the magazine in his Luger without hitting anything. He ejected the clip and rammed a new one into the butt of the weapon. Taking careful aim, he fired two shots. The kubelwagen drifted to one side to avoid being hit, put a wheel on the grass and slowed. The van opened up a slight gap.

Sneijder turned to see the teenager Arnold pull a hand grenade from the sack and remove the pin with his teeth. He dropped the grenade out of the back of the van. It rolled about five metres and settled in the centre of the road, directly in the path of the chasing vehicle. It exploded under the kubelwagen with immense force. The booming explosion filled the night air, slicing through the silence. As the van pulled away, Sneijder saw the burning wreck yaw to the left and career into the trees.

Bruggink reached for the door and pulled it closed, then turned to Van Rijn. 'It's taken care of. Now let's get to the farm before we meet any more of them.'

Sneijder said, 'They were after us just for breaking the curfew?'

'That's right,' said Van Rijn. 'They're really cracking down on us these days. It's a dangerous time for you to return. You are either very brave or very stupid. I'm not willing to guess which one.'

There was not another vehicle in sight for the rest of the journey to the farm and ten minutes later the van turned in through the front gate and moved slowly up a bumpy dirt track. A collection of buildings loomed in the distance, picked out by the moonlight against the night sky; a small cottage, a barn, stables, and a couple of enormous cylindrical grain silos. There was not a light to be seen.

Van Rijn pulled the van up to the front of the cottage and killed the engine. Klara and Jelle climbed out and went over to the door while the three men clambered around in the back trying to gather up their belongings. The man who came out of the cottage was an old farmer in his late seventies, who was slightly deaf and carried a walking stick. He had a youthful face and intense blue eyes. Klara embraced him.

Kees van Rijn lectured his grandfather, 'Grandpa, I told you not to wait up for us. You need your rest.'

The old man waved him away. 'Nonsense, my boy, I'm as fit as the day I was born. Ignore what your mother tells you. Now who have you brought me?'

Sneijder stepped forward and offered a hand. 'Johannes Voorman. Pleased to meet you.'

The old man took the hand and shook it. 'Ah, a good firm handshake. You and I are going to get along. Wesley Lamming is my name. Welcome to my humble home.'

The formalities continued for a couple of minutes, but were cut short by a serious Van Rijn. 'Grandpa, is everything ready? Good, then go back to bed and let us get on with it.'

The leader of the group led Sneijder across the court-yard to the huge barn. It was constructed from grey stone and timber, the roof of slated tile punctured with holes. The building looked to be in a state of disrepair, an appearance not helped by the rusting tractor which lay in several pieces next to it. Inside the barn was piled high with hay and huge sacks of grain. In a corner of the building there was a ladder which stretched up into the loft.

Van Rijn motioned to Sneijder. 'It's up there, I'm afraid. Safest place for you.'

Sneijder replied, 'As long as it's somewhere I can put my head down I'll be fine.' He began the climb up the fifteen-foot ladder, hauling his kitbag with him. The loft was spacious and contained nothing which could be associated with farming. Instead there was a desk and a chair, a battered old mattress to sleep on, a gas stove and a couple of small pots.

Van Rijn appeared behind him. 'It's not much, but at least it's summer so you won't be cold. You haven't seen the best bit yet.' He walked to one end of the room, crouched down and gently eased up one of the floor-boards. 'Here, take a look.'

Sneijder walked over and crouched down. Beneath the floor there was a small secret compartment that went down about four feet, more than deep enough to sit in comfortably. It was padded with soft material of all descriptions, presumably discarded from various other jobs. Sneijder lowered himself in and crawled around, examining the space. In the corner, a large square object was covered with a dirty and tattered sheet. Sneijder lifted the sheet to reveal a wooden box which he knew was a wireless radio set.

Van Rijn grinned. 'All radio sets were seized last year from everyone but NSB members, even ones with no transmitting facility. We've managed to hide this one since.'

Sneijder was impressed with the entire set-up. 'It's incredible; I never saw a gap between the floor and ceiling from downstairs.'

'Thanks to the incompetence of the man who built this barn, the ceiling downstairs is not level; it slopes from one end to the other. Fortunately the difference is very gradual and difficult to spot. It gives us a neat hiding place.' Van Rijn looked at Sneijder's clothes. 'You could do with something dry to wear. I'll borrow some clothes from my grandfather, and I'll take the rest of your kit inside to dry.'

Sneijder climbed out of the hiding place and replaced the floorboard, then turned and shook the other man's hand. 'Thank you. Thank you very much, for everything.'

Van Rijn appeared embarrassed by the comment. 'No trouble. It's good to have another body.' Given the extent of German reprisal murders against the Resistance, it was an extremely poor choice of words, and for a few moments an uncomfortable silence fell. 'I'll go and get those clothes,' he said finally, and disappeared down the ladder.

Sneijder was suddenly overrun with fatigue and collapsed down on to the mattress which lay on the floor against one wall. Van Rijn returned with some spare clothing for him, then bade him farewell for the night and left, taking with him the waterlogged kitbag. Sneijder lay down to sleep, tucking the Luger under the mattress beside his head. He drifted off in an instant.

When he next opened his eyes the low early morning sun was streaming in through a window at the end of the loft space. The air was filled with the sounds of birdsong and the inviting aroma of sweet summer flowers. Sneijder decided he needed to stretch his legs, so he climbed down the ladder to the barn floor and strolled outside. The sky above was clear blue, the sun warm on his face, and for the first time he could see the farm in the daylight. The buildings were all close together, forming a courtyard, with open fields on three sides, the long dirt track making its way through the trees on the other. Sneijder headed for the field behind the farm cottage.

Sneijder returned from his walk just as Van Rijn's van was making its way up the track. He was alone this time and with the boot polish he had sported the previous evening removed, his pale complexion could be observed. Sneijder and Van Rijn had breakfast with the old man Lamming, gathered together everything they needed and prepared to head into Arnhem.

'It's about nine kilometres into the city,' Van Rijn explained. 'We're about halfway between Arnhem and Nijmegen here so we'll be following the early morning traffic in.'

'Are we likely to get stopped?' Sneijder asked.

'Probably not, but the prison raid I told you about released over fifty political prisoners and really shook up the Germans. The Gestapo and the Green Police have been more interested in finding dissenters during the last couple of days.' The Ordnungspolizei, or Orpo, were the regular police of the Nazi state and were nicknamed 'Green Police' with reference to their green uniforms.

'I guess we'll see if the papers they gave me in England stand up to inspection,' Sneijder said. 'Fortunately they were zipped up in the pocket of my jacket and stayed dry.' He took them out and checked them over.

Van Rijn looked surprised. 'That identification card is a forgery? It's perfect. I'm impressed.'

Sneijder put all his weapons inside one of the sacks of grain that filled the cargo bay of the van, and settled in the front seat next to the older man. Together they began the short journey into the city where Sneijder's fate would be decided.

It was a glorious summer morning in the eastern Netherlands, the sun bright in a cloudless blue sky. The van carrying Sneijder into Arnhem joined the line of vehicles making their way into the city for the market; cars, small vans and a couple of large lorries. The German presence along the road from Nijmegen was light and the two of them were not stopped until they reached the bridge over the Rhine which served as the southern boundary of Gelderland's capital.

The Rhine Bridge sprouted up into the sky majestically. Opened in 1936, it was an arched cantilever design constructed from steel which glinted in the morning sun. A black unmarked car was parked at the side of the road a couple of metres before the start of the ramp which led up onto the bridge. A couple of grey-uniformed men of the Sicherheitsdienst or SD, the intelligence section of the SS, were stopping vehicles and questioning the drivers. As their van reached the German officers Van Rijn and Sneijder exchanged tense looks, conveying without a word the need for caution. The first officer signalled for Van Rijn to lower the window which he duly did.

'Can you tell me where you are going?' the SD man inquired in crisp German.

Van Rijn replied in a slightly broken version of the same language, 'To the Great Markt. I am bringing grain from my grandfather's farm to sell.'

The officer looked dubious. 'Really?'

'Would you like to see?' Van Rijn asked. 'Johannes, show him.'

Sneijder stepped out of the van, walked around to the rear doors and opened them up. He selected a sack which he knew was filled with nothing but wheat grain and opened it in front of the German. He took a handful of grain and allowed it to run through his fingers, then smiled at the officer.

The officer allowed Sneijder to return to the front seat, then came back to talk to Van Rijn. 'Are you aware of the prison break that occurred five days ago? We are looking for the perpetrators.'

Van Rijn feigned surprise. 'A prison break? Here in Arnhem?'

'Yes,' the German said sharply. 'Almost fifty prisoners were broken out of the House of Detention on Walburgstraat. Have you heard anything that may help us find those responsible? It is in your best interests to tell me.'

'No, nothing.'

The German officer turned to Sneijder. 'What about you?'

'Nothing,' he replied honestly.

The SD man looked at them both, and then glanced over the roof of the van in the direction of his colleague. For a moment the tension began to build. The officer turned back to them. 'Can I see your papers, please?'

Both men produced their identification cards and handed them over. Sneijder's forgery was identical to the card held by Van Rijn and did not evoke any response from the German officer, who seemed satisfied and waved them on. 'If you hear anything, be sure to report it to an official.'

Van Rijn drove across the bridge slowly. At either end of the structure there was a big concrete pillbox with the barrel of a heavy machine gun protruding from the slit in the wall. The Rhine river drifted by serenely about twenty-five metres below the bridge, the surface of the water as calm as a millpond. Sneijder looked to the left and saw the tall church tower of the Eusebiuskerk that dominated the skyline. The van reached the other side of the bridge and dropped down the ramp between small terraced houses. Van Rijn swung to the left and guided the vehicle through the narrow streets of central Arnhem, avoiding the trolley buses, passing the Great Markt where traders were opening up their stalls.

Sneijder enquired about the situation regarding food rations and was told by his companion that while supplies were short, there was generally enough for everyone to eat satisfactorily. Fruit and vegetables had been rationed since the previous year, meaning that almost all food was now regulated.

'You'll just need to get used to having a bit less energy,' Van Rijn explained. 'As for clothing – shoes and things like that – you just can't get them anymore.'

'The rationing in England is pretty tight now,' Sneijder replied, 'and I spent some time in a German camp so I think I'm used to it.'

'You were in a prison camp?'

'Yes,' Sneijder said, instantly wishing he had never mentioned it. 'Maybe I'll tell you about it sometime.' He looked away, ending the conversation.

The streets were very narrow and flanked on each side by buildings four and five storeys high that blocked out much of the sun, which hung low at this early hour. The style of the buildings was classically Dutch, with tall thin windows, elegantly carved arched door surrounds and elaborately designed gabled rooflines. The ground floors of most of the buildings were taken up by shops, some of which were now unoccupied and sporting a roughly painted Star of David to indicate they were Jewish properties. Sneijder sighed, his mind fixed on thoughts of those who had suffered under the Nazi regime.

Van Rijn eased the van carefully through a series of tight bends before bringing it to a halt alongside a line of similar vehicles. 'It'd be best to go on foot from here. It makes it easier to avoid the police. Leave your things here; we'll get them later.'

Sneijder was led through the city centre, which was busy with people going about their business. The shops that were still open seemed to be doing a reasonable trade considering the unavailability of many goods, and it was not immediately apparent that conditions in the country had got worse since Sneijder left Amsterdam in 1941. As was the case in England there was a visible absence of young men, but for a very different reason. While they were not involved in fighting the war, German labour drafts were becoming increasingly difficult to avoid and men of working age had started to go underground.

There were a couple of Dutch policemen hanging around on one street corner but they allowed Sneijder and Van Rijn to pass unchallenged. They made their way back in the direction of the church, stopping outside a bakery on the corner of the Great Markt. It was an old building four storeys high with the date 1875 carved above the door. To the right of the shop front there was a narrow oak door which led to the living accommodation on the upper floors. Van Rijn knocked hard on the door, and moments later a small man opened it.

'Is he here?' Van Rijn asked.

'Yes,' the small man replied. 'He is taking breakfast upstairs. Come in.'

Sneijder and Van Rijn followed the small man up a dark and dingy staircase, past a couple of doors and up a second flight of stairs. A door on the right-hand side opened into a small sitting room, beyond which was a kitchen with a round table. At the table with his back to them sat a medium-height figure, who appeared to be reading a newspaper. From what Sneijder could tell he was an older man, with grey hair that was almost white, thinning on top. For a moment he ignored their presence, long enough that the small man approached him, but without lifting his head he raised a hand to acknowledge that he knew they were there. The small man retreated to the door and left the room.

Sneijder waited for Van Rijn to speak but for some reason he seemed reluctant to. He looked at the Resistance man, whose expression was one of nerves. Eventually the older man folded the newspaper he was reading and put it down before rising from his chair. He turned around and showed his face. He was a distinguished looking gentleman, probably in his early sixties, whose experience lines gave his face an interesting quality and was well-dressed in a black silk waistcoat and dark plaid suit, with a gold pocket watch on a chain tucked into his jacket. A pair of half-rimmed spectacles rested on his thin nose. 'Good morning, Van Rijn,' he said.

'Mr Helder.'

'And your companion is…?' Helder questioned.

'This is Johannes Voorman – our guest from England. He…'

The older man's face dropped. 'You brought him here?' he said angrily. 'To my house? Bloody hell, man, how stupid are you?'

Van Rijn was flummoxed by the reaction of Helder. 'You told me to come here. I was carrying out your request.'

Helder was furious. 'I wanted you to come alone so I could tell you the arrangements. I did not ask you to bring him. You know what the Germans are like; a new face in town and they're all over it. They could have followed him here. God damn it, they can't know that I'm involved in any of this.'

'It's okay, we weren't followed,' Van Rijn said. 'I would have noticed.'

'Maybe so, but it is still a risk you did not have to take. My standing with the German authorities affords us all a certain amount of protection, but if it becomes obvious I am associating with their enemies that protection could disappear.'

'It's only a matter of time before they find out,' Van Rijn said, attempting to play down his error.

'Not....!' Helder began to shout, before returning his voice to a normal level. 'Not if I can help it. It's only through working for me that you and Bruggink have avoided the labour draft; just remember that. If I lose the reputation I have worked for so long to create, the chances are you'll be on the first train to Germany. With the pounding it's taking from the RAF I shouldn't think that would be too pleasant a proposition.'

Van Rijn did not reply.

Helder turned to Sneijder. 'Mr....Voorman, is it? I'm sorry you have been caught up in this little incident. You must think me terribly rude. Unfortunately the present situation requires appropriate measures.' He moved forward and shook Sneijder's hand. 'My name is Frank Helder. I should explain myself. I am not a young man. I cannot take part myself in any partisan activities, so all I can do is try to make things easier for those who can. To this end, I work with the German authorities, providing black market luxury goods to the pampered officers they like to post around here in return for certain... favours.'

Sneijder nodded.

Helder continued, 'I have an arrangement with the top German official in Arnhem, an Obersturmbann-führer Koestler, that certain employees of mine are protected from the labour draft. They will only turn a blind eye to a point however, and if they suspect I am helping the Resistance my position could be compromised. I'm sure you understand.'

'Of course,' Sneijder said. It occurred to him that Helder probably did very well personally out of what was essentially collaboration, but things were never black and white and one had to pacify the Germans to an extent in order to stay alive. Given the apparent relationship between Helder and Koestler, Sneijder decided he should keep the details of his mission a secret for the time being.

Helder said, 'Van Rijn here is one of my employees so it does not look out of place for him to be here but a stranger visiting me arouses suspicion, particularly when the Germans have a knack of knowing when agents have arrived from abroad.'

'I understand,' Sneijder assured him. 'I dropped straight into a German trap last time I was sent out on operation.'

The older man grimaced. 'How terrible. Now if you want to avoid the police this time, I suggest you go straight away to the house we have arranged for you. Even if we can get my protection extended to you it's much too dangerous for you to stay in the city. You'll be staying in Oosterbeek with a man named Uhlenbroek – a good friend of mine. He is the stationmaster at the railway station, someone the Germans need to rely on to keep the railways operating so they don't give him much trouble. It's a very quiet village, an ideal place to keep your head down. Van Rijn will take you there.'

'It sounds good,' Sneijder said. 'How far is Oosterbeek from here?'

Van Rijn spoke up. 'It's less than five kilometres – probably four or five minutes' drive. It is a nice little place; my cousin used to live out there.'

'I think from now on, Mr Voorman should pose as your cousin,' Helder suggested. 'It may help to explain his sudden arrival.'

Sneijder said, 'This Uhlenbroek; is he discreet? It would be useful to know what and how much I can tell him.'

'It would be wise not to tell him anything about what you do,' Helder replied. 'He'll be safer if he has no information to give. The same goes for me; I don't know what you have been instructed to do here, and I don't want to know. I can deny everything much more plausibly if I am actually telling the truth. Only inform people as and when they need to know.'

'We should go,' Van Rijn said.

'Do you know where the house is?' Helder asked. Van Rijn nodded so he continued, 'Good. Be cautious; the Germans are really on the lookout for saboteurs these days.'

Van Rijn and Sneijder moved toward the door. Helder picked up the newspaper from the table and threw it to Sneijder. 'Here, take that with you – get an idea of what the country's like right now.'

The copy of the underground newspaper *Vrij Nederland* that Sneijder had been given was filled with stories of increasing Resistance activity across the country, fuelled by the Allies ever-nearing advance. For the last four years, a viable chance of victory had been a distant dream so there had been a general acceptance of German rule. To the majority there had seemed little point in endangering one's life if it had no chance of achieving anything. But now there was an air of optimism around the country as the underground press and the radio broadcasts from London reported the struggles of the Wehrmacht in France. Suddenly the Resistance groups in Holland were having no trouble persuading people to participate in subversive activities against the occupying forces. The tide of the war was really beginning to turn against Germany.

Uhlenbroek was not at home when Sneijder and Van Rijn arrived at his house a little before eleven o'clock. It was a small abode on a small tree-lined street just back from the main road to Arnhem, the Utrechtseweg. It was mostly all on one level, with a couple of other rooms set into the space created by the building's sloping roof. Van Rijn parked the old van on a side street about two hundred metres away and they walked the rest of the way. The village was deserted and there was a very peaceful feeling about the place.

Uhlenbroek's wife came to the door when they knocked and took them inside. 'Oh yes, Edwin told me to expect a young man here this morning,' she said. 'We've taken in a few over the years. Only a few months ago we had an American pilot who lost his plane over Germany, until we passed him on to one of the escape lines.'

'Is your husband at work, Mrs Uhlenbroek?' Sneijder asked.

'At the station, yes,' she replied. 'He usually comes back home for lunch around twelve-thirty. You can probably meet him then.'

Van Rijn said, 'Mr Helder sends his regards and asked me to tell you that he will invite your husband and yourself over for dinner when he gets the chance.'

Mrs Uhlenbroek smiled warmly. 'That's Frank for you – always busy with something. Now, Mr Voorman, I should think you'd like to see your room. Follow me.'

'Please call me Johannes.'

The room up in the loft space was accessed by a little staircase at the back of the house. It was not a large room but it was pleasant and had everything one would need to live very comfortably. The window in the room jutted out from the sloping tiled roof, which immediately gave Sneijder the escape route he always liked to identify when he arrived somewhere new. All he would need to do is climb through the window and clamber down to the edge of the roof, which was only around three and a half metres off the ground.

Sneijder sat down on the edge of the bed and was delighted to find it was extremely comfortable.

'If you are all right here I need to get going,' Van Rijn said to Sneijder. 'I have to make an appearance at Mr Helder's factory.'

'I'm sure he'll be fine,' Mrs Uhlenbroek said. 'I can look after him. I've had nobody to fuss over since my son left for Batavia back in 1939.' She smiled good-naturedly and Sneijder laughed.

'I will be fine,' he said to Van Rijn. 'This seems like a good place, out of the way enough that I can avoid unnecessary contact with the Germans.'

'Oh you don't need to worry about that,' Mrs Uhlenbroek said. 'We've never had our home searched despite having many people staying with us. They wouldn't want to upset Edwin, not with the Germans moving equipment by rail.'

'I'll give you a couple of days to get settled in to the new place,' Van Rijn explained. 'We're having a meeting to discuss things on Friday evening so I will come and pick you up. Until then, so long.' And with that he was gone.

Edwin Uhlenbroek turned up at the house around quarter to one for lunch. He walked into the kitchen where he found his wife and Sneijder eating vegetable soup that she had made. He was a tall, thin man with a head of thick white hair and a face dominated by very high rosy cheeks. Mrs Uhlenbroek stood up from the table and made the introductions.

'It's very good to meet you,' Sneijder said. 'Thank you for giving me a place to stay.'

'It's no trouble at all,' Uhlenbroek replied. 'When Frank Helder asks you for something, you do your absolute best.'

The Uhlenbroeks and Sneijder sat around the table and ate lunch together, a meal of chicken, potatoes and fresh vegetables. The old couple were extremely friendly and seemed to relish the chance to take care of a young man, particularly the woman. They spoke warmly about their family, especially their grown-up children who lived in Batavia, the capital of the Dutch East Indies, and Rotterdam respectively. When they asked Sneijder about his family he recited the cover story he had been given, feeling somehow guilty that he was lying to these people after only knowing them for an hour. It was an essential part of the job though – being able to lie convincingly – and it was vital that he stuck to his false identity. After all, his true identity carried with it additional dangers.

Later, upstairs in his room, Sneijder settled down on the bed to catch up on his sleep. His mind would not switch off however, and he found himself rummaging through his clothes to locate the bottle of sleeping pills. With no alcohol to numb his senses he would certainly need the tablets. He washed them down with a glass of water and lay down, hoping to drift into slumber. The dreams would come back.

Chapter Seven

Koestler woke up that morning with very little recollection of the previous night's events. His head throbbed a little as he lay on the leather sofa in his lounge, still roughly dressed in the uniform he had been wearing at the drinks party. Slowly coming to, he dragged his weary body off the chair and moved across the room. There was only one way to clear his mind. Koestler picked up a small bottle of whisky, removed the cap and drank straight from it. The smooth liquid burned his parched throat; he burst into a fit of coughing and the drink ran down his face and soaked his clothing. He took a breath to steady himself and took another swig, then replaced the bottle.

Koestler was disturbed by a loud knock at the door and was alarmed to find his watch said ten-thirty. Putting on his spectacles as he passed through the hallway, he took a look in the mirror. He looked awful, with his black military tunic unbuttoned and his shirt opened halfway down his chest, now stained with alcohol. The little hair that he had these days was ruffled and unruly and he had bags of skin suspended beneath his eyes. The door was knocked again.

Koestler moved nearer. 'Who is it?' he called.

'It's me,' Klimitz replied from the other side of the door.

'Klimitz? What are you doing here?'

'Do you know what time it is?'

Koestler opened the door. 'Yes, I do.'

The captain was shocked by what he saw. 'Jesus Christ,' he exclaimed. 'It's half past ten and you're still in this state. Horvath from Gestapo HQ has been trying to find you all morning.'

'Horvath? What does he want? And what the hell happened to my driver?'

'Your driver was here as usual at eight-thirty but when he got no answer at the door he assumed you were not here,' said Klimitz. 'There was an incident last night; the Gestapo found a kubelwagen this morning on a country road just north of Nijmegen, riddled with bullets and apparently destroyed by a grenade blast. Both occupants dead, the driver and Walter Stracke. They seem to have been in a high speed pursuit.'

Koestler sighed. 'Stracke. I sent him out on night patrol specifically to combat this kind of attack on our forces. His wife is seven months pregnant, you know. Are there any leads?'

'Nothing significant. I don't know if it's relevant, sir, but there were a few reports of a single RAF bomber flying to and from the area, very low. We might find the English have sent us another guest.'

Koestler frowned. 'It'll be relevant all right. An incoming agent is just the sort of reason why the Resistance would be out so visibly beyond the curfew. It seems they need to be reminded once again of the penalty for taking German lives. For God's sake, will these people never learn? Do they think I enjoy having to shoot them?'

'The Americans and English are getting so close,' Klimitz replied. 'The people are expecting liberation.'

The adjutant pushed past his superior officer into the house. 'Horvath is expecting to hear from you. You'd better get cleaned up and get down there. The smell of drink is coming out of your skin.'

'I appreciate your honesty, Sebastien; you know that. But please remember you are talking to a senior officer.'

Klimitz reacted angrily. 'Perhaps you should try acting like it. I have spent all morning being asked where you are by senior officers, and I have had to work extremely hard to avoid telling them you are at home in a drunken stupor. How long do you think you can keep going like this? You are losing control, sir. There are already doubts about your competence, and after your display last night I should think Seyss-Inquart is thinking about replacing you.'

'I am perfectly in control,' Koestler replied tersely, 'and I do not need a lecture from you. If the Reichskommisar had any intention of replacing me I would have heard about it.'

'That's not what I've heard. Besides, it doesn't really matter what he thinks. Everybody knows Rauter is the one in charge and he doesn't like you. He'll be looking for any excuse he can find to get rid of you and put one of his own men in charge of recruitment. An alcoholic officer that goes missing is not going to last very long.'

'You have not told anyone?' Koestler questioned in alarm. 'After the years we have worked together I thought I could rely on you.'

'It is not my place to reveal anything but if you do not do something about it then it will be out of my hands. Somebody whose opinion matters more than mine will notice. Now get ready; I'll be waiting in the car.'

Koestler was taken directly to the scene of the incident to see the damage for himself. The kubelwagen lay in a ditch amongst thick undergrowth, the slightly blackened front end half-buried in the soft earth. The bodies of the two men killed in the incident had already been taken away but the evidence of the attack was plain to see. The left-front wing of the vehicle was caved inwards and jammed on the wheel and there were bullet holes around the area of the windscreen, some that looked to be from a nine-millimetre, others from a higher calibre weapon.

Although the use of a grenade to disable a fast-moving vehicle indicated an unplanned attack, Koestler knew he would have to take strong retribution against the Resistance. He had listened to Klimitz's comments, and he was certainly going to give his superiors no reason to get rid of him. He returned to his office after visiting the crash scene and sent for Horvath.

Franz Horvath was a very aggressive little man and about as complete a Nazi as it was possible to be. While a fairly low-ranking Gestapo officer, he had delusions of grandeur and was extremely insubordinate. He entered the room in an obvious foul mood. 'Ah, you are here now. I have been trying to get hold of you all day.'

'Yes, so I hear. This attack on our people – what is your opinion?'

'From what I have been able to gather, it seems likely that they were following a vehicle which was on the road after the curfew and were engaged. The force used suggests the perpetrators were involved in partisan activity and were evading capture.'

'Do you have any information about partisans in the area?' Koestler asked.

'No. We have no specific information. However, with the way the war has gone recently more and more civilians are taking up arms. This attack could have come from anywhere.'

'That is not good enough,' Koestler snapped. 'What is the Gestapo doing? It is your job to prevent this type of thing, is it not?'

'It is,' Horvath replied bluntly. 'But we can only get so much information from our sources, and we have limited manpower. I don't see how you can expect us to perform better than any other department without giving us more resources.'

'That is a decision dealt with at a higher level,' said Koestler. 'Horvath, I want you to investigate this incident as a matter of urgency. Walter Stracke was one of the SS's finest men. Find those involved, or at least find me some partisans I can make an example of. Somebody will be shot for this, do I make myself clear?'

Horvath gave an evil grin. 'Of course.'

'We must put down all resistance, particularly as military operations in Holland look likely in the near future. We cannot have our army being hampered by civilians. Do you not agree?'

'Certainly.'

Koestler added, 'Please report back to me with your findings. Now what about these reports about a plane being spotted? Did anyone see a parachutist?'

Horvath was expressionless. 'Not that I am aware of.'

'If there is a British agent in this area we need to know about it,' said Koestler. 'We must know their identity and for what purpose they are here. Take care of it. That will be all.'

The Uhlenbroeks were incredibly kind and generous hosts but Sneijder had always preferred his own company and so spent most of his time in his room. He had been pleased to discover that he shared an appreciation of German literature with Mrs Uhlenbroek, and so there were many books in the house with which he could sharpen up his ability with the language. When he was relaxed he did not feel the need for alcohol, which confirmed that he had no physiological addiction. Drinking was just a mechanism for coping with difficult situations. The sleeping tablets helped calm his nerves and he was sleeping slightly better now, but he was far from normal.

Oosterbeek was an extremely quiet village and had very little German presence, which allowed Sneijder to explore the area and walk beside the river. He had been advised that while his exemption from work would probably protect him from the labour draft, at least for the time being, it would be wise to avoid German officers as much as possible.

According to his instructions, in order to get in touch with his contact messages were to be deposited at a dead-drop in Arnhem. Sneijder borrowed a bicycle and rode to the location for the drop, a bench on Onderlangs, a road that ran alongside the river. The message he left was soon collected, but on Friday evening when Van Rijn came to pick him up no reply had yet been deposited.

The meeting of members of the Resistance was held in the basement of a small Catholic church in a village a few kilometres east of Arnhem. There were many attendees, including the church priest who led proceedings. He was a middle-aged man of strong character, who seamlessly moved from giving blessings to discussing German military actions with no lack of knowledge. Klara van Rijn and Max Bruggink were the only other people that Sneijder knew, but Kees van Rijn sat beside him and identified the others.

'That is Father Grooter,' Van Rijn said. 'He served in the army before becoming a priest, so he understands things as they are. Most of the clergy in the country support the Resistance but they often get bogged down in the morals of it all. Father Grooter knows what has to be done.'

'He looks a determined character,' Sneijder observed.

'You'd better believe it. The dark-haired man over there in the hat is Pieter de Jong – a real live wire. His adoptive family were Jewish and so were seized and deported. That includes both his parents who are in their sixties, so he's got a real grudge. God help any German that comes across him. Next to him is Jan Waaring, another man who works for Frank Helder. He's a good man, not particularly useful in a military sense but immensely loyal to the cause. Then there are the Voesman twins – small-time criminals both of them but they've got a habit of turning up the supplies we need to take on the Germans. Michael, the younger one by five minutes, is a real thug. You should stay out of his way.'

Sneijder sized up the two young men in the corner, one of whom had a hard face and sported a dented nose that had obviously been broken on more than one occasion. He was chain-smoking cigarettes as Father Grooter spoke.

'The Germans are already moving military forces into the country,' the priest said. 'They are preparing for a battle here, and it looks as though it won't be long before they get it. We need to think about what we can do to help defeat the German army.'

'We need to take them out – show the bastards we won't let them rest,' a fat man at the front called.

'That's a bad idea,' an older man argued. 'All that will do is make sure the Germans are ready for the Americans and British when they get here. We should do nothing and hope that their rustiness reduces their fighting capability.'

Van Rijn gave his opinion. 'You're missing the point. They're not going to post any military forces in this area. Why would they? Arnhem is a long way from the front line and it is unimportant. I'd be surprised if Allied forces even bother with Holland. If what we're hearing about the Germans is true, the Americans will head straight for Berlin.'

'I wasn't suggesting there'll be a battle here but there may be something we can do to assist in the south,' Father Grooter explained. 'The major problem we're going to face is if the military replace the existing administration. They'll be able to do what they like to us and blame it on military necessity.'

The discussions moved on to the subject of operations that should be carried out. Many of the more conservative characters expressed concern about possible reprisals if anything was done.

'There is just no point,' a tall man sitting next to Waaring said. 'For all the damage we do, the risk to innocent people is too great.'

De Jong turned to him. 'So what do you suggest?' he asked, raising his voice. 'Because they threaten us we should just give up? No way. We stand up to them, no matter what.'

'Are you really that stupid, Pieter?' the tall man responded. 'We're not talking about ideals here; real people's lives are in the balance. Is raiding a Gestapo office really worthwhile if the SS march into a village and murder civilians?'

'You do nothing if you like,' said De Jong. 'My conscience will not allow me to subject myself to an occupier without a fight, and I'm sure there are lots of others in this room like me. I owe it to my country to resist.'

The young man with the broken nose who Van Rijn had identified as Michael Voesman stood up. 'Well let's do something then, instead of sitting around arguing. We've had a tip from a man we know in Amsterdam that in two weeks' time the Germans will be flying a consignment of supplies to Deelen airfield, including ration books and ID cards. The consignment will come on board a Junkers Ju52 transport and be taken into Arnhem on a convoy of trucks. Martin and I are going to hit the convoy but we need more people. Who wants to help us?'

The room fell silent. Father Grooter moved to end the uncomfortable period of quiet, but before he could Michael Voesman exploded angrily. 'What the hell is wrong with you people? Just because I get in trouble with the law I'm not good enough for you? I am doing this, whether anybody helps me or not.'

His older brother Martin pulled him down. 'Please excuse my brother. We can't do this alone; we need at least four more men to do it properly. As well as the ration books, I've been told there will be ten thousand marks in bearer bonds and files on suspected divers, people to be reported if they attempt to obtain ration books.'

Sneijder smiled at the mention of a term he had not heard for some time. 'Divers' was a colloquial term for persons in hiding. It had not been widely used while Sneijder was still in Holland at the beginning of the war as there were not many of them, but now it was commonplace.

'Ten thousand marks,' said the tall man sneeringly. 'So that's why you're interested. You're risking lives to steal some money. It's just plain robbery.'

The Voesman twins were both incensed at the accusation and began to shout at the same time. Dissenting voices were raised all over the room until everybody was screaming at one another.

Father Grooter banged a fist on the table in front of him. 'Quiet! This is supposed to be a secret meeting. If anybody hears us, the Green Police will be here in no time. Now whatever our personal feelings, the fact is we need ration books and blank ID cards to protect those in hiding. I think you should all consider that.'

The room fell silent again. Sneijder got the feeling that nobody was keen on working with the Voesmans. Martin Voesman looked around the attendees one by one. 'How about it, Van Rijn?' he asked. 'We could do with you and Max on our side. It could really be something; one in the eye for the Hun.'

Van Rijn and Bruggink exchanged glances, and the latter spoke. 'Anything that will help the war effort is worth it in my book, but there are conditions. Firstly that you keep that brother of yours under control, and I want Kees in charge.'

The Voesman twins bristled at the comment, but unlike Michael, who had to be restrained by his brother, Martin kept his composure and said calmly, 'Wait a minute, this is our deal. Nobody is telling us what to do. I can handle the planning.'

'Not a chance,' Bruggink replied. 'If I'm putting my neck on the line I want someone I trust in control, and that rules you two out.'

Martin Voesman continued protesting, but under pressure from the other attendees he eventually conceded on the understanding that he could lead the actual assault. 'That still leaves us at least two men short.'

Pieter de Jong raised a hand. 'Count me in. If Van Rijn's in charge, I'm happy to help.'

'Anyone else?' Bruggink questioned.

Sneijder had observed the evening's events carefully, attempting to gage the atmosphere when this collection of men was together. Despite their common interest in defying the Germans there was a tangible air of distrust amongst them, and Sneijder knew he would need to keep his orders to himself for as long as possible. He probably would need help at some point however and needed to start building trust with his comrades. He sensed an opportunity here. 'I could help.'

Van Rijn turned to him. 'Do you think you are ready?'

Father Grooter interrupted. 'Perhaps you should introduce your acquaintance, Kees.'

Van Rijn cleared his throat. 'Gentlemen, this is Johannes Voorman, my cousin from Amsterdam. I asked him to come to Arnhem to help us in our work.'

'I don't know,' Michael Voesman said doubtfully. 'We don't work with strangers.'

'I'll vouch for him,' Van Rijn said. 'He knows how to handle himself, believe me.'

Bruggink frowned and flashed a look at Van Rijn, aware that his friend did not know Sneijder well enough to make that type of call. In return he received a nod. He obviously trusted Van Rijn's judgement and he said, 'That's good enough for me.'

Suddenly the door at the top of the staircase burst open and another priest flew down the stone steps. 'Father Grooter, it's the Gestapo! Right outside the church! A plain-clothes officer and five or six uniforms.'

Father Grooter turned to the assembled group. 'Okay everybody, upstairs and out of the rear door.'

'There is no time for that,' the other priest said.

There was an audible crash from upstairs as the front door was flung open and several sets of footsteps on the stone-flagged floor above. A loud voice boomed in German, 'Father Grooter! I need to speak with you immediately.'

Father Grooter moved towards the staircase. 'Father Vos, the old tunnel. Take them out that way; I'll go up and try to stall them. Hurry.' He placed a hand on his fellow clergyman's shoulder. 'And pray. If we don't get everybody out quickly we're in deep trouble.' He disappeared up into the church to confront the German police, closing the door firmly behind him.

Father Vos barged past the Voesman twins and several others. He pushed open a large wooden double-barred door that opened into a small storeroom. On the far wall, beyond a dusty bookshelf lined with nineteenth century-edition Bibles hung an old and badly worn Flemish tapestry. Father Vos moved it aside to be faced with masonry discoloured by rising damp. It was here that the old priest began pushing on a brick. The Voesmans had followed him in, and the two young men immediately set to work on the surrounding bricks.

Van Rijn entered behind them. 'What are you doing?'

Father Vos replied breathlessly, 'There's a set of old sewage pipes running about two metres from this wall. There is a tunnel leading there dating back to the war of independence from the Spanish, but it was bricked up centuries ago. If memory serves me correctly it's directly behind these bricks.'

'Memory?' exclaimed Van Rijn. 'You mean you don't know?'

'We've never used it before; we only found the plans for the building last year.'

De Jong asked fearfully, 'How do you know the tunnel is even there? Just because it's on the plans....'

Sneijder added, 'If those bricks have been there for centuries they won't shift by hand. We need some tools.'

'Over there, under that sheet,' said Father Vos.

The Voesman twins, the old priest and Van Rijn continued to push against the wall. Sneijder and De Jong scrambled under a huge tarpaulin for something to help them. There were raised voices upstairs as Father Grooter challenged the Gestapo men. It was unlikely that he would be able to stall them for long. Sneijder pulled out a crowbar and pushed through to the wall. He attempted to wedge the sharp end of the implement between the stone blocks and work one free.

'Come on, this is taking too long,' a voice called from the back.

Michael Voesman turned around furiously and charged at the man who had spoken, fists raised. 'Do you want to do it? Do you? We're trying our best, you good-for-nothing old loser!'

'Keep your voice down,' Van Rijn ordered. 'They are not bloody deaf.'

The man pushed Voesman away. The young thug pulled the tarpaulin back, and turned around with a shovel. 'Out of my way!' He ran up behind his brother and raised the tool. Sneijder ducked just in time. The shovel missed his head by millimetres and slammed into the wall with a deafening clang. One of the bricks cracked down the middle and moved a little.

'You damned idiot!' De Jong exclaimed. 'Now they know we're down here. You've killed us all, you little prick!'

Sneijder dropped the crowbar and shoulder-charged the loose brick. It crumbled a little more and with a final push it broke clean in half and disappeared into the darkness, leaving a hole in the wall. The other men ripped at the surrounding bricks and now that they could get decent purchase the hole widened quickly.

'Come on, that's enough,' Van Rijn said. 'Let's go.'

Sneijder stood back and allowed everyone else to go through first, which despite the passage being narrow took less than a minute. Sneijder was just making his way through the hole when there was a loud crash from the next room and footsteps began descending the steps into the basement. Father Vos motioned for them all to be still and remain silent and then he pulled the tapestry back across the hole. Barely two seconds later, the store-room door burst open.

Father Grooter's tone was indignant. 'I told you – there is nobody here. Look, I can't allow you in there...'

Sneijder heard the Gestapo officer march into the room and approach Vos.

Before the German could say anything, Father Grooter spoke again. 'Father Vos, what on earth happened? We heard loud noises from upstairs.'

The old man replied sweetly. 'Please forgive me, Father Grooter. I am very old and not in the best condition. I'm afraid I dropped some of the Bibles, including the Statenvertaling.'

'The what?' asked the German.

'The Statenvertaling,' Grooter repeated. 'It's the state's original Dutch translation of the Bible, published in 1637. A very old book.'

'I'm very sorry,' Father Vos said.

Father Grooter turned to the Gestapo officer. 'Happy? We have nothing to hide. Now get out of my church!'

The Gestapo agent was not satisfied. 'What was all the shouting about?' he asked Father Vos.

'He just told you!' Father Grooter replied vehemently. 'He dropped some books and he cried out. Now really, this is ridiculous – please leave at once!'

Sneijder lay absolutely still, just inches from Father Vos, the elaborately embroidered tapestry all that stood between him and certain capture. He hardly dared breathe. The old tunnel was very hot and sweat dripped down his forehead as he tried to maintain his position. Ahead of him De Jong and Klara van Rijn were crouched in the tunnel; beyond them the bodies disappeared into the darkness.

The Gestapo man continued to question the two priests thoroughly. The voices moved away for a second, but Sneijder knew they could return at any moment. He whispered down the tunnel to the others, 'Go, quickly!'

The message was passed along and the group began to move down into the darkness. The narrow passage was not easy to negotiate. It had obviously been chiselled out with primitive tools and was very uneven in width and surface. Sharp edges protruded out of the stone making it uncomfortable to crawl at any speed. Despite this they all moved along quickly and entered the large sewage tunnel at the end of the crawlspace.

Fortunately the sewer had been abandoned for many years and so they did not have to contend with anything unpleasant. The tunnel was big enough to enable a person to stand up and they could move a great deal quicker. Van Rijn at the front of the group had grabbed a flashlight from the pile of tools in the storeroom before entering the tunnel and he now turned it on. A strong beam of light illuminated the crumbling brickwork that stretched out in both directions for a hundred metres or so before curving around a bend at each end.

'Which way?' Van Rijn asked.

The tall man looked down and examined the bricks under his feet. 'Look at the wear on these. It appears to go in that direction. When this tunnel was used the water probably flowed out that way.' He pointed along the tunnel.

The Voesman twins appeared dubious.

'Do you have a better idea?' the tall man said.

Van Rijn led them along the sewer in the direction the tall man had suggested. After several minutes they rounded the bend and a little later emerged on to the bank of a small canal. It was sunset but still light enough that they could be spotted if they were not careful. The bank was particularly narrow and it required a great deal of balance to avoid falling into the water. While probably not particularly deep, the canal was a hazard as the sound of a person falling in could potentially alert the German officers who were not far away. About twenty metres along the bank there was a bridge over the canal.

Van Rijn led the group under the bridge where they were safe from view, and then he and Sneijder crawled up the bank to take a look at their surroundings.

They were now on the other side of the road from the church. They could see the large black Mercedes and the small truck which had brought the Gestapo to the area. It was several minutes before the uniformed men emerged from the church building and climbed into the truck, and another ten minutes before the plainclothes officer came out and got into the Mercedes. Only when they were all present did the two vehicles pull away from the front of the building and disappear into the night.

While they were waiting Van Rijn brought up the subject of Sneijder assisting in the attack on the German convoy. 'Are you sure you really want to get involved so soon?' he asked. 'You've only just got back into the thick of it and as you have just seen, the chances of us all being caught or killed are quite high.'

'I'm quite sure,' replied Sneijder. He thought for a moment and decided this was as good a time as any to test the water regarding his companion's cooperation. 'I must confess that I have a reason for volunteering. I hope you will not hold it against me when I tell you.'

'I suppose that depends on the reason, my friend,' Van Rijn said.

'As you may or may not have guessed, I have been sent here for a specific purpose,' Sneijder explained. 'I can't tell you what that purpose is at the moment but I think I will probably need your help when the time comes.'

'What kind of help are we talking about?' Van Rijn asked firmly.

'I'm afraid I can't tell you that either; until my contact gets back to me I don't have a lot of information to go on, but I think it is extremely unlikely that I will be able to carry out my orders alone.'

'I see.'

'The point is, I can't really expect you or anybody else to help me without getting something in return. Particularly when I will not be able to tell you what my mission is. I thought that if I volunteered to help on this job....'

'It would buy you some kind of favour with me and the others,' Van Rijn said sharply.

Sneijder said nothing for a moment as he tried to read the other man. His tone of voice was hard and adversarial, but the expression on his face did not convey the same feelings. Sneijder could understand why Van Rijn might be angry with him; each man would be placing his life in the hands of his comrades, and every member of the team needed to be ready for it. If Van Rijn thought he was falsely declaring himself prepared because of an ulterior motive, he would think that Sneijder was happy to risk other men's lives for his own ends.

'I suppose that was what I was hoping, yes,' Sneijder replied. 'But I am ready for it.'

'Johannes, it works like this with me. If you think you can handle this hit, come along. But if you are volunteering just to impress me and get me on your side, forget it because you're likely to get somebody killed. As for assisting with your task, I will do it if I believe it's it the best interests of the country. Whether I like you is irrelevant.'

'Point taken.'

'Good.' Van Rijn smiled. 'Now shall we get the hell out of here?'

CHAPTER EIGHT

'So, Horvath, deliver your report.'

Koestler stood at the window with his back to the Gestapo man, peering out at the vehicles on the road. His mind was not really on the matter in hand; instead it was on the luncheon appointment with Frank Helder he was to attend later that day. Having failed to find a suitable replacement for the deceased Gilbert Krol, he had decided to make Helder work for his privileges. The old man's extensive social network was bound to include someone with National Socialist sympathies, hopefully someone with enough kudos to persuade wavering NSB members to join the Germanic SS.

Horvath cleared his throat. 'Unfortunately we have been unable to locate the perpetrators of the attack on Walter Stracke's vehicle. None of our sources are willing to talk, it seems. The fact is, these people could have come from anywhere.'

Koestler spun around. 'I could have come up with that kind of answer myself,' he snapped. 'I left it to you to get some results. What about the prison break? There were over twenty people involved in that; surely you have some information on at least one of them.'

Horvath shook his head slowly. 'I'm sorry, sir. Without information from our sources I am unable to make any progress. I'm afraid that's the way it works.'

'What the hell do we pay you for?' Koestler said angrily. 'Don't the Gestapo do any investigative work these days? I expected you to get out there and find these people, not sit around waiting for your informers to do your job for you.'

Horvath was infuriated. 'I have been out there trying to find those persons responsible but the information is just not there. The Resistance have become very good at covering their tracks.'

'These people are amateurs - experienced, perhaps, but amateurs nonetheless. Your organisation is supposed to be the cream of German policing. This is not good enough, Horvath. Not good enough at all. I want some answers, so get out there and talk to whoever you need to talk to, but bring me some answers. If you can't find the individuals, then find out which town or village they are from and we will make an example of its people. Someone is going to suffer for taking a German life.'

'I don't think it...' Horvath began.

'This is not a negotiation. Now get out of my office.' Koestler pointed to the door in a rage. For once Horvath did not attempt to argue; he immediately left the room.

When Frank Helder arrived for the luncheon appointment at the Germanic SS's country house on the outskirts of Arnhem, Koestler was already seated at the end of the long dining table. It was a long narrow room with crystal chandeliers hanging from the high ceiling and Nazi swastika banners suspended at each end. The wood-panelled walls were highly polished and embellished with several large oil paintings, one of them a genuine Rembrandt portrait which had been plundered from Amsterdam's extensive collection of art treasures.

Koestler was not in a good mood following a telephone call he had placed an hour earlier. He had called an old friend from his First World War days who was now a staff officer in The Hague to find out whether there was any truth in the rumours relayed to him by Klimitz. After some probing his friend had admitted to him that there was some concern at the highest level about Koestler's behaviour and his ability to continue in his present role. So it was true; the knives were out and he would have to be very careful in his actions.

Helder was shown into the room by an orderly. 'Good afternoon, Herr Koestler. I trust you are well?'

Koestler smiled. 'Yes, thank you. Please, sit down. The cook will be bringing lunch shortly.'

Helder took a seat and immediately set about making the usual small talk that opened these kinds of meetings. The two men were refined gentlemen with a taste for the finer things in life, and shared a love for classical music. Helder used Koestler's weakness for luxury as an asset when trying to negotiate arrangements which suited both the Resistance and himself. Over a starter of mushroom soup Helder produced a wooden box which contained twenty of the finest Cuban cigars.

Koestler was amazed. 'My God, Mr Helder, I knew you were a man who could get hold of many things but Cuban cigars? I am impressed.'

'I have a business acquaintance who is involved in shipping goods in and out of the Netherlands Antilles,' replied Helder. 'He moves shipments from the United States through Havana.'

'However you get hold of it, I thank you.'

Helder smiled warmly. 'Speaking of which, I have a large case of Scotch whisky coming in for you in the next few days. It was not easy to get hold of with things as they are, but as long as your people don't try to arrest me for racketeering it'll get here.'

The three course luncheon they ate was far beyond anything which was now available to Dutch civilians. As a guest of the German administration, Helder could enjoy fine food and wine which he could not have at any other time now that the rationing had become so strict. Koestler had become very accommodating as his dependence on alcohol increased and he had allowed Helder to break the rules on a frequent basis.

As they neared the end of the lavish dessert course, Koestler decided to move in. 'Mr Helder, my superiors have charged me with the task of recruiting young Dutchmen for the foreign legions of the SS. Unfortunately the man who was working on my behalf attending meetings of the NSB to look for candidates was killed recently, and I have been unable to replace him. I would like you to help.'

Helder dropped his spoon and looked up, his face white. 'Me? You want me to do what?'

'I would like you to find me a replacement for the man I lost,' Koestler said. 'You are always telling me about your long list of contacts; now is your chance to prove it. You must know somebody with a good reputation and National Socialist tendencies. The Germanic SS cannot operate without recruits.'

'I will have nothing to do with any Nazi sympathisers,' Helder said strongly. 'What we have is a very good arrangement; you get what you want and I get what I want. You have seriously misunderstood our relationship if you think I am going to help you force young men to turn on their own country.'

Koestler raised his voice. 'Perhaps I am no longer getting what I want. Perhaps it is time you started doing something more useful in return for those special favours you are afforded. Or would you prefer our arrangement to end?'

Helder hesitated for a moment. 'It is all academic anyway; I have always tried to steer clear of the NSB and their supporters. I wouldn't know where to look for the type of person you want.'

'Mmm, I see.' Koestler frowned, and then suddenly a smile crossed his face as an idea hit him. 'I tell you what; why don't you do it yourself? You are a man of un-questionable reputation who could really get through to these young men. In fact, you may even be able to con-vince those who do not have National Socialist leanings to join up.'

Helder pulled the napkin out of his shirt collar, pushed back his chair and stood up. 'Absolutely not. I am frankly insulted that you would think I could possibly agree to this. I am many things but I am not a traitor.'

'Well that is a question of interpretation,' Koestler replied harshly. 'What you consider to be harmless prof-iteering would appear to some to be a bitter betrayal. I am sure there are certain things you would prefer did not become public knowledge. The Resistance can be partic-ularly unforgiving; just look at the number of Dutch collaborators who have been murdered.'

'Are you threatening me?' Helder asked furiously.

'Mr Helder, listen to me very carefully because I will not say this again. The German Reich rules this country, and you and every other Dutch citizen are subjects of Germany. I am in charge in this town and that means you do exactly what I say. If you do not, there will be consequences.' Koestler stood up and walked across the room to where the old man stood. Leaning in threateningly, he continued, 'The sources of your vast income will be revealed to some very unpleasant people, along with some helpful information about where to find you. Your family will be arrested and all members of your staff who have avoided the labour draft through my actions will be shot. Your assets will be seized and your factory burned down. Now do we understand one another?'

After several more days of waiting there was finally a message for Sneijder at the dead-drop location. He still had no idea as to the identity of the person with whom he was conversing but he was pleased to hear from them. The previous week had been spent hanging around waiting, leaving plenty of time for Sneijder's mind to wander into places he did not wish to go. Sleep was continuing to be as elusive as ever.

He took a bicycle into the city on the morning he was supposed to meet his contact. It was a bright and sunny July day, the temperature already high at eleven o'clock. The meeting place was a café just off the Korenmarkt in the city centre, which Sneijder was horrified to find thronging with teenage soldiers of the Hitler Youth. These youngsters were sometimes the most fanatical of all as they had been brought up with Nazi indoctrination; Sneijder just hoped that their lack of years would count against them and that his presence would go unnoticed.

He arrived early to check the place out, going through the routine that had been drummed into him during his training. He stood opposite the café for some time, looking in the window of a flower shop and scouring the reflections for any sign that he was being followed. When he was satisfied that there was no tail Sneijder crossed the square and wandered down the alley next to the café, trying to locate the rear exit so he could plan an escape route. The door was on the corner of the building and opened out onto the back of the alley. There was a wall about two metres high but against it stood a large steel dustbin that would easily support Sneijder's weight if he needed to climb on it. He returned to the front of the café and went inside, trying his best to behave normally. The Hitler Youth were laughing and joking and generally making a lot of noise, and none of them seemed to notice Sneijder enter, walk through to the back to find the passage leading to the rear exit, and leave again.

He returned about twenty minutes later and ordered a coffee, black, as milk was something of a luxury nowadays. He took a table in the corner of the cafe and sat with his back to the wall so he could see the entire room. The contact arrived five minutes later, but there were two of them; a burly man with greying hair and a nervous young man a little younger than Sneijder who did not appear comfortable.

'Are you him?' the burly man asked.

Sneijder nodded slowly. 'Polo.'

The two men sat down and the older man continued to speak. 'My name is Dimitri. This is my son. I asked you to meet us here, in the lion's den as it were, for security. In my experience the Germans are so arrogant they could never believe that anybody hostile to them would meet right in front of them.'

Sneijder did not react. 'Were you followed?'

The older man hesitated and looked at his son. 'I don't think so.'

'Did you check? This is important.'

'Sorry,' the man said. 'I'm new to all this. To be honest I don't think I'm very good at it.' He laughed nervously.

Again Sneijder was unresponsive. 'We should not stay here long - it may be dangerous. Let's get straight to business. I am told that you are close to Koestler.'

'Not me - him,' Dimitri said, pointing to his son. 'He was drafted onto Koestler's staff as his driver.'

Sneijder raised his eyebrows. The young man had not said a word or even reacted to anything that had been said. He continued to look down at the table. Sneijder had expected the contact to be fiery and determined; the sort of person one could imagine putting themselves at risk in order to fight for what they believed was right. What he was confronted with was a shy youngster who was scared to even talk to a stranger. Sneijder directed a question towards the young man. 'How long have you driven for him?'

The young man fired a glance towards his father, receiving a nod in return. 'About seven months,' he said quietly.

'And you always drive for him?'

'That's right.'

'Okay, I need you to tell me everything you can about Koestler's routine. Where he lives, where he works, the times he goes and the routes he takes.' Sneijder leaned in. 'But before we go any further, I need to make sure you understand what you're doing. If we carry this through the Germans are going to hunt us down ruthlessly. How much have you been told?'

'We were told that somebody may come to eliminate Koestler,' Dimitri said. 'Hugo had been relaying messages to the Resistance about him and we heard the

Dutch government in London were looking for someone close to him. But yes, we know what is involved.'

Sneijder responded, 'I need to hear it from your son. He'll be under suspicion immediately and will have to go to ground. He needs to be prepared for that.'

The young man Hugo did not look happy and stared down at the table.

'My boy is prepared for whatever they can throw at him,' Dimitri declared proudly while placing a hand on his son's shoulder. 'It's in the family; my father stormed the Winter Palace in St Petersburg in 1917.'

'Are you ready?' Sneijder asked Hugo, although he knew the answer was irrelevant. This boy was being cajoled into helping by his father but he was frightened. The smell of fear was all over him. This was not a promising sign; when people were afraid they made mistakes. Deep down, Sneijder knew that relying on this young man could be dangerous, but it was all he had to go on.

'I am ready,' Hugo replied. 'I know it's dangerous but I am prepared to do it.'

Sneijder smiled weakly, trying his best to seem positive but failing miserably. 'Good. Now tell me everything you know.'

Once Hugo began talking, his confidence grew and the nervousness that he had initially displayed disappeared. The Hitler Youth soldiers flooded out of the cafe around twelve, leaving them free to talk without the fear of being overheard. The young man told Sneijder about Koestler's home and place of work, the other places he went including the country house on the outskirts of Arnhem, his usual times of departure and arrival, and his usual levels of security. It seemed to be just as De Beer had intimated in London; the Obersturmbannführer was very laissez-faire about protection and often travelled alone with just a driver, or accompanied by his adjutant, a captain in the SS. His journey between his home and the SS headquarters in Arnhem seemed the perfect opportunity to attack him as there was likely to be very little in the way of resistance, but this would involve military force, something which did not sit well with Sneijder's morals.

Sneijder decided to visit each of the relevant locations with the two men who knew them well. Dimitri had an old beaten-up car parked near the cafe and they took it for a drive around the city. They drove past the imposing building which the SS used as their local headquarters, then moved north out of the city centre towards Koestler's place of residence. The urban landscape quickly gave way to open fields and woodland, with several desolate stretches of road ideal for an ambush. The thick forest to each side of the thoroughfares would surely provide adequate protection for anybody wishing to lie in wait and the number of roads crisscrossing at regular intervals would make an escape possible.

Dimitri pulled the car up at the side of the main road and killed the engine. The sun was high in the sky and the trees cast dappled shadows across the roof of the vehicle. The three men got out and Sneijder followed Hugo and his father into the woods adjacent. The trees were mostly of pine, some dense in their foliage and others less so, while one or two had been stripped of branches almost right to the top. In between the mature trees there were small bushes and saplings which snagged on Sneijder's clothing as he passed.

Hugo pointed ahead to a modest two-storey house with large windows and a gabled roof which branched off a narrow dirt track. 'We need to be careful,' he whispered. 'There is always a sentry on duty during the day.'

'A sentry?' Sneijder asked. 'What is he - SS?'

'I think so, but I think he was invalided out from the front line. We shouldn't alert him but I don't think he would cause too much trouble when the time came, if you know what I mean.'

The ground was very dry and sticks cracked under their feet as they covered the four hundred metres to the houses. Smoke drifted out of the chimney of a small cottage away to the right, and an old man stood outside chopping wood with an axe.

In the bright sun the leaves on the trees glowed a vibrant green and visibility was good, but when a cloud passed overhead and it became slightly duller, objects began to disappear into the depths of the forest.

The three men moved in single file as the woods became denser, Hugo leading the way and his father bringing up the rear. Almost by instinct Sneijder reached into the pocket of his trousers and pulled out his Luger. They crept around towards the front of the house, keeping close to the two metre-high fence that surrounded it. Through a gap between two fence posts Hugo pointed out the sentry, who sat on a small wall beside the front path. A Schmeisser machine pistol hung on a strap around his chest. Closer inspection revealed that the man on guard was asleep.

Sneijder turned to Hugo. 'If he is always this alert I shouldn't have too much trouble.' He moved away from the other two and walked right around the house, keeping close to the fence, trying to get a mental picture of the place. The woodland surrounding the building on all sides screened it from the neighbouring houses and

Sneijder noted that it would definitely be possible to stand within five or six metres of the house without being seen from inside, especially after dusk. He paced out the distance from the front path to the dirt track, and from the dirt track back on to the main road. Once he was satisfied that he had investigated the place thoroughly he returned to where Hugo and Dimitri were waiting.

'Is everything okay?' Dimitri asked.

Sneijder nodded. 'Nothing much to report. Seems a quiet sort of place, out of the way. Koestler must really be confident that nobody is going to attack him if his security arrangements are anything to go by.'

'The severity of the reprisals has put most people off the idea of assassinating German officials,' Dimitri replied. 'He knows how unlikely it is that he will be attacked.'

They returned to the car and began the journey back towards Arnhem, taking a slight detour past the entrance to the country estate used by the Germanic SS for training and induction purposes. About twenty metres beyond the front gate there was a small hut painted red and white with a barrier across the road. Two armed soldiers stood clutching Mauser rifles. Sneijder knew that this entrance would be impossible to use. He asked Hugo if there were any other gates into the estate.

'I think there is a rear entrance over behind the stables but the whole place is crawling with soldiers,' Hugo replied. 'You would be taking one hell of a risk if you tried to get in here.'

Sneijder was inclined to agree. It would not make sense to even contemplate trying to breach the security of this place when there were much simpler alternatives.

The house where Koestler lived was obviously a weak point, as was his car when he was making the journey from his home to his office and back. The ideal situation would be to kill Koestler in a way that could be disguised as an accident, but this would be difficult to accomplish. Sneijder knew that despite his own personal reservations about a direct assassination attempt he had to consider it as an option.

Dimitri and Hugo left Sneijder outside the cafe where they had met just after three o'clock. They decided it would be best to communicate through the dead-drop for the time being as it offered security and the ability to deny knowing each other if the Germans got close. Sneijder returned to the house in Oosterbeek to consider his options.

Early the next morning Sneijder was in the woods in front of Koestler's house, roughly dressed in jeans and his leather jacket. It was overcast with a light wind, the sun trying its best to burst through the low cloud. A conversation with Edwin Uhlenbroek had revealed that he kept an old motorcycle in his garage, which after an hour's work with a spanner and some engine oil ran fairly adequately. Fortunately Uhlenbroek also had access to a supply of black-market fuel on which to run the machine, though this increased the chances of the German authorities seizing it if it was left in plain view. For now Sneijder had hidden it in a hedge that ran alongside the Kemperbergsweg.

Just before eight-thirty the Mercedes staff car appeared on the track and rolled to a halt outside the front door. The driver in grey uniform stepped out of the car and walked around to open the rear door. It was

Hugo, and he looked nervous as he waited for his superior officer to come out. The sentry knocked on the front door, and seconds later the door swung open and Koestler walked out. He was thinner than he had appeared in the photograph and far less immaculate; his military tunic was creased and the medal ribbons had been attached with a lack of care. He strode past Hugo without a glance and got into the car.

Sneijder jogged through the trees and pulled the motorcycle out of the hedge, swinging a leg over it and kicking it into action as the car appeared in the corner of his eye. He let it pass and get some distance ahead, then accelerated out of the ditch and followed. The Mercedes kept up a reasonable speed for the majority of the journey into the city. It was straight road most of the way with a few gently sweeping bends, the ground dropping away as they moved towards the river which was situated just south of the centre of town. Sneijder kept well back to ensure he was not spotted, remaining just close enough to keep the car in view. He wanted to observe Hugo without his knowledge, to see the way he really acted when carrying out his job.

The SS headquarters bordered a park on the east side of Arnhem, and was a large four-storey building with a flight of stairs at the front. Koestler was met at the front door by a captain who appeared to be about forty; based on the description given by Hugo, Sneijder assumed this to be the adjutant, Sebastien Klimitz. Above the door there was a small flag sporting the black swastika on a red background with the Iron Cross in the corner; the Third Reich battle flag. A flag pole protruded from the roof and on it hung the black and white double-lightning emblem of the SS.

Hugo drove the Mercedes away. Sneijder followed through the streets to see where Hugo would go after dropping off Koestler. After a couple of minutes the car approached an office building which was also lined with the various logos of the German administration. It seemed to have a civilian use, probably involved with rationing or the processing of decrees from the High Commissioner. Behind the building there was an open yard surrounded by a three metre-high brick wall, the entrance blocked by large wrought-iron gates. A young man in mechanic's overalls opened the gates and the Mercedes moved inside. Sneijder stopped across the road. As the gates swung shut he could see a number of vehicles parked around the edge of the yard. A small garage had been built into the rear of the office building and a couple of men were inside surrounded by vehicle parts.

For the rest of the day Sneijder remained in Arnhem, watching the clock and trying to avoid the police. At a little before six o'clock he was outside Koestler's office in order to follow him back home. It was a fair assumption that he would return to his house along the same route as he had used in the morning, but it was always a good idea to be sure. In reality he more or less went the same way, with just one or two slight variations which made little difference. Hugo dropped him off and left.

Sneijder wanted a closer look, to try to get an idea of what sort of man it was he had been sent to eliminate. He knew that doing so could make it more difficult to carry out the job; at the moment Koestler was just a name, a figure he had seen from a distance. Once he had seen a man close-up, he was a real person in Sneijder's mind and he would have to cope with the moral abhorrence of murder. Even so, he wanted to know.

Sneijder moved towards the house, stepping as lightly on the ground as possible. He crouched in a hedge, only metres from the front path, and watched the sentry smoking a cigarette, close enough to see the whites of the man's eyes. When the sentry turned his back, Sneijder scampered through the undergrowth and moved around to the side of the house to a position where he could see the upstairs windows. It was just at that moment that he was disturbed by a loud voice. It would be a meeting that would change everything for Sneijder, and indeed the man whose life hung in the balance. It was a female voice and spoke in German. 'Who are you?' it demanded. 'What do you think you are doing here?'

Sneijder turned around.

CHAPTER NINE

The woman that Sneijder was faced with was very young, not more than twenty, with dark brown hair a little more than shoulder length. Her skin was pale and soft with a creamy complexion and she had the brightest blue eyes Sneijder had ever seen. She was not beautiful in the traditional sense of the word; her features were oddly balanced and asymmetrical and her nose was too big for her face, but there was a feeling of warmth about her which was difficult to explain.

'I'm sorry...... I,' Sneijder blurted out. 'I was just, er....' The girl was not impressed and she turned to call on the sentry standing at the front door. Before she could, Sneijder grabbed hold of her arm and pulled her down to where he crouched. 'Please don't do that. I can explain, really, I can.'

The girl was taken by surprise by his action and looked at him open-mouthed. She was dressed in office attire, with a matching jacket and skirt and a white blouse which was pulled tight across her large, well-formed breasts. Sneijder had not spent time in the company of an attractive girl for some months, and he was intrigued by the curves of her body.

Sneijder said the first thing that came into his mind. 'This was my aunt's house; at least it was the last time I was here, two or three years ago. I have been away working in Germany and just returned. I realised straight away that it was now occupied by someone from the German administration. I only wanted to see who it was.'

She eyed him suspiciously. 'What is your aunt's name?'

'Maria van der Kamp,' Sneijder replied quickly, quoting the name of a childhood school friend. 'Please, you have to believe me. I was only looking in the window. I didn't realise that this was the house of someone important.'

'Well it is,' the girl said. 'It is the home of Albrecht Koestler, in charge of the SS in Arnhem.'

'You know him?' Sneijder questioned.

'I ought to know him,' she replied smartly. 'He is my father.'

Her answer threw him for a second. *That certainly wasn't in the file.* His interest in this girl quickly changed. Perhaps she could be his way in. 'Really?' he said with a smile. 'So this is your house as well? I'm sorry, I should go.' He turned to leave.

This time the girl grabbed his arm. 'Wait a minute. Who are you? What is your name?'

'So you can report me?'

'Perhaps I will unless you tell me,' she replied.

'It's Voorman, Johannes Voorman.'

'So you are Dutch. You speak German like a native,' the girl said. 'How come?'

Sneijder smiled at her. 'My mother says I have a gift for languages. Working in a factory in Hamburg for eighteen months helps too.'

She frowned, a glint of sadness in her eyes.

'You know, it's usually considered polite to tell somebody your name when they tell you theirs,' said Sneijder.

She laughed gently. 'You know my surname. I think that's enough.'

'I can find out,' Sneijder responded. 'I will find out.'

'You can try.' She looked away for a moment at the sound of a pine cone falling through the branches, and looked back, but by that time Sneijder was already running away through the trees in the direction of his waiting motorcycle. As much as he wanted to continue the conversation with her, he was not prepared to run the risk of being caught by the sentry and having to explain himself.

Sneijder had been running on adrenaline since arriving back in Holland and was waiting for the crash. It duly came a couple of days after meeting the girl who claimed to be Koestler's daughter. Nothing in particular seemed to set it off; he just began to experience the crippling insomnia again that he had struggled with for months. Perhaps he was suddenly struck with the realisation of how dangerous a position he was in, or the gravity of his orders, or maybe he was simply thinking too much now that he had time again, but he was finding it impossible to rest and the sleeping pills he had been taking had run out. Subversive work, like war itself, was one percent action and ninety-nine percent boredom, with the result that there was plenty of opportunity for suppressed memories to drift back to the surface. Again his thoughts turned to his family. He hoped that Wilkinson's promise to locate them had been genuine and not just a device to make him take on the task of eliminating Koestler; only time would tell.

Sneijder spent his time up in his room in the Uhlenbroeks' house, leaving only to visit the dead-drop to check for messages. He had left a note for Hugo and Dimitri requesting further information on Koestler's living arrangements. It was several days before he found a reply. By now it was approaching the end of July.

It seemed that Hugo did not know about the daughter, even though he had been visiting the house morning and night for over a year. The young driver had spoken to several people and had established that she worked as a typist in the administrative offices which also housed the car pool. It was a safe assumption that her assignment to Arnhem had been organised by her father, most probably to save her from the incessant Allied bombing of Germany.

The car pool yard was beginning to interest Sneijder. Harry Wilkinson had suggested tampering with Koestler's Mercedes staff car as a way of killing him without raising suspicions and bringing about terrible reprisals on the civilian population. It would have to be done extremely carefully in such a way that it could be made to look like an accident. The tricky part would be isolating the car for a period sufficient to enable the necessary adjustments to be made, but short enough to prevent him switching to another vehicle. It would also be essential that any break-in to the yard left no evidence, which would of course make it a whole lot more difficult. Sneijder needed to get his hands on a set of plans for the building, but decided against mentioning this to Hugo. It was unlikely the young man could help. There was also another, darker reason not to inform him.

The day before the German truck convoy was due to arrive in Arnhem, the six men who were to be involved met at Father Grooter's church. Van Rijn stood at the front of the room in the basement, marking out details with chalk on the stone wall. Martin Voesman was next to him, doing his best to remind the others that it was his operation and he would still be leading it. Michael Voesman, Sneijder and Pieter de Jong sat on chairs while Bruggink perched on the edge of the table.

'Tell me again, everything you know about this convoy,' Van Rijn said.

Martin Voesman referred to a map pinned to the wall, pointing to a small airfield about seven miles to the north of Arnhem. 'The plane will land at Deelen around noon and the cargo will be transferred to the trucks. The convoy should consist of three trucks and a kubelwagen with an escort of two motorcyclists, or a configuration of similar strength. They will travel due south from the airfield towards Park Sonsbeek and then onto the city centre, the most direct route being along the Deelenseweg, which is an excellent road on which to carry out an ambush.' He pointed to one of the long roads through the woods which Sneijder had considered for his attack on Koestler. 'Here. The road is extremely narrow, with thick tree cover on either side. Perfect.'

'What time will it reach this point?' asked Van Rijn.

'Transferring the cargo from the aircraft to the trucks will probably take about one hour,' Martin Voesman continued. 'It is little more than a twenty minute journey from Deelen airfield to the centre of Arnhem, so if we are to strike halfway through the trip then the time of attack will be a little before quarter past one.'

'And you are absolutely certain about the route?' Van Rijn pressed. 'I mean, as you say, Deelenseweg is an ideal place for an ambush. Won't the Germans try to avoid it?'

Voesman answered: 'I have it on very good authority from my source that this is the route they will take. The only other obvious road they could use if they are heading for the east side of the city is the Apeldoornseweg here.' He indicated a road further to the east which ran roughly parallel to Deelenseweg. 'To get there they must first travel east along the Koningsweg. I will have some friends of mine block this alternative route to make it impassable but as I said, my source assures me that....'

'Source?' De Jong scoffed sarcastically. 'What source? You two are thugs, who is going to trust you with this sort of information? You're probably making half of this up.'

Michael Voesman got to his feet and grabbed De Jong. 'Why you....'

Van Rijn ignored them and questioned Martin Voesman. 'What source?'

The older Voesman brother replied, 'A reliable one, one which has always been accurate up until now.' Spotting the sceptical looks being exchanged he added, 'Look, for once you are all just going to have to trust me.'

Bruggink looked at Van Rijn and shook his head. De Jong pushed Michael Voesman away and sat back down on his chair. For a couple of minutes there was silence. Sneijder considered for a moment the possibility that Van Rijn would refuse to assist him with Koestler. In such a circumstance Sneijder would need to find an alternative source of manpower; he concluded that perhaps it could be advantageous to get on the right side of the Voesmans.

'I know most of you don't know me so my opinion won't count for much,' he said, 'but it seems to me that he knows what he's talking about. It's detailed information that could only come from someone on the inside. Right?' He looked at Martin Voesman.

'Right,' he replied.

Sneijder turned to the others. 'Then I think we need to trust him. As Father Grooter pointed out, we do need the ration books, not least for ourselves if we are forced to go underground.'

Van Rijn hesitated for a moment, and then nodded. 'Okay, Martin. Tell me the rest. How many men?'

'A motorcyclist at the front and back of the convoy. Each truck will have a driver and a guard in the cab, plus another armed guard in the rear. The kubelwagen carries the officer in charge of the transport and his bodyguard. So overall that's two men on bikes, four drivers and eight men of combat strength.'

'With six of us it'll be no problem,' Michael Voesman said confidently. 'They won't know what's hit them.'

'When is the convoy supposed to reach the offices in Arnhem?' asked Bruggink. 'How long until they realise it's missing?'

'About one-thirty,' Martin Voesman replied. 'I assume they will receive a signal when the plane arrives at the airfield, so the delay in the convoy reaching its destination will not go unnoticed for long.'

'So we can say that by two o'clock the alarm will have been raised,' Van Rijn concluded. 'We will need to hit them hard and get away fast. Right, tell us your plan.'

Martin Voesman took the chalk from Van Rijn and drew a quick diagram on the wall depicting the configuration of the vehicles, with the three trucks ahead of the kubelwagen. He marked out the starting position of each member of the raiding party and explained his idea for the attack. A vehicle would be used to block the road, bringing the convoy to a halt. The group would then attack from positions opposite each other on either side of the road. At the end of his explanation the general consensus was positive.

Sneijder stood up. 'Just one problem. May I?' He held out his hand for the chalk. Voesman handed it over and Sneijder moved to the wall. 'Have you ever attacked a vehicle before?'

The Voesmans shook their heads. Bruggink and Van Rijn nodded with a lack of conviction and De Jong stayed silent.

Sneijder continued, 'You've marked out two hiding places directly opposite one another, with the target vehicle in between. That's suicide. Two groups firing at vehicles, which could move at any time, from opposite sides of the road, a few stray bullets – I'm sure you can see where this is going.' As he spoke he drew lines to show the direction in which the bullets would travel. 'Each person is standing right in the other's line of fire. We'd all end up killing each other.'

'So what would you suggest we do?' Michael Voesman said mockingly. 'Come down on them from above?'

'It's really perfectly simple,' Sneijder retorted. 'We arrange ourselves in two groups on either side of the road, just like your brother said; only we do it slightly ahead of the convoy. That way we come at it from the front as well as the side, shooting away from each other. All we have to do is ensure that the convoy is brought to a halt exactly where we want it to be.'

Van Rijn nodded and gave Sneijder a glance as he returned to his chair. 'He's right. This whole thing needs to run perfectly if we're to avoid a disaster. We need to discuss how we're going to arm ourselves.'

The discussion carried on for another hour, and was only concluded when Van Rijn declared himself satisfied with every detail. In truth the plan devised by Martin Voesman had few obvious flaws, only being let down by his inexperience in these matters. It was not the way that Sneijder would have done it but he did not feel that he was in a position to force his viewpoint.

An argument broke out between the fiery De Jong and Martin Voesman about the theft of the bearer bonds, a facet of the operation that the former thought was being given too much prominence. Sneijder pointed out that the theft of the money was the perfect cover for stealing the identity cards and ration books – as long as the trucks were burned afterwards the Germans might not realise the documents were missing.

'If they know the cards have been stolen they will issue new ones in a slightly different design and declare the old ones void, making them useless to us,' Sneijder added, 'but this is expensive and they will not do it if they think the cards have been destroyed.'

Van Rijn agreed. 'Exactly. If we're lucky they'll think we were just after the money.'

The six of them met at a deserted crossroads in the woods northeast of Oosterbeek a little before eleven the following morning. Clouds obscured the summer sun and there was a light wind but the temperature was more than pleasant. Van Rijn and Bruggink arrived in the old van while the Voesmans had turned up in theirs, which was packed full of weapons, most of them stolen from the Germans. Sneijder and De Jong had come on bicycles.

'Is everybody clear on what we're doing?' Van Rijn asked the group when they had assembled. 'There can be no mistakes.'

'We know,' Michael Voesman replied impatiently. 'It'll work.'

'Has everybody got a weapon and enough ammunition?' Van Rijn questioned.

Sneijder carried his canvas knapsack, which held his Sten and three ammunition clips. His Walther was tucked into the waistband of his jeans at the small of his back, covered by his jacket. The others all carried Stens as well, plus their individual choice of handgun. For the majority this was a Luger, though Bruggink carried his old revolver.

While ammunition was passed around, Michael Voesman pulled out his favoured weapon, a six-inch hunting knife with a curved serrated blade. He laughed and said, 'This will do for gutting the bastards.'

'Bloody hell, man,' said De Jong, 'but I hope you're not intending on letting them get that close.'

'I'll kill them before they get two paces, you'll see.'

'Just watch your back,' Van Rijn warned, 'and keep your head. Now we may all have our differences, but today we are putting our lives in each other's hands. We've got to stick together. Right - let's go.'

Sneijder and De Jong put their bicycles in the back of Van Rijn's van and were driven to where the attack was due to take place.

The Deelenseweg ran from the village of Deelen down to Schaarsbergen, a densely wooded area three miles north of Arnhem. The road through the forest was extremely narrow, only just wide enough for two cars to pass one another, and enclosed by dense forest which cast substantial shadows across the road.

Van Rijn ordered each man to his prearranged position, Bruggink and himself hiding in the woods on one side of the road, Sneijder and Martin Voesman on the other. The trees were right up against the edge of the carriageway and provided excellent cover for men laying in wait. Michael Voesman would block the road with the twins' van, while De Jong was to launch his attack from behind the vehicles once they were stationary.

Sneijder was extremely nervous. His heart pumped hard and quick like a drum and his face dripped with sweat. For some reason he had a bad feeling about what was to follow; whether it was the obvious discord amongst the six men or just the instinct he had developed whilst on the run in Europe, he knew things were going to turn out badly. To complicate matters further, his inability to properly rest was beginning to take its toll. He was having difficulty keeping his mind focused. It was not a good condition in which to risk your life and the lives of others.

'You look like hell,' Martin Voesman, crouching beside him, said. 'Are you going to get through this?'

Sneijder forced a weak smile. 'Sure.'

'For Christ's sake, just don't shoot at me.' Voesman looked away in the opposite direction but within fifteen seconds his gaze returned. 'That's it. They're coming. Take a look.'

Sneijder leaned forward and looked along the road. The motorcycle outrider was approaching around two hundred metres away, followed by the three trucks. Behind them a kubelwagen coasted along slowly. Sneijder stood up and gave a hand signal to Van Rijn, who responded in kind, then he pulled the Sten out of his knapsack and threw the strap over his shoulder, allowing the weapon to rest on his chest. He inserted an ammunition clip and cocked the gun. The Sten was an uncomplicated but effective submachine gun which was very inexpensive to manufacture due to its low-cost materials. Its cheapness allowed it to be produced in large numbers but also gave it a propensity to jam, usually at inopportune moments.

The motorcycle reached their position. There was the roar of an engine and Michael Voesman accelerated the van out of its concealed position amongst the trees. The motorcycle was struck by the front wing of the vehicle and swerved violently to the right, smashing into one of the trees which bordered the road. The rider thumped down hard on the asphalt, rolled a couple of times and was still. The first truck in the convoy screeched to a halt, its path blocked. Michael Voesman leapt out of the van, raised his Sten and sprayed the front of the truck with gunfire. The windscreen shattered and the driver was hit in the face.

Martin Voesman jumped to his feet next to Sneijder and threw a hand grenade towards the first truck in line. He dropped to the ground as it exploded. An Orpo officer in the truck caught the full force of the blast and slumped down on the tailgate. Behind the trucks, the kubelwagen's driver and front passenger leapt out and took cover behind their vehicle. The officers and soldiers in the two trucks which until now were untouched began to clamber out clutching their MP40 submachine guns.

Van Rijn and Bruggink opened fire from the trees. A burst from Van Rijn's Sten caught the guard in the second truck in the back and he fell to the ground. The driver stumbled out the other side of the cab and ran as fast as he could towards the front of the line of vehicles. Sneijder fired wildly and missed completely. The German pulled a pistol from a holster on his hip and fired a couple of shots on the run. As he moved past the Voes-mans' van, Michael Voesman popped up from his position of cover and grabbed him from behind. In one swift movement he stabbed him viciously in the neck with his hunting knife. The driver let out a horrific wail as blood sprayed from his severed vessels and his head fell to one side. Voesman laughed as he yanked the blade back out and threw the man aside.

Sneijder looked away in horror at this display of violence and tried to block out the driver's appalling screams. The man writhed around on the ground for about a minute in the throes of death before he finally stopped. Pieter de Jong emerged from the trees behind the kubelwagen, firing from the hip with his Sten. He was running and so his shots were inaccurate but the burst made the two officers in the vehicle keep their heads down. De Jong released his grip on the weapon with his left hand and took a grenade from the bag strapped around his waist. He removed the pin with his teeth and lobbed it upwards. The grenade arced through the air and landed in the back of the kubelwagen, bouncing down between the occupants.

The two Orpo officers yelled at each other in panic. One searched at his feet for the bomb while the other threw himself over the back of the car, catching his foot as he went. The men using the vehicle for cover leapt away from it desperately. The grenade went off, killing the two officers inside instantly and propelling smoke and debris into the air.

The two guards from the third truck were crouched next to it, firing into the trees with their MP40s. The driver fired twice at Sneijder and Martin Voesman with a Luger, the first bullet whistling past Sneijder's ear and thudding into a tree trunk, the second missing by millimetres.

'Get down!' Sneijder shouted at Voesman. Making no attempt to take cover, the big man opened up a burst with his Sten. A couple of shots rang out and then there was a loud click as the ammunition clip emptied. The German driver took aim and shot him in the shoulder. Martin Voesman cried out and let go of his Sten, allowing it to hang on its strap. He turned towards Sneijder. 'What the hell are you doing? Bloody shoot somebody!'

Sneijder lay in a narrow ditch next to the road. He was terrified and had been keeping his head down. This was the first time he had ever been in a combat situation and no amount of training could have prepared him. The Germans were surrounded and stood very little chance but they had managed to organise themselves around the third truck and were shooting back.

Martin Voesman came hurtling towards Sneijder, who was lying prone on the ground just off the road. Blood poured from the bullet wound in his right shoulder. What came out of his mouth was pure fury. 'I am warning you, Sneijder, you better do something or God help me, I'll put a bullet in your head myself!'

Still Sneijder did not respond. He wanted to move but something stopped him, froze him still on the spot. As the bullets flew, all he wanted with every fibre of his being was for it to stop. He felt a hand on his back as Voesman dragged him roughly to his knees and unleashed a barrage of obscenities into his ear. Almost as an automatic reaction, he finally raised his Sten and let off a burst of fire. There was a clanging noise as the shots ricocheted off the steel frame of the third truck. Free from the attention of this German officer for a second, De Jong crawled behind the burning wreck of the kubelwagen.

On the other side of the vehicles, Van Rijn and Bruggink quickly dispensed with the two guards. The Germans had no cover and with the Dutchmen safely ensconced in the gloom of the woods some ten metres away it was all over in a matter of seconds. Now safe from gunfire, Van Rijn and Bruggink ran out from the trees and came around the back of the third truck to assist De Jong.

Michael Voesman moved across the ground towards the same vehicle, bristling with youthful invincibility. The German driver lying underneath the truck fired a couple of shots with his pistol, catching him in the leg. The young man screamed in agony. Another shot bounced off the asphalt.

Sneijder heard another shot, this one much closer. He glanced behind him quickly. Martin Voesman stood holding his Luger, a thunderous look on his face. He fired again, striking the ground right next to Sneijder's foot. 'Listen to me, you piece of shit. My brother is going to die if you don't fire! He raised the gun and pointed it at his head. 'What's it going to be?'

Sneijder was in no doubt that he meant it. He ejected the empty clip from his submachine gun, grabbed another from his knapsack and rammed it into position. He worked the bolt and fired a burst under the truck. The driver dropped his pistol and slumped to the ground. Sneijder spun around to face Voesman.

'There! I killed him, damn it!' Anger and fear tore inside him, and there were tears in his eyes. 'I shot the man. Now get off my back.' He looked back towards the line of trucks.

De Jong emptied his ammunition clip in the direction of the two remaining German officers. He hit one of them in the chest and he slumped down against the wing of the truck. Bruggink appeared around the other side and aimed his revolver at the driver of the kubelwagen. The man cried out in his native language and began to throw up his hands. Bruggink shot him anyway.

With the shooting over, Martin Voesman's main concern was his brother who lay on the road beside the trucks. The younger brother was crying out in pain, the reason for which became quickly apparent. One of the bullets fired by the lorry driver had passed through his ankle and appeared to have shattered the bone. Martin did not seem to care about his own injury, which he had attempted to patch up with a strip ripped off his shirt.

Van Rijn began issuing orders. 'Max, start looking for the ration and identification cards. You too, Pieter.' He turned to Sneijder, 'Johannes, see if any of these vehicles carries a field medical kit. I think we need some morphine.'

Michael Voesman's screams continued, getting louder all the time. His brother crouched over him, trying to reassure him, and then turned to Van Rijn. 'We need to get him to a hospital – he's losing a lot of blood.'

'It's out of the question,' Van Rijn replied firmly. 'The doctors there are ordered to report anything like this to the authorities. In case you haven't noticed we just killed a dozen of their men.'

'You can't just leave him!'

'We'll get him to a doctor we can trust, in his surgery in Oosterbeek.'

There was a crashing sound, followed immediately by a click as a weapon was cocked. A German SS officer leaped out of the rear of the second truck and raised his MP40, aiming the gun at De Jong's back. Sneijder was the only one with a clear shot, but his head was somewhere else and he froze still.

'Shoot!' Van Rijn bellowed. 'What the hell...'

Things seemed to happen around Sneijder but he could play no part; he could only observe. It was all like a dream, and then a flashback shot through his mind, triggered by a situation which was eerily familiar. He was there again, back at the concentration camp, standing over the guard, gun in hand. He had to do it, to answer his urge to punish this man. 'No, no, no...' he mumbled to himself, then louder, 'no, no!'

The gunfire echoed in the summer air as De Jong was cut down mercilessly. It snapped Sneijder out of his trancelike state, and it was suddenly very real. The German spun around to face him. Sneijder fired a long burst which caught him in the heart. He dropped to his knees, then flat on his face.

Transfixed by the dead body for which he was responsible, Sneijder did not even notice when Van Rijn barged past him and ran over to De Jong. He turned and glared viciously. 'He's dead! What is wrong with you? You had the shot, damn it! Are you totally crazy?'

Martin Voesman turned towards Van Rijn and shouted angrily. 'You vouched for him. You said he'd do a good job. He nearly killed the lot of us, and now De Jong's dead and my brother and I are shot.'

Van Rijn glanced at Sneijder, then replied to Voesman, 'I trusted him and believed in him, that's why I vouched for him. Obviously I was wrong.'

'De Jong had a wife and three children, damn it,' Bruggink said to Sneijder. 'You've just let him die. What are they supposed to do now?'

Sneijder would not have had an answer to any of these comments had he heard them, but he was in a world of his own for those few seconds, stunned by what had just happened. His exhausted mind simply could not process the emotions he was experiencing.

'You can forget about any help from us,' Van Rijn added. 'I'm not putting my life in your hands. I don't want you staying with the Uhlenbroeks if they can't trust you.'

Sneijder tried to respond but Van Rijn cut him off. 'Just stay away from us. You're on your own.'

CHAPTER TEN

Sneijder sat at the side of the road and took in the scene in front of him. The road was littered with the bodies of the German soldiers and the kubelwagen continued to burn, filling the air with the acrid smell of petrol. The three trucks were also ablaze, having been set alight once their cargo had been transferred to the two vans; some of the boxes of identity cards had been left behind deliberately in order to give the Germans some evidence to suggest the important documents had perished. The other men had left some time ago, taking Pieter De Jong's bullet-riddled corpse with them and insisting that they wanted nothing more to do with Sneijder. For now it was quiet, but it was well beyond the time when the convoy should have arrived at its destination and a search would surely have begun.

Sneijder buried his head in his hands, praying that his feelings of guilt would subside but they did not. He looked at the two men he had killed, thought of De Jong's death, then he stood up and was promptly sick in the ditch. Searching through a few crates which had been flung out onto the road Sneijder came across a field medical kit which contained several ampoules of morphine. He needed something to dumb his senses, anything to take away the pain he felt. Before he had time to change his mind, he took the hypodermic syringe from the medical kit and injected the morphine into his arm.

The substance coursed through his veins and a feeling of calm descended upon him. His troubled thoughts began to slow down, and soon he was lying on the ground in the woods staring up into the patches of sky which were visible between the trees. His entire body felt as though it had been plunged into a pool of water, with the result that he felt totally detached from reality. It was a welcome relief.

Later that evening, with summer rain falling from the darkened sky, Sneijder reached the front door of the Catholic church used by the Resistance. He hoped above all else that none of the group were there, but he did not feel that he could return to the Uhlenbroeks and had nowhere else to go. He banged hard on the old oak-panelled doors. After a couple of minutes the door swung open and Father Grooter appeared.

'Father, I need your help,' Sneijder said.

Grooter obviously knew something of the day's events as he replied, 'Yes, I rather think you do.'

Sneijder was unsure about what Father Grooter's reaction would be; after all De Jong was a man he knew well, but he was a priest and so would probably listen. In all honesty it didn't really matter; Sneijder had things he needed to get out, and once he started talking it was like a great weight being lifted.

'I just don't know what happened,' Sneijder said. 'I froze. I knew I had to shoot but I couldn't do it. And then...' An agonised expression creased his face and he looked at the floor. 'He shot him.'

'Why couldn't you do it?'

'I don't know!' Sneijder exclaimed, then repeated quietly, 'I don't know. I have a problem taking a life. Once he turned the gun on me, it was him or me, and I had to do it. Even then I couldn't stop looking at his face as he lay there, thinking about the family who will never see him again because of me. For God's sake, he was just a man like me, who happened to be born German!'

'It is wrong to take a life, of course it is, but it is a necessary evil we must bear to overcome the forces of darkness. You do see that?'

'Of course. I understand that, and I know De Jong is dead because I let him down. I wanted to save him, I really did, but I just......I couldn't.'

Father Grooter thought for a moment. 'So if you find it so hard to kill, why are you involved with the armed resistance? Why are you even here?'

'My reason for being here is something I must keep to myself, but what you have been told about me is not all true. I am not a Catholic, but will what I say stay between us?'

The priest nodded. 'The Lord listens to the troubles of all men in confidence and without judgement, and I have sworn to carry out his will.'

'The truth is that I am not Van Rijn's cousin,' Sneijder said. 'Until last week I had never even met him. I am an agent sent here from England to carry out a mission. Two weeks ago I was in London. I work for the SOE-Dutch section – you may have heard of it. Van Rijn was present at my parachute drop, which is how I know him.'

'Why did you get involved in this scheme then?' Father Grooter asked.

'Because they didn't have enough men, and because I know I will need assistance to carry out my mission. I believed being involved with this would earn me some respect and trust. It might have worked had I not messed it up so convincingly.'

The two men sat in silence for a couple of minutes, the only sound the faint tapping of the rain on the window pane. Sneijder smoked a cigarette, something he only did when he was uptight or nervous, blowing gentle swirls of smoke into the room. Finally he broke the quiet. 'I have done terrible things, Father. They come back to me all the time. I get these.... nightmares – flashbacks really. They go away sometimes but they are always there, you know, in the background.'

Father Grooter leaned forward, his face illuminated by the dim glow of a kerosene lamp sitting on the table. 'Tell me about them. You may find solace in sharing them.'

Sneijder stood up and walked to the window. The sun had disappeared and the final light of the day was drifting away. 'I was captured by the Germans on my first mission, back in 1942. They were waiting for me when I parachuted because of some stupid bloody mistake in England. I was imprisoned in a camp near Tilburg for a while, but I tried to escape so they decided to send me to Mauthausen concentration camp in Austria. My God, what a place.' He shuddered. 'Some of the things....' He hesitated.

Father Grooter remained silent but nodded, urging Sneijder to continue.

He did so. 'There is a stone quarry there, about a hundred metres deep. Sometimes the guards would throw prisoners down into the pit just for walking too slowly, women and children. I was badly beaten on more than one occasion. I saw innocent people shot at random for the sheer amusement of the guards – they were just animals. Really unspeakable things happened there, I imagine they still do.' Tears began to form in his eyes. 'The guards that patrolled our section of the camp were monsters. I never really believed that men could be so evil, that they could do such horrendous things to other human beings.'

Father Grooter replied grimly, 'Unfortunately the cruelty of human nature knows no bounds.'

Sneijder continued, his voice wavering slightly with emotion. 'I really thought I would die in there. The man in charge of them was named Kemerling, a real beast. One day a group of prisoners, around fifty of us, were taken outside the camp gates to carry out repairs on the railway track. We were escorted by guards of course, but I knew this was my only chance to get out alive. I don't know how I managed it, but while we were walking I attacked one of the guards and got his rifle from him. I aimed it at one of the others and made the whole lot of them throw away their weapons.' Sneijder covered his face and exclaimed in frustration, 'And then I should have run away!'

'But you didn't?'

'No. I grabbed Kemerling, took his pistol and made him kneel in front of me. I made him beg for his life with a gun to his head.' By now tears were streaming down Sneijder's face. Fear, anger, hate, all the emotions of the event returned, still raw. 'He begged, told me that he was following orders, that he was not an evil man, just weak. Really, you should have seen it, this beast of a man, this cruel and sadistic monster, clutching at my legs, begging for me not to shoot him. I kept him like that for what seemed like hours; it was probably fifteen minutes.

The thing is, the thing I can't get out of my head even now, is that I was *enjoying* it.

'For those few minutes I turned into one of them, Father. I turned into a monster, mocking a man while he looked death in the face.' Sneijder screwed up his nose in disgust.

Father Grooter said, 'Don't be so quick to put yourself in with them. From what you have said they were far from innocent men. That may not excuse what you did but it does explain your anger.'

'I am still a murderer!' Sneijder snapped. 'I made the man beg, I watched him weep and cry in fear and then I pulled the trigger and shot him in the head. I just couldn't stop myself, I wanted him to die. What sort of man does that make me, Father?'

'It makes you a man; a human being,' Grooter replied. 'With so much cruelty and suffering around you, it is natural that you would want to take revenge. Nobody is free from sin. What is important is that you are remorseful and try to make yourself a better person.'

Sneijder spun around. 'But that is exactly the problem! How can I be remorseful for killing a man when I am still expected to kill?'

Father Grooter was firm. 'We are at war, Johannes. Our country has been taken by force and it is our moral duty to free it. Do you think many people fighting around the world really want to kill? Don't think you are the only one who struggles with this. Everyone does, myself included. As a priest, I find the idea of contributing to the deaths of Germans difficult, but it is my duty. We all must find a way to cope with our conscience.'

'Yes,' Sneijder agreed. 'We must.'

'You did not choose this, but it is vital that Nazism does not prevail. What a dark world that would be. Do what you must, and don't be so hard on yourself.' Father Grooter smiled. 'I don't think you are a bad person. Now if you don't want to return to the Uhlenbroeks you must stay here. I will set up somewhere for you to sleep.'

'A convoy of ours attacked? Where?' Koestler was furious.

'Schaarsbergen, sir,' Klimitz replied. 'It was en route from Deelen airfield. The vehicles were burned out and the men are all dead, thirteen of them in total plus the motorcycle outrider. Ten thousand marks in bearer bonds were stolen. The convoy was also carrying blank identity cards and ration books, at least some of which were lost in the fire; it is unknown at this point whether any have fallen into the wrong hands.'

Koestler picked up the telephone, pressed a button and barked, 'Get me Horvath.'

Within a minute the Gestapo officer came on the line. 'Yes?'

'Do you know about this?' Koestler demanded. 'Fourteen German lives lost. Fourteen!'

'Yes, sir. It is extremely unfortunate. I have my best men on the case. We are trying to figure out how these partisans knew the details of the convoy.'

'No excuses this time, Horvath,' Koestler said harshly. 'Find these people. Somebody is going to be punished. You know what Rauter ordered; three Dutch lives for every German. There is a problem in this area and I intend to stamp it out. Now get to work – you have twenty-four hours.' He put down the telephone receiver, and then said quietly, 'I'll show them I'm very much in control.'

As Koestler had expected, twenty-four hours was asking too much and it was a number of days later that Horvath returned the call. 'I believe we have made some progress, sir.'

Koestler put down his pen and leaned back in his chair. 'At last. Go on.'

'I have it on good authority that this atrocity originated from one particular village - Roeden, just outside Elst. A resident of the village has come forward to tell us that he saw two vehicles leaving in the direction of the ambush site yesterday morning and returning later. The times of these sightings are consistent with the approximate time of the attack. We also have a name, a tentative one but it's a start – a man named Max Bruggink who happens to live in Roeden. He's a bit of a local troublemaker.'

Koestler asked, 'Where did you get the name?'

'Someone he talks to and trusts is working for us,' Horvath replied. 'Sir, should I file a report on my investigations?'

'Yes, file a report and bring it to me immediately,' Koestler said. 'I can then make any necessary 'arrangements' for a suitable response. Good work, Horvath. At last we can exact some revenge for our lost compatriots.'

Sneijder did not like to sit around doing nothing. He continued to follow Koestler's car to and from his office for several days, noting the patterns of work the car was used for and when it was parked in the car pool. Obviously it would be preferable to get into the lock-up during the night, as this would afford the most time to carry out any work on the car. However if this proved impossible he would have to consider getting in during the day under some sort of disguise.

It was when he was standing across the street from the administrative building which housed the car pool around midday that he saw Albrecht Koestler's daughter again. She came out of the front door and descended the stairs along with another girl of a similar age, a tall blonde. The two women crossed the street to the small park which lay directly adjacent and sat down on a bench. The blonde lit a cigarette while Koestler's daughter took a small glass bottle from the bag she carried and drank from it. Sneijder was not one for socialising and avoided unnecessary relationships but for some reason he felt able to approach her.

'So it's Frauke, then,' he said, walking up behind the bench.

She turned, surprised, then smiled. 'Oh, Mr Voorman. We meet again.'

'I told you I would find out,' Sneijder said.

'So you did.' She turned to her friend. 'Silke, this is......' She trailed off as the other woman gave an unimpressed look. She turned back to Sneijder. 'We're not really supposed to mix with the local population.'

'I don't suppose any of my people would be too happy about me talking to Germans either,' replied Sneijder. 'I should go.' He began to walk away, a resigned look on his face.

Frauke Koestler sat for a moment, then got up and ran after him. She caught up with him as he walked towards the road. 'Slow down. I'm not going to let you just disappear a second time. How did you find out my name?'

'I know people who know other people who know things,' Sneijder answered. 'Either that or they know who to ask to find out who knows the people who know, and can put me in touch with them, so I can know.'

Frauke laughed, seeing straight through the ploy. 'That doesn't even make sense. You're trying to confuse me so you can avoid telling me how you found out.'

Sneijder shook his head. 'No.' He grinned and added, 'But you're right, it doesn't really make sense, does it?'

'Not at all. So come on, who told you?'

Sneijder continued to walk, ignoring the question. 'You said you weren't meant to talk to me.'

'Oh don't worry about Silke – she's always really tense. Those kinds of rules are stupid; we're in your country so how can we not talk to you?'

Sneijder stopped and turned to face her.

'What?' she asked. 'You're surprised that we're not all ruthless imperialists obsessed with the greatness of Germany? No – that I leave to my father.'

'Unfortunately it is the people who are ruthless imperialists that are in charge.'

'Or the ones who are just afraid of Hitler, but let's not waste breath on discussing such things. I want to know how you know my name.'

'I asked somebody I know on the German staff to find out for me, all right?' Sneijder replied with a smile. 'You challenged me to find out so I did.'

By this time they had reached the motorcycle which Sneijder had left on its stand by the roadside. He moved towards it and swung his leg over so that he straddled the fuel tank.

'Now you know where I work but I know absolutely nothing about you,' said Frauke. 'That's not fair. What do you do?'

Sneijder did not want her looking for information about him. His false identity should hold up so long as he stuck to the back story he had been given, and the forged documents were excellent, but there was still no telling what damage could be done by a bit of digging. 'I have a room at the house of the Oosterbeek stationmaster and I help him out a little, but mostly I keep my head down and try to avoid being drafted back to Germany. Now I'm afraid I must go – I've probably told you too much already.'

'Do you think I'm going to report you or something? If you knew me better you'd know I'm not like that.'

Sneijder gave a stern look. 'I've learned that you can never be too careful. Never.'

As he started the engine she said, 'I like you, but there's something I don't understand, something different. There is a reason why we've met, isn't there?'

Sneijder struggled to contain a reaction. 'I'm not sure I know what you mean.'

She appeared confused. 'No, I'm not sure either. Perhaps it's fate. Come and see me again.' With that she turned and walked back towards her friend. Sneijder rode away.

He had done as much reconnaissance as he felt was necessary, and had gathered enough information about Koestler's general movement to enable him to formulate a plan. What Sneijder now needed to do was figure out a way to get into the car pool, sabotage Koestler's staff car and get out again, all without being detected. Furthermore, the accident would have to be able to stand up to investigation and still look accidental. If the lieutenant-colonel died and it was proven to be an assassination it would lead to dire consequences for the local population.

Sneijder required detailed architectural plans of the German administrative building if he was to successfully break in. From local civilians he had ascertained that the building had been there since the 1850s and had previously served as a local government office and in its original capacity, a police station. Sneijder had no idea where he could get his hands on the plans he needed and the person he would have asked for advice wanted nothing to do with him. There was only one person he could think of who might have the ability to help him out.

It was around nine o'clock in the morning on an overcast day that Sneijder arrived outside Helder's apartment just off the Great Markt. It was quiet as it was a Sunday and the church bells rang out in the tower of the grand Eusebiuskerk, which rose up amongst the houses and overlooked the open square. He knocked on the door several times until it was opened by Helder's housekeeper, the small man Sneijder had met previously.

'Yes? What do you want?'

'I need to speak with Mr Helder,' said Sneijder.

'I'm afraid that is not possible,' the small man replied. 'He will not see visitors who turn up unannounced.'

'It is urgent,' Sneijder added. 'I need his help.'

'I'm sorry,' the small man snapped. 'Whatever your problem is, it's your concern. Mr Helder is not interested. Good day to you.' He attempted to close the door.

Sneijder jammed his foot in, stopping the door, and moved forward threateningly. He was much bigger than the other man and had a strong physical presence. 'I said I need to talk to Mr Helder, now. It's urgent; I believe I said that too. I don't particularly care what you say, or what you've been told to say, but I do want you to take me to Mr Helder.'

The housekeeper had shrunk back into the hallway by this point. 'He isn't here.'

Sneijder looked unconvinced. 'Do you expect me to believe that?'

'It's true, he's not here,' the small man insisted. 'He is at his country house in Driel, where he always spends the weekend. He will be attending Mass this morning but he'll be there afterwards.'

'Driel?'

'That's right.'

'Whereabouts?' Sneijder asked.

The small man smiled. 'I'm afraid I can't tell you that.'

Sneijder pushed him backwards hard and pinned him against the wall, then asked again, 'Where?'

The small man was visibly shaken by Sneijder's physicality and crumbled before his eyes. He told him everything. The man's attitude confused Sneijder, and if it had been directed by Helder made absolutely no sense. The first time he had met the old man, Helder had talked of his desire to assist the Resistance movement in any way he could. It seemed inconceivable that he would now refuse to help.

Later that afternoon Sneijder headed to Driel, a small village south of the Rhine. Helder was a rich man through his factories and had spent a great deal of money on building himself a large country mansion just outside the village, in extensive parkland which appeared to be thronging with wildlife; deer, grey rabbits, birds of prey.

Not wanting to announce his arrival to Helder, Sneijder left the motorcycle outside the property and walked the rest of the way. He approached by crossing the huge front lawn, keeping close to the line of bushes which divided the grass from the gravel thoroughfare. The house was built in a neoclassical style which looked at odds with the surroundings and suggested an

ostentatiousness to Frank Helder's character. As Sneijder neared the front door it swung open and he heard
laughing voices. Instinctively he dropped down behind
a bushy azalea and watched through the branches. To
his surprise three men in field-grey SS uniform emerged,
being shown out by Helder. They concluded their conversation, laughing and joking about an apparently in-
competent colleague in the German administration.

'So, until next week,' one of the Germans said, shaking Helder's hand and adding: 'Don't forget what we
spoke about.' It was only as the German moved away
towards a waiting Mercedes that Sneijder realised his
identity. It was Koestler, and he was flanked by two
young officers whose shoulder flashes identified them as
belonging to the Germanic SS. All three got into the car
and departed. Sneijder waited for Helder to go inside and
get comfortable, then proceeded to knock on the door.

Upon opening the door Helder's expression was a
combination of surprise and horror. 'Er.... Voorman, is
it? What are you doing here, at my home? Did I not make
myself clear the last time we met?'

'You did, but I need some help with something and I
didn't know where else to go,' Sneijder replied.

'Help? You endangered my position so that *I* can help
you?' Helder leaned out of the door and glanced in both
directions. 'Where is Van Rijn?'

'I don't know. Look, it's complicated. The thing is, I
need to get my hands on a set of architectural plans for
that big German administrative office in the city. I've
been told that plans for public buildings are kept on
record somewhere, but I wouldn't know where to begin
to find them. I thought you might know somebody who
could help.'

'Why would you require such plans?' Helder asked impatiently.

'You told me not to tell you anything, so you can truthfully deny all knowledge of my actions. In this case particularly, I suggest you don't ask. You probably would not like the answer.'

Helder appeared alarmed. 'You're not planning on attacking the place, surely? I have no problem with killing the enemy but a collection of typists and bureaucrats? That does not seem right. The reprisals would be terrible.'

'It is the bureaucrats who do the paperwork necessary to deport innocent civilians,' Sneijder pointed out, 'but you can relax, it's nothing like that. I have my orders and I must carry them out, and for that I need those plans. Will you help me or not?'

Helder sighed. 'Of course, I'll see what I can do. But please, I must ask that you don't visit my home again. The Germans are putting pressure on me and the last thing I need is more suspicion. I will make enquiries, and contact you via Edwin Uhlenbroek.'

'Thank you,' Sneijder replied. 'Van Rijn may be in contact with you. Unfortunately everything he will tell you about me is true, but please believe me when I tell you I am doing everything in my power to make it right.'

Helder looked bewildered, as Sneijder knew he would. 'What are you talking about?'

'You will find out soon enough, I'm sure. I will leave your property and stay away from you - the last thing I want is for you to fall under German suspicion. I appreciate your help. Good afternoon to you.' With that parting comment, he left.

Without contact with the members of the local Resistance, particularly Van Rijn, Sneijder felt alone. He had expected someone to inform the Uhlenbroeks about what had taken place but it seemed either they did not know, or they were doing their utmost to hide their knowledge. Whichever was true, the couple continued to display extreme kindness towards their young guest and he appreciated it.

His conversation with Father Grooter had helped him to accept past events a little more than he had previously, and sharing the experience of killing the German guard at Mauthausen had reduced the intensity of the nightmares. However the sheer escapism offered by the morphine was too much to resist. Within seconds of the needle going in he was somewhere else, no longer behind enemy lines, looking over his shoulder. He could be anywhere he wanted to be – back in his family home, his mother and father and his siblings all around. But after these three years he found it hard to picture their faces. No amount of any drug could remedy that.

It must have been the loneliness that drove Sneijder back towards Frauke Koestler. He had intended to strike up a relationship with her in order to obtain information about her father but on the two previous occasions he had spoken to her, Albrecht Koestler had been the last thing on his mind. He found her physically attractive certainly, but she had a way about her which was comforting and it was this that made him gravitate towards her. Sneijder followed her from her office building at lunchtime, at a safe distance, and made sure he bumped into her when she was alone. 'Hello, Frauke.'

She turned around and smiled when she saw him. 'Mr Voorman. How unexpected.' Her eyes narrowed. 'Did you follow me here?'

'Of course not,' Sneijder lied, 'and please, it's Johannes. I just saw you from the end of the street. How are you?'

'I'm surviving,' she replied. 'All I seem to do is type letters stripping somebody or other of their basic rights for no reasons that I can see. If only people in Germany knew the way their own commanders behaved towards occupied people.'

'Isn't that exactly what Hitler promised them though? Germany above all other nations?'

'But not like this,' she answered quickly. 'Not like this. How does life treat you?'

Frauke's surprisingly open demeanour began to rub off on him. She was so honest that it seemed inappropriate and extremely ungentlemanly to tell her anything but the truth. 'Not great. The tighter rationing has hit the couple I live with hard – they've had their telephone disconnected and the electricity will be next. It's getting hard.'

'I'm sure,' she said. 'I'm just on my way back to work. Walk with me.'

Sneijder obliged, and they began the short journey back towards the German headquarters. They walked away from the street and through the parkland opposite the building, making small talk about nothing in particular. Sneijder enjoyed the company and the normality of ordinary conversation which had nothing important hanging on it. For once he did not need to obtain any information from the discussion; he was simply talking.

It was Frauke who made the move which would change their relationship from one of acquaintance to something deeper. 'I see you have the motorbike, but do you cycle? I like to go for a ride when I have time off, to get out of the city and into the countryside. I would appreciate some company - I don't really know many people around here and it would seem neither do you. Of course, you don't have to, it's your choice.'

Sneijder smiled. 'That sounds good.'

She seemed to be pleased with his answer. 'Good, at the weekend then. I'll meet you here at noon. Until then though, I must work.'

CHAPTER ELEVEN

It was a cool evening when they came, dark but for a thin sliver of moonlight. The small rural village of Roeden was quiet and blacked-out, and there was nobody out to see the two Mercedes cars and three troop carrier trucks pull up stealthily fifty metres down the road. The three trucks swerved off the road and parked under the cover of the apple trees which populated the orchard there. Eight men climbed silently from the flatbed rear of each vehicle dressed in plain clothes and long overcoats, MP40 submachine guns tucked out of sight.

The first Mercedes drove into the village and halted in the centre, just opposite the small sixteenth-century church. The driver killed the engine and the headlights were extinguished. The other Mercedes stopped outside the first house in the village. The driver came around and opened the rear door. A grey-haired officer stepped out, dressed much like the others in a long trenchcoat tied around his waist with a belt. He strode up the path, followed by the eight men from the first troop carrier. They now brandished their weapons openly. The second group of eight moved in on the second house on the road, while the final group of eight approached the third house. Simultaneously they banged on the front doors.

The first door opened to the grey-haired officer who spoke in German. A young man behind him repeated his words in Dutch. 'Every man in this house above the age of sixteen needs to come out and show his identification. Let me warn you, failure to comply shall be punished in the strongest terms.'

The same command was repeated at houses throughout the village, and slowly men of all ages began to assemble on the green near the church. In the gloom the presence of the black Mercedes parked nearby went unnoticed. There were widespread protestations about the overtly physical behaviour of the men and the hour at which the whole event was taking place, and it did not take long for it to become obvious that these men were Dutch volunteers for the Germanic SS - traitors.

A middle-aged woman slapped one of them around the face violently and yelled, 'You cowardly pig! Turning against your own people for them.' She spat on the ground in front of him. He reacted angrily and attempted to hit her, but the punch was blocked by two men who leaped to her defence. One of them was older, perhaps mid-fifties while the other was very young. Another Germanic SS man moved forward and swung his gun, catching the young man with a striking blow to the side of the head. He went down, blood cascading from a terrible wound.

A melee was sparked by this act of brutality and apoplectic civilians attacked the two Germanic SS officers involved. Several other officers piled into the confrontation. One of the others released the safety catch on his MP40 with an audible click and fired a burst into the air. It had the desired effect; those fighting ceased their attack instantly and turned around.

The grey-haired man in charge raised his hands to demand silence and spoke in German, his words being translated by a younger officer standing beside him. 'We are looking for Max Bruggink. He comes from this village, we know he does, and yet I have seen no identification bearing that name. Is somebody going to tell me where he is?' There was no response so he took his Walther from his pocket and dragged a small child from the front of the crowd. The child's mother screamed in horror as he placed the barrel against the child's head and added, 'Do I need to ask again? Max Bruggink. Come on, this is important.'

The mother screamed and cried out, 'I don't know him, I swear! Don't hurt my boy, please!'

The German officer thumbed the hammer of his pistol.

'Okay, all right; don't hurt the child,' a voice called from the back, and out of the crowd walked the muscular figure of Max Bruggink, his hands raised above his head. 'I'm Bruggink. I'm the one you want.'

A couple of other people nodded, which seemed to confirm to the grey-haired man that this was indeed the man he was looking for and he released the small boy. Two of the men in long overcoats grabbed Bruggink's hands and tied them together behind his back, then marched him towards the empty Mercedes. The grey-haired officer glanced over towards the other Mercedes, and then followed Bruggink to the car. Bruggink, the two Germanic SS men and he got into the vehicle and it pulled out of the village, disappearing into the black night like a ghost.

In the other Mercedes, Koestler was trembling, having watched the events unfold from his back seat position with a peculiar combination of pleasure and horror. He took pride in performing his job well but was often appalled by his own actions. The German's right hand shook gently as he raised his hip-flask to his lips and emptied the entire contents into his mouth. He looked up at Horvath, who sat in the front passenger seat. 'Right, Horvath, you know what Rauter has ordered. Three men for every German killed. That's fourteen, plus Stracke and his driver. So that's sixteen, which means....'

'Forty-eight,' Horvath finished.

'Y-y-yes,' Koestler stammered. 'Forty-eight. Get it done, and no mistakes.'

Horvath got out of the car. Koestler put his head in his hands for a minute, then regained his composure and got out also, moving towards the crowd.

News of the SS incursion spread rapidly, and it was the early hours of the morning when there was a loud knock at the front door which awoke Sneijder. A light flashed on in the hallway and Edwin Uhlenbroek went downstairs to see who was there. He began to express his displeasure but his voice tailed off and a louder and much more animated voice usurped him. Whoever it was could not get the words out fast enough.

'They did *what*?' Uhlenbroek said when the caller was finished. 'My goodness, this is terrible.' He called on his wife with a tangible sense of urgency and began to explain something to her in an alarmed tone. She gasped.

Sneijder knew something was wrong. He jumped out of his bed and grabbed a white bathrobe which hung behind the door, wrapping it around himself as he descended the stairs. 'What is the matter? I heard raised voices.'

'The Germans have gone into a village near here,' replied Uhlenbroek. 'A reprisal for something or other. They have killed innocent people, burned their homes.'

'Where?' Sneijder demanded. 'Which village?'

Barely five minutes later he descended the stairs again, this time dressed in jeans, shirt and his leather bomber jacket. He knew instantly that it was the village where the Van Rijns and Bruggink lived, and that this was a reprisal for the convoy attack. But how could the Germans have known? As always, the answer would lie with an informant.

'You're not going out, surely?' Mrs Uhlenbroek asked as he approached the door. 'The curfew?'

'I appreciate your concern, Mrs Uhlenbroek, but I'm afraid I'll have to take my chances. A friend may need me.'

Sneijder kick-started the motorcycle on the down-ward stretch of road leading to the river, swung left on to the path that ran along the bank and opened up the throttle. He covered the five kilometres from Oosterbeek to Arnhem in less than three minutes, rode under the bridge and then, sweeping around in a long loop, powered up the bridge ramp and across. As he neared the first concrete pillbox a German voice ordered him to stop and he saw an armed guard standing in the road ahead of him. Sneijder gunned the engine and aimed the motorcycle straight at the guard, forcing him to dive out of the way. A couple of rifle shots rang out. Sneijder was travelling much too fast to hit and the bullets imbedded themselves in the wall of sandbags which lined the road. The motorcycle flew over the bridge without trouble and soon he was speeding along pitch-dark country lanes.

The first light of the day was just beginning to appear when Sneijder got to Roeden but he could still see the flames rising from the rooftops as he approached. His heart sank with the realisation that it was true; the Germanic SS had been here. He thought he knew what to expect, but was overwhelmed by the ruthlessness of what awaited him. The first four or five houses that he passed were completely destroyed; all that remained were blackened frames and smouldering ash. A larger farmhouse a hundred metres along the main road burned steadily with an audible roar interspersed by crackling, like a great spitting dragon. The buildings made from stone and brick did not burn, but white-hot flames flickered inside.

Sneijder noticed a young couple standing in front of a blazing cottage. The woman cried inconsolably despite the efforts of the man, who had an arm around her shoulders in a futile attempt to comfort her. Similar scenes were in evidence at various points along the way. Sneijder passed the church and rounded the green, which was filled with people. He followed the line of distressed individuals and came to a tight right-hand corner. Slowing down and taking the bend, he was confronted with a horrific scene.

Ahead of him there was a school surrounded by a high brick wall and wrought-iron railings. The wall was covered with bullet holes and discoloured patches, obviously blood. On the grassy bank in front there were bodies, lots of them, tied up and blindfolded. All of them appeared to be male and each of them had at least two gunshot wounds, some of them more. A woman was on her knees away to the left cradling a man's body and wailing loudly. Numbed by what he was seeing, Sneijder nearly didn't notice Van Rijn standing in the middle of the road staring blankly into space. His expression was one of agony.

Sneijder stopped the bike and dropped it. He ran over to Van Rijn, hoping his presence would be accepted, and said, 'I just heard what happened. It's awful. Did you - ?' He stopped as he realised where the other man's eyes were pointed. Lying amongst the corpses were two young men, boys really – Van Rijn's nephew Jelle and the boy's friend Arnold. 'Oh, God, no.'

Van Rijn did not react to Sneijder in a hostile manner; he did not really react at all. He continued to look into the distance. It was a couple of minutes before he said anything but when he spoke he made no mention of the death of Pieter de Jong or Sneijder's culpability in it. 'They must have known somehow,' he said matter-of-factly. 'They came and arrested Max, and it was no random act. They knew who to look for, asked for him by name. Somebody must have given him up, but who? I don't see who could have known about us attacking the German convoy.'

A memory flashed through Sneijder's mind; Koestler and the two Germanic SS officers leaving Helder's country home. Now was obviously not the time to bring it up but it was a legitimate suspicion. Helder was evidently in a position in which he might hear of such things. 'They arrested him? Who was it? Gestapo?'

'That bastard Koestler and his bunch of traitorous worms!' Van Rijn replied, suddenly animated. 'He was in charge and he ordered this. They killed Jelle and his father, my wife's brother, right in front of her. How could they just murder an unarmed boy?'

Despite all that Guido de Beer had told him in London Sneijder was still astounded. 'The men that did this were *Dutch*? Are you sure?'

'I saw it with my own eyes,' Van Rijn snapped, and then he exploded into a furious tirade. 'I saw the whole fucking lot of them murdering innocent people. They'd done nothing to deserve it, nothing! The bloody Germans – you'd almost expect it from them – but these were Dutchmen! What the hell is happening, Johannes? Our own people carrying out mass murder – it wasn't meant to be like this. These Nazis – we have to kill them, now do you see? Now do you see?'

'Yes, but all this, their response to our attack. It's horrible. Was what we did really worth it?'

'What choice did we have?' Van Rijn asked, the frustration beginning to tell on him. 'For us to keep fighting them we need the ID cards and ration books, otherwise we can't go underground. We have to fight them. Do you want to live in a country like this?' He pointed to the bodies and tears started to well up in his eyes. 'I don't! Oh, God, I don't!' He fell to his knees clutching his stomach.

Sneijder stood silently and watched the usually dignified and controlled man tearing himself apart. He had no idea what to say, and he knew that nothing he said would make a difference. Looking at the bodies strewn across the ground in front of him, Sneijder was enraged. This was truly diabolical. He felt a powerful pang of guilt; how selfish he had been, putting his own moral concerns before the lives of good, innocent people. He had focused so much on his unease with killing that he had lost sight of the bigger picture. Assassinating Koestler would spare Dutch civilians some of the pain and would slow the recruitment of traitors who would bring terror upon their own.

Sneijder's other major concern was his own security. With Bruggink in German custody, everybody he associated with was in potential danger. Given the strained nature of Sneijder's relationship with the other men involved in the convoy attack, it was not beyond the realms of possibility that Bruggink could decide to give him up in an attempt to save his friends. However he put the idea straight out of his head. Now was not the time to think about it. He moved beside Van Rijn and offered a hand to help him to his feet.

Van Rijn accepted it and was pulled up, but then he pushed Sneijder away. 'That's it. I'm going to get him. I'm going to kill the son of a bitch, right now.'

'Who?' Sneijder asked, but Van Rijn was already striding away purposefully. Sneijder followed him, asking again, 'Who are you going to kill?'

'Who do you think?' Van Rijn replied. 'Koestler. I have a fair idea where he lives. I'm going there to put a bullet in his head – he is not getting away with this.'

'That's madness!' Sneijder exclaimed. 'After something like this he'll be surrounded by security men; you'll never get anywhere near him.'

'I'm damned if I'm not going to try,' came the response.

Sneijder was suddenly afraid of what an attempt on Koestler's life might mean for the people, particularly a botched one. Van Rijn was angry and upset and in no mental state to try anything. 'You'll get yourself killed!' Sneijder protested. 'What about Klara? Hasn't she lost enough tonight?'

Van Rijn spun around in a rage and grabbed Sneijder by the throat. 'Don't you dare talk about my wife,' he growled, 'and do not try to tell me what to do. I let you convince me before and look what happened. Back off.' He threw him to the ground and continued to walk away.

'For Christ's sake, Kees!' yelled Sneijder. 'I made a mistake! A man died, I know. I'm just trying to stop you making an even bigger mistake, which will cause even more deaths. You're probably going to get shot, and even if you do get him, what then? They march in somewhere else and slaughter people; is that what you want? Please don't do this. Let me help you.'

'How can you help me?'

'I'll help you kill him, when the time is right and in the right way. Not yet; it must be carefully planned.'

'You help me kill him?' Van Rijn scoffed. 'Don't make me laugh. You couldn't even shoot a soldier who was about to kill your comrade.'

'I know, and I was wrong,' Sneijder admitted. 'Next time it will be different.'

'Why should I believe you? Why should I let you help me?'

'Because that's why I'm here!' Sneijder cried.

For a moment there was stunned silence from Van Rijn.

Sneijder went on. 'That's why I'm in Arnhem. I'm on a mission to assassinate Albrecht Koestler. I'm working on a plan to get him but it's not yet complete. I just need a bit more time.'

'*That's* your big mission?' Van Rijn seemed genuinely surprised. 'They picked a man like you to assassinate someone?'

'It's not that strange,' replied Sneijder defensively. 'I hold the highest ever score for marksmanship on their training course. I'm not some second-rate operative, you know.'

'It's no good being able to shoot if you don't have the courage to do it when it matters,' said Van Rijn. 'I'll pull the trigger without a second's hesitation.'

'I'm not planning on shooting him,' Sneijder explained. 'That would only lead to another massacre. It must appear to be an accident.'

Van Rijn smiled wryly, turned and continued to walk away.

'Please, don't do this,' Sneijder pleaded. Van Rijn ignored him and kept walking, so he added, 'Look, give me a week. That's all I ask – seven days.'

The other man turned around. 'A week?'

'Yes. I need a few days but within a week I'll have it done. If it works, Koestler is dead and there's no reprisal. If I can't do it, then you do what you want. Agreed?'

'Do you really think you can do it?' Van Rijn asked him. 'I mean, when it really matters? I want him dead.'

'I may need your help, but I will do it, I promise you.'

Van Rijn looked at him for a minute as if trying to size him up, to decide whether or not to take a chance on him one more time. Sneijder had to admit to himself that it was probably the logic of his argument that made Van Rijn agree rather than because he had any faith in him, but nonetheless a potentially incendiary situation had been avoided, at least for the time being. 'All right, a week, but you had better not let me down.'

Sneijder approached the other man and extended a hand to him. After a brief hesitation Van Rijn did the same and the pair shook hands. Sneijder gave a sincere smile and added, 'Don't worry, we will get him. I guarantee it.'

It was a little after seven-thirty on a glorious morning when Frauke came downstairs for breakfast. Koestler was dozing in an armchair in the lounge, dressed in a uniform which had been disassembled gradually and now merely consisted of dove-grey trousers and a white button-down shirt. He stirred at the sound of her approach and quickly pushed the bottle of brandy that he had down his side behind a cushion.

'How long have you been here?' Frauke asked.

'Most of the night,' her father replied. 'I was needed in the early hours and since I returned I have been here.'

'You haven't been to bed?'

'No, I wouldn't have been able to sleep. I've just drifted off occasionally here and I feel all right.'

'Do you want any breakfast?' Frauke offered. 'I was going to have some oats and a coffee.'

'That would be very nice, thank you. You are a good girl, my dear; your mother did a wonderful job.'

Frauke seemed surprised by the compliment. Perhaps sitting in front of the photograph of his wife was making Koestler unusually sentimental.

'I'll get it organised then,' she said and went into the kitchen.

They took breakfast together at the table in the dining room, mostly in a mildly uncomfortable silence. Koestler had not seen much of his daughter during her upbringing, another unintended victim of his dedication to his job and to Germany. She had been close to her mother and her side of the family, and when she died Frauke had moved to live with her mother's sister in Leipzig. Albrecht Koestler's posting to Poland further diminished opportunities for them to see one another, and Frauke had had school to think of. However, with Koestler in the Netherlands and Frauke having finished her education, the tail end of 1943 had thrown up a chance for them to build a relationship. As well as him wanting her away from the danger of

Allied bombing, Koestler was also driven by guilt at the lack of devotion he had shown his family. It was too late for Elsa but Frauke was his second chance. However the shortage of communication over the years meant they had very little in common, and these stunted conversations were nothing new.

Frauke finished eating and got up to leave. 'I'd better be going. We have a lot of work to do today. I may be back late tonight; Silke and I are planning on going to the dance hall.'

'Don't be out too late,' Koestler replied. 'I have instructed the men to enforce the curfew rigorously and it would be a little embarrassing if you were to be arrested. Please stick to socialising with Germans; I don't want you to put yourself in danger with Dutch men who know you are my daughter.'

Frauke frowned. 'Father, you know how I feel about that. If I am going to live here I will talk to everybody regardless of their nationality.'

'Please don't be so naïve, Frauke,' he replied. 'I don't tell you these things to spoil your fun; I am concerned for your safety. The people of this country do not like us and they may use you to get to me.'

'Perhaps we should think about why they don't like us,' she retorted. 'I have to go.'

When Frauke returned home around six o'clock she was obviously unsettled about something. She marched into the dining room where he sat at the table, writing notes in a leather bound file. 'Is it true?' she demanded.

He looked up. 'Is what true?'

'Where you were last night,' she responded. 'You were at that village, and they...'

'They what?'

'Stop playing stupid!' Frauke shouted angrily. 'All those people that were killed. I thought it was some kind of mistake but it's not, is it?'

Koestler attempted to defend himself. 'I was following orders. I have been told how I must respond to attacks on our soldiers, and that is what I did.'

'How could you?' she screamed. 'You stood there and ordered the deaths of innocent people, and what? Watched them die?'

'I told you, it wasn't my decision,' Koestler said. 'I have to do what I'm ordered.'

'It's wrong!' she cried passionately. 'You can't just go around shooting people!'

'Listen, these people were not innocent. There was an attack on one of our convoys and fourteen Germans were killed. These were young men not much older than you; you may even have gone to school with some of them. They deserved justice, didn't they?'

'And the residents of this village did it? All of them?'

'We know somebody in Roeden was responsible, and these people were prepared to remain silent to protect them. They were all complicit.'

'You don't really believe that, do you?' said Frauke.

'I think it's time that you started showing more concern for your fellow Germans and less pity for a race who didn't even try to defend themselves when we took their territory.'

'I can't believe you!' she exclaimed. 'My mother would have been appalled!'

'Your mother knew that sometimes I have to do things that I don't like. It takes courage to do them; that is why only Germans could have accomplished what we have.'

'There really is no getting through to you,' Frauke said, exasperated. 'I'm not wasting my time – I'm going out.' With that she stormed out of the room.

Sneijder's hand had been forced by circumstance, and now he would be obligated to bring his plans forward. Van Rijn was very firm about killing Koestler; he wanted the man dead and he would go to the appropriate lengths to ensure it was done. Sneijder did not like working under pressure. He liked to plan things thoroughly and execute the plan when the time was right. External pressure led to poor decisions, and these led to unnecessary mistakes. However in this case he had made a promise and he could not let Van Rijn down again.

Helder was as good as his word and just three days after confronting him, Sneijder received from Edwin Uhlenbroek a package. Inside there was an original 1853 schematic of the former police station, an updated one dated 1912 with changes made when the building became a governmental office and a hand-scribbled note describing minor alterations performed by the Germans. It was exactly what Sneijder had been looking for. He realised straight away that he would need help, so decided to go straight to Van Rijn.

'I'm hoping to get into the car pool at the rear of the building here,' Sneijder explained, indicating on the diagram. 'I'll sabotage Koestler's staff car in such a way that it won't be obvious when it crashes that it's been tampered with. I've followed him to and from work and his driver likes to drive fast, although obviously the stand-in might not....'

'Hang on,' Van Rijn interrupted. 'What do you mean 'stand-in'?'

'His regular driver is my contact here, the man who gave me all my information. I can't just leave him to have an accident without warning him.'

'You can't tell him,' replied Van Rijn firmly. 'Think about it. If Koestler's fear of attack is heightened in any way by what happened the other night, a sudden change of driver is bound to unsettle him. Even if he does get into the car, if it crashes and the regular driver isn't there, that just looks suspicious.'

Sneijder looked at him incredulously. 'Do you really expect me to send an innocent Dutchman to his death? I'm sorry, but no.'

'He must have known he was putting himself in danger when he agreed to become Koestler's driver. He's collateral damage; I'm afraid that is the way it goes sometimes.'

'How can you be so cold-blooded?' Sneijder snapped. 'Talking about a man's life as if it is unimportant.'

'To defeat these Nazis we sometimes have to sink to their level,' Van Rijn replied.

'If we sink to their level they have already won,' Sneijder said wistfully.

'Maybe so, but we have no choice. If the car crashes and the regular driver isn't there they'll know he was involved, and what do you think they will do to him then? Whatever you do he is probably dead – if anything he's got more chance of surviving a car accident. I know you don't want to let him die but you know I'm right. Anyway, how can you be so sure that Koestler will be killed in this accident, especially sitting in the back seat?'

'I can't,' Sneijder said honestly. 'I can only tamper with the car in some way – drain the brake fluid or damage the steering track or something – that causes real problems and hope speed will take care of the rest. If it works, then it will be the perfect assassination.'

'And if it doesn't?'

'If it doesn't work then we try again, or we try something else,' Sneijder answered. 'We will get him, but if we can make it look like an accident it will save a lot of trouble. All I have to do now is figure out a way to get into the garage, and how to sabotage the car.'

'I may be able to help you with the car,' Van Rijn said. 'There is a man my grandfather knows, a mechanic who fixes his farming machinery. His main expertise is cars, particularly German, and he could probably give you some advice.'

'Can he be trusted?'

'Certainly.'

They had a stroke of luck in that the mechanic Van Rijn had spoken of, a bald middle-aged man by the name of Dressler happened to be at the farm working on Wesley Lamming's ageing tractor when they went there. Van Rijn's grandfather led them into the workshop, his blue eyes sparkling at the thought of being involved in a secret scheme. It was a welcome chance to be involved in a young man's game. 'Mr Dressler, these gentlemen would like to speak with you, but it's very hush-hush.' He tapped his nose and smiled.

'Oh, okay,' Dressler replied. He wiped thick black grease from his hands with an extremely filthy cloth and turned to face them. 'What can I do for you young chaps?'

'You must keep this quiet,' said Van Rijn, 'or it could be very dangerous for all of us. Understand?'

'Of course,' Dressler reassured. 'Your grandfather will tell you I am very discreet.'

Sneijder spoke up. 'We need to arrange a little accident for one of our German visitors; a car accident. It must be done in such a way that it cannot be identified as a case of sabotage. I do not know how it can be done.'

'I suggested that you may be able to point us in the right direction,' Van Rijn added.

'Mmmm,' Dressler mused and sat down on the edge of a workbench. 'What type of car is it; make and model?'

'It's a Mercedes-Benz staff car,' Sneijder replied, 'like the one that you see Hitler riding in on those newsreels.'

'The same type?'

'I think so.'

'The Mercedes-Benz 770 Grand,' said Dressler. 'I'd need to know the exact model. We'll start with a process of elimination. Is the car convertible?'

'No, not the one he uses in Arnhem,' Sneijder said.

'And it has four doors?' Dressler asked.

'Yes.'

'Okay, that helps; it's the Pullman sedan then. Any idea how old it is?'

'It seems in excellent condition so it could be quite new but really I have no idea,' Sneijder answered honestly.

Dressler pondered the response for a moment and then asked, 'Give me a rough description of the vehicle. Is it long, short, wide? Do the front and rear windows slope or are they vertical?'

'It must be six metres long at least, maybe two metres wide. The front window slopes quite a lot, and the rear of the car is kind of curved.'

'Ah, one of the updated models then, post-1938. That throws up some interesting possibilities. You see, the Mercedes-Benz 770 has excellent brakes, but when they were mechanical any tampering would leave obvious tool marks. The newer models have brakes which are hydraulically-powered, so you could simply remove some of the fluid and the pressure would go. The important thing would be to make a hole in the pipe in an area where it might occur naturally, somewhere low to the ground where a stone thrown up by the wheels could strike it.'

'That definitely sounds feasible,' said Van Rijn.

'The only other way I can see that would work would be to damage the coil springs on the front wheels and hope that they break,' Dressler added. 'That would momentarily affect the steering which might be enough, but it would be difficult to do and it is not something which would typically happen naturally. That might make it look a bit suspicious.'

Sneijder appeared deep in thought for a moment, and then he looked up and smiled. 'Right, we'll have a think about it. I appreciate your help because I'm no expert when it comes to cars, or any other machinery for that matter. You seem to be well-informed on this particular model.'

'I'm afraid I can't just claim to be brilliant,' Dressler replied. 'My wife has a cousin who was a financier in Paris before the war. He is a very rich man and bought himself the same car, the Mercedes 770. Being a former Mercedes employee, naturally I was interested. The first time I saw it I was astounded, and I spent hours poring over every inch of it. I've had a keen interest in the car since, even if it is Hitler's preferred mode of transport. Are we finished here?'

'Yes, I think so,' said Sneijder.

'Good, because I really must get this tractor back together.'

Chapter Twelve

Sneijder had spent almost every waking hour since the massacre at Roeden planning how he was going to get in and out of the car pool, so it was a welcome change to be able to get away from it all and just relax. He felt uncomfortable enjoying the company of Frauke while simultaneously plotting the death of her father but there was little he could now do about either. Each had begun to take on a life of its own and he was being carried along, merely a passenger. The way events had unfolded it was now inevitable that Albrecht Koestler would die. Sneijder felt it was his duty however to prevent mass reprisals by carrying it out in the best way possible. In a similar vein he could not change the fact that there was a connection between Frauke and himself, even if he wanted to, which of course he did not.

It was a beautiful Saturday morning, the first in August, and there was not a cloud in the bright blue sky when Sneijder wheeled the bicycle out of the front gate of the Uhlenbroeks' house. As he began to cycle through Oosterbeek he was alarmed to see a group of German soldiers wearing the uniform of the Wehrmacht Heer, the German army. There had been rumours going around that the civilian administration which had been in place since the occupation began would soon be replaced by the military, and this seemed to confirm them.

As Sneijder passed the gentle cream and white structure of the Hartenstein hotel, he noticed a line of German military vehicles in the entrance road. Soldiers moved in and out of the building carrying equipment, an obvious sign that the hotel was being requisitioned for use as a command post.

Frauke was already waiting for him in the park opposite the German administration's headquarters when Sneijder arrived. She looked particularly alluring in a short white floral dress which clung to her voluptuous figure, and her blue eyes brightened when she saw him. 'Good morning, Johannes. I was beginning to wonder if you would come.'

'I was on my way. Just trying to avoid tripping over the Wehrmacht.'

She looked puzzled.

'It appears the military are moving in to the area,' he explained. 'I just passed a line of army vehicles and troops in Oosterbeek. The war is on its way, it seems.' There was a small wicker basket on the front of her bicycle which Sneijder pointed to. 'May I ask what is in there?'

'Just a few supplies,' she said coyly. 'It is a glorious day so I thought we might have a picnic. It's not much obviously, what with the rationing and everything, but it's nice.'

'You get rationed too?' Sneijder questioned.

'Of course; there is only so much to go around. It's nowhere near as strict for us though, and it is possible for us to get certain luxuries that you would be unable to.'

'Yes, I'm sure,' Sneijder said. 'So where are we going?'

'For a ride,' she replied. 'We'll cross the bridge and head along the south bank of the river towards Driel and then out into the country. Have you been out that way before?'

'I've been to Driel but I have never been along the south bank.'

'It's quiet and peaceful once you get out of the city. You'll like it.'

The city was quiet as they cycled through the narrow streets which surrounded the Great Markt. They rode side by side, making conversation about the events of each other's lives over the previous week. As they moved up the steep ramp and on to the bridge, an Orpo officer stepped out to block their path. He appeared too quickly to avoid, and Sneijder and Frauke were forced to stop and dismount. The officer adjusted his body slightly so that his Schmeisser machine pistol pointed a little more in their direction, enough to let them know that he was serious. 'Identity cards, please,' he demanded in crisp German.

'I'm a German,' Frauke replied. 'I work in the administration here, and my father is the SS commander in this area.'

'I'll still need to see your identity card.'

Frauke sighed, turned around and unzipped her bag which was strapped onto the back of her bicycle. She began to rummage around inside. In the meantime Sneijder produced his forged card and handed it over.

The officer examined the card, then looked up. 'Johannes Voorman; this is you?'

'Of course.'

'When did you get this identification card?'

'It was issued around six months ago,' Sneijder replied. 'Is that really important? It's a perfectly legitimate document.'

'You will allow me to decide that,' the Orpo man snapped. 'Where was it issued?'

'In Amsterdam.'

The officer began to ask another question but Frauke stepped forward and thrust her identity card into his hand. 'Satisfied?'

He took the briefest of looks at it and handed it back. 'Of course, *fraulein*. That is perfectly acceptable.'

'Good,' she answered. 'If you've finished harassing my friend I presume we can be on our way?'

The Orpo officer took a step back. 'Yes.'

They crossed the bridge and headed west, following the south bank of the river. The road to Driel ran along the top of a narrow dyke about three metres high; to the right-hand side there was a flat grassy flood plain which stretched the three hundred metres to the waters' edge. On the opposite side there were crops growing in the fields around the farm buildings and several rows of vines stretching away into the distance. The sun was hot at that time of the day, the sky an expanse of radiant blue. They moved through the beautiful countryside, lush green grass and tall trees vibrant with life, cycling alongside one another. The two of them talked a little, laughing with each other and with Frauke gently mocking Sneijder's technique on the bicycle. They were about five kilometres out of Arnhem and had just passed under the Oosterbeek railway bridge when Frauke suddenly began to pedal quickly and pulled ahead of Sneijder.

'Come on,' she called light-heartedly. 'Try to keep up. You're not going to let a girl beat you, are you?'

Sneijder increased his speed and began to follow her. 'Okay. Now you've asked for it.'

'This way.' Frauke veered off to the left onto a small single track road and disappeared around a bend between two large oak trees. The branches grew out many metres and the road beneath the leafy canopy was in shadow, with dappled sunlight struggling to break through. Frauke accelerated away down the hill and was engulfed in the semi-darkness. Sneijder followed her and found himself disorientated for a couple of seconds as his eyes adjusted to the differing brightness. He cycled around the bend, keeping the back of Frauke's bicycle in view. They emerged into the bright sun again and Sneijder was temporarily blinded.

'Are you all right?' Frauke called to him.

'I can't see a thing,' Sneijder responded. 'The sun is so bright.'

'I shut my eyes in the dark bit,' she explained with a laugh. 'I can see fine now.'

'I guess you know this road then,' he said.

'Oh yes,' Frauke replied. 'Silke and I found it while we were exploring one day. Come, I'll show you the best part.'

At the end of the road there was an old narrow bridle path which curved round to the left in a loop, back in the direction from which they had come. Frauke led the way along what was little more than a dirt track with Sneijder just behind. The path continued for about a kilometre until it arrived at a farm. Hanging on the gate there was a sign in Dutch with the inscription '*Private land: Strictly no trespassing.*'

Frauke leapt off the bike, grasping the handlebars and running alongside until she brought it to a halt. She wheeled the bicycle towards the gate which was slightly ajar.

Sneijder stopped and put his foot down, still strad-dling his bicycle. 'We can't go through there. It's private.'

'It's okay,' she replied. 'They won't mind.'

Sneijder eyed the sign again. 'It says 'strictly' no tres-passing. You don't read Dutch, do you?'

'But it's so nice down here,' she protested. She thought for a moment. 'Come on, there'll probably be nobody around.'

'I don't think we should,' Sneijder said.

She gave a mischievous smile. 'Come on. Where's your sense of adventure?'

Sneijder looked at her, feeling a sense of longing he had not felt for several years. Her dark brown hair hung down her cheek, framing her face and contrasting with her pale skin. Her sparkling blue eyes and intensely vivid red lips seemed to leap out to him. He was powerless to do anything but follow her. He stepped off his bicycle and began wheeling it towards the gate. 'All right, come on then, but let's not hang about.'

'Right.' She smiled and moved through the gate briskly, Sneijder just behind. They walked across the edge of a field, keeping to the bushes on one side as much as possible. At the end of the field there was a hedgerow, and beyond it a fresh green meadow through which the narrow stream they had seen earlier passed. Frauke removed the bag and basket from her bicycle and pushed it into a gap in the bushes, then in-dicated for Sneijder to do the same. 'It's best to keep the bikes out of sight, I think.'

They climbed over the hedgerow and walked across the meadow towards the sound of the bubbling stream. Frauke carried her bag and Sneijder the basket, which was a lot heavier than it had first appeared. The grass was long, a metre or more in places and often very dense. As they arrived beside the stream, a dog barked somewhere in the direction of the distant farmhouse. The bark was answered by a man, the farmer no doubt. The dog was already heading towards them and it was too late to run away. The dog would see them for sure; it was just a question of whether or not they were spotted by the humans.

'Quick, lie down!' Sneijder said, dropping to his knees. He put the wicker basket down next to him and lay flat on his stomach. The long grass loomed large above his head and he could barely see Frauke lying next to him.

'What do we do now?' she whispered. 'We'll get caught if that dog picks up our scent.'

The grass around them began to quiver and within seconds the dog was upon them. It was a fast and athletic animal, covering the distance in no time at all and it burst through a space in the long grass and approached Sneijder. He was relieved to discover that the dog was a black Labrador, a gentle and friendly breed. It came right over to him and sniffed around a little, its long narrow tail wagging in the air. Sneijder spoke quietly to the dog and reached out a hand to stroke it. He started to relax but just at that moment the dog began barking.

'That's it, we're in trouble,' Frauke said.

Sneijder reached a hand into the basket and pulled out the first thing that came to hand, a small piece of cheese of some variety. He pushed himself up on to his knees and with a powerful thrust of his arm propelled the cheese through the air in the direction of the farmer's voice. The dog turned and bolted after it. He must have met his master on the way because there was a commotion, and the sounds of the dog barking and the farmer speaking were suddenly coming from the same place.

Eventually the farmer uttered something unintelligible and both he and the dog disappeared. Sneijder lay down and rolled onto his back, breathing deeply.

Frauke burst out laughing. 'Can you imagine if we'd been caught?' she said. 'That would have delighted my father.'

'I hope you weren't particularly looking forward to eating that. It was the only way I could think of to get rid of that dog.'

'No, it's okay. There's a bit more inside. Well, that was fun.'

When he had recovered his breath, Frauke led him across the stream, and through a small line of trees. Moments later they emerged at a pond surrounded on all sides by tall trees with thick, dense foliage. It was a very private location and appeared to be safe from the attention of the landowner. The trees also provided a degree of shade, respite from the now blazing midday sun.

The two of them shared the picnic that Frauke had prepared. It was a collection of various foods which she had been able to find, mostly items left over which had to be used or thrown away. This included half a loaf of bread which was on the verge of going mouldy, a small slice of Edam cheese and some thin strips of roasted chicken, pears, apples and salted peanuts. She had also managed to produce half a bottle of red wine.

'My God, where did you manage to get that?' Sneijder was surprised. 'Is that a vintage pinot noir? My father was once given some by a business associate; it was delicious.'

'Yes,' she replied. 'In Germany we call it *spätburgunder*, but it's from the same grapes. It's one of the best wines to have with this variety of cheese.'

'You seem to know what you're talking about,' Sneijder observed.

'I learned that from my mother.' She hesitated for a moment, considering whether she wanted to speak about her. 'I learned everything from her. She was a wonderful woman you know – caring, compassionate, dignified, and very beautiful.'

'You said 'was'. What happened?'

'She had cancer,' Frauke answered with a hint of melancholy. 'It spread incredibly quickly and she died within three months. I was thirteen.'

'I'm sorry,' said Sneijder. 'You must miss her very much. So did your father bring you up?'

Frauke glanced at him as if he had said something ridiculous. 'Oh no. I hardly ever saw him when I was younger. He was always working, even slept in his office in Munich. Then with the war he was in Poland, and then here. No, I lived with my aunt.'

'Until you moved here?'

'Yes. My father suddenly decided he wanted to get to know me, and get me away from the bombing in Germany. I never knew what his work involved and I figured I wouldn't want to know, but now I can't avoid it.'

'It must bother you, some of the things the SS do,' Sneijder said.

All of a sudden death Frauke seemed to be extremely uncomfortable. She turned away, deliberately avoiding eye contact with him and mumbled something quietly.

'What did you say?' Sneijder asked. 'Frauke, what's wrong?'

'I don't think I should be talking about all this, particularly my father. It's not right and, well, I hardly know you.'

'The only way we can get to know each other better is by talking about the things that make us who we are.'

'It is not so simple,' she replied softly. 'You are Dutch and your country is under occupation. My father is your enemy. As a German and an employee of the administration I am also your enemy I suppose, but my father is in a powerful position. If I were to tell you something which could help the Resistance harm or kill him, you could feel obliged to inform them.'

'What would you think of that?'

'I am not naïve,' she said. 'I know my father is not a good or moral man, but he is still my father, my flesh and blood. That is all that matters.'

Sneijder did not know how to respond, and for a minute the two of them sat in silence. In an effort to end the discomfort that this created, he turned to the open basket and looked inside. Frauke got up and walked over to the edge of the pond, staring out over the water which was very still and had the appearance of polished glass. A light wind picked up, disturbing the water and gently rustling the leaves on the surrounding trees.

Sneijder looked at her silhouetted against the sun, the light seeping through her hair which was blowing in the wind. Her feminine form was accentuated in the well-fitting dress; the smooth, round shoulders, the curvaceous chest and hips and long, flowing legs. It triggered Sneijder's most primitive male desires, feelings which were almost alien to him.

Frauke returned displaying a more settled expression and kneeled down in front of him. 'Tell me about your family. We've spent all our time discussing me. I still know nothing about you.'

Sneijder pondered this for a couple of seconds. His training at SOE's school at Beaulieu had educated him in how to lie convincingly in different situations. It was best to tell the truth as much as possible as this made it easier to recall facts and ensure the story stayed the same with every retelling. 'I grew up in Amsterdam. My father worked in the jewel trade and owed a shop. I worked there for a time after I left school, along with my brothers and sisters, but spending all day every day with your family? Well, you can imagine. I began working as a market trader selling fruit and vegetables, and I was still doing that until the war. I got shipped off to Germany as forced labour.'

'How long were you there?'

'Eighteen months in a factory in Hamburg, putting together engines for ships which were built there.'

'So how did you get out?' she asked.

'I became ill with a lung problem brought on by some of the chemicals used in another part of the factory,' Sneijder answered. 'The ventilation in the building was very poor. I was discharged on the grounds of ill health and let go.'

'Why here?' Frauke asked. 'Why did you not return to Amsterdam to your family?'

'Oh right, yes.' Sneijder took a deep breath and exhaled slowly. 'The truth is, I don't believe they are there any longer. You see, my father disobeyed German authority and actively encouraged others to do the same. This made our family targets. I heard the Gestapo burned down our entire neighbourhood and they had to move.

I didn't want to take the risk of being caught and arrested so I never went back.'

'Never?' She seemed confused by this. 'But you said that you'd got your identification card in Amsterdam so you must have been there.'

'I said that?' Sneijder managed to make his horror at his mistake sound like surprise.

'Yes, that's what you told that soldier on the bridge. You said you'd got it six months ago in Amsterdam, but you told me you just came from Germany a few weeks ago.'

Sneijder thought quickly and used the only excuse he could think of. He grinned and admitted, 'I told him that so that if anything looked odd with the card he might assume it was a regional difference, and I told him I'd had it six months because that would mean it had passed inspection before, increasing the likelihood of it being genuine. You see, it's a forgery.'

Her eyes widened. 'A forgery? Really?'

'Absolutely.'

'Let me see it,' she said. Sneijder took the card from his back pocket and gave it to her. She examined it closely, then passed her fingers along it to feel its texture. 'It's your own name. Why would you have a forged identity card with your own name on it? It is your real name?'

'Of course,' Sneijder replied. 'I lost my old card while I was in Hamburg and when I came back I needed a new one. I was afraid if I went to the authorities they might send me back to Germany so I got a false one, that's all.'

She smiled and chuckled, seemingly relieved by Sneijder's explanation and accepting it. 'A forged identity card? How terrible. If only my father knew.'

He looked at her, in alarm at first and then with a smile as he realised that of course she was joking. 'Stop doing that. You'll make me nervous.'

'Well come and stop me,' she replied playfully. He dived across towards her but she leapt up and began to run away, calling, 'You'll need to do better than that to catch me!' He jumped to his feet and sprinted after her.

They spent the rest of the afternoon at the pond, talking and laughing together and enjoying each other's company. It was a long time since he had relaxed so completely with another person, which seemed paradoxical when much of what he was telling her was untrue. He had expected to be on edge when giving her his cover story, and he had to admit to being unsettled by the ease with which he could deliver total lies. For as long as Sneijder could remember his mind had been filled with negative thoughts; about his family, about his execution of Kemerling at the concentration camp, about the task he had been assigned. Frauke's warm and carefree attitude reminded him that life could be positive and still held pleasures; the beauty of nature, the company of friends, the tenderness of a woman.

He knew that her continuing relationship with him was most likely an act of defiance against her father, who insisted she not mix with Dutch civilians, but as the afternoon wore on her reservations seemed to melt away and her trust in him increased. It was obvious that there was a growing attraction between them but they both resisted, knowing the pitfalls which would present themselves if they allowed anything to happen. For Sneijder it was imperative; killing Albrecht Koestler would become even harder if he fell for the man's daughter. He couldn't do that to himself, and he couldn't do it to her. For her it would be a simpler question but one with potential hazards of its own; her father would obviously disapprove and was in a position to make things very uncomfortable for them both if he found out.

They returned to Arnhem a little before seven o'clock and headed for her house, stopping some way short to avoid unwelcome confrontations. She dismounted and turned to Sneijder, who was still sitting on his bicycle with his foot down. 'I had a good day,' she said. 'Thank you for the company, Johannes.'

'Not at all,' he answered. 'It was lovely, getting out into the country like that. I'm glad you took me there.'

'We'll do it again,' she declared.

For a moment they just looked at each other. Her eyes really were striking, a spectacular deep blue. He was still dazzled by them when she leaned over and kissed him lightly on the right cheek. Her lips were warm on his skin and his nose filled with the sweet aroma of her perfume. 'Goodnight, Johannes,' she added.

Sneijder returned the compliment, knocked out of his stride for the briefest of moments by her unexpected act. He watched her climb onto her bike, and waved to her as she cycled slowly away. He kept his eyes on her as she faded further and further into the distance and then, like an intangible spirit, she was gone.

CHAPTER THIRTEEN

Koestler entered his office early on Monday morning and called Klimitz in to update him on events. A couple of minutes later the captain knocked and entered clutching a file. 'Good morning, sir. A pleasant weekend?'

'Yes, yes,' Koestler replied dismissively with a wave of his hand. 'I have had the latest recruitment numbers. Helder did an excellent job at his first meeting persuading those on the fringes of the NSB that joining the SS would be a good idea. As I predicted, a man of reputation can create a much more positive response than someone unknown. He is actually a terrific actor – he almost had me convinced that he was a National Socialist.'

Klimitz placed the file he was carrying on the edge of the desk. 'I think you'll want to look at this, sir. It's the transcript of Max Bruggink's interrogation, led by Horvath and one of his brutes. Some interesting points came to light.'

Koestler peered over the top of his spectacles. 'How much did he resist? Did they have to push him hard?'

'He wasn't easy to break,' Klimitz answered simply.

Koestler picked up the file and started to read what had been said during the four separate interviews which made up Bruggink's interrogation. It was all written in a formal, official style and there was no mention of any physical coercion or what may have happened to the suspect between interviews. At first Bruggink said absolutely nothing, then gave them a large amount of information which was obviously false. Horvath was not fooled. Eventually Bruggink admitted that he had been involved in the ambush on the convoy, and knew who had attacked Walter Stracke's kubelwagen.

'This is true?' Koestler asked.

'I spoke with Horvath just a few minutes ago,' said Klimitz. 'At present we have been unable to establish whether the names Bruggink gave us check out, but his men are working on it. Read the next page.'

Koestler glanced at him, and then turned to the next page in the file. His face became more serious as he scanned the transcript. His gaze returned to his adjutant and he said, 'There is an agent from England in the area? That is what this says, yes?'

'As you will note, Bruggink admitted to the fact that there is an agent in the area but claims not to know his identity. He has maintained this throughout his interrogation. Horvath also reported to me that he has contacted our coastal listening stations and was told that there was radio chatter on the night in question which might suggest an RAF special duties flight.'

'Now that is interesting. I imagine whoever killed Stracke knows the identity of this agent,' Koestler replied. 'Meeting him would seem to be a likely explanation for breaking the curfew.'

'Perhaps.' Klimitz's response was underwhelming.

'I want to know who this agent is and where I can find him,' said Koestler, 'as a priority. Make some enquiries, Sebastien. I'm not convinced that Horvath can be relied upon. It surely cannot be that hard to find one man with all the informants we have.'

'I will give it a try, sir.'

'And tell Horvath I will come to see Bruggink myself a little later. Perhaps offering some kind of deal will persuade him to be more forthcoming.'

Not wishing to push his luck with the police patrols, Sneijder left the motorcycle behind and cycled to Van Rijn's house in Roeden, where he found him in the kitchen with his wife Klara. She was still struggling to come to terms with the death of her brother and nephew and appeared pale and gaunt. Her eyes were red where she had obviously been crying. Kees Van Rijn looked better, but it seemed to Sneijder as if he were delaying the onset of mourning until he could avenge the deaths of Jelle and Arnold, and also that of his brother-in-law.

Sneijder and Van Rijn moved into another room to discuss business. Before they began Sneijder decided to raise the subject that had been bothering him for days. 'I think I need to find somewhere else to stay,' he said. 'It may not be safe for me at the Uhlenbroeks' any longer.'

'Why not?' Van Rijn's eyes widened. 'Has your cover been blown?'

'No, not yet, but I think the Germans may find out. You know, with Max being arrested and everything....'

Van Rijn cut him off firmly. 'Max is extremely loyal, to me and to our cause. He would never reveal any information to the enemy, never. He would rather die.'

'That may be so but he hardly considered me to be a close ally at the time he was taken,' Sneijder replied. 'Who could blame him if he decided to give them my name?'

'There is absolutely no question about Max Bruggink's integrity,' said Van Rijn. 'I would bet my own life on it. Whatever they do to him he will not break.'

'Everybody breaks,' Sneijder said. 'You can only hold out for so long.'

'He will resist. Besides, even if he gave up your name he does not know where you live. Information is only given to the people who really need to know, for just this reason. The only people who know your whereabouts are the Uhlenbroeks, Mr Helder and myself. Assuming you have not told anybody else, you will be safe.'

Sneijder said nothing. If it was true that Bruggink did not know where he was staying there was no immediate danger, but Sneijder could not shake off his feeling of unease. What he had seen at Helder's home troubled him, despite the relationship with Koestler being something he readily admitted to. It just felt wrong.

'You haven't told anybody, have you?' Van Rijn asked.

Sneijder laughed it off. 'Of course not.' He was not prepared to reveal his relationship with Frauke Koestler, certainly not at this stage. It had taken a lot of persuasion to reach agreement with Van Rijn and the slightest detail could change his mind.

'Then you have nothing to worry about.'

'I guess not.' Sneijder decided to broach another subject. 'Have you got any further with finding out who gave Max up to the Germans? If it is somebody close we could all be in danger.'

Van Rijn shook his head. 'Not yet, but we're working on it. Through one of the clerical secretaries in SS headquarters we've heard that Koestler's office keeps detailed files on every informant who is paid for information. If anyone in our circle has gone to them his name will be in those files. What I don't understand is how any informant could have got hold of the information in the first place. I just can't believe that anyone involved in the attack on the convoy would have let it slip – not De Jong, not the Voesmans and certainly not Max himself.'

Having read through Koestler's personnel file and seen the man in action Sneijder had learned that he was an obsessive organiser, and the idea that there would be such an extensive collection of documents was certainly credible.

'So how does that help us? We haven't got the files.'

'Not at the moment, no, but hopefully we will. The Voesmans have identified a couple of men from their network of dubious characters who might be willing to break in and steal them, provided we can raise enough money to make it worth their while.'

'Break in to SS headquarters?' Sneijder was astonished. 'That's suicide.'

'Why do you think I'm not doing it myself?' Van Rijn countered. 'The advantage of criminals is that although they may excel in their chosen illegal activity, the vast majority are pretty stupid. It is a risk far greater than I am willing to take but if there is the slightest chance of obtaining those files we must look into it.'

That evening, the two of them decided to reconnoitre the German administrative building to assess the security arrangements. If all went well Sneijder intended to break in the following night to sabotage the Mercedes. It was midnight when they approached the front of the building through the park on the opposite side of the street. The lights were off in all but a couple of windows and most of the façade was in darkness. A bright lamp illuminated the large set of doors at the top of the grand stone staircase on the building's exterior. With the rest of the city blacked out the lamp seemed especially luminous and it seemed to cast its light right across the road. There was not a guard in sight.

It was an eerily still night with no discernible wind, and humid. This had the effect of creating perfect silence, not something which would be particularly advantageous for anybody attempting to creep around unnoticed. Sneijder motioned to Van Rijn to follow him and silently sprinted across the wide street. He ran to the corner of the building and stopped, and seconds later was joined by his companion. He peered around the side of the building and down the road which ran along its east side; it too was deserted and in darkness. The office went back about thirty metres, and from there the wall continued right around the large open yard at the rear. Sneijder made his way down the road, keeping in the shadows against the wall.

He reached the enormous solid wrought iron gates which secured the entrance. They were locked shut and fixed into the ground with two large deadbolts, but beneath them there was a gap of about ten centimetres. Sneijder lay flat on his stomach and peered under. The centre of the yard was empty but there were vehicles of various descriptions parked around against the walls; large staff cars, kubelwagens, trucks. In one corner twenty-five or so motorcycles were gathered together, and next to them a few uncoupled sidecars. Sneijder could just make out the figure of a sentry in the gloom and a cloud of smoke rising above him. As the sentry walked towards him, Sneijder could see a cigarette hanging from his mouth. He carried a submachine gun and appeared to be dressed in the green Orpo uniform.

From his vantage point it was impossible for Sneijder to make out anything else. He got to his feet and surveyed the surroundings. Where the main building stopped and the three-metre high wall began, the corrugated-iron roof of the small workshop was just visible. If Sneijder could climb up there it would possibly give him the view he needed. He turned to Van Rijn who stood behind him and whispered, 'Care to give me a hand to get over?'

'Over the wall?' Van Rijn questioned. 'Are you serious?'

'I'm going up onto that roof, see what the situation is.'

'They'll see you for sure, it's madness.'

'Look, do you want me to do this or what?' Sneijder snapped.

He turned and gripped the edge of the highest brick he could reach with his fingers. Van Rijn stooped slightly and cupped his hands under Sneijder's foot. With a tremendous heave he launched him vertically upwards. Sneijder extended his other arm and grasped the top of the wall, dragging himself over. With his head now in clear space above the parapet he could see the sentry walking away. Taking his opportunity, Sneijder climbed right over the wall and onto the roof of the workshop, taking care not to clatter the corrugated-iron.

He moved right back against the adjoining wall of the administrative office, using the roof on which he sat to shield himself from the view of the guard below, and then crawled forward very slowly. As he approached the edge he spread himself out until he was lying prone and crept ahead gingerly. He glanced down. As far as he could tell there was not another sentry but the door to the workshop was ajar and a thin strip of light escaped. Sneijder made a mental note that the mechanics obviously worked during the night when necessary. He remained in the same place for about ten minutes, watching, but there was just one solitary guard for sure. He was surprised by the absence of security, particularly since the attack on the German convoy and it crossed his mind that it could be a set-up, but that was nerves talking. Over a substantial enough period of time people became careless, that was all, especially if their job was dull and repetitive. Physical attacks in the Netherlands had been rare throughout the occupation, a result of the Dutch people's moral aversion to violence, and thus a lack of mental preparedness was only to be expected. All it needed was for the person in charge to allocate his resources badly and suddenly there was a situation like this one, where one man was left to defend over fifty vehicles. His reconnaissance complete, Sneijder's gaze was instead drawn to a manhole cover exactly in the centre of the yard.

It was from this entrance to the sewer that Sneijder emerged the following evening. Using the plans of the original 1853 building he had discovered that the underground sewage pipe which ran under the yard also continued beneath the office and then under the park across the street. The thick undergrowth which thronged the public garden provided the perfect cover to enter the long, dark tunnel. Having assisted him into the sewer Van Rijn waited outside the gates of the yard with guns and a bag of plastic explosives, ready to blast his way through the wall if anything were to go awry. Using the plans for guidance, Sneijder worked his way along the tunnel with just a small flashlight to guide him until he was satisfied that he was beneath the car pool. He scaled the ladder which took him right up under the manhole and waited.

After a delay of a couple of minutes Sneijder heard the pre-arranged signal faintly; a voice calling out in German. The sound of footsteps above his head was clearly audible. There was a metallic clunking as the guard's boots made contact with the iron-clad manhole cover, and then the steps moved in the direction of the gates. Sneijder, with one arm threaded through the top rung of the ladder to support his weight, gently lifted the cover and began to slide it aside. The great hunk of metal was heavy and it required a significant amount of concentration to move it without scraping it along the ground. Once he had slowly moved it clear, he placed the manhole cover down with great care and stuck his head up out of the hole. The sentry stood about twenty metres in front of him facing in the opposite direction, his automatic weapon raised readily. He responded to the voice he was hearing, 'Who are you? What do you want?'

Seizing on the diversion provided by Van Rijn, Sneijder clambered out of the hole directly behind the guard. His heart jumped in his chest like an animal. Trying desperately to regulate his unbearable tension, he replaced the manhole cover, all the time expecting the German officer to turn and spot him. He scurried away across the open yard, dropped to the ground and rolled under a low-slung flatbed lorry which was parked between two larger trucks along the back wall.

Van Rijn kept up the conversation in rudimentary German. 'I am an officer of the SD. I left my military cap in one of your trucks, I believe.'

'That is not my problem,' the guard replied. 'Go away, this is a restricted area.'

Sneijder lay completely still and tried to let his breathing return to normal. The physical exertion of moving while attempting to remain silent had almost caused him to hyperventilate, not to mention the stress and fear that such a dangerous undertaking involved. For the moment he was in a position of relative safety, as he would only be spotted if the guard made a conscious effort to look under the vehicles. His racing heart began to slow, and his attention began to turn towards the job in hand.

The guard left the gate and resumed his patrol. Looking to his right, Sneijder saw a line of five Mercedes parked side-by-side along the side wall, their front ends facing out into the yard towards him. One of those was the car used by Koestler; Sneijder had taken a note of the registration number when he had followed him and it was always the same, so he could be sure that the man did always travel in the same vehicle. Two of the Mercedes in the yard were convertibles, Grand Touring versions of the 770 as used by the Nazi hierarchy in their propaganda films. It had to be one of the other three. They were about thirty metres away, with three or four trucks between them and the lorry under which Sneijder lay. The only way to reach the cars without exposing himself would be to crawl under each vehicle, one at a time. He set off on his way, moving swiftly but quietly and arrived at the rear of the first Mercedes in line.

A brief check of the registration plate revealed that this was not the necessary vehicle. It was parked extremely close to the wall but fortunately the rear of the car incorporated a long boot which Sneijder was able to clamber over. Eventually he reached the other side and was pleased to note that the next car in line was Koestler's. He moved towards the front of the car and peered over the long bonnet to check the whereabouts of the sentry. The German was standing in front of the workshop, which tonight was locked up and in darkness, smoking a cigarette. His submachine gun dangled from the strap around his neck and he did not seem particularly alert.

Sneijder put his plan into action. At the front of the car the running board swept up and met the wheel arch, and at this point there was a space which gave access to the front wheel and the underside of the car. Sneijder rolled onto his back and pushed himself through. He took a small flashlight from his pocket and shone it on the inside of the wheel, then, moving slowly along the axle he found the brake drum. A long hydraulic cable ran out from the brake and disappeared upwards into the darkness, towards the cabin and the driver's pedals.

Sneijder reached into the pocket of his leather jacket and pulled out his miniature knife wrapped in an oily rag. He grasped the hydraulic cable in the rag to catch any escaping fluid and then carefully pushed the end of the knife's blade into the thick tubing. It required a little pressure but he felt it beginning to give and the sharp point started to make a hole. When he was three quarters of the way through making a puncture he stopped and pulled the knife away. In his other pocket Sneijder had a large stone made of some sort of hard sedimentary rock which he had chipped away into a sharp point at one end. He pushed the pointed edge of the stone into the hole he had started with the knife until it broke through the plastic, and jammed it in until it remained there on its own. It was Sneijder's hope that by making the hole with something natural like a stone he could make it appear that the brake line had been cut by accident. It was a long shot but any doubt about it being a deliberate act could serve to soften the enemy's response.

In order for the assassination to be successful the car would need to function properly until Koestler was in it, meaning the leakage of the brake fluid would have to be delayed. Sneijder took from his pocket the two items he would require for this; a length of fine black thread and a stick of chewing gum. He put the gum in his mouth and began to masticate, and then set about work with the thread. Sneijder reached around to the front wheel and wrapped one end of the thread around a large nut which was currently at the top, tying it off. He produced the gum, which was now soft and jellylike, from his mouth and adhered it to the other end of the thread. Removing the sharp-pointed stone from the hydraulic brake cable he immediately covered the hole with the gum, smoothing it out so that there were no leaks but taking care not to stick it down particularly hard. An inspection of his handiwork satisfied him that the arrangement was unlikely to be spotted from anywhere but under the vehicle.

If it went according to Sneijder's theory, when the driver drove the car from its parking space in the morning, the front wheel would rotate and pull the thread tight, which in turn would peel the gum away from the hole in the brake line. The brake fluid would then begin to leak during the car's journey to collect Koestler.

Sneijder dragged himself out from under the vehicle and took his bearings. The German sentry was strolling around the yard in no particular hurry, obviously extremely bored by the job he had been asked to carry out. He stopped outside the workshop and peered through the glass door, cupping his hands around his eyes in an attempt to cut out the glare. He remained there for several minutes then looked up and continued on his way, lighting another cigarette and blowing small puffs of smoke to amuse himself.

Sneijder picked up the rock he had used to puncture the brake line of the car. He took aim and thrust it into the air. It vanished into the dark night sky for a second or two and then clattered down onto the corrugated iron roof of the workshop with a loud clang. There were a few smaller, quieter metallic sounds as the stone bounced and then rolled off the side of the roof. The guard spun round and his head snapped up towards the source of the noise. He disappeared from view around the side of the workshop.

Sneijder did not wait for him to return. He broke cover from behind the row of Mercedes and headed directly for the manhole in the centre of the yard. He lifted the heavy steel manhole cover as if it were made of paper, the adrenalin giving him strength he did not expect. Sliding it aside, Sneijder dropped down into the hole and found his footing on the ladder, reached up for the cover and pulled it into place. It scraped the asphalt as it closed above him but Sneijder was not going to worry about it. He was elated by his success and clenched a fist as he ran away down the tunnel.

It was grey and overcast the following morning when the clock on the mantelpiece in Koestler's sitting room reached half past eight. He was collecting together some papers which he had been working on the previous evening when he heard the familiar sound of his Mercedes staff car pulling up outside. His young driver got out of the front seat and walked around to open the rear door. He stood and waited for Koestler to come out.

The German positioned his military cap on his head, picked up his leather briefcase and left the house. His regular guard Sterchler had just arrived and he nodded to him. 'I'll leave it to you then. See that Frauke gets away safely.'

'Of course, sir,' Sterchler replied formally.

Koestler walked over to the car and pointedly glanced at his watch in front of his driver. He grunted and said, 'Eight-thirty exactly. An improvement.' He climbed into the back of the car without waiting for a reply and felt the door close firmly behind him, removed his cap and placed it on the seat beside him, then settled in for the short journey to his central Arnhem office. Often on this trip he would read through files or communiqués but today he had a lot on his mind.

Koestler had visited Max Bruggink at the Gestapo prison the previous day to try to negotiate with him, to offer him more lenient treatment in return for revealing everything he knew about the agent from England. The man, who had turned out to be a former officer in the Dutch army, had refused to say anything and insisted that he did not know the agent's identity. There was something about his manner though which made Koestler doubt his story and he had told him so. This made no difference; there was absolutely no way Bruggink would tell him anything. When the Gestapo men started utilising their own unique methods of extracting information, Koestler left. He knew that torture was the only way to get through to these enemies of Germany but he didn't need to sit and watch it.

The other issue was the increasing rumour that the Netherlands was about to fall under military control with the general commander of the armed forces in the country, Friedrich Christian Christiansen and his chief of staff Lieutenant-General von Wühlisch in charge. This was hardly unexpected given the speed of the Allied advance in northern Europe but it would constitute a serious erosion of SS influence. There was even talk that the Wehrmacht's Army Command in the West might reassign its headquarters to the Netherlands. This would be a sign if ever one were needed that after four years on the fringes of the war, the country was about to be thrust right into the middle of it.

Koestler looked out of the window as the car picked up speed along the straight, tree-lined Kemperbergsweg. On the left-hand side was thick pine forest which dropped away down a gentle gradient. To the right the line of trees was broken up by green fields stretching for a couple of kilometres with grazing cattle, a little farmhouse in the distance. After a minute or so the Mercedes reached a sweeping bend. The driver took it fairly quickly as usual. He was not careless or reckless but he did like to drive at a reasonable pace, something which Koestler did not mind. He wasn't an especially patient man and did not like to waste time sitting about in cars. Having negotiated the bend the driver straightened the car and reduced speed as he descended a small decline.

Just half an hour before, Sneijder and Van Rijn had been sitting in the latter's house, drinking what passed for coffee these days. A task as simple as heating water was difficult now as the German administration had slashed rations of electricity, gas and coal. Fortunately it was summer and so keeping warm was not a problem. The two of them were sitting in silence when Sneijder could not contain his agitation any longer.

'It's no good,' he exclaimed. 'I can't in any conscience leave a man to die.'

'It's not your fault and there is nothing you can do about it,' Van Rijn replied.

Sneijder got to his feet. 'But that's not true, is it? I could easily inform him and he could call in ill. They'd put someone else in the car.'

'You don't think that would look suspicious? A German officer's Dutch driver gets sick on exactly the same day that he is involved in a car accident? They'd know he was involved in the plot and kill him anyway. Either way, you can't save him.'

'I can try. Maybe I could kill Koestler another way.'

'You don't believe this stuff, I know you don't,' Van Rijn retorted. 'You promised me you'd kill him. For God's sake, that's the whole reason you are here! We've been over this.'

'I've got to do something,' Sneijder said and headed for the door.

Van Rijn stood and blocked his path. 'Forget it, Johannes. Things *are* what they are. You can't save everybody. It's a war – there are always casualties.'

'How can you do that?' Sneijder demanded angrily. 'Stand there and be so cold-blooded. It's unbelievable.'

'I love my country and I'm prepared to do everything necessary to get it back. I will make no apologies for that. As for you –' He paused. 'You're talking about sparing a murdering tyrant for the sake of a traitor. Let me remind you, this man ordered the deaths of my nephew and brother-in-law. Is this man's life worth more than Jelle's?'

'I'm sorry,' Sneijder said.

'You're not going anywhere,' Van Rijn said. 'Not until it is done.'

Sneijder barged him aside, propelling him backwards into the wall. He darted out of the door to his motorcycle, threw a leg over it and started the motor as he began to roll it down the hill. Within minutes he was heading north to Arnhem. He had absolutely no idea what he would do if he spotted the car, but he could not reconcile the thought of letting an innocent man die.

Sneijder crossed the bridge into the city but was halted by a German patrol, this time a soldier in Wehrmacht uniform.

'Identity card, please,' the soldier demanded.

Sneijder rummaged in his pockets hurriedly and produced the required card.

The soldier examined the card and then glanced down. 'The motorcycle – why are you using it? Fuel is for essential vehicles only.'

'It is for my job,' Sneijder replied.

'Where do you work?'

'Look, is this going to take much longer?' Sneijder was exasperated. 'I work at the station in Oosterbeek and my boss telephoned to tell me that a train full of German army equipment has arrived and I am needed to help unload it. I must go.'

The soldier snapped, 'It will take as long as I decide.'

'Fine, but if your superiors wish to know why I am late…'

The guard stiffened, took a breath and said, 'Very well. On your way.'

Sneijder moved through the town and streaked beyond the morning traffic, weaving in and out of a line of cars before heading up the hill out of the other end of Arnhem. After a kilometre he rounded a bend and there it was, coming the other way, Koestler's Mercedes-Benz 770. Sneijder was stuck behind two trucks which were struggling to get up the hill. By the time he managed to turn around the Mercedes had vanished from view. He took off in pursuit.

In the back of the car Koestler was planning his morning, making mental notes of people he would need to telephone. A call to Horvath would be necessary, to find out whether Bruggink had divulged any more information about his accomplices in the convoy attack or the British agent. He thought probably not; the man was tough, which was to be very much admired. It took an incredibly strong will to withstand some of the Gestapo's more unspeakable methods of interrogation. Koestler peered out of the window just as a young man on a motorcycle shot past in the opposite direction. He thought that strange; with the chronic fuel shortages the majority of the Dutch population had had their non-essential transport confiscated. The Mercedes continued downhill towards the city, then hit a small rise as it reached the northern tip of the Park Sonsbeek. The sound of the engine moved up a semitone as the driver pressed the accelerator pedal. The car reached the top of the rise and moved around the slight bend, then began to go downhill again. About a hundred metres ahead there was a right-hand bend. They reached it and began to go round, but this time it was clear to Koestler that they were going much too fast. The car began to drift across the road.

'Hey, slow down!' Koestler yelled. 'What the hell-'

There was a banging sound from the front as the driver slammed the brake pedal to the floor, but with no hydraulic pressure it was to no avail. He desperately tried to reduce his speed by yanking hard on the steering wheel, hoping a series of hard turns might absorb some of the careering vehicle's energy. The engine whined noisily as he dropped it into a low gear and attempted to compression-brake the car, but they were just going too fast. The large, heavy Mercedes ran wider and wider and flashed across the opposing carriageway. On the far side there was a thick hedge which blocked the view of what was beyond. The ground dropped away fairly steeply, with grassy banks leading down to a shallow stream. The car burst through the hedge and flew through the air until the weight of the front-mounted engine block dragged it down. The force of the vehicle striking the ground flung Koestler out of his seat. He suddenly found himself on the floor of the car. He could no longer see a thing, but he could feel the car rushing down the bank.

It smashed head-on into a thick oak tree. The front-left side of the vehicle caved in as if made of paper. The steering wheel was hammered into the cabin, puncturing the driver's chest in a sickening fashion. The momentum of the Mercedes began to propel it up the side of the tree trunk, but the angle of the bank was too much. Slowly, the car toppled over, rolled a couple of times and settled upside down in the stream.

Sneijder rounded the corner and immediately saw the huge, gaping hole in the hedgerow. Beyond it was nothing but clear sky, and he knew before he got there it was going to be bad. He cut across the road and pulled up beside the hedge, steadying himself with his foot. Peering down the bank he saw the Mercedes lying upside down at the bottom, its wheels still spinning slowly. It was in the middle of a narrow stream, mere centimetres deep but fairly fast-moving. There appeared to be no movement down there. Surveying the scene Sneijder observed a significant dent in the side of a large oak tree and pieces of wreckage strewn around it. He realised it would not be advisable to be there when the German police arrived on the scene, so he gunned the engine and began to move. It was time to put as much distance between himself and Koestler as possible.

Chapter Fourteen

It was the middle of the afternoon and Sneijder was upstairs in his room at the Uhlenbroeks' house. The old couple were both out; Edwin Uhlenbroek at work at the train station, his wife fetching groceries in Arnhem. Sneijder was having trouble coming to terms with the lives he had just taken and he had tried to sleep to escape his own penitent thoughts. The curtains in the room were pulled across the windows but daylight crept in through the cracks, and he was unable to drift off. Extreme stress brought back the insufferable insomnia that had plagued him for the past year and he longed for some sort of chemical intervention. Without alcohol and out of morphine, he wondered how he would cope if things really got bad. His only saving grace was that he had carried out his mission, and it was over. Now he could try to find his family.

Sneijder was startled by a loud bang from downstairs. He sat up on the bed but heard nothing. It came again after a few seconds. The sound was definitely somebody at the front door, obviously a visitor for the owners of the house – after all, nobody knew he was there. He was going to leave it but the banging was incessant and seemed a little out of the ordinary. It was almost panicked, like a crashing crescendo of drums. Sneijder went down to see what all the noise was about, and was stunned to find himself facing a hysterical Frauke Koestler.

'Johannes, thank God you're here, oh thank God!' she cried. She looked terrible, with tears streaming down her face, smudging her usually-immaculate make-up. Her shoulder length hair was messy and her office jacket was absent; the blouse she wore was wet and stained. 'I was praying you'd be here. I needed someone, and you were the only one I could come to, and I asked everywhere for the stationmaster's house and....'

This was too much. It had taken everything to kill Koestler, but he couldn't do this - console the man's daughter, who he had begun to feel deeply for. 'Slow down, slow down. What has happened?'

'It's my father,' she replied. 'He had a terrible accident in his car this morning. It was bad, very bad; they thought he was going to die!'

Sneijder's mouth dropped open in shock, and he didn't need to feign that. 'They *thought* he was going to die? So he's alive?'

'Yes, he's alive, but he is badly injured,' Frauke said. 'He's at the German military hospital. Oh, it's terrible, they said his car went down a bank and ended up upside down! It's a miracle he survived.' She stepped forward and put her arms around him, resting her head against his chest.

Sneijder couldn't believe what he was hearing. It was inconceivable that anybody could have survived such a crash, not at that speed. The straight stretch of road before the bend was downhill and without any brakes they would surely have been travelling quickly when they smashed through the hedge. The Mercedes had hit a tree head-on and flipped over. People just didn't come out of accidents like that.

'What happened to the driver?' he asked. He could feel his breath gently blowing on her hair, lifting stray strands into the air, and could smell her perfume as she pressed against him.

She squeezed him tightly for a moment, taking comfort from his big, masculine frame and then loosened her grip and stepped back. 'He was killed. Crushed by the wheel apparently, but probably dead the moment the car hit the tree. It's awful.'

Now Sneijder felt physically sick. Not only had he killed Hugo, he had done it for nothing. An innocent man was dead and Koestler was still alive. Sneijder invited her into the house which gave him an excuse to avert himself from her gaze. He could only imagine how his anguished look might be interpreted. He didn't know what image to put across to Frauke; as she had said herself, he was Dutch and thus Koestler was his enemy. She couldn't possibly expect him to be upset about the accident, and was likely to find it strange if he was. However he was not prepared to cause Frauke further pain by appearing pleased, even if it was to conceal his dismay.

'I'm so sorry to come to you, I just...' she began, then paused and chose her words carefully. 'I wanted to be near you - you make me feel safe.'

Sneijder didn't know what to say but Frauke, appearing to sense his unease, seized upon his thoughts as if she knew them.

'Listen, it's okay. I'm not expecting you to feel bad, or be upset or anything. I'm not stupid and I know how things are. I just want you to stay with me. I can't be alone. Please, Johannes.'

Sneijder smiled weakly. 'It's all right.' She moved past him but he stopped her. 'And Frauke? Thanks.' His gratitude was genuine; that she did not expect the impossible from him came as a huge relief and he began to breathe again.

She tried to return the smile. 'So where do you stay?'

Sneijder led the way up the back staircase to the attic room. He opened the door and showed her in, only now noticing how much of a mess the place was in. His clothes were roughly strewn across a couple of wooden chairs and his canvas knapsack lay against the bed in the middle of the floor. 'I'm sorry about the state of it. I wasn't expecting.....er....you know...'

'Yes, you didn't expect visitors,' she finished. 'It's fine, don't worry about it. Are you home alone?'

'Uh-huh,' he answered, beginning to clear things up from the little table beside his bed. As he pulled a newspaper away he felt something move with it, a solid and fairly heavy object. It fell to the wooden floor with quite a thud and he realised with horror that it was the Luger which he had been cleaning earlier. Dreading the inevitable questions, he looked up to find her examining a painting on the wall. He leapt over, placing one foot in front of the gun to block it from her view.

She turned around. 'What was that?'

'I dropped something, that's all.' Before she could say a word he added, 'You like art?'

'I suppose,' she replied. 'My father does and so did my mother. We had this painting at home – *Bacchus and Ariadne*, it's by Titian. You see this bright blue in the top-left corner? It's called lapis lazuli, and when this painting was done it was...'

'More expensive than gold,' Sneijder said.

She looked at him, her cheeks still streaked with the tracks of her tears, and a small grin appeared on her face. 'How did you know what I was going to say?'

'Well, lapis lazuli is quite a rare gem and with my father being in the jewel business....' Sneijder began, 'Any time a man from the art world came in to the shop they'd mention something like that. I guess they thought they should discuss gems and it was all they knew, how it related to art.'

She looked back at the painting and with her distracted for a second, Sneijder kicked the gun, sending it spinning under the bed. The rough grip of the pistol made a scratching sound on the hard floorboards and Frauke turned again, looking puzzled when she saw nothing. 'I'm hearing things.'

Having made a brief check to ensure there was nothing incriminating in plain view, Sneijder threw the knapsack containing his Sten and the box of grenades into the corner and sat down on the edge of the bed. Frauke walked over and sat beside him, for a moment just looking ahead, then rested her head on his shoulder. 'Oh, Johannes, why is life so unbearable? As if this stupid bloody war isn't enough, now a car accident!'

Sneijder nodded solemnly. 'I wish I could tell you.'

Frauke turned to face him, a matter of centimetres away, and gazed into his eyes. The deep, mystical blue irises she possessed took hold of him and he could not pull himself away as she leaned into him. Her smooth red lips brushed against his, and he could feel an almost electrical energy as she kissed him again, this time a little more forcefully. He placed a hand on her neck, slipping his fingers under her cascading hair and pulled her near.

At the same time he let his mouth fall open and felt her tongue pressing against his.

At the back of his mind, in the darkest recesses, this felt wrong for so many reasons, not least the fact that she had come to him in a hysterically upset state. She probably wasn't thinking rationally and if he let his relationship with her go any further he certainly wasn't, but he wanted her badly, emotionally as well as sexually. He hadn't felt the gentleness of a woman's touch for so long, and the connection between them was strong, perhaps even extraordinary. Frauke's gentleness rapidly gave way to a passionate fervour as she pushed him back flat on the bed and climbed onto him, straddling his body with her long legs. She continued to kiss him strongly while she held him down, pressing her hands onto his shoulders. She moved her lips away, kissing his face and then his neck.

At that point the feelings in the back of his mind came to the surface and he held her away. 'Wait, Frauke, I can't do this. Not with you like....'

She held a finger to his mouth and muttered, 'No, no, don't say that. Please, Johannes...'

'I was just –'

She replied almost desperately, in an odd sort of panic. 'No, no, please Johannes, no, I need this! Please, Johannes.'

He knew he had to stop her, to save her from herself, but she was a beautiful woman with a luscious, ripe body, and he was just a man. He rolled her over so his body was on top of hers, with her legs wrapped around his waist. He kissed her with an insatiable passion, cupping a hand around her backside, her skirt the only thing between him and her warm skin. She started to unbutton her blouse, revealing her fine breasts under a silk brassiere. Sneijder moved down and kissed her lightly on her stomach, causing her to gasp in pleasure. He was not thinking any more, just letting his body guide him. As she cast the bra aside his mind functioned one final time and he went to close the door. She dragged him back, then noticed what he was doing and let him go. Finally he reached the door and shut it, and then, unbuttoning his jeans, submitted himself to the events which were to take place.

Afterwards, Sneijder and Frauke were together in the bed, the thin cotton sheets covering their undressed bodies. She lay against him, an arm across his torso and held him tightly. She kissed him on the cheek and rested her head on his chest, listening to the strong and regular beating of his heart. At that moment in time there was nowhere else on earth he wanted to be but lying next to her.

The previous hour was an experience he would never forget, that was assured. It was many things, not least Frauke's simmering sensuality, that made it special, but after feeling so alone for so long it had been an outpouring of emotion and the satisfying of a myriad of unrequited needs. He had always naturally gravitated towards being a loner and could find it hard to start relationships, particularly with women. He found it easy to be himself with her however, and she didn't share his social reluctance.

He stroked her hair gently. 'What's the matter?' he asked, sensing that she was troubled. 'Did you not enjoy it? Did I do something wrong?'

'No,' she assured him, 'you didn't do anything wrong. It was wonderful. It's just...., oh never mind. I'm all right.'

Sneijder pushed himself up and turned to look her in the eye. 'Tell me. There is obviously something bothering you. Please.'

She looked at him coyly. 'Why do you want to know?'

'Because I care about you,' he replied. 'I don't like to see you upset. Is that a good enough reason?' He immediately regretted the sharpness of his response, which had been triggered by her inquisitiveness. In his attempt to deflect any suspicion of his true identity he had gone too far.

She ignored his tone and said, 'I don't think we should have done it now, not with my father as he is. The accident was only this morning, for goodness sake. He's lying in hospital and look what I'm doing? What was I thinking?'

'You are being too hard on yourself,' Sneijder said. 'He's in hospital receiving medical attention, and they wouldn't let you see him. There was nothing you could do earlier. As you said yourself, you shouldn't be alone.'

'I still feel so guilty.' Frauke was silent for a moment. 'If he knew about you, he would go absolutely crazy. Oh God, what if he finds out? He would be livid with me, but you? Do you realise what could happen to you? My father is a very dangerous man.'

'Listen, Frauke,' he said, 'I know exactly what the SS are capable of, believe me. I also know how to look after myself, so you don't need to worry. Promise me you won't worry.'

'He could kill you, Johannes, do you understand?' She sat up next to him, a pained expression spreading across her face. 'I should never have got you involved – I'm so sorry.'

He reached out with both hands, taking her soft cheeks between them and moved his face close to hers. 'It's okay. I don't care about the dangers, I really don't. You are very special, Frauke, and whatever may happen to me, I want to see you.'

'But you hardly know me. And I hardly know you either. It's not a good idea, with me being German and you Dutch and...'

'None of that matters,' Sneijder said firmly. 'Now please, don't worry, all right?' She nodded and he kissed her lips tenderly. 'Now go to your father before he starts to wonder where you are.'

They embraced, feeling the warmth of each other's skin. Sneijder held her tight to his chest, enjoying the sensation of her body against his for a final minute. He released her and she climbed out of the bed and went to collect her clothes from the floor. Her naked figure was a sight to behold, particularly for a man who had spent the majority of the last three years without female company. She began to put on her underwear, and at just that moment there was a noise from downstairs.

Sneijder tiptoed across the room holding the bedclothes around his waist, pulled the door open a fraction and peered through the crack. 'Oh shit,' he muttered. 'That's Mrs Uhlenbroek back.'

'Who?' Frauke asked.

'The stationmaster's wife; the woman who takes care of the house,' Sneijder replied. 'I think it'd be best if she didn't see you. These people are strong patriots and they might not approve.'

'Yes, right,' she said as she buttoned her blouse. 'What have we got ourselves into?'

'It'll be fine,' Sneijder reassured. 'We have done nothing wrong. It's just that some people wouldn't understand. It'll be a lot less complicated if nobody knows.' He picked up his clothes from the chair and dressed, then walked to the window and slid it up as far as it went. The attic room was at the top of the house, just beneath the tiled roof which sloped down to a point not much more than two or three metres above the ground. The gabled window jutted out, giving access to the roof from the room.

Frauke saw the rain which was falling outside from the dark grey sky and cursed. 'I have to cycle to the hospital in this.'

'First you have to get out of the house,' Sneijder pointed out.

She followed his gaze out of the window. 'You've got to be kidding me. Do you really expect me to climb out of a window?'

Sneijder pulled her over in front of him so he could show her the bottom of the roof line. 'If you get down there you will be able to jump down to the ground. Just be careful with the wet tiles.'

Frauke turned to face him, taking his hands in hers. 'Thank you, Johannes, for everything. I think....' She hesitated for a moment, perhaps doubting whether to continue her sentence, then decided to go ahead. 'I think I'm falling in love with you.'

Sneijder knew she wanted him to repeat the sentiment but he couldn't, not yet anyway. Instead he kissed her softly for a few seconds and then said, 'Goodbye for now. It's probably best that you don't come here again. I'll come and find you at work.'

'Promise?'

'I promise. Now go to your father, and try not to catch a cold in the rain. Do you want my jacket?'

'That could be difficult to explain. I'll be fine.' She climbed out of the window gingerly, sat down on the ledge and slid carefully down the rain-soaked tiles. When she reached the bottom she turned, gripped the edge with her fingers and lowered herself down, disappearing from Sneijder's view for a brief time. He caught a glimpse of her again as she crept cautiously towards the front of the house, dodging the raindrops under the trees, and then she vanished.

Koestler was put in a private room at the military hospital with two armed guards placed at the door. He was lying in his bed in a state of semi-consciousness when one of the nurses showed Klimitz in. The captain approached the bed but on noticing that his superior had his eyes firmly shut he backed away.

Suddenly Koestler spoke. 'Sebastien,' he mumbled. 'You are here.'

'Yes, I'm here, sir. How are you feeling?'

Koestler's eyes were heavy from the sedative he had been given and he continued to open and close them as he said groggily, 'I've got one hell of a headache. My ankle hurts too but the painkillers have taken the edge off.'

A rather morose-looking man with grey hair was standing in the corner of the room in a white coat, reading through a chart. He glanced up over the top of his thick spectacles, 'You are Herr Koestler's adjutant – Hauptsturmführer Klimitz?'

'That's correct,' Klimitz replied.

'Lieutenant Hortl. I am a doctor in the SS and the senior medical officer here. I am overseeing Herr Koestler's treatment personally.'

'I see. And what is your opinion?'

'He is exceedingly lucky to be alive. He has a serious concussion and some cranial swelling, but I expect him to make a full recovery. However, as with all head injuries there can be unseen complications so he is not out of danger just yet.'

'And what of his other injuries?' Klimitz enquired. 'His ankle...'

'His ankle is broken, and he has a few cracked and bruised ribs and a slight whiplash,' Hortl explained. 'He got off remarkably lightly considering. Herr Koestler's driver, a Mr...' he looked at the chart in his hand, 'er, Petrovsky was killed outright when the steering column went through his chest. Most unpleasant.'

'Indeed,' the captain agreed.

Hortl grimaced slightly and scratched his head thoughtfully. 'There is one other thing, Herr Klimitz.' The doctor glanced over towards Koestler who was dozing, then turned back to Klimitz. 'Perhaps we might discuss it outside?'

Klimitz hesitated for a moment and looked at Koestler, and then he left the room with Hortl. He returned about five minutes later, alone this time.

Koestler lifted an eyelid with difficulty and mumbled, 'What did the doctor have to tell you?'

'Oh, I shouldn't worry about it...' Klimitz began.

Koestler mumbled again with a weary irritation. 'Damn it, Sebastien, just tell me.'

The captain took a deep breath. 'The doctor was telling me that he found a very high alcohol content in your blood. He was seeking an explanation.'

Koestler averted his gaze from his adjutant. 'I see.'

'I think I managed to persuade him not to inform the High Commissioner,' Klimitz declared matter-of-factly.

Koestler's head snapped around and he mouthed the words, 'High Commissioner?'

Klimitz nodded. 'He wanted some advice as to whether he should report it. I gave him some bullshit story about you negotiating with partisans and drinking with them to win their trust, and told him to forget about it. It's a poor story but the only one I could come up with.' He looked down at his feet for a couple of seconds, then continued, 'With all due respect, sir, if you really want to maintain your position you need to do something about your drinking. I can only cover for you so often. And if you continue to give our friend Rauter ammunition, eventually he is going to use it on you.'

Koestler did not reply and for a minute neither man broke the silence.

Eventually Klimitz asked, 'About the accident - what do you remember?'

'Accident?' Koestler jerked forward as he coughed a couple of times, and he croaked, 'That was no accident – somebody is trying to kill me!'

'Kill you?' Klimitz asked incredulously. 'You think so?'

'I know so,' Koestler said weakly. 'I don't just have accidents. I want that car taken apart and checked for signs of sabotage.'

'So you don't think it could just have been an error by the driver, or a mechanical failure?'

'Certainly not,' Koestler replied sharply. 'I am extremely important around here, and someone wants me dead. Surely you can see that, Klimitz?'

'With all due respect, sir, I think it is rather unlikely that the Resistance would attempt to kill you. All of our previous experience suggests that the severity of our recent reprisal will keep them quiet for a while. I don't believe they would risk another one so soon, not least for fear of alienating their own people.'

Koestler waved him away dismissively. 'Nonsense. A man in my position will always attract violence. Check the car - I can assure you that you will find it has been tampered with.'

'If my understanding is correct I'm not sure there is that much of the car left to check,' Klimitz replied. 'The lack of skid marks on the road indicates the problem may have been with the brakes, but unfortunately the brake assemblies are very badly damaged. It will be almost impossible to determine if any damage was caused to the car before the accident.'

'Exactly!' Koestler cried, and an agonised expression creased his face. He held his hand to his ribs and sank back down into the bed. 'Oh, it's no use.'

'I think you should rest, sir,' Klimitz advised. 'I'll come back later.'

Koestler was still dozing when Frauke arrived around quarter past four that afternoon. They spoke for a while in their usual way, their conversation punctuated by silences. Frauke had tried to get across to him that she cared and that she had been afraid of losing him but he had never been one for sentimentality and he brushed her comments off. Since she had moved near him in

Arnhem he had tried to open up to her but the unavoidable truth was that it was too late for him to change.

After one of the extended silences Frauke finally said what had obviously been bursting to get out. 'I'm sorry I wasn't here earlier, father.'

'It's okay,' Koestler answered with a weak smile. 'Where were you?'

'They told me this morning that I couldn't see you until later,' she explained, 'so I didn't think there was much point in coming. I was at work and then I went to see a friend from work who had the day off.'

'You must be careful, Frauke,' said Koestler. 'Someone is trying to kill me. Do not trust anybody.'

'It was an accident,' she replied. 'You are just confused from the concussion. Don't worry – the doctor says it will pass.'

'I have been the victim of a murder attempt!' Koestler insisted. 'Why won't anyone believe me? Oh, you're all the same. I wish to be left alone now.' He closed his eyes and turned away.

CHAPTER FIFTEEN

As the summer drifted through August, Sneijder's mind was a confused and tortured place. The events that had gripped him since his arrival in Holland six weeks ago were pulling him in so many different directions and he was struggling to keep things on an even keel. He had always prided himself on his clear understanding of right and wrong, of what was morally justifiable and what was not. However the lines were becoming more and more blurred on an almost daily basis and he was no longer sure in his convictions.

Hugo's death sickened him. On the evening of the crash he had gone back to Van Rijn to challenge him. Sneijder was furious with him for convincing him to sacrifice Koestler's driver, but when it came down to it he couldn't honestly say that Van Rijn had been wrong. As much as it fundamentally disagreed with his principles, the act had been necessary in order for Sneijder to get at Koestler. The fact that the target of the assassination had survived was merely an uncomfortable stroke of bad luck.

His relationship with Frauke could not be justified however. By continuing to see her while he simultaneously plotted the death of her father he was being deliberately duplicitous. Deep inside, he knew that it could never lead to anything but trouble but his desire for her was incredibly strong and he could not consider the idea of not seeing her. He was trapped in a whirlpool from which there was no escape.

It was now just over a week since the car accident had failed to kill Koestler and Sneijder was planning another assassination attempt. He wasn't altogether sure that he could bring himself to have another go but Van Rijn insisted he would do it if Sneijder did not. This was a bad idea in Sneijder's book; the Resistance man's emotional attachment to the task was likely to interfere and cause him to botch it. No, if the job had to be done it would have to be done properly, and the only person Sneijder trusted to do that was himself.

Once again the pair were sitting in the kitchen of Van Rijn's house, listening to a small wireless radio which had survived the large-scale German confiscation of May 1943. The broadcast was the daily fifteen-minute radio program from the BBC in London, 'Radio Orange'. This was news of the war tailored to a Dutch audience, although today they were reporting on the fighting in northern France. The German garrisons in Brittany, particularly those at Brest and St Malo were holding out strongly against the formidable American onslaught, although it was expected that they would fall within the next couple of days. There was also news of significant Allied success in the Italian campaign. All of this pointed to a potentially swift conclusion to the war in Europe.

The program ended and Klara Van Rijn switched the wireless off. 'The Germans must realise now that they can't possibly win,' she said. 'Why don't they just surrender and stop all the suffering?'

Her husband leaned back in his chair and answered, 'They don't think like the rest of us, love. The Germans think that they are better and that they cannot lose. Somehow they feel that they will be saved. I really don't care; as long as it's them suffering and dying that's fine by me. The sooner Hitler and his gang are in the ground the better.'

Sneijder took a sip from his weak coffee. 'If the British and Americans keep up this pace they will be in Berlin by Christmas, surely. I'm not sure that we will have to put up with the occupation for too much longer. And I'll tell you one thing; the SS officers who have been going around killing innocent people are going to get their judgement.'

Van Rijn nodded. 'You're not wrong there. The people around here will tear them apart.'

'I just hope the Allies make their way into the Netherlands soon,' Klara added. 'Every week the rations for the gas and electricity get reduced. Once winter arrives it'll be terrible.' She cleared up the plates which lay on the table before them and moved to the sink to begin the washing up. This could only be done with hot water as soap products had long since become unattainable luxury items.

Van Rijn stood from the table and walked to the kitchen door, inviting Sneijder to follow him outside. They moved through the rear garden and entered the garage which was situated at the side of the house. In it was parked a decrepit old 1920s truck which was missing its entire engine block.

'I started fiddling around with this thing years ago,' explained Van Rijn, 'but then the war began and I've ended up stripping it for spare parts. The Germans steal everything for their military; you can only use what you've got that they don't know about.' Hearing his own words, he began pulling the ripped tarpaulin down over the front wing of the vehicle.

'Nice old machine,' Sneijder commented.

'That wasn't what I wanted to show you,' Van Rijn replied. 'Take a look at this, a little something from my grandfather.' He clambered around behind the truck and pulled out a long, slim item wrapped in dusty brown sackcloth. It was around a metre in length and with the way he was holding it Sneijder recognised it at once as a rifle of some sort. He tossed the sackcloth aside and held up the weapon, a beautiful old bolt-action Mauser rifle, the wooden body polished to a shine. 'It's my grandfather's old hunting rifle. Bearing in mind what you told me about your shooting skills I thought it could help us. It's a bit of an antique but it still fires nicely.'

Sneijder took the rifle from Van Rijn and passed it from hand to hand to get a feel for its weight and balance. He held it in front of his eye for a moment, and then examined the mechanisms. He ejected the five-cartridge magazine, looked it over and then popped it back in, working the bolt expertly. He was impressed.

'We'll take it over to my grandfather's farm for you to have a practice and get your eye in,' Van Rijn added. 'I can handle small arms but shooting from distance? I'm not sure.' He turned away. 'Wait there. I'm just going to look for something in the house.'

Sneijder was left alone. He wrapped the rifle back up in the sackcloth and placed it on the bonnet of the truck. When he walked out to the front of the garage it was approaching early evening and the sun was beginning its descent across the clear sky. He observed the peaceful tranquillity of the village, contrasting it with the memory of the bullet-ridden bodies that was etched into his mind.

He disliked the thought, and he turned around and walked back into the garage.

Unnoticed by Sneijder, a figure had been crouching in the undergrowth at the front of the house waiting for him since he had gone in over half an hour before. Despite being a large and burly man, the intruder had managed to keep his presence a secret until the moment he was ready to reveal himself. Sneijder heard the sound of somebody approaching behind him. Before he could even begin to turn around he was grabbed roughly around the shoulders and propelled headfirst into the front of the old truck. He struck his skull painfully as he went down and felt a sharp blow to his stomach as a boot flew into him. Sneijder struggled to move as he was kicked another couple of times. He managed to pull himself free and rolled away behind a wooden crate which he kicked hard against the shins of his assailant, drawing a cry of pain from him. Sneijder leapt to his feet with his fists at the ready. It was only then that he realised that he knew the man he faced, with his stocky frame and greying hair.

'Dimitri?' said Sneijder in astonishment. 'What the hell....?'

The man's face was pure fury, his round cheeks somewhere between purple and red, his jaw fixed tight. Sneijder knew at once he would not be able to talk him around no matter what he intended to do, and that there was no way he could defend the death of his son at the wheel of Koestler's car. Whether or not it was necessary in the wider context, it was naïve to think that Dimitri could accept it. That would leave only one option.

'You traitorous liar!' the older man yelled. 'My son put himself on the line and he lost his life, because of you! We knew it would be dangerous, but the danger was meant to come from the Germans!'

'Wait, I don't know what you're talking about,' Sneijder replied calmly. 'Koestler's crash was an accident, wasn't it?'

'Don't give me that; the innocent act!' Dimitri fumed. 'You were looking for a way to kill him, and then his car crashes off the road. You think that's a coincidence?' He moved towards Sneijder menacingly.

'Look, I swear I don't....'

Dimitri pulled a four-inch knife from a pocket and flicked it open. 'Perhaps this will remind you of the truth.'

'For God's sake, man, what are you doing? This is crazy, really.' Sneijder tried to stay calm in the hope that he could slow Dimitri down but he knew he was in trouble here and his heart rate was rising.

'Crazy? My son goes out to help you, gives you all the assistance you want and then you arrange a crash and don't tell him. I'm upset and angry to lose my son and you say that's crazy? You kill somebody on your side for nothing, that's right, nothing, and *you* call *me* crazy?'

'I had nothing to do with it,' Sneijder insisted. Dimitri launched forward with the blade and Sneijder jumped back, using his hand to deflect the older man's arm. 'Okay, okay, you want the truth? Here it is – Koestler would never have got into the car if Hugo had not turned up; he'd have been suspicious at least. Even if he had, if he'd had an accident on the one day that his regular driver was missing it would have suddenly seemed like a deliberate attempt to kill him. Think of the reprisals.'

'Screw the reprisals, you murdered my son!' Dimitri exclaimed.

'They would have known that he was a part of it and killed him anyway,' Sneijder pleaded. 'Do you think I wanted this? It is the hardest decision I've ever made!'

'I don't care, he's still dead! I ought to give you up to the Gestapo, you bastard!'

'If you want to side with the enemy, fine,' replied Sneijder. 'If your son hadn't he...' He tailed off, unable to complete the sentence.

'He'd still be alive? You're blaming him? Jesus, what sort of man are you?'

'No, I didn't mean that,' Sneijder told him. 'I just wanted to...' He couldn't find the words to explain what he meant, and maybe there were no words. To kill an innocent person was inexcusable - it was as simple as that, most of the time but not here and not now. Sneijder was not sure how much more of this he would be able to stand.

Without another word, Dimitri hurled himself at Sneijder. He caught him midway up his body with the point of his left shoulder and slammed him against the concrete wall. Sneijder's head crashed against a wooden shelf, sending some old paint cans flying. Dimitri thrust the knife towards Sneijder's stomach in an upward jabbing motion. Sneijder twisted his body away at the last second, avoiding the blade. Spotting an opportunity, Sneijder struck the older man in the head with an elbow and kicked his legs away from under him.

Dimitri fell to the ground heavily and avoided the truck by millimetres. Sneijder leapt upon him, pinning him down with his knees and grasping him around the neck. He thought he heard something behind him and looked around, expecting to see Van Rijn coming into the garage. He saw nothing. His momentary lack of attention was seized upon. Dimitri flung his free leg up into the air and caught Sneijder in the side of the head, in the same place as the wing of the truck had hit him a few moments earlier. A sharp pain shot up through his skull and he fell to the dusty floor clutching his head.

Behind him Dimitri clambered across towards the knife which had fallen from his hand. He grabbed it and raised it above his head, obviously preparing to plunge it down into Sneijder's prone body. Sneijder saw him coming from the corner of his eye and tried to get out of the way, but he had left it a little too late and he felt the blade catch him in the side. It was a glancing blow which only created a flesh wound but the pain was savage. The older man had expected a more substantial connection and was thus off-balance, and his momentum carried him beyond Sneijder.

Sneijder turned and stood up in one movement and reached the truck. Instinctively he picked up the rifle which lay on the bonnet. Grasping the barrel firmly he spun around and swung the weapon viciously. Dimitri was beginning to rise from the floor at precisely that moment, and with a disgustingly audible crack it connected with his head. His face almost seemed to explode with the sheer force of the impact; his left cheek-bone vanished into the side of his head as did his eye socket and they were replaced by a bloody red pulp. He was flung backwards and his head hit the concrete of the floor, spilling yet more blood. Instantly he stopped moving and his eyes were still, staring blankly into space. He was dead.

Sneijder dropped the rifle on the floor and stood there motionless, transfixed by the horrific sight in front of him. He was almost waiting for the body to move again, for there to be a flicker of life behind the faded pupils. It could only have been a minute later that Van Rijn returned to the garage but the time seemed to pass interminably slowly. He walked in and began to explain that he hadn't found what he was looking for but then he saw the body.

'What the hell....!' Van Rijn exclaimed in disbelief, a stunned look on his face. 'Who is he? Do you want to tell me....?' He was visibly flabbergasted and unable to get the words out.

'He just came out of nowhere,' Sneijder replied. 'He had a knife; what was I supposed to do?'

'He just attacked you?' Van Rijn was incredulous. 'Do you know him?'

Sneijder twisted around to face his companion and gasped in pain as he jerked the open wound in his side. He reached a hand down and yanked it back when it stung, then studied his fingers which were covered in blood. 'Yes, I know him. His name is Dimitri. He's the father of my contact, you know, Koestler s driver.'

'Oh God,' said Van Rijn. 'And he's lying here dead, in my house? We've got to get rid of him before the shit really comes down. How did he find you here?'

'I've no idea. He's involved with partisan groups so I suppose he knows someone who knows that you and I have contact.' Sneijder attempted to move again but the agony was too great; he couldn't stand straight without it being unbearable. He groaned, 'He got me in the side. It's no good.' He hobbled over to a pile of boxes and sat down, noticing that the blood was starting to soak through his shirt.

Van Rijn's eyes widened and he asked: 'Is it bad?'

'No, I don't think so, just a flesh wound.'

The Resistance man examined it closely and grimaced. 'It's going to need stitching, that's for sure. We can't go to a doctor but there is a man I know. For now though we'll have to patch it up – go inside and I'll get Klara to help you. Do not tell her what happened out here.'

'What about you?'

'I'm going to clean up your mess.'

Klara managed to patch him up reasonably well with cotton wool and sticky tape and the bleeding was brought under control, though without medical attention it would become more serious. The wound stung from the alcohol-based fluid that she had used to clean it and it was made worse by the pressure that he tried to keep on it. While he had been inside attempting to make excuses for the injury, Van Rijn had remained in the garage to tidy up. The amount of blood on the floor and the walls made it extremely difficult to remove evidence of the killing. After fifteen minutes of thorough scrubbing it appeared only marginally better when Sneijder hobbled back into the garage with a pained expression.

'You never make things bloody easy for me, do you?' Van Rijn commented in a tone somewhere between humour and irritation.

Sneijder came around the truck and saw the body with its battered head again, and this time it really struck him. 'Oh God.' He covered his mouth with his hand and averted his eyes as he felt the nausea rising. 'It's horrible. I didn't mean...'

'Don't be stupid,' Van Rijn interrupted. 'He had a knife and he tried to kill you, so you defended yourself. There's nothing wrong with that, but don't say you never meant to kill him. What choice did you have?'

The two of them approached the body of the large man and taking an end each, they tried to move him. He was extremely heavy and the exertion caused Sneijder to let out a loud cry of pain. He dropped Dimitri's legs and bent over double.

Van Rijn sighed loudly. 'Look, Johannes, this is not going to work. You can't manage.'

'Well how the hell else are we going to get rid of him?' Sneijder snapped. 'He is far too heavy for you to move on your own. Let's just keep going.'

It was quickly apparent that there was no way Sneijder would be able to lift in his present condition. Instead they dragged the body across the garage and out to the front garden. The Van Rijns' house and the five other houses in the same row were connected by a six-metre wide stretch of grass which essentially constituted the front lawn of each property. A narrow driveway in front of each house where each owner could keep his car divided the lawns from each other. At the end of the row the grass gave way to a heather-covered bank and eventually a sparsely wooded orchard. In order to reach the trees they needed to cross the front of three houses, an unenviable task when dragging a dead body.

The added resistance of the softer ground compounded their struggle and Sneijder was forced to stop several times when the pain became too much, but within a couple of minutes Dimitri's corpse lay at the foot of the bank. As they began getting themselves in position to move again, however, they were disturbed by the sound of a petrol engine from further up the road. Sneijder looked up and spotted a German open-top car coming towards them. The driver, an SD officer, could not possibly fail to see them.

'What now?' Sneijder yelled to Van Rijn. 'If we get caught with a dead body we are in trouble.'

'Do you think I don't know that?' he shouted back angrily. 'We're just going to have to dump him here.' He scrambled halfway up the bank to a point where the heather grew thickest and pulled some of the plant from the ground. When he had a large handful he returned to the body and spread the heather across, covering the head first. 'The best we can do is disguise it and hope he is not discovered.'

Having covered him with as much heather as the time allowed, Sneijder and Van Rijn left him and returned to the garage to clean up.

It was not long before the body was discovered and within half an hour the village was thronged with German soldiers. The change from civilian to military rule was continuing and there were a number of soldiers from the regular German army, though they did not seem like front-line troops. The body was quickly taken away and residents of the village briefly questioned about what they saw, but acts of brutality by the police and security services were becoming so widespread that it was often wise for them to first check if a crime had been committed by another German organisation. Between them Van Rijn and Sneijder succeeded in cleaning up the majority of the blood, but by the end of it Sneijder's own slow but continuous blood loss was beginning to take its toll. He was now feeling light-headed and weak and he needed medical attention.

The doctor in Oosterbeek of whom Van Rijn had spoken when the Voesmans had been wounded was where Sneijder was taken; however it quickly emerged that he was used to treating patients of an entirely different sort. The Germans sealed off the village for two hours after the discovery of Dimitri's body and it was only after they departed that travel anywhere was possible. Sneijder was somewhat alarmed to find out that the man Van Rijn knew was in fact a veterinary surgeon who specialised in horses but when they arrived at his house, which also doubled as his surgery, he proved himself exemplary in his profession. Despite some initial unease about the unexpected arrival of Van Rijn with yet another injured colleague he set about cleaning the wound and stitching it up after injecting Sneijder with a local anaesthetic. His technique was anything but gentle having been perfected on much larger animals but within ten minutes all that was left was a scar about seven centimetres long. Exhausted by the exertions of the afternoon and having lost a significant amount of blood, Sneijder was left to rest in the surgery's recovery room.

He dozed fitfully for most of the afternoon, and awoke later that night to find himself alone in the dark. The house was silent, and he was careful not to make a sound as he moved to the door into the corridor, which was slightly ajar. He pulled it open a fraction and peered down the hall. It was gloomy, the only light a dim one coming from a room at the end. Sneijder felt a dull ache from his side and was a little dizzy, presumably a result of the painkilling tablets he had been given earlier. As he started to walk out into the hall he stopped suddenly, taken by an urge he knew he should in all conscience ignore. He retracted his steps into the room and closed the door behind him, shutting out the light from the hall in the process. At one side of the recovery room was a narrow door which connected through to the surgery and although Sneijder did not expect to be able to get through, it came open easily to his touch. On the other side he closed it behind him and moved over to the cupboards where the veterinarian stored his drugs.

They were of course locked but with his surgery closed the vet had left the keys lying on a side table. Sneijder checked through several of the cupboards before locating what he was looking for. On a shelf near to the top was a small glass bottle containing morphine. He took it down and examined it. He had no medical knowledge and hence did not know about the appropriate strength or dose, but the intense feeling of release which he had obtained when injecting morphine previously was something he needed, particularly if he was going to be forced to kill people. Sneijder knew his own mind and he knew that the way he had killed Dimitri would dominate his thoughts for at least the next couple of days; therefore it was likely that he would need something to help him switch off. He found a couple of syringes which he put into his pocket along with the bottle and turned to go. The guilt he felt about stealing the drug was suddenly tremendous, and he took thirty guilders from a roll of banknotes and dropped them in the cupboard in place of the morphine. He closed and locked the stores and went off to thank the veterinarian for his help.

Koestler and his daughter sat opposite one another at the dinner table, eating in silence. The opportunity to sit was welcome as he was struggling to get around on crutches, his broken ankle in plaster and still unable to bear weight. He was a proud man and his physical weakness irritated him intensely, although he had recovered quickly from the crash and was now just faced with painful ribs and the occasional headache, remarkable considering the scale of the accident. His conviction that it had been a deliberate attempt to kill him continued to be dismissed by officers including Klimitz and the Gestapo man Horvath and a thorough examination of the car had provided no irrefutable evidence. The line containing the brake fluid was damaged but there was no way to tell how this may have happened or whether the damage had been picked up during the crash. So much of the front of the car was wrecked that really there was no chance of detecting any subtle acts of sabotage.

Koestler finished his meal and put down his cutlery, then wiped his mouth clean with a napkin. He dropped it on to the plate and said to Frauke, 'I have told you my feelings about you socialising with the Dutch civilians, have I not? I mean, my position is quite clear?'

Frauke paused, replied: 'Yes, quite clear,' and continued to chew through her food.

'Good,' he said. 'Then perhaps you'd like to tell me about this Dutchman you have been seen with, this Voorman fellow?'

Frauke was shocked but kept her emotions in check. 'Sorry?'

'A few of the men have reported seeing you with him; one in particular said you seemed close.'

Frauke put down her fork angrily. 'Have you had your men reporting to you on everything I do? We agreed when I came here that-'

'Don't change the subject, Frauke,' her father interrupted firmly. 'I want to know about this man.'

'There is nothing to tell,' she answered irritably. 'He is just somebody I met, that's all. We get on well so I see no reason not to speak to him.'

'So you don't know him well?'

'Not particularly, no.'

'Are you in the habit of taking cycle rides in the country with people you don't know?' Koestler asked. It was a pointed accusation.

'For goodness sake, Father, why do you ask me if you already know everything?' She pushed her chair back and stood up. 'I'm not going to apologise for wanting to talk to people; it's perfectly natural. I'm nineteen years old – didn't you want to have friends when you were nineteen?'

'I didn't want to be friends with our enemies in a war,' he replied.

'Screw the damn war!' Frauke yelled. 'This is my life, and life is too short to ignore people because of their nationality. German, Dutch, British, American – we're all human, aren't we? Really, I wish you would see that.'

'It doesn't matter,' said Koestler. 'What matters is that I told you not to mix with the locals and you deliberately disobeyed me, your father. Even now you are not telling me the truth. It seems I will have to find out about this man myself, in my own way.'

'Oh my God, Father, you are not going to do anything to him, are you?' she pleaded. 'Please, he hasn't done anything. I began talking to him, not the other way around. You're not going to hurt him?'

Koestler grinned menacingly, an idea flashing through his mind. 'Certainly not. You are going to invite him to dinner.'

CHAPTER SIXTEEN

'No way. Absolutely not.' Sneijder's answer was emphatic.

'I don't think he meant it as a request,' Frauke replied. 'He is a very powerful man and he expects to get his own way. The best thing you can do is to agree.'

'I told you, I'm trying to keep a low profile and avoid being sent back to Germany,' Sneijder explained. 'Having dinner at the home of a high-ranking officer in the SS is not exactly what I had in mind.'

They were sitting on the grass in a clearing in woods north of Arnhem, basking in warm summer sun. There was not a cloud in the sky and it had been a beautiful morning on which to stroll through the forest near her home, listening to the calling birds and observing the many types of wildlife which lived there. With the world around him becoming ever more tumultuous, his relationship with Frauke was the only positive thing he had to hold on to and he was determined that he would.

This latest development however had the power to tear everything apart. How could he sit opposite the man he was trying to kill and make small talk with him, particularly having seen his work first-hand in Roeden? It would at best be extremely uncomfortable, at worst a disaster; were his nerves to get the better of him there was every chance he would do or say something that would appear suspicious and it would be all over. There were other dangers too. His story about doing forced labour in Germany stood up to examination from most people – after all, he had the papers to prove it – but more detailed investigation, the kind a man like Koestler could initiate, might prove otherwise. Regardless of this there was the possibility that Koestler would arrange for him to be deported anyway in order to prevent him from seeing his daughter.

The other factor to consider was how he might view Koestler after meeting him. He had struggled with the concept of assassinating the man from the beginning, and that was when he was just a name and a photograph in a file. Seeing him for the first time from a distance had brought it home that this was a real human being, and being close to him, actually speaking to him, was likely to increase those feelings. It could definitely make the job significantly more difficult.

'Johannes, please listen to me,' Frauke said. 'I know my father. I know what he is like and unfortunately I also know what he is capable of. You must come – for your sake and mine.'

'What if I don't refuse?' Sneijder suggested. 'We just have to think of an excuse.'

'Believe me, the only excuses that would satisfy him would be that you were dead or had been arrested.'

'That is not a bad idea,' said Sneijder; at first serious but then breaking into a wide grin. 'I just need to find a suitable crime.'

'Thinking you are a criminal would just antagonise him and then it would be much worse,' Frauke told him.

Sneijder collapsed backwards, yelling: 'Damn it, there's got to be some way out of this!' He lay flat on the grass staring up at the solid expanse of blue, squinting slightly against the glare of the beating sun.

Frauke rolled over on top of him and kissed him warmly on the lips. After a moment she broke off, said, 'I'm afraid not, my dear,' and then kissed him again.

He wrapped his arms around her and pulled her tight against him as they continued to kiss, then reached a hand to the back of her head. It was a sign of his growing moral ambiguity that as he enjoyed a passionate embrace with a woman he cared for deeply, he resolved that the only way to avoid having dinner with her father was to kill him before it.

Koestler sat at the back of the room, observing Frank Helder at work. They were in the main hall of a local social club which was mostly frequented by young agricultural workers, and the old man was explaining the virtues of service to the SS. He was a man of extremely good reputation in Arnhem and hence when he spoke, people tended to listen. Of course this also meant that he had an awful lot to lose by appearing to collaborate with the enemy. Fortunately Koestler was in possession of information which would cause more severe damage to his standing, as Helder had done things which could not be excused by being under duress.

The room however was mostly empty. Despite the majority of the population not having a radio set, news of the war in France and Belgium was gradually filtering through and there was a genuine expectation of an Allied thrust into the Netherlands in the immediate future. The result of this was that the young men who may have been drawn towards working with the Germans in order to give themselves an easier life under occupation were staying away, and those with genuine right-wing tendencies were keeping quiet about it for fear of retribution after liberation.

For a threatened man who was being forced to spout views and ideologies which were contrary to his own, Helder's nerve was extremely firm. It must have appalled him to stand up in public and criticise his own country's government for their failure to defend their homeland against the German invasion, and particularly the Dutch royal family for the speed with which they had fled, but he did it nonetheless and managed to hold an air of authority. He then added that National Socialism was the only way forward for the so-called Germanic nations and that service in the SS was a good way to support this. He stood down from the stage at the end of the hall to muted applause from the half-dozen or so in the audience.

Koestler turned to his adjutant and said, 'He is really rather good, isn't he?'

'Yes, sir,' replied Klimitz. 'If only there were a few more people here to hear it.'

Koestler nodded. 'Unfortunately most of them are already in Germany doing forced labour, which makes the entire scheme rather pointless. However I must be seen to be trying.'

A Germanic SS private approached Koestler. 'Telephone call for you, sir.'

Koestler moved slowly on his crutches into the corridor and picked up the receiver. 'Yes?'

'Horvath here, sir. I thought you may want to know about a discovery made by the SD three days ago. A body was found in the village of Roeden where we carried out our reprisal, where we arrested Max Bruggink.'

'I presume you are telling me this because he didn't die of natural causes,' Koestler stated.

'He certainly didn't,' Horvath replied. 'He was killed brutally with a single but extremely powerful blow to the head, possibly with the butt of a rifle or shotgun. To be honest, sir, it might be a while before we can identify him – his face is quite badly damaged.'

'Why did you not inform me about this sooner?' Koestler demanded.

'I have only just found it about it myself,' Horvath said. 'The officers involved in the recovery of the body and the investigation wanted to make sure he was not a victim of the Gestapo.'

Koestler sighed. 'Very well. Let me know when you find out more.'

Sneijder lay on his bed in his room, the curtains drawn across against the afternoon sun. He was haunted by the image of Dimitri's face after he had struck him with the rifle and had not been able to sleep for several days. He hadn't meant to kill him, at least he hadn't thought so, but the more it played on his mind the less he was sure. After all, to inflict such a catastrophic injury with a solitary blow he must have used some force, far more than would have been necessary to immobilise him. Perhaps he had killed him deliberately - he just didn't know any more.

It was difficult to estimate how much the Germans would deduce from the discovery of Dimitri's body. They would soon realise that he was the father of Koestler's driver and that would raise suspicions, but with only Bruggink in custody they had nobody who knew about Sneijder's attempts to assassinate Koestler. The trouble would only come if they managed to link Bruggink to Van Rijn. If the latter was picked up by the SS, it would be time to think about getting out.

Sneijder needed to escape from it all; for a while at least. He found the small bottle of morphine and the hypodermic syringes in a drawer and placed them on the desk beside the window. Taking the first syringe he slowly drew some of the liquid out of the bottle until it was half full.

Amongst the substantial collection of books in the Uhlenbroeks' home he had found an old edition of a pharmacology journal which contained a chapter on the usual doses for various different drugs. Using this and some basic arithmetic he had calculated roughly the amount of morphine he would need in order to feel its effect, taking care not to overdose. He removed the belt from the dressing gown which hung on the back of the bedroom door and tied it around his left arm just above the elbow, then grasping it between his teeth he pulled the end until he felt the knot squeezing his arm with sufficient force. As the blood flow became constricted Sneijder began to feel a tingling sensation in his fingers, and his feeling started to disappear. He took the syringe and gently pushed the needle through his skin, grimacing as it scratched a little, then pushed down with his thumb to deliver the medicine.

Closing his eyes and holding his breath for a few seconds he felt the narcotic wash over him. Instantly he felt a detachment from reality. As his respiration continued to slow, a glorious calm spread across his body. The shafts of light which crept around the curtains became hazy and then melted away into the gloom as the pupils narrowed in his eyes. Freed from the painful musings in his head, he spread himself out on the bed and allowed himself to drift.

It was evening now and Sneijder was still feeling the euphoric effects of the morphine. After much torturing he had decided that the only way to ensure his own personal safety was not to meet with Koestler face-to-face, and the only way that could be achieved was to get rid of him before that time. Koestler would be at home and though his security had never been particularly good in the past, Frauke had told him of her father's fears of assassination since the accident. It was therefore almost certain that there would be a stronger presence of officers on guard duty. If he had been thinking clearly he would have dropped the idea of trying to break in there and then, but the morphine clouded his judgement.

It was obvious that Sneijder had to conceal his identity now that Frauke knew him. He ripped a square out of one of his white shirts to create a mask, covering it and the remaining areas of his face in black boot polish so as not to attract attention. When he looked in the mirror he appeared fairly anonymous, but from his eyes and hair Frauke would still be able to recognise him. That particular problem was solved by rummaging through an old chest in the corner of the room and finding a soft felt hat with a wide brim which covered his hair and left his eyes in deep shadow. Satisfied, he dressed. Mrs Uhlenbroek had invited him to make use of some old clothes which had belonged to her son and this was a good time to take up her offer. Ten minutes later he was standing outside the house wearing dark slacks and a thick black sweater, plus the hat, knowing he looked ridiculous but confident in the disguise.

The six kilometre journey from Oosterbeek to the Koestler house took about fifteen minutes on the motorcycle and the last remnants of sun were visible as he arrived at around nine o'clock. He left the bike in the woods some way away and walked the rest, taking care to be as silent as possible on his approach. The route he had taken brought him around the back of the property and he crept up and peered through a small hole in the two-metre wooden fence. The rear of the house was in deep shadow at this late hour and it was difficult for Sneijder to make much out. There was a well built soldier in Waffen-SS uniform positioned next to the back door. Hugo had spoken of Koestler's regular guard being removed from the front line on medical grounds and there was always the possibility that this soldier was of similar quality, but Sneijder was not going to test him unless it was absolutely necessary.

He skirted around the side of the house until he found himself with a view of the front. Seated on the wall beside the front door was the officer who had been there every time, smoking a cigarette, his Schmeisser laid across his lap. There was no sign that he intended to move, and as Sneijder watched the guard from the back walked around to check on him.

'Jesus, Sterchler,' he said in the harshest German, 'are you just going to sit there all night?'

Sterchler blew a cloud of smoke into the air and replied, 'Give me a break, will you? All I have done since bloody Stalingrad is stand outside this damned house. Can't you just walk around a few times?'

The other officer muttered something in frustration and strolled away, returning to his post at the back door. He settled back into his watch, seemingly refusing to do his colleague's work for him. Sneijder walked around to the other side of the house, keeping pressed up against the fence. A light flashed on in an upstairs window and Frauke appeared as she made her way across the room. Sneijder watched her for a moment before realising that he was standing in her line of sight; if she were to look down she would see him and raise the alarm. He moved quickly out of view. As he did he suddenly experienced acute vertigo. His head spun and for a brief second he did not know where he was, and then as quickly as it had come it was gone. He breathed deeply and steadied himself, dismissing the episode as a side-effect of the morphine. When he was confident that the moment had passed he scrambled over the fence into the garden.

It was only now as he was crouched behind a tall conifer that Sneijder heard the music. It was extremely soft but it was definitely there, the beautiful mournful melody of a violin. He looked around, expecting it to be coming from one of the surrounding houses but they were all too far away; the nearest was at least thirty metres down the dirt track. It had to be coming from the house in front of him. Frauke hadn't mentioned being able to play the violin, and the sound appeared to be coming from downstairs. Intrigued, Sneijder drew his Walther from his waistband and moved closer. As he bent low and scurried across beneath a window he recognised the piece of music– Schubert's *Ave Maria*. He peered in the corner of the window and was surprised by the sight which greeted him.

Seated on a wooden stool in the centre of the sitting room with his back to him was Koestler, still wearing his dress shirt and trousers but no longer his tunic. There was a table within reach of him and on it stood a half-empty bottle of Scotch whisky which was open, though there was not a glass in sight. He had a pair of crutches propped up against the same table and Sneijder could just make out a plaster cast around his left foot and ankle. The German held the violin under his chin and was playing it with some passion, guiding the bow across the strings skilfully. He was evidently something of an expert with the instrument as he did not appear to miss a note.

Sneijder watched him play for a few minutes and was unable to deny a feeling of admiration. As he observed Koestler more closely he realised how completely consumed by the music the man was; in that moment it was all that mattered to him.

Sneijder turned away and sat down below the window with his back against the wall, listening. Koestler moved through the piece masterfully, the wonderful soaring symphony simply oozing from the violin's skin. It seemed almost inconceivable that such beauty could come from a man of such darkness, the creation of flawlessness from someone more inclined to destruction. Those thoughts however quickly gave way to memories of his mother. *Ave Maria* was her favourite piece; how she would have loved to have heard it being played so perfectly. Immediately a feeling of loss struck deep inside him, a true despair which took hold of him and squeezed him to the core. He had kept so many feelings suppressed for as long as he could remember but the music brought it all to the surface and tears formed in his eyes. He was reaching the point where he would be unable to go on.

Before the war Sneijder had been a young man plotting a future in the family jewel business; now he was lost, a traumatised and tortured drug addict in permanent grief for his family, a man who had killed five people, two of them innocent compatriots who had been assisting him in his task. The death of the concentration camp guard Kemerling had affected him deeply but now he had taken so many lives. It was all too much.

Inside, Koestler was immersed in the music. The piece he was playing was a personal favourite which he had learned as a schoolboy and the sound filled his senses. He had not touched the violin in months but today it had felt right; his wife had always encouraged his interest in music and it would have been their twenty-fifth wedding anniversary had she been alive. The melody coming from the strings of the instrument were the perfect accompaniment to his thoughts and memories about her, the good times and the times when he had failed to be there for her. Every note seemed to conjure up a different image; walking in the mountains of Bavaria, the day he became a father, the expression on Frauke's face when he had come home to discover his wife had passed away. He missed her terribly. If only he had had her counsel on all those occasions when he had been forced to make appalling decisions in the name of the Fatherland, perhaps he could have been a stronger man.

Koestler reached the end of the piece and gently lowered the violin. He put down the bow and picked up the bottle of whisky, taking a large gulp from it. The liquid burned the back of his throat and he coughed, allowing a little to spill down his chin. Wiping the whisky away with his sleeve, he turned his head towards the window. Out of the corner of his eye he saw a figure dressed all in black flash across the garden.

'Hey, Sterchler!' Koestler yelled at the top of his voice. 'Where the hell are you?' He slammed down the bottle and grabbed his crutches, and began hobbling across the room to the window. He could not see anything in the near-darkness, especially with the reflection of the interior light in the glass. A second later the door behind him burst open and Sterchler came in brandishing his Schmeisser.

'What were you doing out there?' Koestler demanded. 'Did you not see the man outside the house?'

Sterchler frowned. 'What man? There was nobody there.'

'Nonsense!' Koestler blasted. 'I have just seen somebody with my own eyes.'

Frauke entered the room. 'Are you okay, Father?' she asked breathlessly. 'I just heard you shouting. What is the matter?'

'You must have seen the intruder,' her father replied. 'In the garden, literally seconds ago.'

She shook her head slowly. 'No, and I was just looking out of my window.'

Koestler was frustrated. 'Somebody is trying to kill me, I'm telling you, and nobody else ever seems to notice! Don't tell me, you didn't see anything either?'

He was addressing the other guard who had just come in also; he shook his head as well.

'Oh, you're all bloody useless!' Koestler shouted. He remained at the window for some time looking out into the darkness. Later, once everybody had gone, he walked back to the table and inspected the whisky bottle, then grimaced and put it back on the table. Perhaps it really was the alcohol.

When it came down to it, Sneijder just could not do it. It would have been easy to shoot him; a couple of shots through the window into his back and he would have been away before either of the sentries had noticed anything. Koestler wouldn't have known anything about it; it would have been clean and tidy. But listening to him playing the violin so perfectly reminded Sneijder that this was not just a target, he was a real human being with talents and troubles and people who cared for him. Sneijder had no desire to be a murderer and especially not when to be one would hurt terribly the woman he realised he loved.

He wanted to forget all about killing for a while, to try to remember what it was like to be a human being. All of the death which he had been surrounded by was tearing him to shreds, stripping him of the humanity he had left. He tried to spend as much time with Frauke as possible. She too was trying to escape, to get away from her father's paranoid delusions about a plot to kill him. Sneijder listened to this only fleetingly, thinking that if he did not hear what she was saying he could not possibly give anything away with an unfortunate look. As he saw it, it was not unreasonable for a high-ranking official of an occupying power to be in fear for his life anyway but she evidently did not feel the same.

For Sneijder, being with her was freedom. He felt enlivened by her optimistic and carefree outlook and suddenly felt that anything in the world was possible. A depressed and murky mood could be lifted by her mere presence and the innocence with which she spoke of the world was refreshing. She had never even had to consider taking the life of another.

Every time they were together it was as if they were the only two people on earth. Sneijder had always thought that a clichéd sentiment but with Frauke it really felt that way. He could lose himself in her remarkable blue eyes for an eternity, and her achingly feminine body seemed to draw him near. They made love out in the summer sun on many of their long walks through the countryside, where they explored the forests and the fields and the waterways. Every time felt like the first, beautiful and satisfying if a little awkward and hesitant. For an afternoon they could simply enjoy being young people, away from the struggles of the world.

One of their walks brought them along the north bank of the Rhine to the west of the city one early evening. They had just managed to get through a patrol of Wehrmacht troops who were stopping all men of working age. Their questioning had been intense and they had not accepted Sneijder's story about already having worked in Germany until he had produced his *Rücktehrschelme*, but with a suspicious eye they had sent him on his way. As they strolled down Onderlangs, beside the river, Sneijder glanced at a bench and had an idea.

'You know, it may not be safe for us to come and find each other soon,' he said. 'If they stop everybody of my age whenever they see them I'm going to have to stay underground as much as possible.'

'How will we contact each other?' Frauke asked. 'You already told me I couldn't come to your house.'

Sneijder stopped and turned to her. 'Do you know what a dead-drop is?'

'Yes,' she replied, 'where you leave messages for someone so they can pick them up, right?'

'Exactly. That's what we'll do.' He took her hand, ran over to the bench and sat down. 'We'll use this bench. Obviously we'll always try to arrange our next meeting when we are together, but if you want to see me leave an envelope under the seat. I'll do the same.'

'Don't we need some kind of signal that there is a message waiting?'

Sneijder thought for a moment and said, 'Okay, you know the Musis Sacrum, that huge music hall just up from the bridge? There is a great ornamental lamppost right outside the front entrance. Leave a mark on it, a big 'x', with chalk or lipstick or something. I'll do the same. Make sure you look there every day, as I will.'

She smiled. 'You really do think about these things, don't you? Where do you learn it all – some kind of spy school?' She laughed.

'It means we can make sure we always meet some-where quiet. Just keep your messages slightly cryptic in case they are discovered.'

'What is going to happen to us, Johannes?' Frauke asked suddenly. 'Even if we get through this war, I'm still German. We're hated in this country now and nobody is going to be happy with us being together.'

'We can't think about that,' he answered. 'The future could bring anything. All we can plan for is the here and now.'

'But what do you want from your life? Don't you even think about it?'

Sneijder turned himself away from her and put his head in his hands. He did not want to lie to her any longer. She seemed to put so much trust in him and he was throwing it back in her face by deceiving her, but the truth would have to stay hidden forever. He knew in his heart of course that their relationship could never be real while he kept his true identity a secret from her but if he told her then it would surely be over. She had come to him for comfort when her father's car crashed and he had listened to her outpouring of emotion, had allowed her to give herself to him. How could she forgive him if she knew he had been the one trying to kill him?

Sneijder replied: 'I don't know what I want anymore. I am a different man from the one I used to be. I had hopes and dreams but somewhere I lost them – I suppose I'd like time to find them again.'

Frauke reached a hand out to his cheek and turned his face towards hers. 'Why do you hide from me, Johannes? You can tell me those things, those dark secrets you have. If you just opened up…'

Sneijder got to his feet and spun around, displaying irritation with her for the first time. 'Frauke, please!' he exclaimed. 'I've told you before; there are some things I cannot tell you. You can't help everyone.'

'Why not?'

'You just can't!' He looked down at his hand, which was shaking a little, and tried to stop it. It was no use, so he ignored it and looked back at Frauke. 'I'm sorry, I…'

She was upset but said, 'It's fine. Are you all right? You're sweating.'

'I'm okay,' he mumbled. 'Look, I've got to go. We'll try using the dead drop idea, see how it goes.'

'Remember, you're coming to dinner on Sunday,' she said. 'Just don't do anything to upset him and it'll be fine.'

'Yes,' he grunted. He kissed her on the forehead. 'I'm not myself – just give me time.' He rubbed her head affectionately and walked away.

CHAPTER SEVENTEEN

'Yes, sir.... Of course, I understand.... Yes.... Okay.....
Understood.' Koestler put the telephone down, instantly
dropped the courteous tone and growled in frustration,
'Bloody stupid.'

He pressed a button on his desk and summoned
Klimitz into the office. Within a minute one of the great
three metre-high doors opened and he walked in, obviously eager to say something. It was some time before his
superior noticed – he had already launched into one of
his increasingly common rants.

'That's another sector being taken over by the military,' he told Klimitz. 'The Reichskommisar tells me Field
Marshal Model has just been made commander-in-chief
of Army Group B, replacing Von Kluge - can you believe
he was involved in the plot to kill Hitler? He's heard
rumours that Model might set up his main divisional
headquarters right here in Arnhem. That's just terrific,
isn't it? I'll be taking my orders from a Hitler fanatic.
They just want me out – I'll bet it's that bloody Rauter.'

Klimitz said, 'Sir, Horvath is here to see you. He seems
to think it is pretty urgent.'

Koestler sighed with resignation. He probably
wanted to hear what the Gestapo agent had to tell him
but wasn't in the mood for him at this early hour. He
really could be a thoroughly disagreeable man. 'You had
better show him in.'

Horvath literally flew into the room. 'We have made a positive identification on the body we discovered in Roeden and you will not believe it. The man's name is Dimitri Petrovsky – forty-four years old, a Russian immigrant in 1919.... and the father of Hugo Petrovsky, the young Dutchman who was your driver.'

Koestler's eyes had widened as Horvath spoke. 'His father? Dead as well?'

'Yes. The strange thing is that the village where we found him – well, he had no reason to be there. He did not live anywhere near and to the best of our knowledge he was not acquainted with anybody there.'

Koestler leaned back in his chair and pondered this for a moment. 'This is not a mistake? I mean, there is no doubt about the identification?'

'None.' Horvath's demeanour verged on indignant. 'It took us some time as it appeared he had been underground for a couple of months but three of his neighbours identified him independently of one another. It is definitely Petrovsky, no question.'

'It proves it, then,' Koestler declared. 'My accident was no such thing – it was a deliberate attempt to kill me. I knew it.'

Horvath raised his eyebrows and said: 'I'm afraid I don't follow you.'

'Think about it. I am involved in a terrible car crash in which my driver is killed. Less than two weeks later his father is also killed and his body is found in Roeden, the village from which we know the Resistance attack on our convoy originated. Do you not think that is a little odd?'

'The Resistance are active in every town and village in the country. No, I was thinking that it may prove a plot to kill these two Petrovsky gentlemen,' said Horvath. 'Perhaps the accident was a deliberate attempt to kill not you, but your young driver.'

Koestler laughed and said patronisingly, 'Really, Horvath. Is that the best you can come up with? A lieutenant-colonel in the SS, the local chief, is in an accident and you think it is the driver, a private, who is the target? Come off it.'

The tone of his superior angered the Gestapo man. 'He was a Dutch collaborator - a traitor,' he said pointedly. 'Men like him are regarded as the main target of the Resistance, it is a perfectly legitimate theory,' he added.

'I was the target of this assassination attempt. I am convinced of it. Finding the body of this Petrovsky in this particular village gives us a connection between the accident and an active Resistance cell.'

'Okay, then. Tell me why Dimitri Petrovsky was in Roeden and how he came to end up with half of his face missing.' Horvath was becoming confrontational.

'I have no idea at the moment, but there is a connection. Even you cannot deny that.'

Horvath sighed. 'What would you have me do?'

'Obviously this attempt on my life had nothing to do with Max Bruggink, as we had him in custody at the time, but I think I will go and speak to him nonetheless. It would seem to be related to members of his cell. I think what you should do is investigate every single male in Roeden and look for links to Bruggink - anything which connects anybody else to him. That way we may be able to uncover more partisans. Then we shall question them. Somebody must know something.'

Horvath frowned and said, 'Do you have any idea how much manpower that will take?'

'I don't care. This is the attempted murder of a senior officer - me. The military will soon be taking over some of your duties anyway so it will not matter. Now please do as I say. You're dismissed.' Koestler waved him away and muttered under his breath as Horvath left, 'That bloody man.'

Klimitz showed him out and closed the door, then returned to stand in front of Koestler.

'What do you think, Sebastien?' Koestler asked. 'Is my logic correct?'

'I wouldn't like to criticise your logic....'

'Oh, can you leave out the bullshit?' Koestler said. 'I want your honest opinion.'

Klimitz smiled half-heartedly. 'I agree that there is a connection between your accident and this village. The deaths are too close together for it to be a coincidence but as to the reasons for them?' He shrugged.

'Come on – you've always been good at this sort of thing. What does your investigative nose tell you?'

Klimitz was deep in thought for about thirty seconds and then replied, 'It seems to me that if somebody had gone to kill this Petrovsky we would have found his body in a place he frequented often. The fact that we found him somewhere he had no reason to be suggests two possible scenarios. The first is that he was lured there, probably by a person he knew, for reasons unknown – perhaps to silence him because he knew about the attempt on your life? The second is that he went to find somebody, and the violence with which Petrovsky met his death would indicate that this person he had a serious quarrel with.

'If we assume the latter, just for argument's sake, and then also assume the matter he was so angry about was the recent death of his son, it suggests that the man he went looking for – the man that ultimately killed him – was involved in the plot to kill you. For Petrovsky to know who this man was he must have been involved himself, and it would seem likely that his involvement would be down to his son being your driver.'

Koestler seized on his train of thought. 'So perhaps my driver was involved in the plot too?' He frowned. 'No – why would he agree to something which would lead to his own death?'

'Well you would have to assume that your driver did not know that he would die. Obviously the father did not know that his son would die, hence his anger.' His mind was now moving faster than he could speak. 'It would make perfect sense if you think about it. If some-one wanted to make it look like an accident they would want to keep everything the same as normal. If your usual driver suddenly didn't turn up it would raise suspi-cions – certainly afterwards it would be obvious he was involved and that it wasn't an accident.'

Koestler nodded.

'Of course, this is all just conjecture,' Klimitz added. 'I could be on completely the wrong track.'

'No, it's certainly feasible.' Koestler grinned slowly. 'In fact, I'm sure you are correct. As always, Sebastien, you have convinced me. We shall go and talk to this Bruggink man at once.'

Koestler lifted himself out of his chair and fetched his crutches, and then left the office with his adjutant.

Sneijder had been woken early that morning by the sound of military vehicles pouring past the house in Oosterbeek. He walked through to the bathroom which had a view of the main road outside, arriving just as the turret of a Panzer III tank cruised by, the German Iron Cross clearly painted on the side. Its large five-centimetre main gun protruded from the front menacingly. Behind it trundled two large troop carrier trucks filled with soldiers, most of whom seemed very young. A military motorcycle and a black Mercedes staff car pulled off from the back of the convoy and disappeared along the road in the direction of the hotel being used as their headquarters.

Sneijder had arranged to meet Van Rijn at his grandfather's farm in order to get in some practice with the rifle, so after breakfast he took his bicycle and headed into the city in the direction of the bridge. As he approached he noticed that the road ahead had been blocked off by German troops. Moments later the air was filled with the roar of diesel engines and a line of heavily armoured vehicles rumbled over the bridge from the south bank of the river; Tiger tanks and half-tracks of a Waffen-SS Panzer unit. They vanished behind the group of houses which were clustered around the bridge ramp and were gone. Recently there had been a noticeable increase in the Germans' military presence in the area, old men and young boys unfit for the front line mostly, but this was something different. The Waffen-SS were fanatic, battle hardened veterans.

Sneijder found Van Rijn at his kitchen table surrounded by files - thick wedges of paper tucked into brown manila folders. There were at least thirty of them, some fatter than others but all containing a significant amount of information. The titles written in German in bold text on each one immediately caught Sneijder's attention.

'What are these? They didn't....'

Van Rijn grinned. 'Yes. They came through for us, Voesman's people. I don't know how they did it but they got in and out and got the files without any of them being caught.'

Sneijder did not hide his surprise. 'Really? I thought that would be impossible, I really did. I know their security isn't always the best but this is their headquarters. Who knows what sort of information they keep there?'

'Quite.'

Sneijder leaned forward to look at the typed list that Van Rijn was scanning and asked, 'Have you found anything interesting, anything that might help us?'

The other man shook his head. 'Not so far, but there's so much to go through and my German is not the best. This is a list of named informants and the amounts of money they were paid at various points, and these go all the way back to April 1941. The remaining files contain more detailed knowledge about the most prolific inform-ants; photographs, where they can be found, the sort of information they have access to - that sort of thing. On each list there are hundreds of names and I want to make sure I don't miss any. Even if the payment for the tip-off about Max is not listed, our man might have volunteered information before so I must check.'

'Can I help?'

'Not really,' Van Rijn replied. 'You won't recognise the majority of names even if they are men linked to our group. No, I'll have to do it by myself.'

'You say they go back to 1941?' Sneijder asked rhetorically. 'That is disciplined filing. It must be true what they say about Koestler's administrative skills.'

'Here, take a look.' Van Rijn handed a file to Sneijder. 'I'm not kidding, this stuff is meticulous.'

Sneijder opened the manila folder and began leafing through the pages. The first half were all just lists but the sheer number of names on these lists appalled him. When the Germans had first invaded his country he had hoped that the people would resist and avoid collaborating with them, but over time there had been a general acceptance that they were here to stay and so it was prudent to work with them. The trouble was that in their haste to better the situation for themselves many people either did not consider or did not care about the repercussions of their actions. Some could simply not imagine that informing on their neighbour would lead to that neighbour's brutalisation or even death. Others just saw the opportunity to make money or gain favour as too good to turn down.

Once he had reached the thirteenth page he pushed the file away from him. 'Just look at this,' he exclaimed in exasperation. 'There are hundreds of names here and this is only 1941. From what I've seen the problem has got worse as the occupation has gone on so how many are there now?'

'That's what I was just telling you,' Van Rijn said irritably. 'Weren't you listening?'

'I know, I was, it's just.....' Sneijder struggled to find the words. 'It just really gets to me. We're putting our lives at risk to stand up to the Nazis while others are profiting from giving us up. It makes me ashamed to be Dutch sometimes.'

'Yes, I know how you feel.'

'I mean, some of these people were hardly paid anything, and yet other people probably died because of

them.' Sneijder grabbed the file again. 'I can't believe.....'
He stopped abruptly and stared at the bottom of the list
in front of him; suddenly the colour drained completely
from his face.

'What is it?' Van Rijn asked. 'What's wrong?'

Sneijder was speechless and appeared totally stunned.
'No, surely it can't....' he finally managed to blurt out.
'Not....'

'What?'

Sneijder ignored the question and stood up from his
chair. He moved to the pile of folders and starting flinging them open one by one. With each he scanned the first
page, flicked through the rest and tossed it aside, scattering loose sheets of paper. He was searching desperately for something but evidently not finding it.

'Johannes, stop!' Van Rijn urged him. 'Those are in an
order, I need them in that order! What are you doing?'

Sneijder's eyes continued to jump from side to side
erratically. 'The detailed documents about informers,
where are they? I need to find them.'

Van Rijn raised his hands. 'Slow down. What do you
want them for? If you've found something...'

'I'll explain in a moment. Please, where?'

Van Rijn pointed to a pile in the corner of the table.
Sneijder grabbed them and began to rummage through,
quickly discovering that the characters in the files were
listed alphabetically by surname. He flicked through
rapidly, got to the correct letter and then slowed down,
taking extra care not to miss a single page. He turned over
a sheet and was suddenly looking at a familiar face; the
balding head, the slightly chubby cheeks, the round silver-
rimmed spectacles. It was crushing. Sneijder slumped
down in the chair and reached both hands up to his face.

'What's wrong?' Van Rijn asked again.

Sneijder slammed a fist down on the table angrily and swore. 'This is unbelievable!' he exclaimed. 'How could this happen?'

'Tell me what the problem is,' Van Rijn instructed him.

Sneijder took a deep breath. 'I was sent here on a mission to assassinate Koestler as you know. My superior was approached by a man who works for the Dutch government-in-exile in London, who wanted an agent outside his organisation for the job. That man is named Guido de Beer.'

'Go on.'

Sneijder turned the file containing the list of names around so that the other man could see. 'Look at this page from June of 1941 and these three entries down here. Then turn over to the next month and look – here, here and here.'

'My God,' Van Rijn said, 'Guido de Beer.' He looked up. 'You were sent here by a German informant?'

'This picture,' Sneijder indicated, pointing to the photograph in the more detailed file, 'is him. He's a bloody collaborator! I'm here because of a damned traitor! I never did see the reasoning behind killing Koestler; he's not a nice guy certainly but important enough to assassinate? I just followed my orders but this....'

'Koestler deserves to die – don't convince yourself otherwise,' said Van Rijn.

'Whether he does or not is irrelevant, don't you see? I have killed two innocent men because I thought I was serving my country, not trying to cover up for traitors! This is why he wants Koestler dead, to keep it quiet that he sold them information. Look, it says in his file that his information led directly to the arrest and execution of Underground members. Imagine if the government in London found out.'

Van Rijn frowned. 'Killing Koestler wouldn't get rid of the files though, would it? They would still implicate him.'

'An understandable oversight on his part,' Sneijder explained. 'How many officials actually file everything so thoroughly, particularly when it is three-year-old information? Most people would have disposed of it by now, especially when there is so much newer stuff. It would be reasonable to expect that the only record existed in Koestler's mind.'

'So why now? Why not get rid of him sooner?'

'It's obvious now that the Germans are going to lose the war. I dare say important officers like Koestler might talk in an effort to save themselves if they are captured, and who knows what they could reveal. It was obviously time to take care of business, and he used me. The bastard.'

'And you're sure it's definitely him?'

'Of course I'm sure,' Sneijder replied tersely. 'Now what do I do?'

'Listen, Johannes,' Van Rijn said firmly, 'this changes nothing. It is still your mission to assassinate Koestler and you should follow it through. Come on – you've witnessed first-hand what he is capable of. He must be killed.'

'Before, I thought I was serving my country. Now I find I am serving one corrupt man's self-interest. That makes me very uncomfortable.'

'Well that is something to sort out later,' Van Rijn replied. 'You can't do anything about it now, and it is not as if he'll get away with it now that we've found the files.'

'I'm not at all happy about killing a man to cover up treason.'

'What are you telling me, Johannes?' Van Rijn was irritated. 'That you won't do it? Because I will. Koestler is going to die; that is for certain.'

'I honestly don't know,' Sneijder replied, rising from his chair. 'I'm going to go outside and get some air, and think things through.'

When he returned half an hour later he still didn't know how he felt about his mission. There was so much to think about and it would take a couple of days before the fact that De Beer had deceived him would really sink in. Sneijder wanted to avoid the subject altogether so he mentioned the line of military vehicles he had seen that morning to Van Rijn as he was setting up some targets in front of the barn wall.

'It looks like there is something happening. What do you think?'

'I heard on the wireless last night that the Germans have already lost most of Belgium,' Van Rijn responded. 'Something may happen here but the Allies might just go straight for Germany.'

'If the Germans have all these units nearby, they must think they will need them,' Sneijder speculated. 'They obviously expect a fight.'

'Not necessarily. They could be sending them here to rest, specifically because they *don't* think there will be any action here.' Van Rijn motioned towards the rifle standing against the wall. 'Now are you going to show me what you can do with that thing?'

Van Rijn had set up a line of tin cans on a long wooden trestle table in front of the crumbling brick wall of the barn. From a range of twenty-five metres Sneijder picked off the first six with ease, taking his time to get a feel for the weapon. The bolt was stiff to begin with but softened up as he worked it each time. He doubled the distance to fifty metres and tried again. This time he had to be a little more careful when taking aim but the remaining four cans were dispatched clinically.

'Good shooting,' Van Rijn commented, 'but if you were that close you wouldn't need a rifle. Try from further away.'

Sneijder continued his target practice from one hundred and then two hundred metres. At the further distance his accuracy faltered and this irritated him, as he knew it was well within his capability. Indeed the type of rifle he was using was designed to hit targets up to five hundred metres away. He put it down to rustiness and had another go, although they did not have an excess of ammunition.

'Not too bad at all,' said Van Rijn.

Sneijder scowled. 'You don't need to congratulate me for the sake of it. That was pretty terrible.'

'No, it was a good effort. You are probably out of practice - that is perfectly understandable. Come on inside, we'll have lunch. My grandfather makes a wonderful vegetable soup, even with the few vegetables we can still get.'

Just as Van Rijn had promised, the old man Lamming's soup was indeed delicious and Sneijder enjoyed it immensely. Afterwards, just as he was about to leave, Van Rijn motioned to him.

'Johannes, come with me for a moment,' the Resistance man said. 'There's something I'd like you to see.'

He led the way into a small copse which lay behind one of the large grain silos, keeping to the dirt path which had formed along the most worn route. After they had gone about two hundred metres into the forest Van Rijn branched off to one side and took about fifty paces, pausing beside a tiny sapling which grew between two larger trees.

'What is it you want to show me?' Sneijder asked.

'Take a step back,' Van Rijn commanded him.

Sneijder did what he had been ordered to, and was surprised when Van Rijn crouched down in front of him and began sweeping dirt and leaves aside with his hands. Eventually he found a hard corner which he slipped his fingers under and lifted; a metre-square section of the ground came away and folded back like a hatch cover to reveal a set of concrete steps descending about two metres down to a rickety wooden door.

'What's this?' Sneijder inquired with interest.

Van Rijn grinned. 'Go down and take a look. You'll need this.' He took out a small flashlight and tossed it over to his companion.

Sneijder descended the steps gingerly and pulled open the door, shining the torch into the darkness. Facing him was a room about six metres long and four metres wide which was packed full of weapons; the floor was covered with machine guns and what appeared to be home-made mortars and shelves lining the walls were piled high with wooden boxes. 'My God,' he said.

Van Rijn pointed to the boxes. 'In those we have German fragmentation anti-personnel mines and stick grenades which we stole from a facility just across the German border, British Mills bomb grenades and ammunition belts for machine guns. Then we've got more

German machine guns – five or six MG-42s – and a British Bren which we recovered from a military transport plane which crashed near here. Apparently it had been destined for the Resistance in Poland so it only seemed right to use it.'

'You could start a war with this lot.'

'Or hopefully finish one,' Van Rijn responded. 'We've not had the opportunity to use any of this yet – it's not really suitable for subversive operations like sabotage which we want to keep low-key. If we get to a situation of open warfare though, we'll be ready. Perhaps that will be soon.'

'Yes, perhaps,' Sneijder replied. 'Does your grandfather know about this?'

'Of course. I like to keep him out of things which he doesn't need to know about; the less he knows the safer he is, but it is his farm. It only seemed right to tell him.'

Sneijder closed the door and climbed back up the steps and Van Rijn pulled the hatch down behind him. After a couple of minutes of spreading dirt and leaves it was impossible to tell that the entrance to the bunker was there. The two of them returned to the farm.

A month being held at the pleasure of the Gestapo had taken its toll on Max Bruggink. He was very pale with dark, sunken eyes and his face was badly bruised. A large cut ran down his left cheek and intersected with his dry and cracked lips. He puffed pitifully on the cigarette Klimitz offered him, allowing the smoke to drift out of his nostrils and mouth. The entire time he was in the room he was hunched over as if straightening would be too painful, and his voice was a low, agonised drawl.

'You cannot want to put yourself through this,' Koestler said. 'If you just tell me what I want to know, I can make it stop.'

'Screw yourself,' Bruggink grunted.

Koestler sighed. 'That sort of answer will not help either of us. Someone tried to kill me - they did kill two of your fellow Dutchmen. I want to know who that person is.'

'Well I can stop you right away with that one,' Bruggink answered. 'I honestly know nothing about that. For goodness sake, I've been in here over four weeks. How could I know about anything that has happened since then?' He turned away from Koestler and blew smoke into the air.

The room in the basement of Gestapo headquarters was gloomy and bare, the only natural light coming from a window high up in the wall which led out to ground level. A weak electric lamp dangled above the wooden table, either side of which sat Bruggink and Koestler. Klimitz leaned against the cold concrete wall some way behind his superior officer. Koestler just wanted to talk; he left the more aggressive forms of questioning to men for whom empathy was an alien concept.

'And nobody mentioned anything to you before?' Koestler asked. 'Sabotaging my car cannot have been an impulsive thing; it was carefully planned.'

'Your guess is as good.....ah,' he clutched his stomach, obviously in pain, 'as good as mine.' His face creased.

Koestler said nothing, and neither he nor Klimitz made any attempt to move.

'Then you can tell me the names of your associates,' Koestler demanded when Bruggink had recovered. 'We know that it was one of them that tried to kill me. Give me all their names, everyone in your cell, and I can find out which one.'

'Go to hell,' the Dutchman croaked. 'You've got enough damned informants in this country, you certainly don't need me and you are not going to get me.'

'Mr Bruggink, I'm afraid you are leaving me with very little option. I will have to let the Gestapo's finest do what they do best.' A look of genuine distaste appeared in his expression. 'Please, I know there is an agent from England in Arnhem. You have confirmed this yourself. Tell me his name.'

'Are we finished here?' Bruggink was dismissive.

Koestler stood up in frustration. 'Very well. But if you are not planning on giving us any information, you are no use to me. You will be executed for the murder of sixteen Germans.' Klimitz passed him his crutches and he began to leave. He turned and added, 'If you change your mind, I will be back. If not...'

He left the sentence hanging in the air.

Chapter Eighteen

Sneijder could not believe he was actually going to dinner with the man he was trying to kill, a German and a committed Nazi at that. He had read so many terrible things about him, details of the killings of civilians he had arranged and so forth, and had seen the work of his men first-hand. The sight of all those bodies in front of the schoolyard had stuck with Sneijder, particularly those of Jelle and Arnold, mere boys whom he had liked in the short time he had known them. If it hadn't been for the awful things he had witnessed in the concentration camp it might have surprised him that humans could do such things to one another.

It seemed that Frauke was more nervous about the evening than Sneijder. She really did not know what to expect from her father, or so she said. Koestler had tried to allow her space to be her own person, if only so as not to alienate the only family he had left, but his controlling tendencies had got the better of him. His attitude towards non-Germans was anything but positive and he seemed determined to ensure the same would be true of his daughter.

Sneijder decided that the best course of action would be to behave agreeably at all times. Playing down his own opinions on all matters to the point of being slightly dull would hopefully give Koestler nowhere to go with regards to attempting to unsettle him. He dressed smartly in his dark double-breasted suit, shirt and tie and cycled to the Koestler house, declining the offer of a car to pick him up as he did not want the authorities to know where he was staying. It was around seven o'clock on a pleasant Sunday evening when he arrived. The two sentries who had been on duty outside the house when Sneijder had last been there were standing either side of the front door. One of them moved forward and approached him as he pushed his bicycle up the front driveway.

'Are you Voorman?' he asked in German.

'I am,' Sneijder replied. 'You are expecting me?'

'Of course. Obersturmbannführer Koestler is inside. He asked me to show you in, but first....' The sentry swung his submachine gun behind his back to allow free movement of his arms. He patted Sneijder down to check for any hidden weapons.

'I am unarmed,' Sneijder said with a hint of a laugh. 'Do you really think I would be crazy enough to attack a German officer in his own house, surrounded by soldiers?'

The sentry's expression did not change. He obviously did not see the humour. 'We must check at all times. You can go in now.'

Sneijder rested his bicycle against the fence and entered the house. The kitchen was straight ahead and the smell of roast chicken drifted out of the open door. He could see a middle-aged woman chopping vegetables, probably a cook. He imagined that most of the high-ranking German officials had cooks. There was conversation in German coming from a room on the left and Sneijder recognised one of the voices as that of Frauke.

He walked through the door and found himself in the sitting room. Frauke was sitting in a chair beside the window; opposite her sat her father.

Koestler was no longer wearing a plaster cast around his ankle and rose from his chair with only a very slight difficulty. 'Mr Voorman, I presume.' He extended a hand and went on, 'I appreciate you coming. I am SS Ober-sturmbannführer Albrecht Koestler. I am pleased to meet you.' He was dressed in his black SS uniform, the red armband with the swastika catching Sneijder's attention. His breast sported an array of different coloured medal ribbons and at his throat was the unmistakable Iron Cross.

Sneijder shook his hand. 'As am I pleased to meet you.'

Koestler smiled. 'What a quaint idea. I do not think that is true, however, is it?'

Sneijder said nothing.

'Father,' Frauke warned him gently. She turned to Sneijder. 'Thank you for coming. Would you like a drink?'

'I have a bottle of crisp white wine being nicely chilled as we speak,' Koestler announced. 'I trust you will indulge me.'

Sneijder replied, 'Of course.'

Koestler left the room and went into the kitchen. Frauke leaned over and kissed Sneijder, brushing a mark off his jacket at the same time.

'You look very smart,' she whispered to him, adding, 'I wasn't sure that you would turn up.'

'Neither was I. To be honest, I am still not certain that this is a good idea.'

'It's not, but we have to make the best of it. Just be yourself.'

She stopped abruptly as her father came back into the room clutching a wine bottle wrapped in a tea towel. Frauke moved over to the sideboard and produced three glasses which her father filled. They all sat down and sipped the wine.

'Helena will have dinner ready in about twenty minutes,' Koestler informed Sneijder. 'In the meantime, tell me about yourself.'

Just as he had planned, Sneijder kept things simple. He spoke in a deliberately convoluted manner which took time but revealed little, making a conscious effort to deliver his words in a dull and monotonous fashion. He mentioned his home in Amsterdam and doing labour in Germany, and gave the same story he had given to Frauke about an aunt in Arnhem. He omitted his family's disappearance as he felt this could be a point of disagreement with Koestler. He would have preferred to have given a less truthful account but this was impossible with Frauke sitting there. Most of the story would have to match what he had told her, although she would understand his reluctance to tell him everything.

'It sounds like you have had an interesting war,' Koestler commented.

Sneijder would not have used that particular term to describe forced labour. 'Yes,' he replied. 'Quite a war.'

'So what are your feelings about the German occupation?'

'Father,' Frauke said irritably. 'How is he possibly supposed to answer a question like that?'

'Why? What was wrong with my question?' Koestler snapped.

'Please, can we avoid disagreements at least until after we've eaten?' Frauke said. 'Look, I think Helena has it ready. Shall we?'

Frauke led the way through into the dining room where the table had been set for the three of them. It had been done extremely professionally as if in an expensive restaurant, with shiny silver cutlery either side of a thick red serviette in each place. Polished glasses stood in the centre of the table. They were seated and within minutes the cook brought out a starter of prawn cocktails; afterwards they ate roast chicken with potatoes and mixed vegetables. Sneijder was hungry living on the meagre rations that Dutch civilians were given and it took a good deal of self-discipline to stop him wolfing it down in an undignified manner. They sat mostly in silence, Frauke occasionally attempting to make small talk with each man. There was a definite tension in the air and she quickly gave up trying to lighten the mood.

The cook came and removed the plates from the table. As they waited for the dessert course Koestler challenged Sneijder with another probing question. 'So, Mr Voorman, what is it you do for work? I assume you must have a job.'

'I work for the stationmaster at the Oosterbeek railway station - cleaning, loading and unloading, sweeping the platform, that sort of thing. Menial tasks.'

'Ah, small things,' Koestler replied. 'Where do you live then?'

Sneijder's instinct was to lie to him, to give him some false story, but if Koestler decided to look into it and found that he did not live where he said he did, it would be obvious that something was not right. Instead he went against his better judgement and told him the truth. 'At the stationmaster's house. I have a room there.'

'Really?' Koestler almost sounded surprised. 'It is very kind of him to offer you accommodation.'

'Yes, it is,' Sneijder agreed.

'And does he make you pay for this arrangement?'

'I do a proportion of my work for free, in return for the food and board. It seems to work well for us both.'

'More agreeable than labour in Germany, then?' Koestler commented. He was almost laying down a challenge, waiting to see whether Sneijder would criticise German methods to his face.

Sneijder remained diplomatic, replying, 'It is always preferable to work in one's own country, serving one's own people.'

Koestler smiled. 'Of course.'

The conversation continued for the next few minutes in a similar vein, Koestler asking questions and Sneijder answering without an inflammatory word. Each was perfectly courteous, but distrust simmered below the surface; neither wanted to reveal his true feelings; each man was waiting for the other to make the first move. Frauke sat on the sidelines wearing a worried expression but keeping out of the crossfire. The cook brought out the dessert course, a sponge pudding with fresh fruit and whipped cream, and again they fell into silence.

Later, when the cook had taken away the plates and brought out another bottle of wine, the third of the evening, Sneijder decided to question Koestler. 'So as the SS chief in this area, what are your particular responsibilities?'

'I am in charge of all matters,' Koestler replied, 'especially recruitment of foreign volunteers into the service and suppression of Resistance activities.'

Sneijder made an educated guess in an attempt to unnerve the older man. 'I suppose some of your duties will be curtailed by the increasing Wehrmacht presence.'

Koestler grinned. 'I can see that you are a very observant man, and a thinker. However on this occasion your assumptions are incorrect. I will remain in charge. Nationalistic uprisings must be ruthlessly crushed.' His expression had become hard.

'When people see freedom is near,' Sneijder said charmingly, 'their spirit toughens. It becomes much harder to put them down. Fear alone will no longer be enough.' His smile was infinitely disarming, precluding Koestler from any kind of angry response.

The German leaned forward and with a terrible look replied, 'I believe you underestimate just how ruthless we can be.'

'I do not think that would be possible.'

Frauke suddenly cut in. 'For God's sake, can we stop all this talk of ruthlessness?'

Koestler chuckled. 'Frauke, my dear, we are just playing.' He turned back to Sneijder. 'Tell me, Mr Voorman, do you play chess? It is a passion of mine, one that I do not get much of a chance to indulge. My adjutant Klimitz plays, but certainly not to my level. Unfortunately he does not make much of an opponent.'

Sneijder gave a small smile and answered, 'It seems you are in luck. Chess was also a passion of my father's – he taught me to play.' He added flippantly, 'But I doubt I play to your level either.'

'I fear you may be setting up my ego for a fall,' Koestler said, 'but we shall have a game. Frauke, perhaps you would leave two gentlemen to a good-spirited confrontation?'

She glanced at Sneijder, who nodded.

'If you wish,' she said curtly, and she got to her feet. 'I will be upstairs. Johannes, please don't leave without saying goodbye.' She looked at her father, warning him to be reasonable, but he either did not see or chose to ignore her.

'I will not be too hard on him,' Koestler called to her as she reached the door.

This time she ignored him and disappeared. He laughed.

They set up the chessboard on the dining table once it had been cleared after dinner. It was now approaching nine o'clock and with it being the third day of September darkness had fallen. Koestler switched on the lights.

He had an elegantly carved chess set, beautiful wooden pieces in a Gothic style which reminded Sneijder of a set he used to admire in a shop window near his home in Amsterdam. Koestler suggested that Sneijder play as white, allowing him to open the game, while he would take the black pieces made from darkened hardwood. The opening skirmishes saw Sneijder make a traditional start, matched by the older man.

'A very cautious beginning,' Koestler observed. 'Do you always play this way?'

Sneijder did not look up; he scanned the board with his eyes, contemplating his next move. 'I like to consider a strategy before I jump in - take the long view.' He moved his knight ahead of his line of pawns. 'Your move.'

Koestler had evidently been planning his next move as straight away he advanced a pawn on the right side of the board. Sneijder did something similar. Koestler brought a bishop into the centre of the action.

The German's sudden attack surprised Sneijder, but in turn he executed a defensive shield, placing his other knight in front of his king. 'I do not easily get drawn in to an offensive game,' he commented with a smile.

'So it appears.' Koestler moved a rook forward from the corner of the board. 'I shall have to do the attacking for the both of us.'

The two men studiously continued their game, the odd comment passing from one to the other. While neither mentioned it, it was clearly a battle that they were each desperate not to lose. Koestler's early attempts to put pressure on Sneijder began to unravel as he carelessly sacrificed several pieces. Sneijder made his first set of attacking moves and soon was closing in on Koestler's king, which the German had left trapped behind his pawns. Using one of his knights, Sneijder caught Koestler's king and queen in a fork; the king was in check and hence Koestler had to move it, leaving Sneijder free to capture his opponent's queen.

Koestler's good-humoured approach had suddenly vanished, and he was plainly irritated. 'Good move,' he said bitterly through gritted teeth, then rather aggressively took the knight with his rook. He wrinkled his face as he analysed the position before him.

Sneijder made another cautious move.

'Tell me,' Koestler began, 'what is it about my daughter that interests you?'

Sneijder hesitated, wondering how he should answer this unexpected question. Finally he replied, 'She has a kind nature, and takes an optimistic view of the world. I think that is refreshing in the current climate.'

Koestler executed a move which Sneijder had not seen coming and took one of his bishops. 'She is an incredibly naive young woman,' he said harshly. 'She does not understand the way things are. You do not agree?'

Sneijder raised an eyebrow. 'No, I do not.'

'You two have a very close relationship,' Koestler stated. He waited for the younger man to answer. Sneijder thought Koestler was just fishing but he couldn't be sure; perhaps he knew. He didn't reply, he just got on with the game.

Koestler leaned forward in that way of his, when he wanted to emphasise a point. 'No good will come of it - for either of you,' he growled threateningly in a low tone.

For the next few minutes Sneijder tried to channel his growing anger into the game but Koestler had succeeded in unbalancing him and his moves were not carefully considered enough. He left several pieces exposed and Koestler broke out with his rooks, mopping up the stragglers.

'It seems your attack on my king has stalled,' the German announced. 'You have lost the initiative.'

'I wouldn't be too sure of myself if I were you,' Sneijder replied without looking up, for the first time showing signs of frustration.

This appeared to please the other man. He grinned and said sarcastically: 'Why? Is this all part of a master plan to defeat me? I must say, this is not one I have seen before.'

Before Sneijder could rise to the jibe the lights suddenly went off. After a few seconds it became apparent that they were not going to return straight away.

Koestler got to his feet and walked towards the kitchen, feeling his way along the wall in the pitch-darkness. The lounge door burst open and the guard named Sterchler shone a flashlight in.

'Stay there, sir,' he called out. 'Let us check it out.'

Koestler scowled and called back: 'For goodness sake, Sterchler, it's just a power cut. How many times does it happen?' He continued to move into the kitchen, returning moments later. 'Yes, all the electricity has gone.'

Sneijder was standing looking out of the window. 'The lights are off in all the other houses too I think. It's hard to tell with the blackout curtains.'

Frauke came into the room to find out what was going on with the lights. 'Is it just us or the whole road?' She looked out of the sitting room window and added, 'Oh, right, it's everyone. There are some candles and matches in that cupboard over there.' She squeezed behind Sneijder's chair and crouched down to access the relevant door.

Soon the chessboard was illuminated by five candles on an ornate candlestick holder which Frauke left in the middle of the table. She spread a few small tea lights around the sitting room which created a ghostly glow, then collected three more candles on a smaller holder and returned upstairs.

The dim flickering light from the candles was enough to enable Sneijder and Koestler to see the game in front of them but their faces were now partially obscured by shadow. Sneijder could now just make out the other man's nose and his prominent cheeks and chin. His eyes seemed to vanish into the gloom, the pale irises occasionally glittering when the flame blew in the right direction. Everything but the chessboard and Koestler's face had disappeared from view. The conditions lent the game a certain mystical quality and heightened Sneijder's feelings of uncertainty. Koestler was beginning to step up the intensity of his conversation, seemingly no longer happy to spar with his opponent. They were moving into unknown territory, a fact mirrored by the darkness which now enveloped them.

'Where were we?' Koestler asked. 'Ah, yes, your master plan.'

Sneijder made a face but ignored the comment. He concentrated on the task in hand. However his earlier loss of focus was hurting him now. He had left himself badly out of position and Koestler, proving himself a skilled player, was punishing him for it. He collected another couple of Sneijder's pieces for a similar loss, but he could afford to.

Sneijder had now just his king and queen, a rook and a smattering of pawns remaining. With black pieces closing in on a pawn situated at the edge of the board, Sneijder inexplicably moved away the rook which was protecting it. It was a suicidal move. Koestler pounced on it with glee. Sneijder cursed and slapped the side of his head a little immaturely.

Koestler laughed. 'Getting to you a touch?' he mocked.

Sneijder was raging inside, his fury at Koestler's arrogance beginning to bubble over. He clung to his composure with his fingertips, motivated only by a desire to avoid unfortunate consequences for Frauke or himself. For the next minute or so he didn't say a word, fearing that if he did he would say something regrettable. The resulting increase in his concentration levels started to pay dividends and his luck in the game began to change.

Koestler was enjoying himself and evidently believed that he had Sneijder beaten. He rubbed his hands together with a stupid smile on his face as he moved his bishop into a position which put Sneijder's king in check.

Sneijder could not believe what he was seeing. It was a ridiculous move to make for what seemed like obvious reasons; the bishop was now directly in the line of fire from Sneijder's queen. What was more, by taking the bishop, Sneijder's queen would be in the perfect position to capture Koestler's rook. He took the bishop.

'Complacency is the enemy of victory,' Sneijder said without emotion.

'And victory is something a Dutchman would know about?' Koestler answered, displaying a nasty expression. 'By subjecting himself to the rule of Germany? By allowing his Queen to flee with her household to England within hours of the invasion?'

'Germany's rule will soon be over.'

Silence fell again as if the darkness had snatched Koestler's words away. The candle flames danced and weaved like a cobra charmed by a flute, throwing their glow back and forth. Peculiar shadows appeared and melted away at random.

Koestler moved the rook, he had to, but it was another poor choice of move. He put it directly in the path of one of Sneijder's pawns and that too was taken. Koestler swore in Polish, betraying his presence in Krakow early in the war. Sneijder recalled that information from Koestler's file.

'Our spirit is far stronger than you may think,' Koestler insisted. 'We do not intend to go down without a fight.'

Sneijder continued to decimate Koestler's pieces. By now his desire to pacify the German had been usurped by a need to get at him, to rattle him. The man was too arrogant for his own good and Sneijder was determined to defeat him.

'I hope for your sake that you fight better than you play chess,' he mocked. He was playing a dangerous game here; Koestler had the power to make life extremely unpleasant for him.

Koestler leaned in. 'I would advise you not to push me, Mr Voorman,' he said forcefully. 'I can do things that you cannot even imagine. I have men under my command who like nothing better than inflicting pain upon others. Do you understand?'

Sneijder leaned forward too, bringing his face into the light. 'Those would be the men who murdered almost fifty civilians then? The best, most honourable Germans?'

'That was a simple matter of evening the score,' Koestler replied with a twisted smile. 'Well, perhaps swinging it in our direction a little. Still, we must respond to any attack, mustn't we? It surely would not be prudent for us to allow the murder of sixteen Germans to go unpunished. We would quickly have anarchy.'

'Surely the most sensible solution would be to withdraw from other people's countries,' Sneijder suggested dryly.

Koestler laughed patronisingly. 'Really? Perhaps I should suggest that to the Führer. I'm sure he would love the idea.'

They were now in the closing stages of the game, the endgame. Koestler's complacency and over-adventurous style had left him with no pieces with which to defend his king. Sneijder had a single pawn in addition to his king.

It was now impossible for Koestler to win; the best he could hope for was a draw. In order to win the game Sneijder needed to get his pawn to the other side of the board where it could be converted into a queen, or promoted. This would allow him the chance to check-mate Koestler's king.

It took five minutes, all of which were in silence, for Sneijder to promote his pawn. He now had a queen as well as his king.

'Okay then,' Koestler said. 'I'm invoking the fifty-move rule. I hope you are good.'

'We shall see.'

The rule in question stated that a game in which no pieces were captured by either player for fifty consecu-tive moves would be declared a draw. In other words, to defeat Koestler, Sneijder would need to reach checkmate within fifty moves. He set about the task.

Suddenly, totally out of the blue, Koestler came out with something very curious and equally alarming. 'Mr Voorman, I cannot put my finger on it, but there is some-thing that tells me you are not all you seem. You are sitting here in the home of the local head of the SS, surrounded by armed German troops, and yet you are not afraid to challenge or mock me. I must say that I find this unusual.'

'You do, do you?'

'I do, yes. I will tell you a few things now, so that I do not have to at some later juncture. Whoever it is you are, whatever it is you do, I will find out. I guarantee you of that. I will make it my business to find out. And you will not under any circumstances drag my daughter into any scheme you may have. I absolutely assure you of that. Are we clear?'

Sneijder moved his queen, trapping Koestler's king in a corner. 'That's checkmate.'

Koestler did not even look at the board. He didn't say a word – his eyes were totally focused on Sneijder's, as if searching for a hint of what lay behind them. 'Yes,' he finally said, 'I think we shall probably be seeing more of one another.'

Sneijder rose from his chair, then reached for his king and laid it carefully on its side. 'I think I will now take my leave. But first, I shall go and bid farewell to your daughter.'

'Remember what I have said,' Koestler warned him. 'If any harm should come to her, there will be consequences.'

Sneijder left the room without acknowledging the threat and went upstairs to say goodbye. When he returned and finally departed from the house, it was eleven o'clock.

CHAPTER NINETEEN

It was just after noon. Koestler was again seated at his dining-room table, this time with files and loose pieces of paper scattered in front of him. Klimitz was seated opposite him with another batch of files, although his were arranged in a far more methodical manner, a testament to his logical mind. Koestler's skill in administrative matters lay in his being able to find the one relevant piece of information in a sea of irrelevant ones and concentrate solely on that; the downside to this was that the items he dismissed often ended up in a pile on the floor and he was forced to spend countless hours putting them back in the correct order. The files they were going through contained information collected by the Gestapo about the male residents of Roeden.

Koestler's reasons for examining the evidence personally were two-fold. Firstly, having discussed matters with Horvath on many occasions, he did not have much confidence in the man's ability to draw satisfactory conclusions from the information he was presented with. He had an uncanny knack of misinterpreting what he was told, such as his ridiculous idea that the deaths of Koestler's driver and his driver's father indicated a deliberate plot to kill them, rather than an assassination attempt on Koestler himself.

Secondly, having been heavily defeated in Normandy by the Allies, the commander of Army Group B, Field

Marshal Walther Model, had indeed set up his head-quarters at the Hartenstein and Tafelberg hotels in Oost-erbeek. On Hitler's orders he had established military rule over the Netherlands and, according to rumours, was intent on dividing the country in two along a west-east axis; his forces, having retreated from France, would control the front. The Wehrmacht's presence in the coun-try effectively neutralised Koestler's influence; many of the tasks which the SS had been charged with were now taken over by the army, and those in the civilian admin-istration were placed under the command of the military. In Koestler's eyes, if his opinions and orders did not matter, he was not particularly interested in giving them. From now on, he would concentrate on his own matters.

They had been reading through reams of information, most of it useless, for over three hours now, trying to cross-reference it with their other files. Most of the morning had been spent in silence as the pair concen-trated on the various pages of notes, reports and inter-view transcripts which had been collated during the Gestapo investigation. So far, they had not found any firm links between Max Bruggink and the other men in his village besides their shared residence.

Klimitz closed the file in front of him and sighed. 'Perhaps we really are on the wrong track here, sir. Every possible connection I have seen can easily and plausibly be explained by something perfectly innocent. To be honest, even if we found the correct link, I'm not sure we would even be aware of it.'

Koestler did not look up from the paper he was read-ing. Almost absent-mindedly he replied, 'No, it's got to be here. It's all too much of a coincidence.' He reached the end of a sentence and glanced up. 'Don't you think?'

Klimitz got to his feet and began to stroll slowly around the room, stretching his legs. 'I thought so - I really did. But there's just nothing. Coincidences do happen - we must entertain that idea if we have no alternate theories.'

Koestler put down his file and removed his spectacles as if he intended to say something profound, but the words seemed to escape him. There was a pause. Finally he said, 'Maybe we are too close to see - wood and trees and all that. We need a break. Perhaps we could go and see another of Helder's extraordinary performances.' He laughed.

Klimitz spun around looking absolutely astonished. 'My God, you're right. You're absolutely right! How could we have missed it? Sorry, how could *I* have missed it?' He practically flew back to the table, leaned across from the other side and roughly grabbed his neat pile of documents. He tossed a couple aside and flung the next one open.

Koestler was intrigued and desperate to find out what his adjutant was talking about. Klimitz began to speak, launching into a commentary of his thoughts as he searched through page after page, evidently looking for something.

'Before Helder started doing all this recruitment stuff for us, he was providing black-market goods, doing favours for us - you know; all that stuff. And what was he getting out of it? You agreed to stop the deportation to Germany for labour of several of his factory staff, yes?'

Koestler nodded.

Klimitz continued, 'We assumed that this was a genuine reason, we thought that this was just Helder being Helder, trying to protect his profits, looking after his lifestyle. But what if there was a more sinister reason for this? What if Helder was just trying to protect these men?'

'What is it you are trying to tell me here, Sebastien? For God's sake, spit it out.'

'This Bruggink fellow - I knew that I had heard his name before when Horvath mentioned it. Then he said he was a local troublemaker, and I thought that I must have heard the name in relation to some incident. But now I remember where I saw it. It was on a document given to us by Helder. Max Bruggink was one of the men that Helder stopped us from deporting.'

Koestler was aghast. 'What? You're telling me....'

'Exactly.' Klimitz pulled a sheet of paper from the file in front of him and placed it down in front of his superior. 'There.'

Koestler put his glasses back on and began to read. At the top of the page there was a handwritten note which read:

For The Attention Of Obersturmbannführer Koestler:

Please Find Below The Particulars Of The Gentleman We Discussed At Our Previous Meeting. I Would Be Much Obliged If You Could Process This Information In Order For Us To Continue His Employment.

Signed, Frank Helder

Below there was a list of various personal details relating to Max Bruggink and some legal information concerning his employment status. At the bottom there was a line on which were the initials 'S.K.' in handwriting Koestler knew to be Klimitz's.

Koestler turned to his adjutant in exasperation. 'Why have I never seen this before now? It is marked for my attention. Why did you not show it to me?'

Klimitz frowned. 'You asked me to take care of the paperwork at the time, sir. I believe you agreed it with Helder verbally over dinner and left it to me to sort out. I may even have attempted to show you but you were satisfied that I had done it correctly.'

'So Frank Helder was employing this Bruggink?'

'He still is, I suppose,' replied Klimitz. 'Now if we can just identify the other men protected from deportation by Helder we might get somewhere.'

Koestler seemed to be having difficulty with the suggestion. 'You're telling me that Frank Helder is involved with the Resistance?' He suddenly broke out in a broad smile and added: 'Well, I'll be damned. I didn't think he had it in him.'

His adjutant looked up from the document he was fingering through and replied, 'He's being playing the whole lot of us, working for them on the one hand and us on the other. He gets comfortable treatment from us and his conscience is eased by thinking that he is being patriotic. It's actually very clever; why would we ever suspect a man who was collaborating with us? '

Klimitz produced six other letters from Helder, all identical bar the date and the details of the individual concerned. Neither Koestler nor Klimitz recognised any of the names but when they listed them and compared them with a register of male residents of Roeden, it emerged that four of them lived there. Two of them had coincidentally been executed as part of the German reprisal but the others were alive and well; a thirty-three-year-old named Kees Van Rijn and another older man by the name of Alberts.

'It is time to test your hypothesis,' Koestler announced. 'We shall have these two men arrested at once, and Helder as well. I certainly think he owes us an explanation at least.'

Klimitz nodded, but a sheepish expression was evident on his face. 'I must apologise for not deducing this sooner. I just never connected it all up.'

'Nonsense,' Koestler insisted, waving his comments aside. 'At the time you saw these documents there was nothing to suggest that Helder was up to anything other than protecting his interests. Let's face it; it is not exactly out of character for the man to attempt to profit from unfortunate events.'

'Even so....'

'There is nothing left to say, Sebastien. You have worked it all out eventually - that is what matters. If I had left it up to Horvath, we would still be nowhere. However there is no time to lose. If we are right and somebody is out to kill me they could strike again at any moment. Now is our chance to stop them.'

Things happened very quickly for Sneijder. The time from his arrival in Holland until the day he had arranged Koestler's accident had seemed to drag forever, but since then it had gone in a flash. His quiet, introspective existence had exploded in a maelstrom of action; his killing of Dimitri, the unstoppable development of his relationship with Frauke, the dinner with Koestler - all these things had happened so rapidly and all totally out of his control.

That week Sneijder's world descended into total anarchy. Having spent an evening in Koestler's company, killing him seemed like a particularly attractive proposition. He really was a pompous, arrogant man, totally lacking in empathy for the people around him. If he were to be eliminated it would be a good thing for all concerned. It would also be morally justified as a response to the heinous German reprisal which had robbed Van Rijn of two members of his family.

On the other hand, to do so would mean the end of the relationship with Frauke, the most special woman he had ever known. This was unthinkable to Sneijder; he had waited so long to experience the feelings he got from being with her and could not entertain the idea of never seeing her again. It also did not sit well with him that he would be helping a traitor like De Beer cover his tracks by killing Koestler.

As had been the case since the day he had watched the Mercedes lying upside down in the stream, he was in limbo, unsure as to the best course of action. He was caught in two minds, the result of which was that he did nothing; he assured Van Rijn that he was working on a plan, but in fact spent most of his time either with Frauke or in his room injecting himself with morphine.

Since the beginning of September it had become substantially more difficult to move freely in the Netherlands. The Germans had dropped back from France and were reinforcing their lines with more and more troops. Arnhem, being near to the German border, was towards the rear but it was still being patrolled by army units. A Resistance meeting at the church had given rise to reports that the Waffen-SS were refitting and recuperating in the area around the city. Somebody had heard a rumour that the British and Americans were planning an operation soon and it was agreed that a message needed to be sent to England warning them about the German regiments; no reply had been forthcoming.

Seeing Frauke had become fraught with danger. They exchanged messages at the dead drop periodically, always arranging to meet in secluded locations in the woods or out in the country. Sneijder never told her about her father's threats. Their feelings for each other were their business and nobody else's; he had no interest in bringing Koestler into it or even mentioning what his opinions were.

The day that Van Rijn was visited by the Gestapo was cool and overcast; it had rained in the morning and there was still moisture in the air, suggesting that another downpour was imminent. Sneijder had ridden his bicycle to Roeden, taking a roundabout route in case he was being followed.

He had a feeling that since their evening together, Koestler might take an interest in him and organise some sort of tail. He had no idea why the German suspected him of having something to hide but he supposed he had gathered a lot of counter-espionage experience in Poland and Holland and knew what to look for.

Sneijder rounded the corner and immediately saw the large black car parked in front of the house. An officer in plain clothes was walking towards the vehicle along the front path. Behind him two uniformed Gestapo men followed holding Van Rijn between them, his hands restrained behind his back. He turned his head towards Sneijder as he cycled by but maintained his sombre expression, giving no hint of recognition. Slowly he was put into the back of the car and disappeared from view.

There was the sound of a commotion as Klara Van Rijn yelled at her husband's captors but it was already behind Sneijder. He continued on his way without as much as a hesitation. It was too dangerous to go back, and was now just a matter of time before he was blown.

He went straight to see Frank Helder. With Van Rijn in Gestapo hands it was likely that Koestler would soon know the identity of his would-be assassin, and would come for him. For God's sake, he had even told him where he was staying; what a fool. Sneijder needed another place to stay quickly while he tried to plan an escape, and had to arrange a way out for the Uhlenbroeks; they were good people and did not deserve the treatment they would get for harbouring an agent.

Sneijder was too late. The small and unpleasant man who worked as Helder's housekeeper opened the door at the flat near the Great Markt and dragged him inside. He was distraught and obviously very afraid.

'He's not here,' the man told him. 'They.....they took him.'

'Who? Who took him?'

'The Gestapo! This morning at six o'clock they just burst in and took him. Oh, it's terrible! Do you think they will torture him?'

Sneijder was struggling to take it all in. For a few seconds he just stood there and tried to process what he was being told.

The small man would not stop. 'I don't believe this..... They said he had done something.... I don't know what. Do you think they will torture him? Do you?'

'I don't know!' Sneijder snapped. 'Will you just shut up and let me think?' He had no time for pleasantries and did not like this man at all. 'They just came this morning? No warning?'

'Of course there was no warning!' the small man wailed. 'You know how the Gestapo work - they just turn up and drag you out of bed if they have to. Oh, what will they do to him?' He was beginning to become hysterical.

'Will you bloody well pull yourself together?' Sneijder yelled, hoping to shock the man out of his panic. 'Now, do you think they will come back?'

The small man had calmed down, but he hesitated.

'It's a simple enough question - do you think they will come back?' Sneijder asked again.

The housekeeper shook his head. 'No, I don't think so. They looked around while they were here.'

'Right, I need to stay here for a couple of days. I'm blown - for all I know the Gestapo are at my place already. Is there somewhere you can go?'

The small man seemed terribly worried at this comment. 'Stay here? I'm afraid..... No, it's simply out of the question. Mr Helder....'

Sneijder finished the sentence for him. '..... is not coming back. When they get someone, well, you know what happens. Besides, it was not a request. Now, is there somewhere you can go?'

The housekeeper shook his head. 'I have nowhere.' He added, 'I'm a Jew. If I run and they catch me...'

'Okay, I get the picture,' Sneijder replied in a resigned tone. 'I'd better warn you - it might get a little danger-ous.'

The small man shrugged and repeated, 'I'm a Jew.'

'Quite. Now I have to go and collect some things - I will be back in an hour. Do not let anybody in. Understand?'

Sneijder cycled quickly to Oosterbeek, avoiding troops and police as much as possible. Whether they were already on to him was anybody's guess but he did not wish to find out. He rode past a line of military vehicles as he made his way along Utrechtseweg but they did not seem to care about one civilian on a bicycle. As a precaution he cycled past the house and looped around the block, but there did not appear to be anything out of the ordinary. He repeated this measure, this time looking out for any sign that the house was under surveillance. He left the bicycle in a narrow alley between two houses, vaulted the fence and approached the Uhlenbroeks' property from the rear.

It was lunchtime and both Edwin Uhlenbroek and his wife were home, in the kitchen, eating. They looked up as Sneijder entered through the back door. They could immediately tell that there was something wrong.

Before they could ask he began to speak. 'Please, you must listen very carefully to what I am about to say. It is very important.'

'Sorry?' Edwin Uhlenbroek began.

'Please, let me explain,' Sneijder pleaded. 'The Germans are on to me. I'm not sure how it has happened but they will be coming here to pick me up, and soon. I must leave, and so must you. It is not safe.'

'Not safe?' Mrs Uhlenbroek asked, and then she frowned and said, 'where will you go?'

'I think it will be safer for all of us if you don't know,' Sneijder replied. 'Now, you must leave. The Germans do not take mercy upon those who hide partisans. They have already arrested Helder and Van Rijn.'

Edwin Uhlenbroek stood up from his chair. 'They arrested Helder? But why? How did they.....'

'They know!' Sneijder exclaimed. 'They know everything, like they always do. I don't know how. I guess when they found the body they worked it all out.' He was beginning to ramble and saying far more than he ought to, but he had to get it out, to somehow clear his mind.

'What body?' Uhlenbroek was astonished. 'What are you talking about? Is this why you are here? To kill people?'

'To kill Koestler!' Sneijder answered. 'I was sent from England to kill SS chief Koestler! The accident he had - it wasn't an accident. I sabotaged his car.'

'Dear God,' Mrs Uhlenbroek mumbled.

'So now you see, don't you? You need to leave.'

Edwin Uhlenbroek shook his head emphatically. 'I'm not going anywhere. This is my home and nobody is going to force me out.'

Sneijder was exasperated. 'They'll kill you. You do realise that, don't you? Or even worse, they will send you to one of their camps. I've been there, and believe me; you don't want to get sent there.'

Mrs Uhlenbroek gasped. 'You've been there? Oh, my dear boy.'

'Please, please don't stay here,' Sneijder pleaded. 'If something happened to you both and it was my fault, I would never forgive myself. Please, you are good people.'

The way Edwin Uhlenbroek spoke the next sentence it was obvious that no amount of persuasion would sway him. He had made up his mind. It was also obvious that his wife would stand by him no matter what; their fates were inextricably intertwined. 'Listen to me, Johannes. When we agreed to take in young men like yourself, we did it because we believed that a fight must be continued against the occupiers. We believed that giving refuge to those who were able to do what we could not was our duty. But we also knew that one day this could happen, that one day we could be in danger; we were prepared for it. So do not blame yourself. However we will not abandon our home.'

Sneijder began to protest, but fell silent when he saw the couple's faces. Finally he told them, 'I'm sorry, I must go. I have to apologise for this, for everything. It is not fair that you have been brought into it.'

Mrs Uhlenbroek replied: 'You have been no trouble. It was our decision to get involved with hiding enemies of the German state; whatever happens is the result of our own actions.'

Sneijder moved forward and embraced her warmly. 'Thank you for your great kindness. I will never forget it.' He added, 'May God be with you.'

He shook Edwin Uhlenbroek's hand and repeated his sentiments, then quickly went upstairs to gather his things. He stuffed the Sten and the Luger into the bottom of his kitbag along with the grenades, piled some clothes on top, and then wrapped a couple of socks around the bottle of morphine and the glass syringe. The rest of his clothing went in at the top.

He inserted a fresh clip into his Walther and tucked it inside his waistband, pulling his shirt down to conceal it. With a brief check of the room completed he promptly left the house without looking back. Things would be very different now.

The Mercedes drove along the tree-lined avenue towards the city centre, Koestler and Klimitz seated in the rear.

They had made the journey from Koestler's home in silence, each of them occupied by his own thoughts. For the Obersturmbannführer, the knowledge that he had allowed himself to be fooled for so long by Frank Helder, a man he had always considered as intellectually inferior, was a bitter pill to swallow. As well as making him feel cheated and used it was also a hammer blow to his professional pride. If it was to come to the attention of the wrong people that he had personally authorised the protection of partisans who had amongst other things killed sixteen Germans and stolen ten thousand marks from the Reich, he was finished.

Klimitz turned to him and opened his mouth to say something, but he evidently thought better of it and remained silent. His gaze returned to the window.

'What is it, Sebastien?' Koestler asked.

Klimitz was deep in thought but was interrupted. He turned to his superior as if he had not heard the words. 'Sorry?'

'You were going to say something.'

The captain shook his head. 'It was nothing really – just a thought that occurred to me.'

'Well?'

'I was just wondering about all these things we are looking into – the attempt on your life, the Resistance cell in Roeden, and the agent from England. Mightn't they *all* be connected?' Klimitz received a look of interest from Koestler so he went on. 'Let's examine each constituent entity one at a time, for the sake of clarity. You were involved in a car accident which you believe to have been an attempt to assassinate you, in which your driver Hugo Petrovsky was killed. The violent slaying of his father Dimitri Petrovsky less than two weeks later is in all likelihood connected.' He raised a finger. 'That is the first link.

'Next, the body of Dimitri Petrovsky was discovered in the village of Roeden, a place with which he had no obvious association. That gives us our second link. The theory that these events are related is strengthened by our third link – the fact that there is clearly an active Resistance cell in Roeden. We know this because Max Bruggink cannot have attacked our convoy alone. So we have a violent argument involving an angry man who just happens to have lost his son, which takes place near the homes of members of the Resistance, the obvious suspects for an attempt on your life.'

Koestler frowned and waved a hand. 'Yes, yes, you've already told me your theory.'

'Yes, sir, but there is a fourth link. From the interrogation of Bruggink we know that the Roeden cell probably provided a reception committee for the agent sent here from England. For all we know they have remained in contact; perhaps the villagers have even harboured him. With these four links we have a chain which connects your accident, Petrovsky, the village of Roeden, the Resistance cell and the agent from England.'

'Yes, I see that.'

'So my point is, we have connected both the accident and the agent with the Resistance, but we have not entertained the possibility that they could be connected to each other. You see what I'm getting at?'

An expression of realisation spread across Koestler's face. 'You're suggesting that this agent is the one who sabotaged my car? That this agent is here to kill me?'

'It does fit, doesn't it, sir? We always believed that nobody would try to kill you because of our reprisals, because anyone tempted to would fear retribution being taken on their family or friends. A foreign agent would not have that fear. Besides, what other reason is there for a British operative to be sent here?'

Something had obviously occurred to Koestler because he slammed a fist against the window and swore. 'The bastard. I knew there was something about him, I just knew it!'

'Who?'

'Now that you've joined it all up it seems so clear,' Koestler declared. 'That's why he acted so strangely around me, why he got close to my daughter. Johannes Voorman, the man I had around to dinner – he is the bloody British agent! He must be.'

Klimitz frowned. 'Are you sure about that, sir? We have no evidence to support such a conclusion. Are you sure your judgement is not being impaired by his relationship with Frauke? I mean, it's a possibility....'

'Then we shall find the evidence,' said Koestler firmly. 'We shall find the evidence and tie up this whole sorry mess once and for all. It ends now.'

Chapter Twenty

The room into which Van Rijn was led was dark and oppressive with hard, grey concrete walls and a cold stone-flagged floor. The only source of illumination was a powerful spot lamp which cast a harsh white light, slicing through the pitch-blackness like a sharpened blade. In the centre of the room there was a rickety wooden chair onto the arms of which were bolted steel wrist restraints. Along one wall there was a metal medical trolley covered with a white sheet, a black leather briefcase on top. An enormous steel bath filled with water stood in the corner, next to a rubber hose which was connected to a rusting tap.

Koestler stood to one side and watched as two burly Gestapo officers dragged Van Rijn over to the chair and sat him down. They clamped down the restraints on his arms to immobilise him, then withdrew from the room, closing the heavy wrought-iron door behind them. A huge blonde haired man, at least six feet four, emerged from the gloom and peeled off his shirt, exposing a toned and muscular physique dotted with tattoos. He had a large swastika emblazoned on his chest with a German phrase written in an unintelligible ancient script beneath it.

Koestler stood in front of Van Rijn and asked gently, 'Do you know why you are here?'

Van Rijn shook his head. 'Absolutely not. I assume you have arrested the wrong man.'

For a moment Koestler managed a smile. 'Of course we have.' His expression changed and he leaned forward until he was just a couple of centimetres away from him. 'You do not want to test my patience,' he hissed venomously.

Van Rijn looked away.

'I will ask you again,' Koestler said. 'Do you know why you are here?'

There was no response from the Dutchman, and Koestler nodded to the blonde haired man, who stepped forward and punched him square in the face. Van Rijn grunted as a small cut opened up above his eye. The man struck him again and there was a crack as his nose took the blow; he cried out in pain.

Koestler pulled the muscular man back and stepped forward. 'Mr Van Rijn, I will tell you something. Lind here is not a very nice man; he likes nothing better than causing pain to others, which I shall let him do unless you become a lot more responsive.'

Van Rijn spat on the floor and replied, 'Then I suggest you let him get on with it.'

'As you wish.' Koestler stepped back and allowed Lind to hit Van Rijn again. He punched him hard, once in the face and then a couple of times in the stomach. Van Rijn bent double and groaned loudly. The huge tattooed man struck him with an elbow which flung his head back against the chair. His nose was broken and blood was running from his nostrils; the cut above his eye was opening up more and more with each strike.

'Perhaps we should try something a little different,' Koestler suggested. 'How about I tell you what I know, and you stop me if I go wrong? Does that seem fair?'

Van Rijn said nothing, just let out a low groan.

'Okay. I know that you are an associate of Max Bruggink's, that you are involved in Resistance activity and that you are both employees of Frank Helder's. You were involved in the attack on a German convoy along with Bruggink, and you also know the identity of the agent from England who has been here since the beginning of July – the agent who has come here to kill me. I want his name.'

'I don't know what you're talking about,' Van Rijn said, gasping as a wave of pain swept over him. 'There is no agent - not as far as I know.'

'Save me this nonsense,' Koestler snapped. 'Bruggink has already confirmed to us that there is an agent from England here in Arnhem. You know who he is. I want you to tell me.'

'You're getting nothing out of me!' Van Rijn cried out. 'Get it? Nothing!'

'Listen, your refusal to give up your comrades is admirable, but ultimately futile. I already know the identity of the person concerned. I simply want you to confirm it. So you see, it is quite pointless for you to withhold this information. Lying to me is also pointless, as I shall know the difference.' There was no response from Van Rijn. With a deep breath, Koestler touched Lind on the shoulder and walked to the wall, turning his back to the other men.

Lind grabbed the back of the chair roughly and dragged it across the room towards the huge steel bath. In a single movement he thrust it to one side and plunged Van Rijn into the water. His hands still fastened to the chair, the Dutchman was unable to move; he began to thrash around violently, his head and shoulders beneath the surface. He let out a panicked cry which was muffled by the water. After about twenty seconds, Lind pulled the chair upright again.

Van Rijn gasped for air, his mouth wide open like a goldfish. He was obviously terribly frightened and began to hyperventilate. His head swung from side to side uncontrollably and between breaths he continued to let out anguished cries.

Koestler went over and shouted right into Van Rijn's face: 'For God's sake, man, just tell me what I want to know!'

Van Rijn was having difficulty breathing, never mind trying to speak. He made his best attempt, 'I..... I can't..... I'm not, I'm not.....'

'Tell me and I will make it stop,' Koestler ordered him. 'It's the only way.'

'Never! I won't....'

'Very well,' Koestler said regretfully. 'Herr Lind?'

The big German flipped the chair over again and once more Van Rijn went head first into the water. This time Lind grabbed the back of Van Rijn's neck and forced him under, trying hard to fight his fierce resistance. Water splashed up over the side of the bath as Van Rijn wriggled around desperately. Lind kept him under for what seemed like minutes, only pulling him out when his movement began to slow.

He coughed hard for ten seconds or so, spitting out large amounts of water from his lungs, then cried out and began to shake. 'Stop it! Please, you bastards, stop it!'

'You know what to do to make it stop.'

'But I don't know anything!' There were tears streaming down Van Rijn's cheeks now and his chin rested on his chest. Lind slapped him hard around the face in an attempt to calm him down.

Koestler pulled the big blond-haired brute away and placed another chair directly in front of Van Rijn. He sat down opposite his suspect and spoke to him in a quiet and gentle tone. 'Listen to me, and listen well. Some of these Gestapo folk have methods which you and I can barely imagine. Eventually you will tell me what I want to know. Save yourself the punishment. Now, there is an agent from England, yes?'

Van Rijn hesitated for a moment but then nodded.

'And his name?'

The Dutchman took a deep breath, smiled bitterly and answered, 'You will never hear it from me.'

Without a word but with an angry scowl Koestler stood up and kicked the chair away. He spun on his heel and went to the door, pulled it open and left the room. Behind him Lind dragged the rubber hose over, stuffed the end into Van Rijn's mouth and turned the tap. As Koestler made his way along the darkened corridor towards the room where they were holding Helder, he could hear the agonised screams being cut short as the suspect began to choke. It made him shudder.

Frank Helder was being held in a room much different to the one in which Koestler had spoken to Van Rijn. It was light and airy, with pleasantly coloured walls and antique furniture. The old man was still dressed immaculately in a two-piece suit and silk waistcoat and puffed on an elegant pipe as he waited to be interviewed. He tapped his fingers slowly on the polished mahogany table which reflected the bright fluorescent strip light above.

He checked the time on his pocket watch and called out to the single guard who stood beside the door, 'How long is this going to take? Is somebody coming to speak to me?'

There was no answer from the guard. At precisely that moment the door swung open and Koestler marched in; he told the soldier to wait outside and went over to the table. With a smile that swiftly disappeared he sat down opposite Helder.

'Well, well, Mr Helder. We did not expect to meet each other in such circumstances, I think.'

'No,' Helder answered abruptly. 'Would you like to tell me what I'm doing here? This is totally unacceptable, and not at all in our arrangement.'

'I think you should be telling me,' Koestler said. 'I think you should be telling me everything.'

'What the hell are you talking about?' Helder scoffed. 'Stop wasting my time.'

Koestler slammed his fist down on the table and jabbed a finger into Helder's face, yelling angrily, 'It is you who has been wasting *my* time! You have been playing everybody, including your own people! All those favours you were allegedly doing for me and all the time you were working with the bloody Resistance!'

'Pardon?' The old man seemed genuinely stunned.

'Do not even try to deny it. Bruggink, Van Rijn, Alberts, Lerstapper - these are all men that you stopped us from deporting and all are involved in Resistance activities. This is not a coincidence. You have tricked and deceived me for too long. It will not happen again.'

'This is absolutely ridiculous, Koestler,' Helder replied strongly. 'I have done nothing of the sort. Who has been feeding you this nonsense?'

Koestler rose from his chair and went over to the door. He opened it and put his head out, calling out into the corridor. Seconds later it opened wider and Klimitz came in with a small batch of files. The two Germans came back over and sat down in front of Helder.

'Right, if you don't believe that we know, I will present you with the evidence,' Koestler declared. 'Herr Klimitz here has been busy collating everything.'

Koestler and his adjutant laid out the sheets of paper before Helder; first the six letters signed by him which had stopped the men from being deported, then the testimony of the villager who had given up Bruggink, then a transcript of Bruggink's own interrogations. This was more or less a true record of everything he had said and confessed to, but near the end Klimitz had cleverly changed the wording in such a way as to suggest that Bruggink had implicated Helder.

'That is your evidence?' asked Helder. 'All he has said is that I saved him from deportation, which is true; I needed him in my factory, just like I told you. He has not said anywhere that I knew what he was up to.'

'Because he doesn't want to give you up!' Koestler insisted. 'That much is obvious, but still, read his words - 'Mr Helder kept us in the Netherlands so we could carry out subversive operations against German forces.' That seems pretty clear to me.'

Helder was not deterred. 'Look, it's a transcript - you could easily have twisted his words or misrepresented him. If you put a comma in there it's totally different. 'Mr Helder kept us in the Netherlands, so we could carry out subversive operations against German forces.' If you put it that way, what he is saying is that my actions gave them the *opportunity* to do such things, not necessarily that those were my motives.'

Koestler laughed. 'Are you serious? You have been protecting these people for years, taking advantage of my goodwill. Besides, we do not just have Bruggink's word for it - Van Rijn has also been most helpful. Show him the transcript, Sebastien.'

Koestler and Klimitz had concocted a false interrogation record before the lieutenant-colonel had even spoken to Van Rijn, to use on Helder if the Resistance man did not reveal anything. In it Van Rijn admitted to having been protected by Helder and insisted that the old man knew all about the activities of his employees. Van Rijn also accepted responsibility with Bruggink for the convoy attack.

'Do you still deny it?' Koestler asked.

'This is all a set-up,' Helder roared. 'You have made it all up.'

Koestler got to his feet and stood over the old man. 'Enough! I have had enough of your lies! How dare you lie to me? After all I have done for you, all the strings I have pulled, and still you slap me in the face! We have got you, and I will personally see that you are punished.'

Helder snapped. 'I will speak to you in any way I like,' he growled furiously. 'You think you are so special, such an important man, but you are just an impotent bully, a useless alcoholic has-been. Even your own superiors can't wait to get rid of you. The military want you out of the way, don't they?'

Koestler ignored the jibe and continued to pressure the old man. 'You know that what I am saying is true. Now you can either admit to it, or every collaborative act you have ever done will be leaked to those who will not forgive them. Your life would not be worth living.'

'You are going to kill me anyway – why should I tell you anything?'

'How do you think people will treat your family once they know that you are a damned traitor?' Koestler said. 'Do you think they will be kind or respectful? No - your wife and your sons will be pariahs in their own country. When it emerges that they are living off the proceeds of your work for us, the Netherlands will become a very dangerous place for them.'

Helder breathed deeply and replied: 'You are absolutely right. Some of the things I have done over the years have been inexcusable, and I deserve everything I will get. But that is precisely why I will never tell you anything you want to know. If I am to die I will die a patriot, not a traitor - so do whatever it is you want to do.'

'That is not a challenge you want to put to me, Mr Helder, so I will give you one chance to answer. We know there is an agent from England here in Arnhem - Bruggink confirmed this to us. We also know that he has come here to kill me, and I want his name.'

'I don't know.'

'I do not believe you. What is his name?'

'I don't know.'

Koestler replied, 'Very well, but I am sorry that it has come to this. I did not wish for this.'

When Koestler went back into the dark room a little later, Van Rijn had gone and had been replaced in the wooden chair by Helder. He was not in a good way after twenty minutes of beating from Lind; blood poured from a wound on his head, staining his pure white hair and there were cuts to his eyes and lips. His tailored suit jacket had been roughly slashed off with a knife and his shirt and waistcoat were ripped. The old man was slumped forward and his head lolled to one side; he was showing signs of a concussion.

Koestler crouched down in front of him. 'You don't want this to continue, surely? Just tell me the truth - I know everything already, there is really no point in denying it.'

Helder groaned. 'I won't...... I won't tell you.....'

'Yes you will,' Koestler replied harshly. 'It is just a question of when. Now tell me who is trying to kill me. Who arranged my accident?'

Helder's speech was slurred. 'I don't know, honestly.'

Lind tilted the chair over and plunged Helder under the water in the steel bath. The old man opened his mouth to shout something and immediately began to choke as the water poured down his throat. He shook his head around viciously, swinging his legs in a desperate panic. Eventually the big blond-haired German pulled him out of the bath.

Helder coughed several times, and cried, 'All right! All right! I'll tell you!'

'Well get on with it then!' Koestler retorted.

'You're right, you're right about all the men!' Helder answered. 'I stopped them from getting deported to Germany so that they could fight you lot. I admit it. I've been leading you on all the time.'

'Who sabotaged my car?'

'I don't know, you must believe me,' Helder pleaded. 'I don't know anything about that.'

'What about the agent? I know you know who that is. Give me his name.'

'I can't.... I can't tell you.'

Lind punched him hard in the face. His head snapped back with the force of the blow. The blond man grabbed the side of the chair and lifted it, this time putting the whole thing upside down in the bath. With Helder face down in the water, the chair on top of him, Lind walked away. The old man's muffled screams filled the air as he started to drown and water shot up out of the bath, soaking the floor around it. Lind left him for almost a minute before dragging him out. Helder began to cough violently, ejecting large amounts of water from his nose and mouth. He was in a terrible panic, and Koestler knew that he would tell him what he wanted to know.

'Come on, Frank!' Koestler pressed. 'I already know who the agent is. All I need is for you to confirm it. Just say the name and it's all over.'

'Okay, okay. Voorman, that's his name! You want to know? Johannes Voorman, all right!' Helder was terrified, and tears were running down his cheeks.

'Voorman? Are you sure, one hundred per cent sure?'

'Of course I am bloody sure!' Helder exclaimed. 'Johannes Voorman! He is staying.....'

'At the home of the Oosterbeek stationmaster, I know,' Koestler finished.

'Right, now you know, please stop all this!'

'And it was Voorman that tried to kill me?' the Obersturmbannführer asked forcefully.

Helder professed no knowledge. Lind hit him square in the stomach; he leaned forward, bending over double and groaning. Suddenly he shot back in the chair and sat bolt upright. His eyes widened, almost surprised, and he began gasping for breath. He shook dramatically; all of a sudden his eyes rolled back in his head and he lurched to one side.

Lind turned and looked at Koestler for guidance.

'Bloody hell, Lind, he's having a heart attack! I told you to be careful!'

The big German placed a hand on Helder's chest, glanced at Koestler and nodded. As the old man panted and gasped, his face began to drain; he foamed at the mouth, then seconds later passed out. Koestler felt for a pulse. There was none.

'Clear this up,' Koestler ordered, and left the room.

Klimitz raised an eyebrow when his superior told him what Helder had said. 'Johannes Voorman? He confirmed it?'

Koestler grimaced. 'He confirmed that Voorman is the agent from England, but he claimed to know nothing about any attempt to kill me. To be honest, I'm inclined to believe him – by the end of the interrogation he was terrified. He'd have told me if he knew. Lind's techniques are very persuasive.'

'So you were right,' Klimitz remarked. 'Have you sent Horvath to arrest this Voorman?' Klimitz asked.

'Certainly not. If this were just another agent, maybe, but not this one - the moment he involved my daughter he made this personal. I am going to get him myself.'

'Have Van Rijn or Alberts given you anything?'

Koestler shook his head. 'Alberts squealed but he doesn't know a thing, I'm convinced of that. Van Rijn definitely does know more but so far he hasn't cracked. I'm sure he knows about the attempt to kill me. I just need to get it out of him.'

'Do you think he'll talk?'

Koestler shrugged. 'I guess we'll find out. So far I've kept quiet about what we know – I didn't want to pre-empt any of them. I wanted to hear Voorman's name from them. Now I've heard it from Helder we can be a little less subtle.'

Van Rijn looked in horror as the Gestapo officer took a pair of pliers and a large meat cleaver out of the briefcase and laid them out on the medical trolley. The huge blond-haired Lind had left earlier and been replaced by a fat man with thick dark-rimmed spectacles who was dressed in a long white coat. He looked like a librarian or a postal clerk or some other low-level worker and spoke like somebody well above their station, in a squeaky effeminate voice.

'Before we begin,' he started, 'I must tell you that I have done this many times before. I know how to remove fingers in a way which reduces blood loss, so you will remain conscious for the duration of your,' - he laughed - 'experience.'

Van Rijn did not know how to react. The sight of the shiny instruments on the trolley and the words coming out of the man's mouth were terrifying, but the ridicu-lous voice made him want to burst out laughing. He managed a masochistic smile. 'Really?'

The fat man shrugged his shoulders and replied, 'Everyone needs a hobby. We Germans even have a word for this sort of thing – *Schadenfreude*. It means deriving joy from the misfortunes of others.'

Suddenly the door flew open, crashing off the wall behind it. Koestler, who had been watching from outside the room, walked in fast in something of a rage and immediately launched into a violent tirade.

'Johannes Voorman, is it not? Is that not the agent from England? The man you would not give up? See - we know everything, there is no point in trying to lie to us.'

Van Rijn cursed in frustration.

'Stop me if I go wrong. Voorman was sent from England to kill me, that was his mission - I assume Bruggink and yourself were part of the reception committee for him, and you ran into a German patrol that night. Then there was the attack on the convoy; presumably you were involved in that too, along with Bruggink. Voorman too? Well, perhaps.'

Van Rijn did not reply.

Koestler continued, 'Fourteen German soldiers were killed, but you know that, because you were there. Voorman became very friendly with my daughter so he could get to me, didn't he?'

Van Rijn smiled. 'That is a lot of rubbish.'

'Voorman then planned and organised an accident for me, with the help of my driver, Hugo Petrovsky. He was never told that he would have to die though - how could he be told? He would have compromised the whole operation. That was why Dimitri Petrovsky came to your village; he came to confront his son's killers, but he ended up dead himself. Voorman's work, I suppose. What a dreadful irony - with all the dead bodies you people have left in your wake, one of them leads us straight to the whole lot of you.'

'You tell a terrific story, but alas, it is just a story,' Van Rijn replied. 'Not a word of it is true.'

'That's not what Frank Helder tells me.' Koestler gave a nod. Without a word the fat man walked to the table and picked up the cleaver, then returned to stand beside Van Rijn. 'Tell me that it is true, now,' said Koestler firmly.

Van Rijn shook his head. The fat man took hold of his little finger on his left hand, swung the cleaver without hesitation and chopped it clean off his hand at the knuckle. Blood spurted out and Van Rijn screamed in agony. 'Aaaaah! You bastard! You swine, oh, God!'

'I know everything, you fool, just admit to it. This is not necessary.'

'Well don't bloody do it then!' Van Rijn cried. 'Just stop him!'

'Tell me what I need to know and it's over,' Koestler ordered him.

Van Rijn bit his lip and shook his head. The fat Gestapo agent raised the cleaver above his head, lining it up with Van Rijn's next finger. As he began to bring it down, the Dutchman yelled. 'All right! Okay, I'll tell you, I will tell you. Just, please, don't do it anymore. Please.'

Koestler smiled and replied, 'I'm listening.'

Chapter Twenty-one

The morning of the seventeenth of September was bright with light winds and very quiet in the centre of Arnhem until the bells began ringing out in the tall tower of the Eusebiuskerk. There were few people around in the street below when Sneijder peered out of the attic window. Just before nine o'clock the peace was disturbed by the wail of an air raid siren; an unusual moment for such an occurrence. Bombing raids were almost always carried out at night, particularly with the prevalence of anti-aircraft defences in the Netherlands. Sneijder heard the sound of distant planes, then the dull thuds and rumbles as bombs exploded somewhere not too far away. They got louder and louder as they moved nearer, then stopped. A minute later there was an almighty boom in the vicinity of the city centre and black smoke began to rise above the rooftops. The noise of the aircraft engines receded.

Sneijder dressed and went downstairs where he found Helder's housekeeper Bassen having breakfast and reading a newspaper.

'I have to go out for a few hours,' he informed him simply.

Bassen replied, 'I should be very careful if I were you – there are troops all over the place. You'll be lucky to get anywhere.'

'It's something I need to do. I won't be long.'

Since Van Rijn and Helder had been arrested Sneijder had been keeping his head down, staying upstairs in the attic room. His fear of a Gestapo raid on the house was very real and so he had been attempting to stay out of sight as much as possible. He needed to keep his wits about him and had been trying to keep off the morphine; the resulting withdrawal symptoms made him nervous and irritable, but he decided this would be preferable to feeling drowsy if he had to make a run for it.

It had been over a week since he had seen Frauke and he was beginning to think that she had found out the truth about him. It seemed inevitable now that Koestler would discover his true identity and hence inevitable also that Frauke would find out too, but at the back of his mind there still lay a tiny illogical hope that he could hold on to the woman he loved. This hope had been strengthened the day before when he had found a message from her at the dead drop asking him to meet her. There was always the possibility that any meeting could be a trap but he had to see her, to feel her touch. He needed her.

The location where they were to meet was a farm about eight kilometres to the north-west of the city which had been abandoned since the owner was arrested for selling fuel on the black market. They had discovered it by chance some weeks earlier when looking for a quiet spot to be together and had been back more than once since.

Sneijder left the house and picked up his bicycle from the alley behind. He cycled quickly north up Bakkerstraat, past the Korenmarkt and across the railway line before turning west, hoping to get out of Arnhem without coming upon a German patrol. Happily he was able to do so and rapidly make his way through the countryside towards the farm.

It was a little before twelve noon when he arrived at the gate, dismounted and put the bike out of sight behind a metre-high hedgerow. He climbed over the fence and headed for the barn, a three-storey nineteenth-century wooden structure which had well stood the test of time. The double-barred door was padlocked up but there was enough slack on the chain to enable Sneijder to pull it open a fraction and squeeze through. Inside it was a touch gloomy, the only natural light coming in from a partially-open skylight high up in the building. The floor was covered in thick hay and there were huge bales at one end of the long barn; a ladder around five metres in length was positioned so as to give access to the second level through a square hatch. Sneijder walked to the centre of the room and looked around. There was no sign of Frauke yet. He waited a few moments for his eyes to adjust to the lack of light and then went around the barn once more. Perhaps she was yet to arrive.

Suddenly there was a voice behind him and a familiar figure stepped out from the shadow of the bales of hay. 'Looking for me, Johannes?'

Sneijder turned and smiled at her, replying warmly: 'Frauke, darling, how long have......'

He stopped dead in his tracks when he saw the hard look on her face, then he glanced down a little. In her right hand, and pointed at him, she had a Luger pistol.

'Frauke?' he said in astonishment.

'Don't move,' she ordered him as she advanced into the room.

'Is this some sort of joke?' Sneijder asked. Of course it was no joke; she knew.

'Does it look like I'm laughing?' she snapped. 'I told you not to move,' she added as he turned to face her.

'Okay, okay,' he replied, raising his hands. 'I'm still. Now do you mind telling me what the hell's going on?' It was all far from convincing, and he knew it.

'You and I are going to have a little chat, Johannes,' Frauke told him. 'In fact, is that even your real name?'

He wanted to act surprised, shocked even, but the walls were closing in fast. It was over for certain now; to draw it out would benefit no-one. He said nothing.

She stood in front of him, just inches away, and touched him with her free hand. This time though it was not in a romantic way, there was no chemistry at work; she patted him down and came away with the Walther he had tucked in his waistband. She held it up in front of him, and then dropped it into her pocket.

In an instant her angry expression became wistful and she exclaimed, 'Oh, Johannes, how could you? How could you do this to me?'

He frowned and answered, 'I never meant for this to happen, I didn't plan on getting you involved.'

'But you did, didn't you?' she said. 'For God's sake, I thought you loved me.'

'I did. I do. Please, you must believe me.'

'How can I possibly do that?' she asked. 'You've been telling me lies from the start. I thought you were some-one in trouble, someone I could help, and now it turns out you are a bloody secret agent here to kill my father!'

'I never lied,' he replied. 'Everything I told you about me was true; about Amsterdam, about my family, every-thing.'

'About your aunt in Arnhem? About doing labour in Germany?'

Sneijder shook his head sheepishly. 'No, but....'

'Do you even know what the real truth is, Johannes?' Frauke raised her voice again. Sneijder took a step towards her; she stepped back and raised the gun. 'Stay where you are.'

'Listen to me,' he began.

'Tell me it's not true,' she said, interrupting him.

'Sorry?'

'Tell me it's not true,' she repeated, 'all of this.....madness. Tell me it's just my father's paranoid delusions again. Tell me that.'

Sneijder's words were deeply impassioned and sorrowful. 'I can't. I wish I could but....'

'Tell me it's not true!' she cried. 'Please, Johannes, please!' Hysteria was starting to take hold of her and she was shaking, tears streaming from her eyes.

'What do you want? More lies?'

Frauke fired millimetres wide of his head. The bullet embedded itself in a wooden pillar behind him. The sound of the gunshot so close to Sneijder's right ear deafened him for a second.

'I want you to tell me it's not true!' she screamed at him, her eyes wide in unmitigated fury. 'I want to know that I didn't fall in love with a lie, that I didn't give my soul and my body to a murderer!'

'I can't, okay?' Sneijder yelled in return. 'I can't tell you that – I won't. I'm sorry.'

'But you made love to me, right here in this very room! Did it mean nothing to you? Was it just a bit of fun to you, a pleasurable experience? Was that all?'

'Of course not,' he tried to answer.

'The day of my father's accident, when I came around to your house for comfort, we slept together then as well! And it was you that nearly killed him! Really, how could you be so cruel?'

'Because I wanted you so badly!' Sneijder exclaimed. 'I saw you that first time and you were so beautiful, I just had to have you. There was nothing I could do, even though I knew it was wrong.'

'And you don't think killing people is wrong?' she questioned.

'Of course I do!' he answered in frustration. 'Do you really think I *like* all this? I hate it more than you can possibly imagine. I see all their faces, all the time – every man I have ever killed is etched into my mind, burned through my brain. I despise everything about taking a life. But this is a war – I am serving my country.'

Frauke raised the gun. 'Perhaps it is time I served mine.'

'What, you are going to shoot me? Listen, it doesn't have to be this way. It doesn't have to end between us. I love you.'

Tears poured down her cheeks. 'And I love you, Johannes. But it's too late to go back. That's the thing about life, you see, sometimes something happens and nothing can ever be quite the same again.' She seemed to be in another place for a second but then she snapped out of it. 'Right, over there, against the post, Mr.....'

'Sneijder. Johannes Sneijder.'

'Sneijder. Put your back against there, and your arms around behind the post.' She produced a short length of rope from the pocket of her jacket and proceeded to bind his wrists together behind his back, with the wooden pillar in the middle.

'What now?' Sneijder asked.

'Now I go home and tell my father where you are. You will be arrested.'

'Frauke, please! They'll kill me!'

She stepped forward and kissed him on the lips firmly, wrapping her arms around him in a passionate embrace. Eventually she broke off. 'Goodbye, Johannes, my love.' Then she was gone.

Klimitz put down the telephone in the hall of Koestler's house and walked through to the sitting room. His superior was sitting in an armchair beside the front window looking out, a large glass of whisky on the table next to him.

'That was Horvath, sir,' Klimitz told him. 'There's no sign of Voorman anywhere – not at the stationmaster's house, not at any of the Underground safe houses we are aware of. He seems to have disappeared.'

Koestler cursed gently to himself. 'Of course. This is what these men are trained to do – to vanish, to be like ghosts, then to strike hard. It is imperative that we find him before he does any more damage.'

'He evidently knows we are on to him, which is why he has gone underground. Surely he is long gone by now.'

'I would not be too sure of that,' Koestler replied. 'Something tells me that this man will not leave without completing his task. I think we have not heard the last of him.'

'Perhaps I should increase the guard detail around the house, sir,' Klimitz suggested.

Koestler nodded. 'Yes, that would be wise. On a different note, has anybody seen my daughter? Unfortunately, the revelations about her friend Voorman were not warmly received.'

'I'm afraid not, sir.'

Koestler sighed. 'Remind me, Sebastien, how old are your daughters?'

'Twelve and nine, sir.'

'Whenever it is you get home, enjoy them before they reach a more troublesome age. Right, that will be all.'

Sneijder pulled at the restraints around his wrists but the rope was thick and tied tight. He kicked his right foot backwards against the pillar but as he expected it was solid, with no give in it whatsoever. Throwing his entire weight forwards he attempted to snap the rope against the wooden post. Of course this was ridiculous; all he succeeded in doing was wrenching his shoulder painfully. Sneijder cried out and then stopped to think.

There would not be much time before the Gestapo or the SS arrived to arrest him, and he was not expecting to be treated well. All German military and police forces were under direct orders from Hitler to shoot spies on the spot; there were to be no prisoners and no trials. This seemed like the best Sneijder could hope for given his attempt on the life of a senior German officer - it was more likely that Koestler would have him tortured before killing him, if only just for revenge. He had been tortured before, when he was captured by the Abwehr, and it had been a horrifying experience.

It really did not bear thinking about. He simply had to escape, and quickly. Perhaps the wooden pillar would be weaker at the ends; Sneijder crouched down slowly, sliding the rope down to the floor. He yanked his arms forward hard, feeling his shoulder pull again but he did not stop. Using all his weight he shook the pillar, praying that either the wood or the rope would give way. They did not. He stood up straight again in resignation.

'Come on, man, think!' he pleaded with himself.

Looking desperately around the barn for inspiration, for anything, Sneijder realised that this was it; Frauke had left him for dead. In an ironic way he deserved nothing better given the way he had treated her, and it was fitting that it was her who had stopped him. For the next couple of minutes he stood there in acceptance of the situation. He was captured, and there was absolutely nothing he could do about it.

Finally Sneijder's survival instinct kicked in. This was wrong - he would not die here, not like this, not tied to a post like a stray dog. Certainly not without fighting for every moment he had. Once more he pulled the rope tight against the pillar, and then dropped to the floor quickly, hoping to chafe the fibres a little. A sharp pain shot up his arm as a pointed splinter of wood punctured the skin above his wrist and he swore. It was a nasty piercing sensation and for the briefest of seconds he feared that it had cut a blood vessel, but he could feel no liquid running through his hands. Wincing for a moment, Sneijder suddenly realised that it could be the opening he was praying for. If it could slice through his skin with such ease, maybe it could do some damage to the ropes. It was all he had.

Sneijder adjusted his body carefully so as to position the jagged piece of wood between his wrists, then lowered the ropes onto the point. It was bound to break off easily from the pillar, he knew that, but as he began to slide the rope up and down it surprisingly held. After managing to push the splinter through the centre of the knot, now all Sneijder required was patience and a large degree of luck. For the next five minutes or so he rubbed the rope against the wood, concentrating as hard as he could to ensure that it did not slip. He obviously succeeded in cutting away a few fibres from the edge of the rope because he felt it move a little, then all of a sudden the knot came apart and his wrists came free.

Sneijder sighed in relief; Frauke had evidently tied a bad knot. It was an enormous reprieve, and he was not going to let it go to waste. Without a moment's hesitation he headed for the door; it did not budge when he attempted to open it, as Frauke had obviously pinned it shut from the outside, but with a hard shoulder charge it shifted and he went outside.

The first thing Sneijder noticed was the noise. The idyllic silence of the countryside which he had enjoyed on the way into the barn had gone; now the air was filled with the drone of aircraft engines - lots of them. He looked up and was absolutely astonished by the sight which greeted him. Less then five thousand feet up and within three or four kilometres, the sky was filled, literally filled, with aeroplanes. All displayed the markings of the Royal Air Force. Sneijder was confused; all of the planes appeared to be C-47 Dakotas - transport planes, not bombers. What was happening here? Before he could think through his own question, dark objects began to fall from the aircraft, and then suddenly there were parachutes. As Sneijder looked closer he realised that the objects were in fact men - paratroopers.

By the time he had climbed back over the fence surrounding the farm and had fetched the bicycle from its hiding place, there was a sea of parachutes below the planes. They vanished from view behind the tall pine trees as they neared the ground. From the distance and the direction Sneijder guessed that the landing zone was probably around Wolfheze, a small village around twelve kilometres from Arnhem. He thought through the situation as he cycled away furiously, repeatedly checking over his shoulder to make sure he wasn't seeing things. There was bound to be an Allied operation soon given all the rumours, but a full-scale airborne landing? It seemed unlikely, it had to be a small force here for a specific purpose; on the other hand there certainly were a lot of them.

Somewhat paradoxically, it was this uncertainty about what might happen next that made Sneijder certain about what he would do. If there was to be a major battle in the area he had to get out quickly, and in that moment he had to decide whether he would kill Koestler or leave him and make an escape. There would be no second chances, no changing of his mind. It was suddenly very clear to him; assassinating Koestler was his mission and he was going to complete it. Despite his moral concerns and his outrage at being manipulated by De Beer, he owed it to Wilkinson, he owed it to Van Rijn and he owed it to his country to kill the German official.

Besides, it was now an inescapable fact; he had lost Frauke and he could never get her back, no matter what. One could hardly blame her – he had deceived her, used her even, and when it came down to it Albrecht Koestler was still her father whatever his failings. There was nothing quite like your own flesh and blood, and it was an individual's duty to defend it. However, Sneijder had his own duty to consider now.

He headed back to Frank Helder's flat in Arnhem to get the rifle which he had hidden away in the attic, with no real idea of how he would get through any road-blocks once he had the weapon. A full-size rifle was not the sort of thing one could easily conceal when riding a bicycle. The Germans would see right through the obvious disguises – a fishing rod, a musical instrument – but what else was there? Oh, to hell with it, what did he have to lose? He would just have to hope he got lucky. He abandoned the bicycle outside the front door and barged in, climbing the stairs to the sitting room. Bassen was reading a book.

'They are here!' Sneijder said breathlessly. 'Twelve........twelve kilometres.'

'Who is here?'

'The British, the bloody British!' Sneijder bent double, panting furiously, his hands on his knees. 'Falling out of the sky, near Wolfheze I think.'

Bassen was shocked. 'What? Paratroopers? What is there in Wolfheze?'

'Nothing, nothing at all – they must be coming here.'

'Why?'

'I don't know!' Sneijder exclaimed. 'The bridge, Model, because it's near Germany - who can say?' He turned and headed for the stairs.

'Where are you going?'

'To do something I should have done a long time ago.'

Sneijder went up to the attic at the top of the building. At one end there was a plasterboard wall beyond which was the brick external wall. There was a hole near the skirting board which he had cut using a knife; in front of it, covering it from view was an old and battered chest of drawers which should have been discarded years ago. Sneijder pulled the furniture aside, crouched down and put his arm through the hole, then reached up and felt around. Eventually his hand came upon the long rifle wrapped in sackcloth and he gently pulled it out of its hiding place. He located the ammunition and turned to leave but paused, deciding to be cautious. If he were to be caught with the rifle he would need to take urgent and direct action. He took the Luger and a grenade from his kitbag and returned downstairs.

Sneijder tied the rifle onto the frame of the bicycle, on the crossbar below the saddle, hoping that it would not attract attention at first glance. He tucked the Luger into the waistband at the back of his trousers and pushed the solitary grenade into a pocket. It was madness of course, to go for Koestler now when the man was out to arrest him, to head straight for the lion's den, but it was a peculiar sort of relief to be so certain about something. For weeks and weeks his mind had been in turmoil, struggling with the concepts of right and wrong, of death and murder and killing and guilt. Now he was resolved to doing what he simply had to do, however he had to do it.

Sneijder headed north at speed, leaving the city behind and moving out into the wooded countryside. It was uphill all the way and required all his strength and stamina to keep going, but he was an extremely fit young man and his mind was totally focused on the job in hand. Some time into his journey he came around a bend and was confronted with a sight that made his heart sink; at the side of the road were parked a black Mercedes and a troop truck, both with SS registration plates, and there were two uniformed policemen blocking the road. It was too late to turn around but they were bound to see the rifle and he would be finished. He brushed his hand gently against the grenade in his pocket to remind himself it was still there.

'Can I see your identity papers please?' one of the policemen asked as Sneijder came to a halt in front of him.

Sneijder responded immediately, rummaging in his pockets for the relevant documents. This was delicate; assumedly Koestler had issued orders for his arrest, and these men would act as soon as they saw his identity card. He passed the man a couple of pieces of paper, then dismounted his bike and crouched to tie a shoelace.

The policeman glanced at them and replied, 'This is a ration book and an exemption from work certificate. I asked for your identity papers.' At exactly the same moment he spotted the long item wrapped in sackcloth which was attached to the bicycle. He raised his MP40. 'Wait. Show me that. Show me that now.'

Sneijder reached into his pocket and gripped the metal ring which was connected to the fuse pin of the grenade. As he stood the grenade came free, then the two pieces separated and the pin came out. Sneijder allowed the weapon to drop to the road and then kicked it. He watched as it rolled and spun away and settled underneath the Mercedes. At the same time he laughed out loud and answered the question with, 'What? You want to see that? Excuse me just one second.....'

He dropped to one knee again. A mere quarter of a second later, the grenade went off under the car. Sneijder was hit by the blast and knocked flat against the road; behind him the two German policemen were thrown back off their feet, one of them ending up several metres away. The Mercedes was wrecked by the explosion; the windows shattered and a huge dent was put in the bodywork. When Sneijder glanced up the vehicle was in flames. He leapt to his feet, yanked the bicycle up off the ground and began to run with it, climbing aboard after getting up a little speed. One of the policemen shouted for him to stop and then presumably opened fire; there were gunshots but he was already away.

Sneijder left the road about a kilometre before the dirt track which led to the Koestler house and cycled through the woods. At this point the trees were some distance from one another and it was easy to navigate a path. The ground was dry and hard, not muddy at all and the bicycle went over it with no problem. Looking ahead he could see nobody. For a moment he thought that Koestler was no longer there, but then he caught sight of a guard in Waffen-SS uniform standing about one hundred metres from the house. Straight away he stopped and dismounted; riding the bicycle created far too much noise, particularly here where the roots of the trees penetrated from below the ground. He took the rifle off the bike and slung it over his shoulder, made sure he had the ammunition and approached the house.

Sneijder circled the property a little, putting some distance and some cover between him and the guard. There were a couple of other men standing at the perimeter, just outside the back fence surrounding the garden, but with the rifle he would not need to get so close. Sneijder moved around towards the side of the house, hoping to find a convenient angle for a shot. However the tall trees and obstructive fences made things extremely difficult. He continued around the house towards the front, all the while glancing up to see if he was clear of the fence. Sneijder kept himself hidden amongst the trees, treading silently to avoid detection. To his alarm, as he moved along there was a sudden gust of wind and a couple of pine cones dropped to the ground noisily. He threw himself down and froze still. For about a minute Sneijder did not dare to move a muscle; he could almost feel the sentry's gaze penetrating the forest. When he was finally satisfied that he was still safe Sneijder rose to his knees, and with a grin found himself with an unobstructed view of four windows and the front drive of the house. Now he would just have to wait.

'You are absolutely sure?'

'Of course I am sure!' she replied, tears running down her cheeks from red eyes. 'I've just seen him.'

'What?' Koestler was incredulous. 'After everything I have told you about him? He tried to kill me! Bloody hell, what more reason do you want not to see him?'

'I'm sorry, father!' Frauke wailed. 'I didn't want to believe it - I love him. I thought somehow....., somehow.... Well, I don't know what I thought. I thought I could get an explanation from him.'

'And?'

She shook her head in dismay. 'I tied him up and left him there. You can go and get him.'

Her father was not in the mood to give her sympathy. 'You are a silly little girl, Frauke,' he said cruelly, 'a child. I am very disappointed in you. I just hope you have learned from your mistake and will listen to me in future.'

'Just because you are incapable of feeling love does not mean I have to be,' she replied angrily. 'You might be able to live like this – cold, lonely, only holding on to hate and spreading death. Perhaps you do not need friendship or laughter or fun or anything like that. But I can't stand it! I can't stand you, not anymore!' Her face was contorted in an agonised expression as the words poured out of her. 'I have had enough!' She turned to storm away.

Koestler grabbed her by the wrists fiercely. 'You are going nowhere, young lady! You are coming to show me where you left Voorman.' He started to drag her through the hall towards the front door.

She struggled against him, trying to wrestle her arms free and dig her heels into the carpet but she simply didn't have the strength to overpower him. 'His name is Johannes Sneijder!' she yelled. 'And you can't make me do anything! Not anything!'

'Pull yourself together, Frauke,' Koestler ordered. 'I am your father and you shall do as I say.'

'You haven't been interested in being my father for most of my life,' she retorted. 'Why should you be interested now?'

Koestler dragged her to the front door, releasing her with one hand so that he could open it. As he did he shouted: 'Captain Klimitz, where the hell is my car?'

Footsteps approached from behind. Klimitz hesitated as he was faced with his superior physically restraining a defenceless girl. He said nothing.

'Well?' Koestler raised his eyebrows.

'It should be here any minute, sir.'

Koestler grabbed his daughter again and pulled her out of the door into the driveway. She continued to fight against him and dug her heels into the gravel, trying everything she could to stop him.

'Get off me! Leave me alone!' She would not stop shouting. 'You can arrest him on your own!'

He pulled her hard; she resisted and threw her weight to one side; she spun around, circling her father. That was when the shooting started.

Koestler had no idea where it came from; he just heard a bang, and a crack as a shot thudded into the wall mere centimetres away from him. Two more shots followed in quick succession; one ricocheted up off the gravel, the other shattered the window next to the front door. He still had his right hand around Frauke's wrist and still the pair of them were spinning around. When they stopped Koestler began to drop to the ground; he realised that she had suddenly become heavy and was already on the way down. Another bang, another shot; it was definitely high-calibre, a rifle - he couldn't forget that from the first war, those damned snipers who took out anybody who ventured into No man's land. He lay face down on the ground for a couple of seconds but the shooting had stopped. Rolling over on to his back, he glanced first at the bullet hole in the wall, then in the opposite direction to see where the shot had originated from.

Through the leaves, around sixty metres away, he saw a figure pop up from amongst the pine trees. From this distance it was difficult to identify him, but it had to be Voorman or Sneijder or whatever the hell his name was. How he had got there was anyone's guess but he had; who else could it possibly be? The figure turned on his heels and began to run, letting the rifle in his hands fall to the ground, seemingly perfectly content to leave it behind. After a couple of seconds he disappeared from view.

'Guards!' Koestler screamed at the top of his voice. 'Intruder, intruder! He's got a gun - where is everyone? Over there, through the trees!'

A couple of men in Waffen-SS uniform sprinted past across the gravel; from his prone position Koestler saw their boots flash by. Sterchler came over to check that his superior was uninjured.

Klimitz emerged from the doorway to see what all the commotion was. 'Sir, what is going on? I heard shooting.'

Koestler sat up and replied: 'It's Voorman, it's bloody Voorman! I don't know how but I know it was him.'

'He shot at you? Really?'

'Yes, he shot at me and..... Frauke.' He said his daughter's name and then turned to find her, as if the mention of her had reminded him of her existence. She was lying crumpled on the ground next to him; her breathing was loud and laboured and she made an unpleasant bubbling sound each time she inhaled. Her neck was covered in blood and still more ran from a wound in her throat. Her eyes were clear and wide in alarm and fear.

'Oh, God,' Koestler muttered in despair, 'Frauke, no. No.' He crawled over to her and touched her face, then opened his hand and laid the palm upon her cheek. Her skin was warm and soft yet she shivered with every troubled act of respiration. Still she had a look of surprise upon her face. There was a sound, an inaudible whisper from her lips. He leaned closer.

'I...... I'm...... sorry,' she croaked, choking on blood.

'No, no, don't say that,' Koestler answered. He tried desperately to hold back his tears, to retain some authority. 'There is no need. You're going to be okay.' He turned his head towards Klimitz and yelled, 'Come on, Sebastien, we need some help here! Get a medic here quickly!'

'Of course.' Klimitz sprinted back into the house to use the telephone.

Koestler turned his attention back to his daughter.

Her breathing was slowing now and becoming shallower, the glow in her bright blue eyes beginning to disappear. He took hold of her hand, squeezing her fingers gently, and spoke to her reassuringly.

'It's okay; you are going to be fine. I promise.' Inside he knew it was not true, she was not going to last long enough for help to arrive, but he wanted to believe it. Surely she couldn't die now, not when he had said some of the things he just had. That would not be fair. 'I'm so sorry, if I hadn't pulled you out here…. It's not right, please, stay with me, please. Frauke, you are going to be fine.'

She shook her head almost imperceptibly. A second later she was gone.

CHAPTER TWENTY-TWO

The first thing that alerted Sneijder to Koestler's presence was the shouting, first the German's voice, then a loud female one – Frauke's. He saw nothing for several seconds although he could be sure where they were; his memory of being at the house told him that the front door was behind the wall which currently blocked his view. Perhaps he should have taken up a better position. Still, he would have to make the best of it now.

The two of them appeared in the driveway, Koestler obviously dragging his daughter against her will; she was yelling and flapping her arms around in an attempt to break free of him but he grabbed her firmly and spun her round, the fury evident on his face.

Balancing on one knee, Sneijder worked the bolt of the rifle. He raised the weapon in front of his eye and fired, aiming for Koestler's head in the hope that he could finish him with a single shot. He was moving too quickly; the bullet missed and struck the whitewashed wall behind him. Sneijder flipped the bolt up, dragged it back and rammed it forward again with the flat of his hand; the cartridge casing sprung out to be replaced by another. Just as he squeezed the trigger for his second shot his supporting foot slipped and he lost his balance. The bullet squirmed away, kicking up gravel as it struck the ground, a good half-metre wide. He regained his balance and reloaded.

Sneijder should never have taken the next shot – his aim was out, whether through nerves or lack of practice, and he had a moving target in increasingly close proximity to an obstacle he had to avoid. It would have been a difficult undertaking in even the most ideal of conditions but when the stress of the situation was taken into account, along with his personal involvement with the people concerned, it was extremely ill-advised. It was his last chance however, now or never – he either fired or he left Koestler alive. He fired.

It seemed to happen over several hours, hours which were somehow compressed into half a second. There was the feeling of the steel trigger rubbing against his finger, the explosion as the firing pin propelled the projectile down the barrel, the recoil pressing the weapon into his shoulder. With horror he watched Frauke spin around as if in a ballet, performing a dance which would culminate with her hitting her mark. The bullet struck her in the neck, went straight through and smashed into a window. She didn't make a sound, just began to fall to the ground slowly, going in stages, first dropping to her knees then toppling over sideways. Behind her Albrecht Koestler threw himself to the ground in an attempt to protect himself. The tears forming in his eyes blurred Sneijder's vision and his fourth shot dispersed into the air. Still Frauke did not move.

There wasn't time for another shot – the opportunity had gone and now two Waffen-SS soldiers were running in his direction. Koestler rolled over and looked straight towards him. Sneijder immediately threw the strap of the rifle over his shoulder, turned around and without so much as a glance behind started to run, heading out through the trees towards the bicycle. The rifle slipped down off his shoulder and he pulled it up again, but it was heavy and he had no further use for it so he dumped it. Freed from its restrictions his pace increased. There were shouts and panicked cries and the sound of military boots on the ground behind him.

'Hey, stop right there!' one of the pursuers called. There was the dull rattle of automatic fire as he opened up with a Schmeisser, but it was all too late. Sneijder leapt onto the bicycle and headed directly for the road back to Arnhem.

Taking a slightly convoluted route back to Helder's flat in order to be sure he was not followed, he cycled in a sort of introspective trance, finding the appropriate roads by instinct, certainly not actively aware of the decisions he was making. He couldn't think, couldn't even be upset about Frauke – he was too numb for any of that at the moment. All he had was the knowledge that he had been changed forever in the time it had taken for one bullet to fly through the air.

The entire period Sneijder had spent in Arnhem had been a profound experience. He had gone through every sense and emotion a man could – moral disgust, apprehension, fear, duty, love, hate, friendship, sexual desire, anger, vengeance – and been moulded by each. Now, though, with that shot, he had gambled everything he loved and wanted in order to carry out a duty, and he had lost. A part of him, the part only she could reach had died, and he had pulled the trigger himself. It was torture, and he hadn't even begun to process it yet – that would need to come later, when it was over.

In the distance there were still many planes, now not only C-47 Dakotas but Stirlings and Halifaxes too, some of them trailing ropes to which were attached large gliders. This was obviously a major operation of some kind, the sort of operation for which paratroopers would require equipment - artillery pieces, jeeps and the like. This assumption was confirmed to Sneijder as soon as he returned to the flat.

Bassen was next to a wooden cabinet in the sitting room, listening to a radio set which was concealed inside. He glanced up and said, 'They're here all right - they have just been broadcasting messages encouraging a general railway strike, to slow down the Germans, stop them moving men and armaments.'

'So it's real - a genuine proper invasion?'

Bassen shrugged his shoulders. 'It would certainly appear so.'

'I wonder what they are after,' Sneijder mused. 'We'll need to think about getting out of here.'

'And go where?'

They both left that question hanging. Sneijder headed straight up to the attic to get his things together, hoping that the time spent up there would generate some idea about what he should do now.

It was early evening when Sneijder saw the first British soldiers in Arnhem. They moved slowly and carefully through the narrow streets from the west, in the direction of the river. He looked down on them from his position on the fourth storey of the building, noting their green infantry uniforms and steel helmets camouflaged with grass and leaves. A man leading them wore a distinctive red beret; if Sneijder's memory served him correctly this was the attire of the British First Airborne Division. Prior to the Normandy landings in June he had got talking to an officer from the division who had let slip his annoyance at being held back from an impending operation; of course at the time Sneijder had not known the significance of this - only later did it transpire what a disaster this indiscretion might have been.

As paratroops they were only lightly armed and would of course stand no chance against the mechanised vehicles available to the Germans, particularly when they were used by the mighty SS Panzer Corps. With a sinking feeling Sneijder realised that the lack of response from England to the Underground messages informing them of German strength might indicate that those messages had failed to get through. In that case the British would be expecting far less resistance – after all it was only three weeks ago that the military presence in the area had been negligible. He considered going down and telling them, to make them understand what they were up against but concluded that they would be unlikely to listen to a civilian.

Just after six o'clock the quiet evening was disturbed by chugging diesel engines and the high-pitched squeal of tracked wheels. A long German convoy consisting of thirty or so armoured vehicles and half-tracks powered up the northern ramp of the bridge and swept across the Rhine in a southerly direction, heading for the opposite bank and beyond, Nijmegen. This seemed to indicate either a similar airborne drop there or the imminent arrival of the ground forces which would be necessary to reinforce the lightly armed paratroops, perhaps both. The vehicles were each painted dark grey, the Iron Cross emblazoned at various points on the exteriors.

There were currently no German troops in the streets around the bridge and the British paratroops moved without impediment. Sneijder went to the window on the other side of the attic and looked down. The officer in the red beret knocked at the front door of a house about fifty metres down the Eusebius Binnensingel from the bridge, flanked by two soldiers with rifles. They stood for a second talking to the still-concealed owner of the house and then went in, followed moments later by about fifteen others. It was three or four minutes afterwards that they emerged onto the flat section of roof which served as a balcony terrace, overlooking the ramp at the northern end of the bridge.

So it was the Rhine Bridge they were after. It was the logical target – the success of any invasion of the Netherlands would be largely dependent on securing crossings over the innumerable waterways that traversed the country. Capturing the river crossing would open up a path for tanks and armoured vehicles, but where would they come from? As far as Sneijder knew the German lines stretched the whole way across the Belgian-Dutch border, and between here and there were many rivers and canals which would also need to be crossed. His gut feeling seemed to be correct; there would need to be other landings further south in order to capture those bridges as well.

Sneijder found a window which would open and eased it ajar. Immediately the sound of the small arms fire drifting across the city became louder. Every so often there would be an explosion, a grenade or a mortar, and if one were to look closely one could see light smoke hanging on the air. He had to get out of Arnhem if there was to be an all-out pitched battle but it would be impossible until he could find out which areas were controlled by the Germans. They would surely have sealed off the city centre by now to prevent reinforcements from reaching the bridge, so he probably needed to stick it out a few hours at least. All things considered, there was also the possibility that the British might actually win and take Arnhem which would render any dangerous escape unnecessary.

As darkness began to fall the British paratroopers made their first attempt to attack across the bridge, led by an extremely courageous soldier who ran forward enthusiastically with his bayoneted rifle raised. Attaching bayonets was a well-practised method to increase morale; charging at full speed with a stabbing weapon, usually yelling at the top of the lungs, was bound to get the adrenaline going. Behind this soldier the others followed, some holding back more than others. There was the deep baritone rattle as the machine guns in the concrete pillboxes opened up and the attack leader was cut down, followed by several of his colleagues. From the grandstand view that Sneijder had, elevated above the bridge, it was clear that there was no way any of them would even make it to the end of the ramp. He winced as men began to fall, then the air was full of different cries as the survivors retreated; they shouted obscenities at one another and encouraged each other back to their own lines. The bridge fell silent once more.

It was just after five o'clock when Koestler first heard about the Allied landings. He was laid out on the sofa in his sitting room with a large brandy in his hand, going through the afternoon's events in his head. His neatly pressed tunic was in a pile on the floor, draped over the now empty bottle. It had still failed to sink in that Frauke was dead; it did not seem possible, however he looked at it. She had been so alive, so full of energy and conviction - how could all that have been wiped out in a second? Koestler was beginning to ponder how he could have acted differently when the telephone rang; Klimitz answered it in the hallway and ten seconds later entered the room.

'Telephone call for you, sir. I believe you will want to take this.'

Koestler got up, feeling his head spin a little from the alcohol, and walked through to the telephone. 'Yes, this is Obersturmbannführer Koestler.'

The voice on the other end of the line had a gruff Bavarian tone. 'My name is Grundheim. I am with the 2nd SS Panzer Corps under General Bittrich. As I believe you are aware, we are currently based in the area.'

'Go on.'

'I am calling you on General Bittrich's behalf,' the man who called himself Grundheim explained. 'British para-troopers began landing north-west of Arnhem, near Wolfheze, around four hours ago. The general would like to know if you can spare any men to bolster our forces.'

Koestler was stunned. 'British paratroopers? You can't be serious.'

'I'm afraid so. As far as we can tell it is part of a much wider Allied offensive here in the Netherlands - we are getting reports of similar airborne landings by the Amer-icans around Nijmegen and Eindhoven. At this stage we don't know the purpose of this operation but obviously we must ensure it does not succeed. However we are extremely short of men – that is why the general would like your assistance. The British seem to have come in numbers.'

'It is out of the question,' Koestler replied strongly. 'All of the men under my command are from the civilian administration – most of them have had no military training. You are asking me to sacrifice them. I'm afraid I must refuse.'

Grundheim was taken aback. 'You do understand the seriousness of the situation, don't you? The entire country could fall into the hands of the enemy. If that were to happen they could be in Germany within the week.'

'That is a military matter – I am responsible for purely civil affairs, as are my men. Besides, they are all currently engaged in a large-scale operation to locate a saboteur. It is extremely important.'

'More important than repelling this attack?'

'Yes, extremely important. I have provided substantial numbers of men to the many Dutch SS units in the area who can reinforce your battalions, but I cannot allow any of the others to abandon my operation.'

Grundheim's reply seemed to be a veiled threat. 'General Bittrich will be very disappointed, Herr Koestler. He expected greater cooperation from a man of your reputation.'

The man was trying to play to his vanity but Koestler was having none of it. 'What reputation is that?' he asked.

'I was told you are a man who is totally loyal to the cause and to the Führer, a man who is dedicated to the victory of Germany. Allowing some of your men to support the defence of Arnhem would be the best way to achieve that victory.'

'I have given you my answer, Herr Grundheim,' Koestler said. 'Please give my apologies to the general but I cannot spare my men. Good day to you.' He hung up before the officer could argue and returned to the sitting room where Klimitz was standing. 'Well I'll be damned. The British have begun dropping paratroops to the west of the city.'

'When?'

'This afternoon, apparently. General Bittrich wanted me to send him some of my men.'

Klimitz raised his eyebrows. 'And will you?'

'Absolutely not. The SS Panzer Corps with their tanks and armoured vehicles should easily be able to defeat a lightly-armed infantry force. I need all the men I can gather to hunt down this Voorman or Sneijder or whatever his name may be.'

'Will the Waffen-SS accept that?' Klimitz asked.

'Possibly not; this is why I am going to telephone the Reichskommisar right away.' Koestler hadn't thought of that until the words came out of his mouth but it was an excellent idea so he set it in motion. Seyss-Inquart had told him to call him if he needed anything; now was the time for him to make good on that particular favour.

Koestler dialled the direct number which the Reichskommisar had given to him. Seyss-Inquart was no longer in a position of particular power as the military had now taken control, making decisions based purely on war strategy and tactics; orders were now issued by Field Marshals Model and Von Runstedt. However his word would still carry more weight than Koestler's.

Seyss-Inquart answered cautiously. 'Albrecht, this is most unexpected. How are you? I hope you have recovered from your accident.'

'To be honest, sir, I am not all that well.'

'Oh?' His voice conveyed surprise and a little trepidation.

Koestler took a deep breath and tried to hold himself together. 'My daughter was killed today – shot right in front of me. There was nothing I could do.'

Silence. Finally: 'That is awful. I am so sorry, Albrecht.' His tone changed and became harder. 'The work of partisans?'

'In a way,' Koestler replied. 'It's a very long story, but it was the work of an agent sent from England. It has emerged that he was sent here to assassinate me – he was responsible for sabotaging my car, for causing my crash, and for the deaths of sixteen German soldiers. It would be fair to say he has made it his business to get at me.'

'Good God. The Führer has issued an order declaring that all spies be shot – you are perfectly within your rights to execute him immediately.' He paused. 'You do have him in custody?'

'No, not so far,' Koestler explained. 'Actually, sir, that is what I am calling you about. I assume that you have been told about the Allied paratroopers landing near Arnhem?'

'Of course, I was just going to ask you about that.'

'I just received a telephone call from a man named Grundheim on behalf of General Bittrich, asking me to provide some of my men to him to reinforce his ranks. I told him this was not possible but I expect I have not heard the last of it. You see, this agent must still be in the area - with the movement of troops, the road blocks and the short time he has had to escape he cannot have got far. I need every man I can muster to locate him before he can get away.'

Seyss-Inquart sighed. 'I see. Yes, I do see. What is it that you need from me?'

'I need you to issue a directive placing the men I require under my command, which will supersede any order I receive to provide them to the military,' Koestler answered forcefully. 'This man must be caught. In any case, these officers are not military men - they are police-men and security staff. I don't see that they would be a lot of use to the SS Panzer Corps.'

'You must understand, Albrecht,' the Reichskom-misar began, 'my position has been significantly compromised since the beginning of the month. I am not sure I have the authority to give such a directive.'

'You are still the head of the government, appointed by the Führer,' Koestler insisted, his confidence to speak his mind increased by his intoxication. 'Your word is still important.'

'Hitler will side with his generals, particularly Model,' Seyss-Inquart argued, 'but I will see what I can do. However, no matter how much you want to catch this agent, you should not make it personal.'

'Personal?' Koestler raised his voice. 'The man has murdered my daughter and twice attempted to kill me! How much more personal can it get?'

Seyss-Inquart did not attempt to answer. Instead he asked, 'Which men will you require? Obviously some of the divisions under your command are on the re-serve list for the Waffen-SS; I shouldn't think I can do much about them.'

'All of the Gestapo, SD, Orpo and Abwehr officers in and around Arnhem for sure,' Koestler answered. 'I will make no attempt to prevent the Dutch SS volunteers from joining up with their respective battalions.'

'All right, Albrecht, I shall see what I can do about your request,' Seyss-Inquart concluded, 'but you may have to discuss it in more detail with Rauter - he is coming over in person to take charge of your Dutch SS regiments. If you want to avoid trouble for yourself I suggest you find this agent as soon as possible.'

'Yes, sir. Thank you, sir.'

The fighting around the bridge intensified throughout the night. German infantry began to close in from the north and west, presumably in an attempt to cut off the British battalion from their reinforcements. The attic in the house had windows on all sides and Sneijder was able to see the events unfold, illuminated with every flash of fire. As dusk evaporated into the blackness of the night the Germans started to attack the British positions in the houses with machine guns and grenades; mortar fire started to blow holes in walls and roofs. The paratroopers returned fire with the few weapons they had.

The German pillbox at the northern end of the bridge had been inflicting heavy casualties and a small contingent of British troops launched an assault on it with a flamethrower. As soon as they got near, the machine guns opened up on them and they were forced to seek cover. The soldier in charge of the weapon let off a burst and a jet of flame erupted from the nozzle with a tremendous roar. It had no effect on the reinforced concrete bunker but the wooden structures around it caught fire, going up like gunpowder.

The SS troops positioned on the southern bank of the river launched a couple of attacks across the bridge with armoured vehicles, firing into the occupied houses on either side of the ramp. The British soldiers opened up with a barrage of withering fire, cutting down the enemy troops mercilessly. An armoured half-track swerved to avoid the kubelwagen in front whose driver had been struck by a rifle shot and collided with the barrier; moments later it was hit by a shell, probably a PIAT anti-tank round, and exploded. A badly burned German soldier began to crawl out but was shot and killed. Even from a distance, Sneijder could hear the man's screams dying away and it chilled him to the bone. Another car burst into flames further along the bridge, billowing thick black smoke into the sky.

It was around three-thirty in the morning when Sneijder went downstairs. The continuous gunfire and bombardment made it impossible to sleep and he wanted to find out whether the city centre was closed off. It seemed only a matter of time before the Germans brought artillery fire to bear on the houses surrounding the Great Markt and he would need to start planning an escape route. Bassen was dozing in an armchair in the sitting room and did not flinch even when Sneijder stepped on a squeaky floorboard on the staircase. The young agent went right down to the front door, eased it open and peered out. Before he had taken so much as a step into the street there was a rifle shot from high up in an adjacent building; the wooden door frame to his left exploded into splinters as a round smashed into it. Sneijder leapt backwards and slammed the door breathlessly. His heart skipped a beat.

It was a stupid thing to do; going outside when there was a battle going on, particularly in the dark. Snipers on either side would be unable to make out much detail on any of their targets, so would make their choices as to whether they should shoot depending on the location of the man. If he was near to the British positions he would easily be mistaken for one of their soldiers. Sneijder would have to wait until morning.

The following day dawned with a light but chilly mist. Sneijder, having finally drifted off to sleep during a lull in the fighting, was awoken by a blast of cold air through the window. He stood up and stretched, wandered over to the window and looked down to the street. For a couple of minutes he saw and heard nothing. All of a sudden a company of German infantry appeared on the far side of the bridge ramp. The first soldier around the corner raised an arm, a stick grenade in his hand. A burst of gunfire cut him down. The grenade hit the ground and exploded, catching two others in the blast. The rest of the company continued their charge towards a row of houses held by the British, opening fire on them with MP40s and Sturmgewehr assault rifles. The paratroopers began to shoot back and for the next ten minutes there was a constant deafening roar as a pitched battle ensued.

Sneijder watched as an old couple emerged from the front door of their house across the street. There was a terrific amount of firing going on around them and the man stopped his wife. She was obviously extremely frightened and for a while they argued at a great volume, but suddenly she pulled away from him and began to run out into the open. The man shouted at her in despair. It must have been the confusion of battle as she was evidently a civilian, but Sneijder watched in horror as she was caught in the crossfire. The man moved after her.

The frustration suddenly got to Sneijder up in the attic and he thumped the window. 'For goodness sake, no!' he yelled out loud. 'Don't do it!'

The old man was cut down in a hail of bullets and collapsed next to his wife, both of them dead. Sneijder closed his eyes and tried to clear the appalling image from his mind. He shut the window and moved away, not wishing to witness any more death. From this position high up in the building he was detached from the battle and was watching it take place as a man might watch a play, not altogether grasping the terror of the situation and he had to remind himself that these were real people losing their lives down there.

For the remainder of the morning the fire from either side continued, getting harder and more concentrated. The Germans started to pound the encircled British soldiers with mortar fire but the shots were inaccurate and scattered far and wide. At one point there was a loud rumble as a shell landed close to Sneijder's building and then another as the next shot landed long. A line of German vehicles again attacked over the bridge but the British were ready for them; their artillery positioned just outside the city centre decimated them, destroying every one. It was a death trap for the SS battalion, caught between the big guns and the PIAT-equipped paratroopers. Several of their soldiers took the only escape open to them, jumping off the bridge into the river.

As the day wore on the German numbers seemed to be increasing all the time, as were the ferocity of their attacks. One by one the houses around the bridge ramp were pummelled by shellfire and mortar projectiles and the focus of these attacks was expanding. Sneijder knew he had to get out soon before Helder's house fell inside their range. Once that happened either he would be killed or trapped within a German-occupied zone, which would prove equally fatal for him. The question was where he would go. The bridge was obviously unusable so he could not cross the river; to the east lay Germany and certain capture. He would have to head west and try to find a way through the German lines, hoping that he could somehow link up with the British.

At just that moment a huge explosion rocked the house next door, shaking the very foundations of the entire row. For a brief few seconds it seemed that the roof would certainly cave in. Sneijder threw himself to the floor. The shockwaves rippled through the brickwork, loosening dust into the attic. Sneijder coughed and spluttered, and made up his mind to go at once.

CHAPTER TWENTY–THREE

Sneijder knew he had to leave the house before it got dark, after his near-miss with the sniper the previous evening. There seemed little hope that there would be any sort of let-up in the hostilities so he decided just to make a run for it at the earliest opportunity. It was important that he travelled with as little baggage as possible as every single item he carried would reduce his mobility and his ability to conceal himself effectively. After emptying his kitbag of all the things he could do without - the double-breasted suit, four shirts and a couple of pairs of trousers, the box of grenades – Sneijder realised that all he had left should fit comfortably into his canvas knapsack. He dressed in an old pair of slacks and his thick woollen jumper, zipping up his leather jacket on top, and stuck the Luger in its usual place in his waistband. The Sten went into the bottom of the knapsack, the two pieces wrapped up in the legs of a spare pair of trousers, along with the flashlight and compass.

When he was satisfied that he only had the essential items he returned downstairs to the kitchen to make himself something to eat before he departed. It was impossible to know when he would next get the chance to have a meal. Bassen sat opposite him in silence, his face ashen.

'You are going to have to get out of here soon,' Sneijder told him. 'The Germans will flatten the whole area before they'll give up the bridge to the British.'

Bassen remained silent.

'Did you not hear me?' Sneijder continued. 'I said....'

'I heard what you said,' the housekeeper snapped.

'Well?'

'Well what?'

'Where are you going to go? This building will not be standing in two days' time.'

As if to emphasise the point, there was the unmistakable whistling noise of an artillery shell flying through the air and a giant booming sound as it exploded not more than fifty metres away. The floor shook beneath their feet and a picture fell from the wall, the glass shattering.

'If I knew where to go I would not still be here,' Bassen replied. 'As I told you, I am a Jew - until the Nazis are defeated there will be no place safe for me.'

'This place is not safe, that is for sure. You must go somewhere.'

'But if I leave, what about Mr Helder?' Bassen asked.

Sneijder replied quietly: 'Mr Helder is dead, believe me. The Gestapo would never let him go. Now is the time to think about yourself.'

'Where will you go? I could come with you.'

'Not where I am going,' Sneijder said. 'I am a wanted man as far as the SS are concerned; to tell you the truth, the chances of me making it anywhere alive are very slim indeed. My only way to escape is through the German lines to the British. No, it is much too dangerous - I cannot ask anybody else to do it.' He stood up from the table.

'Then I have nowhere. I am a dead man.'

'In the end, we are all dead men,' Sneijder answered philosophically with a weak smile. 'War just brings it to some people sooner.'

And then Bassen was no longer there. The wall beside him just seemed to explode, a devastating blast which tore the room apart. Sneijder heard the initial impact, a terrifying rumbling which was the loudest noise he had ever heard, and then nothing but a high-pitched ringing in his ears. The floor split open almost exactly down the middle, caving in on the side nearest to the external wall. Bassen was plunged onto the level below. The gloomy room was suddenly illuminated by daylight flooding in through an enormous gap in the ceiling above. A wooden beam collapsed directly above Sneijder, missing him by millimetres and smashing a hole through the tiles around his feet. It had to be one of the larger artillery pieces which had launched the shell; the damage from one shot was incredible. Sneijder spun on his heel and headed for the staircase as another shell hit the building. The force of the blast hit him in the back and propelled him headfirst down the steps, slamming him into the wall at the bottom with tremendous velocity.

Suddenly filled with fear he scrambled to his feet, ignoring the pain in his ankle and his throbbing head. Dazed and more than a little confused he headed to the front door and pulled it open, only thinking about getting out of the house before it was struck again. His knapsack slung over his shoulder, Sneijder ran out into the street and headed south through the Great Markt towards the river. He passed a house which no longer had any glass in the windows; instead the barrels of two Bren light machine guns protruded out, manned by

British paratroops. As he rounded a corner a German MG-42 machine gun fired at him from behind a pile of sandbags, striking the wall. A ricochet tore a small hole in the knapsack.

Sneijder ran for all he was worth, only now beginning to feel his injury. His route to the river took him through the Sabelspoort, the last remaining gate of the old city fortifications. It was an ornate construction, an arched central section flanked on either side by a round turret reaching up to a point. He made his way through the arch and found himself on the bank of the river, then turned west and headed away from the bridge. An SS machine gun detachment had set themselves up at the side of the road and they watched suspiciously as he passed.

Sneijder only made it a few streets before he came across a vicious confrontation between divisions of British paratroopers and SS Panzer Corps. The British soldiers were situated in a building on the corner of two streets and were firing with machine guns and mortars on the attacking Germans. It was a scene of absolute carnage, black smoke rising above the houses, dead and wounded men littered across the street. A shell struck the occupied building, tearing down a section of wall and sending a cloud of dust through the broken windows; when it cleared the two soldiers who had been there were gone. There was an appalling scream from the same direction.

There was no way through without taking a huge risk, the battle was so fierce. Gunfire came from all directions, interspersed with tremendous explosions and Sneijder decided to wait a while. He walked back a street and sat down on the front step of a butcher's shop.

It was going to be very difficult to get anywhere with the battle raging so he had to choose his route carefully. His hope was that the British might be able to help him get in contact with London, and through them he could organise passage back to England. It was unlikely that the airborne troops were planning on securing Arnhem without some sort of ground support and that would mean that the front line had advanced into the Netherlands. All he would need to do would be to reach the Allied side and he would be safe. If his calculations were correct the paratroopers had dropped to the north-west of Arnhem; if he continued to walk in that direction he would eventually come across them.

An hour later the sounds of battle had receded a little so Sneijder began on his journey once more, passing the now demolished house which had earlier been filled with soldiers. It was now abandoned, the fighting by this stage having moved further up the street. After following the river for half a kilometre he headed north towards the railway line, picking up Utrechtseweg, the main road connecting Arnhem and Oosterbeek. He was undisturbed for a while on this stretch as there was no evidence of any soldiers from either side. The air carried the sounds of small arms fire and exploding ordnance, mortar rounds and anti-tank rockets. Occasionally there would be a deep booming sound as one of the howitzers brought in by the Germans found its target.

He passed the front entrance of the St Elisabeth's hospital, a tall and grand building in red brick with a gabled roof. The curved driveway swept up each side to a large central arch beneath which was a set of glass doors. Out of the corner of his eye he saw something in the reflection of the glass. He heard the growl of the engine and turned to see a German Panzer tank driving up the street slowly, a military helmet sticking out of the hatch beside the main gun. Sneijder quickly disappeared up Zwarteweg, the narrow residential street which ran along beside the hospital. A group of British paratroopers emerged from an alley between two houses and ran across the cobbled street, one of them carrying a PIAT launcher. Sneijder continued on his way through the quiet residential area, hearing the sounds of gunfire as they engaged the tank, then the bang as the anti-tank weapon was used. A moment later there was another explosion as the tank inevitably fired back and the cries of the soldiers.

After rejoining the main road he moved along Utrechtseweg into the outskirts of Oosterbeek. It was after seven-thirty and darkness had almost fallen. Sneijder knew he could not go on much further and needed to find somewhere to stay overnight. By chance he found himself just a couple of blocks away from the Uhlenbroeks' house so he walked round to see if there was anybody there. As he had feared the front door had been broken down and the place was deserted, evidence he assumed of a Gestapo raid and the arrest of the occupants. He entered the house cautiously, aware that Koestler might have left someone to watch it in case he returned, but after several minutes there was no sign of anyone and he relaxed a little. The refrigerator in the kitchen still contained some meat and vegetables, although it appeared that the electricity had been disconnected as the appliance was switched off and none of the lights in the house were working. Sneijder found some bread and was able to make himself a plate of raw ham sandwiches.

That night he slept up in his old room in the attic with the Luger under the pillow. His slumber was constantly disturbed by the terrible memory of the previous day, the shooting. Even though Frauke had been about to hand him over to her father, his feelings for her had been undiminished and the idea that he had killed her left him hollow, as if a part of him had been wrenched away. It was the most dreadful sort of grief it was possible to imagine, loss and sorrow and heartache combined with the guilt of knowing he was culpable. He began to think of all the things she might have done with her life had she not been struck by the bullet, but it was all too much to bear. Everyone he ever cared for ended up dead – that was what the last few months had taught him. His mother had always said that life was a gift, a beautiful experience to be savoured but it wasn't true; she was wrong. Life was hard and cruel and painful, a miserable and tortuous chore from which there was only one escape. He couldn't stand it for much longer, he knew that much; the stress of being in constant danger had nearly destroyed him. He broke down in despair, and just let it all out.

The following morning was foggy and when Sneijder looked out of the window visibility was down to less than fifty metres. Now would be his chance to make up some ground. As long as the weather continued there could be no fighting, and neither side's snipers were likely to take a shot in such poor conditions.

He left the house and headed west along the same road into the centre of the village, passing a couple of German tanks which were parked beside the road. Two or three soldiers sat up on top of them smoking cigarettes, rifles lying beside them. One of them raised his weapon instinctively as Sneijder appeared suddenly out of the swirling fog.

Sneijder put up his hands and called out in German, 'Don't shoot. I'm a civilian.' He kept walking forward with his arms above his head until the soldier could see that he was not in uniform.

The soldier frowned and replied, 'Where are you going?'

Sneijder shrugged his shoulders. 'I have no idea. My home in Arnhem has been destroyed and I just want to get away from here.'

The German lowered the rifle and waved him on with a warning: 'Watch your back; it's a disaster out there.' He returned to enjoying his cigarette.

Sneijder vanished into the fog again and was alone until a foxhole dug into one of the front gardens loomed into his view. A Bren machine gun defended the nest and beside was arranged a mortar, its hollow tube pointed into the sky at a steep angle. A group of four British infantrymen occupied the foxhole.

Sneijder approached them, now speaking in English. 'Excuse me, where are your divisional headquarters? Near here?'

A tall fair-haired man with a moustache gave him an extremely dubious look. 'Of what interest is that to you?'

'I need to get there. I am a Special Operations Executive agent.'

'Who? Special Operations.....' The man chuckled. 'Pull the other one.'

Sneijder did not understand the quip. 'I'm sorry? Pull the other what?'

The fair-haired soldier looked at the others, and they all began to laugh. Sneijder was not in the mood for amusement and he reacted irritably.

'Listen, I don't have time for this - I need to get to your headquarters,' he explained. 'Are you going to tell me where it is or not?'

The British soldier's smile vanished instantly. 'I don't think I like your aggressive attitude,' he commented.

Sneijder scowled and snapped, 'Never mind my attitude. Where is it?'

One of the other soldiers climbed out of the foxhole and pointed his rifle vaguely in Sneijder's direction, as if to give him a slight warning. 'We are under orders not to talk to civilians under any circumstances,' he said. 'It's for security. You see, you could be a German for all we know. It would be pretty stupid of us to point you in the direction of our commanding officers.'

'Do you have any idea how many Germans I have had to kill to get here?' Sneijder was exasperated. 'I was dropped here to do a job, and I have been behind enemy lines for almost three bloody months. I've got half the Gestapo on my tail now, determined to kill me, and the only way I can get out is by contacting England. Do you think you could be a little more helpful?'

The fair-haired man shook his head. 'I'm sorry, we are under strict orders. We have a job to do like anybody else.'

Sneijder walked away along the road, unable to see what was ahead through the fog. However it slowly began to lift and gradually the sounds of gunfire erupted once more. The woods either side of the road were slightly thicker here and with a more considered look, Sneijder noticed the camouflaged German soldiers dug in between the trees. At the side of a small track three SS conscripts were crowded around a seventy-five millimetre gun. As he came upon a crossroads he realised that this was the main German line between the paratroopers' drop zones and Arnhem itself.

The battle for Oosterbeek was intense and fierce. Machine gun fire and mortar rounds came from all directions as the British and German soldiers fought for control of each individual street, facing up to each other from houses opposite one another. Artillery shells arced through the air with deadly accuracy, bringing down death and destruction on the soldiers dug in to the banks and gardens. Every time Sneijder came to another junction he found himself unable to pass because of the sheer devastation being unleashed. He watched as a line of British paratroopers leapt out from their trench and ran across a wide road towards the Germans encamped on the other side; one threw a grenade at his enemy before the MG-42 machine gun opened fire with a noise like canvas being ripped. The first couple of men went down like sacks of coal, collapsing to the ground hard; another fired with his rifle, killing the machine-gunner and the soldier feeding the ammunition belt. The gun fell silent.

Sneijder kept to one side of the road where he thought he was safe. Suddenly, without warning, he heard the popping sound of a mortar being launched. He spun around, frantically searching for the projectile but could not see it. There was an explosion less than ten metres away and a tree just disappeared. Sneijder threw himself down in panic, keeping his head well down as he heard more gunfire in his direction.

This was foolish; trying to walk slowly through a battle zone. What did he think he was doing? Instead he scrambled to his feet, veered away from the main road and began to run through a small copse, his route taking him around behind the line of German foxholes. Though now away from the crossfire he remained in danger every time a British shell or mortar round exploded nearby. Over to his left he saw two heavily armed half-tracks on the road but this was the end of the German-held territory. Three hundred metres further on he returned to the main thoroughfare, passing a column of British jeeps, some of which were towing six-pounder guns.

Sneijder found himself on the wide open part of the Utrechtseweg that ran along in front of the Hartenstein hotel, which last time he had passed had been a German command post. Now there were Allied jeeps parked up the drive and plenty of green-uniformed men milling around. Sneijder reasoned that the British would most likely have taken over the German headquarters; it made sense to do so. Overwhelmed with relief at having got through alive and uninjured, he began to walk up towards the big white house.

The grounds of the hotel were filled with men of various regiments according to their differing uniforms and badges. Some of them were paratroopers of the First Airborne with their distinctive red berets, while there were a couple of soldiers displaying the crest of the King's Own Scottish Borderers. At the foot of the flight of stairs leading into the hotel there was a soldier in a uniform that Sneijder did not recognise; he blocked his path and gave him a stern look.

'No, you can't go in there,' the soldier said. 'It's been requisitioned for the British Army now.'

'Is this your headquarters?' Sneijder asked.

'That's right.'

'Thank God for that,' Sneijder replied with a smile. 'It's been a nightmare to get here. I need to speak to whoever is in charge.'

The soldier frowned. 'I doubt that will be possible. As you have noticed we are in the middle of a battle and our senior officers are extremely busy. Besides, orders from the top are that nobody speaks to civilians.'

'I'm not a civilian, I'm an agent of the government, intelligence,' Sneijder explained, reminded from his previous conversation that SOE was secret and hence unknown to regular soldiers. 'It is very important that I talk to someone.'

'Look, I've told you....'

'Please,' Sneijder pleaded. 'I've been undercover here for three months, I've done what I was ordered and now I'm on the run. The German police are searching for me and I need to get in contact with London. It's vital. Please.'

The British soldier thought for a moment and told him, 'Wait here.' He disappeared into the building, returning five minutes later. 'Okay. Major Barclay will be out to speak with you in a few minutes.'

Sneijder took a seat on a bench in the gardens and waited. It was nearly twenty-five minutes later that a dark-haired officer about forty years of age came down the stairs and approached him, an agitated expression on his face. Sneijder's heart sank.

'Corporal Black tells me you wish to speak to me,' the officer said. 'You will have to make it quick – I am trying to run a battle here. Major-General Urquhart has given me two minutes.'

Sneijder stood. 'I'll get straight to it then. I am an agent of the British government and I have been undercover here since June. I've been blown and the German police are after me, and now with the battle going on I need to get out. I must get in contact with London and I was hoping you could signal them for me. I assume you have radio sets and….'

'That's all you have to tell me?' Major Barclay was hugely irritated. 'I thought you had some sort of useful information to give me. I'm sorry, you must excuse me.' He turned and began to walk away.

'Did you not hear what I said?' Sneijder said. 'I need to contact London. You do have radio sets, don't you?'

Barclay turned to face him. 'Listen; perhaps you don't fully understand the situation here. We've got a battalion down by the bridge being pulverised by an SS division across the river, there are units spread out all over Arnhem under attack from far more heavily armed Germans and there is another airlift coming down onto landing zones which are now surrounded by German anti-aircraft guns and artillery. We have not had proper radio communication until a few hours ago, and even now my radio operators are struggling to keep up with all the messages they are receiving. Somehow we have to try to co-ordinate this God-awful mess before everybody gets wiped out. Do you really think we've got time to send signals around on behalf of civilians?'

'I'm not a civilian.'

'Yes - so you say.'

'For God's sake, they are going to kill me!' Sneijder exclaimed.

Barclay pointed towards the road in fury. 'I've got thousands of men dying out there, friends of mine, good men,' he blasted. 'Don't talk to me as if you are more important. My responsibility is to them and them alone.

Whatever situation you find yourself in may be regrettable but it is your concern. Now I really must be getting back inside. Good day to you.' He stormed away.

The ongoing battle seriously hampered Koestler's attempts to find Sneijder. He had originally intended to block off all the roads leading into the city to prevent an escape, realising that the river would provide a useful natural obstacle. Sealing off the bridges over the Rhine would prevent Sneijder from travelling south, and a group of men spread out in a semicircle could then close in from the north and squeeze him out. The reality was that while the battle raging at the road bridge in Arnhem made it impassable and the railway bridge at Oosterbeek had already been destroyed, there could be no roadblocks on any of the roads without getting in the way of the military. Instead the semicircle had to be much larger, encompassing the entire city, and was unable to close in. They would just have to remain in place and hope that Sneijder would run into them.

Koestler and Klimitz stood around a large table in one of the outer offices at SS headquarters along with Horvath, an Orpo officer called Prinz and an Abwehr officer by the name of Prahl, peering over a detailed map of the city and the surrounding area. A thick red line drawn on with a marker pen indicated the police perimeter around the northern suburbs, which stretched out as far west as Oosterbeek. Pins of various colours denoted the latest positions of both the German and British forces, giving some idea as to which areas should be avoided; the last thing Koestler wanted was a disagreement with Field Marshal Model.

Koestler was frustrated by the lack of a breakthrough and made his feelings clear. 'This is not good enough. He is just one man. Surely we can find one man.'

'That is precisely the problem,' Horvath replied. 'He is just one man in a city of thousands, and a war zone at that. He could be hiding anywhere. How can we even begin to look?'

'Well he is unlikely to be anywhere near the city centre, not now anyway,' Koestler said. 'With the pounding it's taking from our guns it is far too dangerous.'

Horvath did not agree. 'Sir, we are talking about a man who will now be in fear for his life. It would not be unreasonable for him to think he would be safer to remain in hiding and risk the bombing than to run.'

'Maybe so but it is my belief that he will run at the earliest opportunity,' Koestler countered. 'The presence of British troops so close is bound to attract him. I think he may head straight towards them. It would obviously be his best chance to get out of the country - presumably the British have some sort of exit strategy in case their attack fails.' He looked for an ally. 'Sebastien, what do you think?'

'I'm not sure that we can presume anything with this man,' Klimitz answered. 'As you have said yourself on more than one occasion, these agents are trained for just this sort of scenario. They are experts at remaining hidden. We may just have to wait and let him come to us. If he doesn't turn up then we'll know he is still in Arnhem, and our next step will be to go house-to-house once the battle is over.'

'And what if the British win the battle?' Koestler asked in frustration. 'Arnhem will be in their hands, and Sneijder will have got away. That simply cannot be allowed to happen. He killed my daughter, remember.' Saying the words made his blood run cold; he still was struggling to accept the reality of what had happened to Frauke, and was struggling more with the thought that it was because of him.

'If the British win the battle, Sneijder getting away will be the least of our worries,' Horvath put in.

The Abwehr man Prahl spoke up. He was a studious man of great intelligence who used his words sparingly but purposefully. 'All of the information we have received from England suggests that since our infiltration of SOE's Dutch section there is a great mistrust of the Dutch Underground. I wouldn't have thought that the British military would have any interest in assisting him.'

Koestler pointed to the map in front of him. 'Right. The main British command post is here in Oosterbeek, yes?'

'That's what we've been told,' Klimitz replied. 'They have taken over Model's headquarters at the Hartenstein hotel.'

'So if we assume that by now he has reached this point and been refused assistance, where will he go now?' Koestler looked at each man in turn. All remained silent. 'Come on; where will he go?'

'Well obviously he cannot cross the river so he will not go south,' Horvath answered.

Klimitz pointed to a marking on the river further to the west. 'What about this ferry here at Heveadorp? That would give him a route across.'

'Our troops are bound to have secured that already,' Horvath observed. 'Otherwise it would give the British a bridgehead over the Rhine.'

'Indeed,' Koestler agreed.

'If he heads further west he is in danger of running into the battles around the British landing zones,' Horvath added.

'So what we are saying is that he will probably head north from Oosterbeek,' Koestler stated. 'Are we agreed? Excellent. Right, Horvath, take some of the men away from the east side of the city and double the patrols to the north-west. Ensure that they are extra vigilant.'

Klimitz asked, 'Sir, are you sure that is a good idea? I am not questioning your judgement but we are basing this on many assumptions, none of which we can be certain about.'

'Sebastien, the time for detailed consideration is over. We have no choice but to take a few risks and hope that they pay off. I will go and take charge of the search myself. Please arrange for my car.' He turned to the other men. 'Gentlemen, thank you for your time. You are dismissed.'

Just as Koestler had deduced, Sneijder headed north after being refused assistance at the Hartenstein hotel, believing that his only hope of escape was into the thick woodland there. Arnhem and Oosterbeek were too dangerous now, and it would surely not be long before the civilians were evacuated and his presence became suspicious. Heading towards any of the other towns in the vicinity would leave him open to arrest as he would likely be a wanted criminal now.

Sneijder was tired and broken, and had absolutely no idea how he was going to get out. With his family lost, his mission failed and Frauke dead he really had nothing left to live for. Perhaps the best he could hope for was a quick and painless death but that was not the way the SS worked, especially not when one of their officers was out for revenge.

It was in this confused state of resignation that Sneijder approached a road through the forest as dusk was falling. He had been making his way through the trees for the last half an hour and it was a relief to emerge out of the gloom for a few seconds. Usually he would stop and check that all was clear before stepping out onto the road but this time he was careless. There was a slight rise leading up to the wide track with large boulders at steadily increasing heights laid out on the ground. For his own amusement, rather than check his run as he normally did, he increased his speed, took them two at the time and launched himself feet first onto the road. To his left, no more than twenty metres away, there was an SS patrol.

The two SS officers standing in front of the kubelwagen seemed as surprised as Sneijder about the turn of events. For a moment they just looked at him openmouthed, then one of them commanded him to freeze and began to raise his rifle. In no mood to allow them to question him, Sneijder already had his hand behind his back. He brought it forward again grasping the Luger. The single shot he fired at the one who had spoken caught him in the left ear. The officer screamed in pain and clutched at it as blood spurted from between his fingers.

Sneijder was already across the road and back amongst the trees by the time the second officer took a shot at him. The bullet thumped into a tree behind him and the birds scattered. There was another shout in exceptionally harsh German and the man appeared to give chase; Sneijder did not look, just continued to run. He was still heading roughly north. After about five minutes he thought he had lost the tail and he began to relax. However, as he moved through the woods he suddenly caught sight of a bespectacled man in a tailored suit and long flowing trenchcoat. It was very much the wrong dress for a stroll in the countryside and the man looked every bit the stereotypical Gestapo agent. Trusting his instincts, Sneijder paused and stepped behind a tall pine tree.

The man passed by about twenty-five metres ahead, followed a few seconds later by a similarly dressed man and then another in Gestapo uniform. After about a minute they were gone and Sneijder took several more steps forward towards the next group of trees. Suddenly he heard the sound of a man laughing and another voice answering with a playful insult, followed by a far more troublesome shout.

'Hey, you there, stop!'

As if conjured up by a magician the forest ahead was suddenly filled with German policemen; Gestapo, SS, Orpo – they were all there. There were at least fifteen of them and all were armed. The only thing that saved Sneijder was the thin screen of trees which made it difficult to line up a shot. He could not go any further in this direction; that was for sure. He turned about and fled. To his relief the expected barrage of gunfire never came.

The wireless operator raised a finger in the air to request silence and reached up to his headphones. The other men in the small front room of the hunting lodge obeyed. All focused their gaze on him expectantly. For thirty seconds he said nothing, just sat there with a look of intense concentration on his gaunt face and listened intently to the message he was receiving. Finally he pulled off the headset and said hurriedly to his superior, 'I think we've found him, sir. A man matching his description just walked into the patrol north of Oosterbeek and refused to stop when ordered to.'

Koestler was reclining in an easy chair beside the door and spoke without waiting for the message to be relayed to him. 'Where? Who found him?'

The wireless operator gave him the name of the officer and the exact coordinates of the location.

'That's less than a kilometre from here,' Koestler observed. 'In which direction is he now headed?'

There was a pause while the wireless operator sent out a message and waited for the reply. 'They believe he is going almost exactly due south, back towards the village. It's the only way he can go if the perimeter holds.'

Koestler struck the arm of the chair with his fist and broke out in a broad smile. 'We've got him,' he exclaimed. 'If he keeps going in that direction he will end up trapped between our men and the river.'

Klimitz gave a warning. 'Sir, there is every chance that he will seek refuge in one of the houses in the northern suburbs of Oosterbeek. We must be extremely careful.'

Koestler rose from his chair and walked over to the map which was pinned onto the wooden wall of the lodge, beneath an enormous stuffed deer's head mounted on a board. With a shaky hand he pulled his hip flask from his pocket and took a couple of gulps of whisky. 'All right then. He has to cross the Amsterdamseweg at some point - we'll try to cut him off there. I wish to be present at the arrest. Sebastien, my car.'

'Of course, sir.'

The two men walked out of the building, passing the owner of the lodge and his wife who sat on the porch; an old Dutch couple. They were wrapped up in thick woollen clothing against the evening cold and wore frightened expressions, no doubt inspired by the SS guard standing beneath the outside lamp clutching a machine pistol. Koestler felt no sympathy for them.

Sneijder kept running. It was pitch-black, total darkness all around, and it took all his concentration to find his way between the pine trees. The sound of his laboured breathing filled his ears. His heart pounded furiously. Sticks cracked beneath his feet, piercing the still night air like gunfire. The mist was settling over the forest now, reducing visibility to just a few metres; looking over his shoulder he saw nothing but the impenetrable cloak of night. He had no idea if they were still behind him but he couldn't risk stopping to find out. The thought of what they would do to him was too much to bear.

The choice was made for him. As he moved between two trees, he caught his foot on something and fell to the ground heavily. Rolling over on to his back he sat up, looking back in the direction he had come from. Nothing. Feeling a sharp pain in his lip he instinctively reached a hand up. His fingertips were tinged with blood, the barrel of his weapon bloodied where it had hit him in the face.

He heard a dog bark somewhere out in the fog. A voice called out and the dog barked again, closer this time. He pulled himself up on to his feet and stood still, listening for a moment. Another voice called out nearby. He turned around and starting running again. It began to rain, softly at first but as he reached a clearing in the woods it was getting heavier. The ground that had been firm underfoot was softer here; the going became more and more arduous.

Without warning his legs collapsed from under him and he dropped to the ground. He tried to move, to get away from the spot where he had fallen, but he couldn't; his arms and legs did not respond to his commands. Looking up and finding himself lying in the undergrowth beneath a giant oak tree rather than in the open, he breathed a sigh of relief. The rain was driving hard by this time and he hoped that might put the dogs off his scent. It was a lot to hope for. He put his head down and passed out.

The powerful headlamps on the front of the Mercedes cut a path through the darkness, illuminating the light mist that drifted across the forest. The driver accelerated up the incline at the end of the narrow lane and swept to the right, joining the wide thoroughfare of the Amsterdamseweg. Spread out along the road, every fifty metres or so, there was a policeman or security agent with a flashlight watching the woods to the north. So long as everyone did their job and Sneijder was not allowed to slip through the perimeter he would be forced to come this way – it was just a matter of time before he was captured.

Koestler sat in the rear of the car next to his adjutant but not speaking; he was deep in thought, contemplating the way things had turned out. For years he had carried the guilt of letting his wife slip away from him and it had torn him apart inside; now he also had the burden of knowing his decision to bring Frauke to be with him in Arnhem had killed her. His life was spiralling out of his control more and more each day, what with his alcoholism and the acceptance that Germany's inevitable defeat would bring personal repercussions for him. He could do nothing about either and he knew it – focusing all his energy on apprehending the man responsible for Frauke's death gave him a welcome distraction.

All of a sudden gunfire erupted to the right, out of the woods. A policeman about twenty metres up the road fell to the ground. The Mercedes was still travelling at thirty miles per hour and everyone in the car was thrown forwards when the driver slammed on the brakes. There was a loud thump from the front end.

'What the hell was that?' Koestler demanded.

Before the driver could reply, a figure scrambled up off the road in the full glare of the headlamps and looked directly at them through the windscreen.

'It's him!' Koestler cried, pointing furiously. 'We just hit him! Look!'

Sneijder was carrying a Sten submachine gun. He pointed it at the front window; though dazed he loosed off a burst of fire. Klimitz spotted the danger and acted instinctively, throwing his body forwards in front of Koestler. He caught two bullets in the stomach and dropped down into the foot well. Sneijder vanished into the night as swiftly as he had come.

Chapter Twenty–Four

As the road came into view, the line of flashlights alerted Sneijder to the presence of many German policemen. They were spread out in a chain, one every fifty metres, and presumably all would be carrying guns. Although it was dark there was little chance of slipping through unnoticed; the only possible way through would be using force. This was no longer the time to ponder the morals of taking lives - that had gone a long time ago; it was now a question of survival, every man for himself. The hunt was on, and any hesitation would be fatal.

Sneijder had the Sten strapped around his chest. He reloaded as he ran through the woods. Without breaking step he aimed at the Gestapo officer standing at the edge of the road about ten metres ahead and opened fire, hitting him several times in the chest. He went down quickly, the flashlight smashing on the ground beside him. Sneijder sprinted beyond, encroaching on to the road just as there was a roar from the left-hand side.

He saw the black Mercedes for a split-second before being blinded by the headlights. There was no way he could stop; his momentum carried him into the car's path, there was the shriek of tyres skidding on the asphalt and then the impact. The front wing of the car struck him in the shins and then he felt the grille against his body. Sneijder was flung backwards down the road, landing painfully. Fortunately the driver of the car had slowed it considerably in the second which had been available to him and the only injury Sneijder sustained was a twisted shoulder.

There was no time to recover his breath. Footsteps behind him warned him of the approach of another German officer and he scrambled to his feet, finding himself looking directly through the front window of the car. To his amazement, in the back seat was Koestler himself. Without hesitation Sneijder rattled off a short burst and then the chamber ran empty. He spun on his heel and sprinted away, ignoring the sharp pain in his ankle, and disappeared into the woods again. There was gunfire this time and a sudden burning agony in his left arm which he recognised as a gunshot wound.

Injured, exhausted, disorientated and scared, Sneijder continued to head due south through the woodland. He had been through here in the opposite direction a matter of hours ago but now his mood was quite different; the trap was closing around him and he was out of ideas about how to escape. The night was cold and blood continued to drip from the wound which he had hastily patched up with yet another strip from his shirt. The sound of the battle at Oosterbeek gave him something to aim for, in that so long as he continued towards it he would know he was going in the right direction. In his current state his progress was painfully slow. He was aware that the Germans could easily outflank him, but the reality was that they would probably not bother. After all, once he reached the river, where was he going to go?

All that Sneijder could think of was the tiredness and the pain in his legs and arm. His stamina levels were impressive - it was something the instructors at Arisaig had particularly commented on - but there was a limit to what any man could do. More than twelve hours of continuous walking, interspersed with sudden bursts of sprinting had taken all he had. Only fear and adrenalin were keeping him going now. He tried to focus his mind on other things but all he found were feelings about Frauke. That shot replayed over and over again in his mind, every single aspect of it. Why had he taken it, why? It tore him up inside, causing him pain like he had never known, the realisation that he would never experience the joy and passion again. She was a beautiful person inside and out, he loved being with her, and yet he had betrayed her. It was that simple. And now she was dead and he could never explain.

Sneijder skirted around the various battles, crossing the railway line and making his way down a narrow corridor between Wolfheze and Oosterbeek, using the woods as cover. The Utrechtseweg was deserted at the point he crossed it and he was soon back in the woods and on his way towards the river.

Dawn was breaking as he approached the Rhine and it was raining heavily from a leaden sky. While the trees had provided shelter there was a hundred-metre expanse of grass leading down to the bank, and any advance towards it would expose him to the elements. Sneijder decided against it, realising that this would be unpleasant and only serve to put him in the open. What he really needed was some rest and time to plan his next step. He slumped down behind a row of thick bushes and laid himself out flat.

Koestler had to ride in the car for the whole journey to the German military hospital with Klimitz slumped in the seat beside him crying out in agony. In the end it took almost half an hour for him to die, with the bullets lodged in his abdomen and the doctors unable to do anything to save him.

Afterwards Koestler sat outside in the corridor for a while, looking into space and allowing the incident and the loss of his closest confidant to sink in. Having emptied the hip flask of its contents he put it back in his pocket and took out Klimitz's silver cigarette case - a family heirloom embossed with the seal of Otto von Bismarck. He opened it and removed one of its contents. Koestler lit the cigarette with a match, inhaled and blew out a stream of smoke. It was a testament to the captain that his sacrifice did not come as a surprise - indeed, Koestler did not expect anything less from such a man. That was not to say that laying down one's life for one's superior was an expectation of service for everybody, just that Klimitz's own personal morals demanded it.

In a way, Koestler felt honoured that his adjutant would do such a thing. However he found it difficult to reconcile. Deep down he knew that he did not deserve it and for a man like him it was a waste - soon he would find himself punished for his actions during the war and would likely face a death sentence. That was the problem with life; it was all so futile, so meaningless. An act of chivalry could quickly be rendered pointless by events which were uncontrollable, and it would fade away into the passage of time.

Koestler scolded himself for allowing sentiment to enter his head. What was important now was catching the person responsible for all of the death and misery. To do so would be the best way to honour a fine man, and to find vengeance for having his daughter stolen away from him. More determined than he had ever been before, he stood and dropped the cigarette to the floor, stamping it out under his boot. He turned and marched down the corridor, barging his way through the set of doors at the end. As he moved out of the front entrance of the hospital a young officer named Spohnheimer who had been involved in the search for Sneijder approached him.

'Get a message through to Horvath,' Koestler ordered him. 'Tell him I want as many men as possible at the Rhine around Heveadorp, as soon as possible. If my feelings about this Sneijder are correct I think he will look for a way to cross the river. We should apprehend him before he abandons this plan and goes into hiding.'

'Very good, sir.'

Koestler continued across the gravel driveway and climbed into the back of his waiting car, his third Mercedes in the last six weeks. The driver quickly pulled out and drove away into the last of the darkness before morning.

Sneijder had managed to sleep for a while but was woken by the sounds of artillery fire coming from the northeast. The rain was still falling heavily and he was soaked to the bone, though the hawthorn bush had protected him from the full torrent. The sharp burning pain in his left arm had now receded to a dull ache. The tightness of the sleeve of his leather jacket had held the makeshift tourniquet in place, preventing any further bleeding. It was a minor miracle that the bullet had failed to hit an artery - the second time Sneijder had experienced such a happening in his life - but one which he appreciated.

The rest had allowed him the time to consider his options. It would be a massive undertaking to get back to

England, and in his eyes it was foolish to try when the British Army were so close. The best course of action would be to contact London and see if they could arrange to help him. In order to achieve this he would need access to a wireless radio set, and this meant he would need to get to Wesley Lamming's farm. Unfortunately this was not possible without somehow crossing the river.

Sneijder crawled out from his hiding place, got to his feet and strolled over to the edge of the woods where he could look out over the Rhine. He was standing around one hundred metres from the bank, with a flat stretch of grass between the water and himself. The river snaked around a bend at this point and was about two hundred metres wide, and beyond that was polder, drained bog land, topped by a row of tall poplar trees which appeared like spectres through the rainy mist. Rain rippled across the water, each drop piercing the surface like a needle.

Sneijder collected his kitbag and wandered down to the edge of the river, listening to the artillery and mortar fire coming from the vicious battle at Oosterbeek five or six kilometres away. Where it was usually blue the Rhine was today grey under a dull and overcast sky. Sneijder started to walk along the bank in a westerly direction, hoping to come across a boatyard or someone who could assist him in getting across to the other side. There were a group of buildings in the distance, perhaps two kilometres away and he continued to move towards them, feeling thoroughly miserable as the wind blew the rain into his face. In places the thick grass was turning to mud beneath his feet and he had to concentrate to keep his footing. After walking about a kilometre he stopped to rest and turned to once more look out across the river.

Out of the corner of his eye he saw movement away to his left, from the direction in which he had come. For ten seconds he kept looking and saw nothing, but then he saw it again, a figure appearing from behind the trees. At first it was little more than just a dot at the top of a rise but as it continued to move towards him he realised that the figure was in uniform, coloured dove grey. Suddenly there was another man and then another, and once more the area was swarming with German police. An armoured car bounced towards him over the rough terrain and behind it there was a troop carrier truck which pulled to a halt and unloaded around twenty men.

Sneijder had nowhere to go. With vehicles heading in his direction he could not possibly outrun them, and the nearest cover was some distance away. There were so many of them that he would not be able to disappear in the woods for long in any case. He turned and looked out across the river. It was shallow near the shore but quickly became significantly deeper and the bank opposite was very steep. While there was not a strong current the swirling wind and rain made the surface of the water choppy and uneven, and it looked cold and miserable. If he was honest he had no idea if he could swim that far; he was so exhausted. It was madness surely, an impossible task and yet it was the only option left. Without considering it any further, Sneijder dropped the kitbag to the ground, reached into his waistband and took out the Luger. Unceremoniously, he tossed it into the Rhine. He stripped right down to his underwear, casting off his sodden wares, and steadied himself. With a deep breath and a quick prayer, he launched himself into the river and started to swim for all he was worth.

The Rhine was bitterly cold and contemptuously un-forgiving. While it had looked calm on the surface there were one or two fairly strong currents in the deeper areas which took Sneijder by surprise. To swim the two hundred metres to the south bank took every ounce of energy he possessed and an unflinching desire to survive. The pain from his gunshot wound became almost unbearable about halfway across but to stop would be fatal and he ploughed on. It was an act which in the past would have been beyond him but af-ter all he had gone through since returning to his homeland he was now a stronger character. He never once looked back but he heard the German voices yelling at one another in an attempt to find out what course of action they should take. He did not realise that Koestler was there nor did he hear the command to hold fire but the sound of silence from their guns was like beautiful music to him.

When he finally dragged himself out on the other side and collapsed breathlessly to the ground, Sneijder was about fifty metres downstream of where he had begun his crossing. For the next ten minutes he lay there near naked in the pouring rain, coughing and spluttering but safe from the Germans trapped on the other side. Snei-jder comforted himself with the thought that the blocked Arnhem road bridge would slow down Koestler's forces and allow him the space to disappear. This time he had to make it count.

To Koestler's frustration, it took more than two hours for Horvath to organise the men he had requested and assemble them at the river. For a man so experienced in the area of administration and organisation it was a source of bewilderment to him that people could find a simple task so difficult to complete. In the case of Horvath, the Gestapo man's narcissistic need to be in charge always prevented him from following orders efficiently; it was only because he was a distant relation of Rauter that he still held his position.

The continuing battles for Arnhem and Oosterbeek made access to the river difficult and it required a sweep around to the north and west to complete the journey. The ferry that connected Heveadorp and Driel had been captured by a small band of British troops and was still in their hands and so also had to be steered clear of. All the while there was the accompaniment of bursting shells and exploding mortar bombs, ever increasing as the number of tanks brought in by the Waffen-SS steadily grew. At a little before eight o'clock the search westwards along the river bank began, led by uniformed Gestapo and SD officers and bolstered by four armoured cars taken from the SS car pool. In many places there was thick woodland right down to the water's edge and the passage of the vehicles was impossible; they were forced to return to the main roads, approaching the river once again several kilometres downstream. Despite this it was not long before they spotted Sneijder making his way along the Rhine and they closed in quickly.

Despite Sneijder obviously being a tough and determined individual it surprised Koestler to see him turn and dive into the river. On a wild day such as this it looked very uninviting indeed, and it was a distance that all but the strongest of swimmers would surely find too much. If one were to get into difficulties there would be no hope of rescue and death would quickly follow; after spending the entire previous day and night running and being shot Sneijder could not possibly be in a good physical condition. In short, it was a huge risk.

The men closest to Sneijder reached the bank and raised their rifles to shoot. Koestler ordered them to stop; this was not what he had in mind, to kill the man when he was trying to escape and see his body washed away down the river. No, that would not be vengeance - giving him an easy way out would not redress the balance which had been disturbed by the murders of Frauke and Klimitz. Sneijder had to be caught and know he had been caught; he needed to feel fear and terror and know he was going to die before he actually received the *coup de grâce*. Nothing else would do.

Now wearing nothing but a pair of underpants Sneijder would have been cold were it not for the extreme physical exertion of crossing the river. However he did not wish to run into a German patrol in his current condition and headed into the first village he came across, hoping he could acquire a set of clothes from a helpful soul. That village was Driel, the location of Frank Helder's country house, and he was greeted warmly at the first house he called at by a plump and kindly housewife. Fortunately she was used to not asking questions, simply providing him with a towel and a set of her farmhand husband's clothes and sending him on his way, after insisting he have something to eat.

During his time on the run in central Europe Sneijder had honed an excellent sense of direction and it led him quickly to his destination. It was not quite eleven o'clock when he vaulted the locked three-barred gate and walked up towards the farmhouse. Over to his right was the huge barn against the wall of which he had practised his rifle shooting. With a grimace he remembered his below-par performance with the weapon. If only he had taken heed of the warning and not taken those shots at Koestler - once more, the memory of Frauke and her demise was like a dagger to his heart.

In the courtyard at the front of the little cottage there was a figure with his back to Sneijder; he had a slight stoop and was wielding an axe a little unsteadily. On the large block in front of him was a log taken from an oak tree, now in two pieces. The grey-haired character was puffing and breathing heavily.

Sneijder afforded himself a chuckle and said loudly, 'Are you not a little old for that sort of thing?'

Wesley Lamming turned around slowly. At first his face betrayed surprise, then after a small frown his blue eyes brightened. 'Did your mother never tell you to respect the elderly?' he replied good-humouredly. 'Mr Voorman, isn't it?'

'Sneijder,' the young agent told him. 'Johannes.'

For a second the old man looked confused, and then there was a flash of recognition. 'Ah, I see. I thought.... well, I thought the Gestapo would have picked you up along with my grandson.' For the first time he looked at Sneijder properly. 'My God, you look awful. Did they get to you?'

Sneijder shook his head. 'Not yet - when they arrested the others I went underground but they are after me. To be honest I am putting you in jeopardy by coming here but I didn't know who else to trust.'

'Will they know you are here?'

'I should clarify what I mean,' Sneijder said. 'I've literally got the entire German police apparatus of Arnhem after me right now. I had to swim across the Rhine to get away from them. I came here because I need to use the wireless set in your barn to contact London.'

Lamming raised his eyebrows.

'Perhaps I'd better explain,' Sneijder added.

The best way to establish trust with the old man and acquire his cooperation was to lay everything out exactly as it was which is precisely what Sneijder did. He told him about working as an agent for the British government, about the assignment to assassinate Koestler, about the Petrovskys, about the car accident which failed to kill the SS chief. He explained how he had shot Koestler's daughter by mistake but omitted his own relationship with her – that would only cloud what was at present a clear and untarnished situation – and completed the story by telling him about the battle in Arnhem and his escape and being on the run.

Lamming listened intently until he was finished then replied: 'My, that is quite a story you tell. I see why this Koestler chap is so determined to catch you. And yet the British still won't help you despite the fact you're working for them?'

'I am hoping they will organise something if I can get in contact with our home station,' Sneijder told him, 'even if I have to continue into France and then meet up with the appropriate unit.'

Lamming frowned. 'The gentleman on the next farm tells me the German military are holding a firm blocking line just north of the Waal river, between Arnhem and Nijmegen. He tried to get through this morning and couldn't. I don't think you'll be getting any further south.'

Sneijder sighed. 'Then I'm afraid I shall have to ask something of you which I have no right to. I must stay here and take whatever it is they wish to throw at me – running is no longer an option. I must ask you to leave your own farm for a while.'

'I shall do nothing of the sort,' Lamming replied a little indignantly, raising a hand when Sneijder started to interrupt. His face softened as he continued, 'That is not to say however that you cannot stay. Sometimes a man must make a stand; he must turn around and say to his adversary 'I will not run from you anymore.' I admire that sentiment. But the Germans will not force me from my home.'

'They will come here in numbers and use extreme force,' Sneijder told him, 'and they will kill anybody they think has helped me. Are you certain you should stay?'

Suddenly the old man's eyes lit up, like a schoolboy's after being given a peashooter for the first time. 'Johannes, I am very nearly eighty years old. The most excitement I get these days is...... well, actually I don't get any. You are offering me the opportunity to battle it out with the people who have killed members of my family. Do you think I really want to leave? Besides, you are not planning on losing are you?'

'I hope not.'

'Good. Neither am I. Go and send your message and then we shall plan our defence.'

'There is one more thing,' Sneijder said, removing the jacket he was wearing and pulling down his shirt to reveal the bullet wound in the top of his arm.

Lamming gasped, but on closer inspection he seemed less concerned. 'It's not too bad; it looks like the bullet has gone straight through. Come inside and we will get it cleaned up.'

As the old man had said it was a clean wound and after attending to it with cotton wool and antiseptic he bandaged it up tidily. Sneijder went over to the barn and climbed the ladder to the attic. At the end of the room he located the loose floorboard, lifted it and crawled down into the secret compartment beneath. The wireless set was still in the box beneath the old dusty sheet, apparently untouched from the last time he had seen it.

He carefully eased the box open and was confronted with an array of wires, dials and switches. It was a different type of radio to the one which Sneijder had been trained on but it worked on the same principles. After checking that the crystals were in place in the electronic oscillator which controlled the frequency, Sneijder found the aerial antenna, a long thin cable about seventy feet long which needed to be fully extended in order to operate satisfactorily. He unfurled it across the length of the loft, found a hole in the wall to poke it through and dropped the rest down the outside of the wall of the barn. He then returned to the radio set, flicked the power switch and was relieved to see a small red light indicating life in the battery.

The batteries which were installed in these sorts of transceivers could not provide much power and would rapidly run down so Sneijder knew he would need to work quickly. Placing the headphones over his ears, he turned the volume dial upwards and heard the familiar electronic buzz which moved up and down in tone. He decided to transmit on an open frequency in order to maximise the reach of his broadcast, though this would be far less secure and could possibly alert the Germans. With a deep breath he began to tap out a message in Morse code, not making any attempt to encrypt his words.

Calling Home Station Poundon Calling Home Station Poundon Stop This Is Polo Stop Repeat This Is Polo Stop My Cover Is Blown Stop Am Surrounded By Police And Require Urgent Assistance Stop Ongoing Battle In Area Prevents Escape Stop Have 48 Hrs At Most But Probably Less Stop Repeat Require Urgent Assistance Stop Location Is As Follows Stop

Sneijder then proceeded to give the precise longitude and latitude co-ordinates for the farm which Lamming had read to him from a map. He felt incredibly foolish doing so, knowing that he was giving away his position to anybody that cared to listen but Koestler and his men would find him eventually. As far as he could see, the only hope he had was that help would come his way.

Sneijder packed up all the components of the wireless set into the box and replaced it beneath the sheet in the secret compartment, then returned to the farmhouse. A peculiar feeling of relief began to come over him as he strolled across the open ground, as he realised that he had done everything it was possible to do. From now on his destiny was out of his hands and he could attribute no blame to himself.

The old man had made a quick meal while Sneijder had been out at the barn and they discussed what they would do as they ate. Afterwards they walked out into the copse behind the grain silos and opened up the small weapons bunker which Van Rijn had shown to Sneijder. As Lamming's grandson had explained, most of the items in there had never been used, as the majority would only have been useful in a time of open warfare. Throughout the German occupation, resistance had always been an underground activity; sabotage and attacks with small arms. There had been no place for the use of the more substantial items which lined the bunker; now however they would finally see action.

With just two of them it would not be practical to use the mortars, and while Sneijder had been trained on the use of such weapons he was not prepared to risk his life on his ability with them. He took a couple of boxes of mines, some grenades, the Bren and one of the MG-42s from the bunker and gradually transferred them to the farmhouse.

The anti-personnel mines were of the German S-type. These were relatively small devices the size of soup cans which were designed to, when activated, spring three to four feet in the air before exploding. On detonation the mines would fragment, sending hundreds of ball bearings across an area of several metres. American troops had nicknamed them 'bouncing Bettys' while their propensity to maim soldiers' genitalia had led British forces to crudely christen them 'debollockers'. They could be set up with standard pressure switches which responded to a man's weight or connected to tripwires via a specially made adaptor.

Sneijder used a combination of these methods. Any force which came to the farm would obviously heavily outnumber himself and Lamming and would in all probability attempt to encircle them. It would be extremely difficult for the two of them to defend a position against a group of men coming from several directions at once, so Sneijder decided to ring the farm's perimeter with mines. Mine clearance was a laborious and time-consuming enterprise, and in order to save time the Germans would be likely to clear one area and then send all of their men through at this point. Sneijder and

Lamming would thenceforth only need to fight an enemy which was coming at them head-on.

Sneijder spent the next five hours laying the mines, setting them up with pressure switches in the open areas, such as in the fields behind the farmhouse, and with trip-wires stretched out between trees in the woods. His para-military training had taught him how to work with such explosives and so it was not a difficult undertaking. Each time he laid a mine he marked it on a diagram of the farm to ensure he did not step on them himself.

Afterwards he returned to the farmhouse. With the old man Lamming's help, Sneijder barricaded all the windows in the house except the two in the downstairs front room either side of the main door. In front of these two windows he placed the Bren and the MG-42, each propped up on its barrel-mounted bipod. The MG-42 in particular was a terrifying weapon with an astonishing rate of fire, being capable of well over a thousand rounds a minute. While the Bren gun took cartridges the German gun required long belts of ammunition to sustain it; Sneijder piled up four such belts within easy reach.

By the time all this was accomplished it was almost eight o'clock. Sneijder gave Lamming some quick instruction on the use of both weapons and was pleased to discover that the old man was quite a good shot.

'What do we do now?' Lamming asked when they were finished.

Sneijder gave a tense look. 'Now we wait.'

Later, Sneijder and Lamming sat at the kitchen table, illuminated by a flickering gas lamp. On the table in front of them there was a collection of pistols and two shotguns, one of which was double-barrelled, along with some ammunition. It was coming up to two o'clock in the morning according to the tall grandfather clock which ticked noisily in the hallway. The old man's wrinkled face caught the half-light, the shadows of his experience lines exacerbated by the dull glow.

For the past two hours they had each been discussing their lives up to this point. Sneijder had told Lamming all about his family, the prison camp and Mauthausen and his execution of Kemerling, and all that had happened since he returned to the Netherlands at the beginning of July.

Lamming had regaled him with tales from his youth, as a young man sailing across the world on merchant ships. He told Sneijder of Southeast Asia, of China and Japan and Malaya, and of trips to the Indian subcontinent. Afterwards he spoke of his life as a farmer and his family; his children and then his grandchildren. The old man was warm and kind and obviously extremely proud of his three sons and one daughter, the woman who had given birth to Van Rijn.

'Yes, I have lived a long and good life,' Lamming concluded. 'I have enjoyed many great experiences, and endured some not so great. But overall, I cannot complain.'

Sneijder had consumed several glasses of alcohol and was beginning to lose his usual inhibitions. He spoke more openly than ever. 'I always thought I would grow old and experience the best of life. It is funny how things never turn out the way you expect.'

Lamming chuckled. 'You're not wrong there. I could never have predicted the way my life would pan out. However you will still have the chance to experience it all. This is not the end for you; I am quite convinced of that.'

'I would like to believe you but there is no escape. They will come for me. Koestler will not rest until one of us is dead.'

'Then we must make sure it is him and not you,' Lamming replied. 'You will leave here alive.'

'And what about you?' Sneijder asked. 'I can't say I understand why you are still here. This is not your fight.'

Lamming said nothing for a while, obviously searching for the right words. 'For four and a half years we have been occupied. All of that time my grandson and young men like him have been resisting, more so throughout the past year. But I am an old man, a fossil who has simply had to sit back and accept the conquest of my country – a country I have helped to build. While more able men have gone out and made an attempt to liberate the Netherlands I have become useless, a burden.

'I have been searching for a purpose – some opportunity for me to stand up and prove that I am still a man, that I still have courage and a will to fight for my nation and for my Queen. Keeping you alive is that purpose. You got out when things became bad – you could easily have remained in Switzerland and ignored your country but you obviously felt ashamed to do that. I have felt that shame for years.'

'This is not resistance,' Sneijder insisted. 'This is a suicide mission. We will both die here.'

'Then so be it,' Lamming declared. 'I will end my eighty years fighting, going down with a gun in my hand. Look at it another way if you wish. I will be killed for allowing you to hide out at my home; I may as well take a few of them with me.'

For a couple of minutes they were silent. The ticking clock in the next room was the only sound in the dark house. Lamming struggled up from his chair and hobbled over to the window to peer out. He returned after thirty seconds and shook his head.

Sneijder took another drink of whisky. Eventually he asked a question which had been going around in his head for the past few days. 'What do you believe happens when we die?' It was a very direct question to ask a man of a very different generation but death seemed so near that it was an extremely pertinent issue.

Lamming took his seat opposite Sneijder once more. 'That is an interesting question but one which for a man of my age, brought up in the 1860s and 70s, is easy to answer. I do not share my grandson's communist and atheistic ideals. I believe that if you are deserving you will go to be with the Lord.' He studied Sneijder's face and added matter-of-factly: 'But you do not believe.'

Sneijder shook his head. 'I want to – believe me, I do – but I have seen too many terrible things for that. My parents, my brother and my sisters were..... are all good, innocent people. What sort of God would let them be taken away? What God would allow prison camp guards to kill children?'

'It is so difficult for us to comprehend,' the old man replied, 'but human free will allows these things to happen, not God. We must have free will.'

'I wish I could believe in *something* though,' Sneijder told him. 'I find it hard to cope with the idea that this life is the be-all and end-all, particularly at a moment like this.'

Lamming leaned forward and explained, 'When I wake up early in the morning and see the beautiful sunrise, hear the birds singing in the trees and smell the flowers, I am convinced that there is some higher power.

I can only go by what I have been taught, and that is to believe in Jesus Christ.'

Sneijder said, 'It must give you a greater peace when facing death, that knowledge you will go to a better place.'

'I couldn't tell you – I've never faced death before,' Lamming answered. 'And I don't know if I'm deserving.'

'I'm sure you are.'

'Perhaps I will soon know.' Lamming pulled the drink away from his companion, changing the subject. 'Right, you should get some sleep. I'll take the first watch and wake you in four hours.'

'Are you sure?' Sneijder asked. 'Maybe I should.....'

'Nonsense.' Lamming quashed Sneijder's response a little harder than he intended. 'I am not an invalid. Now go upstairs and I shall see you in four hours' time.' With that he picked up a Sten gun and a couple of magazines from the kitchen table and shuffled off into the sitting room.

Chapter Twenty-Five

It was over two days before the report from the direction-finders reached Koestler. In this time he had become very agitated by the failure to locate Sneijder and had begun to fear that he had allowed the agent to slip through his fingers. He had instructed Horvath and the Orpo man Prinz to carry out an extensive search in the villages south of the river while he remained at his home and awaited news. Without Klimitz to stop him Koestler drank and smoked heavily, plagued by the despair of losing Frauke, the apparent escape of her killer and his own impending doom.

Over the same two days the Allied offensive at Arnhem had fallen apart under considerable German pressure. The attempt to capture the Rhine Bridge had failed and been abandoned, and the troops involved in the assault had all either been killed or taken prisoner but for a few isolated pockets of resistance. The rest of the British forces were now surrounded in Oosterbeek, defending a rapidly diminishing perimeter, and it was now just a matter of time before they were defeated.

The Gestapo had trucks with radio detecting equipment driving around the area on a regular basis and one of them had picked up a suspicious message coming from a farm to the west of Elst. Eventually the report had found its way to an officer involved in the hunt for Sneijder and then to Horvath. The radio broadcast had been addressed to England on an open frequency, and a little detective work had revealed the farm belonged to Kees van Rijn's maternal grandfather.

Koestler went into SS headquarters to check the status of the search. He was in his office when Horvath was shown in, a bottle of scotch on the desk in front of him. 'Ah, you are here,' he said. 'Do you have something to report? I should hope that by now...'

Horvath interrupted him. 'We think we have a good lead, sir. I believe we may have found him.' The Gestapo officer explained the details to his superior.

Koestler listened to the information and began nodding. It had to be the place; of that he was sure. It made perfect sense – the German blocking line between Arnhem and Nijmegen would make it impossible for Sneijder to travel any further south, and his visit to the British headquarters in Oosterbeek showed that rescue was clearly in his mind. It was perfectly logical for him to try to contact London in the hope that they would arrange for the army to assist him. 'Finally, some promising news,' Koestler said. 'Now we must deal with the situation. How soon can you have a battalion of men ready to go to this farm?'

'It's going to take some time,' Horvath replied. 'I have men spread out from here to Nijmegen and the continuing military action in that area is making movement difficult. None of the major roads are currently passable.'

'How long?'

'Several hours at least.'

In his intoxicated state Koestler did not even attempt to disguise his disdain for the man in front of him. 'That is unacceptable. Damn it, Horvath, why must you always be so difficult? This man has made himself an enemy of the German people and it is our duty to apprehend him. We must not give him a chance to escape.'

'Well I don't know what you expect me to do,' Horvath snapped. 'It'll take as long as it takes.'

Koestler answered harshly, 'I expect you to see that it doesn't. Gather together as many men as you can, arm them as heavily as possible and then report back to me, and make it quick. I will lead the assault personally.'

'How many men do you require?'

'As many as you can assemble – twenty or thirty,' Koestler responded.

Horvath eyed him warily. 'Twenty or thirty? To capture one man?'

'One man who murdered my daughter,' the Obersturmbannführer said firmly. 'Catching him is an absolute priority and I am taking no chances. These people are trained to be invisible, Horvath, remember that. We shall need as much help as we can get.'

Horvath hesitated, a look of frustration upon his face. Koestler gave him a challenging glare, daring him to argue, and he folded. 'Yes, sir,' he answered frostily.

'Good. You are dismissed.'

Koestler made a few phone calls, repeating his order to Horvath's Orpo and SD counterparts. Afterwards he returned home and freshened himself up, had a meal and dressed in his spare black uniform. This was to be a great hour for him after the hell of the last few days, as he would be the one to arrest a British agent and bring him to justice. Koestler took great care as he pinned his badges and ribbons from the Western Front to his breast. If this was to be the final success of his career, perhaps even his life, he wanted to look the part, like a military man of some consequence. He went into a drawer and brought out his Iron Cross second class, his most prized possession. Standing in front of the mirror, he put the ribbon around his neck and positioned the decoration at his throat. He glanced up at his reflection and sighed.

Despite the immaculately cut tunic and the gleaming acclamations of the past he was still a tired middle-aged man who looked even older. The vices he could not shake off were displayed for all to see on his face. The pale and dishevelled complexion, the reddened nose, the slightly bloodshot eyes – all pointed to a man whose drinking was now out of control.

Finally he opened a shoebox in the bottom of his wardrobe and produced an old black First World War service revolver in a tattered leather holster; the weapon he had used to defend his trench and win the Iron Cross. He pulled the gun out of the holster and examined the base of the handle; scratched into the metal were the words 'Verdun 1916'. Koestler shuddered at the memory of those dark tunnels full of misery and death and rotting flesh. Slamming the revolver to the bottom of the leather pouch he decided that this would be the weapon with which he would execute Johannes Sneijder. Then things would be as they should be.

It was dusk before the required numbers of men were assembled in Arnhem. The fighting in the city centre had all but ceased entirely and so it was now safe for the security forces to be there. The contrast between the area around SS headquarters on the east side of town which had escaped damage and the area around the bridge was startling. The houses on either side of the bridge ramp had been occupied by the British troops and so had subsequently been completely demolished by German artillery. In addition, the use of flamethrowers to clear out the most stubbornly defended buildings had led to devastating fires. Eventually the Germans had brought up a huge 105mm gun which had flattened the schoolhouse and ended the resistance of the paratroopers.

Koestler's Mercedes spearheaded the German police convoy which roared across the bridge heading south. Behind were four kubelwagens and two huge troop carriers, the rears of which were full of men from the various police organisations. There were over twenty-five officers in total, each armed with a rifle or MP40 and prepared to storm the farm. Bringing up the rear was an armoured car from the Gestapo pool.

In the back of his car, Koestler studied a detailed schematic of the farm which he had obtained from the local land registry. Although it was dated 1938 it was reasonable to assume that the property would not be fundamentally different and so the map could be used to plan an assault.

The farmhouse was in the centre of the plot, with a wide courtyard in front flanked by a large barn and stables. There were fields on three sides, protected from the nearest road by a thin screen of woodland. The woods grew denser towards the front of the property, the dirt track – the main vehicular access – cutting through the middle. Another dirt track divided two of the surrounding fields at the back of the farmhouse.

Koestler began to draw on the schematic, indicating where he would position his troops during the operation. He decided on a heavy thrust up the main drive with vehicles while a small group of men would approach from the rear through the fields, in order to encircle Sneijder.

A little after nine o'clock, with darkness now having fallen, the convoy of vehicles slowed to a halt outside the three-barred gate. The tailgates of the trucks were dropped and the officers climbed down. Horvath strolled up to the window of the Mercedes.

Koestler shone his flashlight on to the diagram so that the Gestapo man could see. 'This is what I want to happen. Take ten or so men and go around here, behind the main farmhouse. Approach through the fields but keep it quiet. Wait for my signal. When you hear us open fire, move in. Is that understood?'

'Yes, sir,' Horvath replied. 'Will you lead the frontal attack?'

'That is correct. Between us we shall encircle him.'

Horvath followed his orders and disappeared into the woods with a group of Gestapo officers. Koestler stepped out of his car and walked over to where the remaining policemen stood. The commanding Orpo officer Prinz stepped forward to speak to him.

'We'll go up the main entrance road with the vehicles – the troops behind,' Koestler ordered. 'Spread some out either side too, through the forest. Right, let's go.' He turned to the kubelwagen parked beside him. 'You – what's your name?'

'Schmidt, sir,' the young man in the driver's seat replied.

'You lead the way in, Schmidt. Ram the gate down and keep going until you get the buildings in sight.'

The kubelwagen's engine roared as it pulled out from behind the other vehicles. It swung to the right and crashed through the weak three-barred gate with ease.

Prinz waved for the men to follow and they began to jog in the same direction, guns raised for action. As they all started to vanish into the night Koestler walked back to his car, taking a swig of whisky from his hip flask before climbing in. It was at that moment that he heard the explosion.

The sound of the explosion woke Sneijder with a start. He glanced at the small alarm clock beside the bed and realised he had been asleep for almost five hours. He sat up and glanced out of the bedroom window. Seeing nothing he got up and moved closer but there was still just the darkness of night. Sneijder went downstairs to find Lamming standing next to the front window.

'Is this it?' he asked the old man. 'Are they here?'

Lamming shrugged his tired shoulders and replied, 'I don't know – I presume so but I haven't seen anyone yet. Sounds like your mines have claimed their first victim.'

For two and a half days the pair of them had watched and waited, hoping for a sign of the Allies coming to the rescue but expecting the German police under the command of Koestler. Sneijder was surprised at the time it had taken them to locate him, particularly given his radio broadcast - the Gestapo were renowned in the occupied countries of Europe for their excellent radio direction-finding.

Sneijder moved across to the other window and looked for himself. There was another explosion a touch closer and a man's cry, definitely this time.

Lamming looked up. 'You heard that?'

Sneijder nodded. 'Poor sod. They have stumbled upon my little surprise, it seems.' He sighed. 'Well, it was just a matter of time before they tracked me down.'

'What should we do?' the old man asked.

'Let's wait and see how brave they are with the mines while it is dark.' He checked the mechanism on the MG-42 machine gun in front of him, making sure it was ready to fire. 'In the meantime, let's check that we have everything ready.'

The blast from the anti-personnel mine which had been buried under the road blew the wheel off the kubelwagen and seriously injured the young driver. The wrecked vehicle now blocked the entrance road into the farm. Koestler's heart sank. It was likely that there would be other mines, a fact confirmed by the second blast just a minute later from amongst the trees. The troops standing along the road froze exactly where they were.

A couple of minutes passed before Prinz appeared from out of the woods looking distraught. 'Sir, the area appears to be heavily mined,' he said. 'One of them just took out three of my men. We must wait for daylight before we proceed.'

Koestler shook his head. 'We cannot afford to wait. He will have heard the explosions; he will know we are here now.'

Prinz answered firmly. 'Sir, I cannot order my men blindly into a minefield in the dark. The mines are connected to tripwires - in daylight we will be able to see them and we may have a chance of avoiding them. We must wait.'

Koestler was not swayed. 'It is absolutely out of the question. He could get away if we don't go in now.'

Prinz was becoming exasperated. 'Sir, with all due respect, we have the place surrounded – where can he possibly go?'

Koestler considered this for a moment. He had to admit that Prinz had a point, and it did seem foolish to risk the lives of any more men when it could be avoided by waiting until dawn. 'Very well,' he responded resignedly. 'Pull your men back. But we go in at first light – do I make myself clear?'

'Quite clear, sir.'

Koestler turned to a junior officer who was standing behind him. 'Corporal, do you know Lieutenant Horvath, the Gestapo officer?'

The young man nodded. 'Yes, sir.'

'Good. I have sent him around here with a group of his men,' Koestler explained, pointing to the schematic of the farm which he held in front of him. 'I would like you to go to him and warn him that there may be landmines in the fields between the farmhouse and himself. Tell him that my orders are for him to remain in position and await further instructions. But let him know that he may not hear from me until morning.'

'Is that all, sir?' the corporal asked.

'Yes, that's all. Be as quick as you can.'

The corporal went immediately, returning forty-five minutes later without comment. Koestler was surprised that Horvath had apparently accepted his orders without question. However there was a first time for everything and the threat of landmines made it foolish for the Gestapo officer to argue.

Koestler ensured that the men who had withdrawn from the farm held a perimeter which would prevent any sort of escape by Sneijder. They set up camp in surrounding fields and built fires to protect themselves from the cold, drinking coffee and smoking cigarettes when it was not their turn to sleep. The night seemed to drag. Koestler tried to sleep in the back of his car but thoughts buzzed around his head and he remained awake, impatient to get into the farm and capture Sneijder and end the terrible ordeal which had claimed the life of his only child.

Dawn broke just before seven o'clock, allowing the Germans the first proper look at the farm and its surrounding area. Koestler sent for all his senior officers and gathered them around him at the front gate to discuss the situation. After an uncomfortable night sleeping outside in cold conditions neither Prinz nor Horvath were in a particularly good mood. Prahl from the Abwehr listened quietly.

'So what is the present situation?' Koestler asked. 'We must get into this farm building as soon as possible. Will we be able to encircle Sneijder or not?'

For a second the two other men looked at one another, and then Prinz spoke. 'It may be possible to move men through the woods if they are extremely careful and can avoid triggering the tripwires but it would be a huge risk and unlikely to succeed. I would strongly advise against it – these mines could be booby trapped in some other manner or there could be others buried out of sight. If one were to go off in such an enclosed space the damage would be enormous.'

Koestler displayed no expression. 'The safety of these men is of secondary importance, is that understood? However, I will not risk their lives needlessly if there is little chance of success. Horvath, how are things on your side?'

'We will be unable to proceed, sir,' the Gestapo officer replied, shrugging his shoulders. 'It is impossible.'

'That is not your decision to make,' said Koestler in an acerbic tone. 'I did not ask you what we should do; I asked what the situation was currently.'

Horvath continued. 'It is impossible to approach the farm from the rear, sir. As well as there being a very real danger of stepping on one, these mines have a devastating psychological effect and the men are refusing....'

'For God's sake, Horvath, can you not answer a simple question?' Koestler exploded, gesturing angrily at his subordinate. 'Just tell me the situation so that *I* can make a decision as to the best course of action.'

'Our initial belief is that there may be a large number of mines in the fields and along the rear access road. There are no tripwires to indicate where these explosives might be buried so attempting to walk through this area would, in my opinion, be nothing short of suicidal. Clearing the mines will take several days at least.' Horvath gave Koestler a smug grin.

The Obersturmbannführer ignored him and instead turned to Prinz and Prahl. 'So if we cannot encircle the farm, how else should we attack? Any ideas?'

Prinz spoke up. 'The armoured car.'

'Sorry?'

'We should put three or four men in the armoured car and just drive up the road to the front of the farmhouse. Once they get within twenty metres or so they can get out and launch their assault from there, using the car as cover. The vehicle should be well able to survive contact with any of the mines as they are only designed to be effective against infantry.'

Prahl put in, 'It is an excellent idea, sir. The officers in the armoured car will at the very least be able to draw his fire which will enable the others to approach safely. If we can get enough men within ten or fifteen metres our numbers will overwhelm him.'

Koestler took a couple of minutes to consider the opinions of each man. He wandered over to the foot of the dirt track and glanced up, following the gentle bend with his eyes until the road was swallowed up by the burgeoning forest. Finally he came back over and nodded. 'Okay, that could work. I think it may be our best hope for a swift resolution. Prinz, please see to the arrangements. Horvath, return to your post and hold the perimeter. Sneijder must not under any circumstances be allowed to slip away.'

Horvath made one last attempt to make his opinion heard. 'Why don't we just wait for him to come out? It surely will not be that long.'

'Why not?' Koestler retorted. 'It is a farm which contains wheat fields and two very large grain silos – he will be rather unlikely to run out of food, wouldn't you say? In any case, if I wait, the Wehrmacht and the Waffen-SS will probably reassign all the men and Sneijder will get away. I will not allow that. We shall go with Prinz's plan.'

In the farmhouse, the tall grandfather clock struck eight o'clock. Lamming was snoozing on the sofa in the front room while Sneijder sat at the window keeping watch. After several days of being constantly alert he was exhausted, and was really struggling to hold himself together. The tension was unbearable. Knowing that every minute might be his last was extremely difficult, and he longed for it all to be over.

Sneijder was brought out of his trance by the sound of an engine, which gradually became louder. There was an explosion from the direction of the entrance road as one of the mines went off. Moments later the front end of a dark grey armoured car appeared around the bend and started to emerge from the woods.

Sneijder released the safety catch on the MG-42 with a loud click. Lamming stirred at the sound. Sneijder was relieved to notice that the car did not have guns of any sort; he opened fire with a short burst. There was a loud metallic clanging as the rounds struck the steel armour of the vehicle. Despite the ineffectiveness of the shots the armoured car swerved hard to one side and slowed to a stop. A group of men appeared from behind and started to move towards the farm.

'Are they coming?' Lamming asked.

Sneijder did not need to answer. When the German officers were about a hundred and seventy-five metres away he fired another burst with the MG-42 but failed to hit anything. They dived to the ground and covered their heads with their hands. Sneijder raked the ground with machine gun fire and then turned to Lamming who was struggling to his feet. 'Are you all right?'

'Yes, no problem. Keep an eye on them.'

The first German got to his feet and sprinted forward; Sneijder fired at him and he fell to the ground. The other three headed back down the track and disappeared from view.

'Is that it?' Lamming asked.

Sneijder opened fire once more on the stationary armoured car, only stopping when the ammunition belt ran out. As he reached for another belt he heard gunfire. Bullets struck the wall outside the window. He dropped down out of sight until the firing ceased.

Lamming reached the other window where the Bren was situated and began to prepare it for firing. He glanced quickly over to Sneijder. 'Good luck, my boy.'

'And to you,' Sneijder replied. 'I think we're going to need it.' He fed the next belt into the machine gun and closed the feed cover, opened the bolt and sprung up again. The armoured car was moving towards him once more, rapidly closing the distance. It provided cover for two or three men who were gathered behind it. Sneijder took careful aim and let off a two-second burst, striking one of them with a head-shot as he struggled to keep up with the car. Lamming fired too but was well wide. The Germans returned fire from their position a hundred and fifty metres away. Sneijder took cover.

'My God,' Lamming suddenly exclaimed. 'There are so many of them.'

Sneijder peered gingerly over the edge of the windowsill. The armoured car slowed down and drew to a halt about twenty-five metres away in the centre of the courtyard, with its left side facing towards the farmhouse. Sneijder kept his machine gun trained on it, expecting to see the car's occupants appear from behind it at any moment. A dozen or so men began to appear from the edge of the woods, following the path taken by the vehicle. Sneijder did not know who to aim at.

As the larger group approached the courtyard they started to spread out, making it impossible for Sneijder to cover them. He called over to Lamming, 'You'll have to take them, especially the ones on the left-hand side, next to the barn!'

'I'll give it my best shot,' the old man replied. He let off a burst with the Bren and caught two of the Germans though his aim was generally a little off.

Three figures popped up either side of the armoured car and shot at Sneijder, forcing him to drop out of sight once more. He fired blindly while he had his head down, then grabbed a grenade from a pile on the floor and pulled out the pin. With great care he swung his arm up and propelled the grenade out of the window in the general direction of the enemy. There was a loud boom as the Mills bomb exploded; when Sneijder looked up two of the Germans were lying face down on the ground not ten metres away. One looked to be dead. The other started to get to his feet. Sneijder mowed him down with an arc of withering fire.

Away to the left, three men approached rapidly. Lamming shot at them; however he was obviously struggling with the recoil of the weapon and he shot well over their heads. They continued to bear down on him, shooting back with their MP40s and he took cover.

Sneijder and Lamming were fighting a losing battle. Facing an enemy with such superior numbers, they were continually forced to seek cover which gave the Germans the opportunity to close in. Soon they were close enough that they could use the walls of the barn and stable to protect themselves. The old man Lamming was putting up a brave display but his age and the weight of the Bren were starting to tell. Understandably his shooting was wayward.

'Keep it up the best you can,' Sneijder shouted to him. 'We've got to hold them off as long as possible. If we're going, let's take some of them with us.' It was futile, he knew that, but he wasn't going down without a fight. He was scared, and had it not been for the adrenaline coursing through his veins the fear would have gripped him entirely. Instead he was forced on by his sheer will to survive.

The old man found the target with a couple of shots, driving the German officers back. He began changing the magazine on the Bren. 'Perhaps I am too old for this nonsense,' he puffed.

'Listen, you really don't need to do this,' Sneijder reassured him. 'It's not too late to go. You owe me nothing.'

'I owe it to my grandson and to my people,' Lamming answered. 'Kees was prepared to risk his life; so should I be.'

'You have risked your life but it's all over,' Sneijder said. 'In five minutes they'll be coming through the door.'

Lamming did not reply. He popped up to fire the machine gun. Before he could release a single round there was a rifle shot from behind the stable wall. Sneijder turned to see the high-velocity round hit the old man in the forehead, tearing away one side of his skull with horrifying ease. The speed of the bullet knocked him backwards, away from the window. He slumped down on top of a wooden table. Blood poured from his head.

Sneijder looked away in horror, but there was no time to be upset. A couple of Gestapo officers were heading across the courtyard. He tried to fire at them with the MG-42 but as it was prone to do on a weapon with such a high rate of fire, the barrel had overheated and the gun would not operate. In desperation Sneijder took a grenade in each hand, removed the pins with his teeth and tossed them over his head and out of the window. There was a Walther P-38 pistol on the floor and Sneijder picked it up and cocked it; as the two grenades went off he scampered to his feet and moved through to the kitchen.

His body literally shaking with fear, he stood with his back pressed against the wall beside the doorway. All of a sudden, the place fell silent. The guns ceased firing. He waited.

Sneijder considered all that had happened in his short, eventful and ultimately painful life. He had always felt guilty about leaving his family behind and fleeing to Switzerland, but at the time he had expected them to join him within weeks. He had acted with the best intentions, hadn't he? Sneijder quickly put that to one side. He could not blame himself for the way things had turned out. His decision to go to England once they failed to arrive was also sound; he could never have forgiven himself for sitting back and not contributing to the war effort. Everything after that had been beyond his control - he had done what he needed to do in order to survive, not all of it particularly palatable but that was surely the nature of war.

The thought of all the men he had killed tore him up inside and made him feel physically sick. He had been brought up in a strictly moral family, always being told what was right and wrong, but he had done things which fell very much on the dark side of that divide. But could he have done things any other way? Sneijder consoled himself with the knowledge that he had served his country the best he could, and every time he had killed it had been necessary.

Sneijder's introspective musings were halted by the unmistakable click of a revolver being cocked, and there was now the gentle whisper of a man breathing. He knew beyond all doubt who it was.

'Mr Sneijder, it is time to surrender,' Koestler called into the house. 'You cannot possibly escape and you know it - I do not believe you are an idiot.'

Sneijder did not move. He shouted back, 'And you expect me to believe you will not shoot me on the spot? You do think I am an idiot.'

'This is where it ends,' Koestler replied harshly. 'You have killed everyone that is close to me, you have tried to kill me and I shall have my revenge. How unpleasant that revenge is will be up to you. Come out at once.'

Sneijder breathed deeply. 'You know I never meant to kill Frauke,' he shouted, tears forming in the corners of his eyes. 'I loved her – really, I did.'

'Don't you dare even speak her name!' the German exploded. 'She was far too good for the likes of you so don't even pretend she felt the same.'

Sneijder rested his head back on the doorframe and managed a bittersweet smile. 'She loved me. And she hated you, for all the evil things you have done, for all those innocent people you have murdered. The way you act sickened her.'

Koestler gave a small laugh. 'You and I are not so different, Mr Sneijder. We are in an ugly business and we get our hands dirty. Don't delude yourself into thinking you can condemn me as something you are not.'

'I am nothing like you! You have destroyed entire villages, killed and deported innocent women and children, brutalised thousands! Don't try to tell me I'm like you. I could never be like you.'

'You are a murderer, plain and simple,' Koestler told him. 'A cold-blooded killer.'

'I am a patriot!' Sneijder answered, peering around the corner. He could just about make out Koestler's shadow on the far wall. 'I came here to serve my country and that is exactly what I have done.'

'Why do you think I have done all these things you speak of?' Koestler asked. 'Because I enjoy it? I do my duty for the Fatherland and I always will. This, however, is not for Germany but for me.' There was a gunshot as

Koestler fired through the window, striking the wall, and sending Sneijder sprawling. 'This is your last opportunity to give yourself up.'

There was silence for a few seconds, and Sneijder did not respond. He leaned around the door and fired a shot in the general direction of Koestler's voice.

'Final warning!' the German shouted. 'If you surrender now I shall not have you tortured before I kill you. We do not need to find out if you squeal like Van Rijn.'

Still Sneijder did not answer. After a minute there was movement outside, and then came the sound of a grenade being dropped on the other side of the front door. Sneijder threw himself under the kitchen table and covered his head as the initial boom gave way to the sound of wood being ripped apart. An MP40 opened up and shredded the fabric of the sofa standing behind the now-nonexistent door. The Germans flooded into the sitting room of the farmhouse and Sneijder raised his pistol to fire, but suddenly there were shots from behind the policemen.

Koestler saw them at the last minute. He gave the order for his men to storm the farmhouse, but at the exact moment the grenade dropped to the ground outside the door the gunfire began. The sound was not that of any German weapon; he recognised that immediately. Koestler spun around to see four officers being cut down. Two more sprinted ahead but they too were shot. Koestler watched in horror as one of them stumbled to the ground less than a metre from him, his eyes wide in surprise and shock.

Koestler saw the green flash of a British uniform, then another. A Browning pistol fired at him. Instinctively, he ran. Koestler entered the farmhouse, stepping over the German soldiers as they were cut down. He ran straight through the kitchen, wrenched the back door open and sprinted out into the fields. There were bursts of fire behind him but he didn't look back. Although he knew there were mines here he did not break step. If he stopped he was a dead man.

From his position hiding under the kitchen table, Sneijder saw Koestler rush by. He fired a wild shot, striking the wall. Without a thought he leapt out from safety and gave chase. When he got outside Koestler was already halfway across the field and moving at a surprisingly quick pace. Sneijder veered to the right and followed the tree-line to avoid the mines he had planted.

Koestler disappeared into the woods ahead. Sneijder reached the same point about twenty seconds later, running hard and breathing heavily. He darted into the trees and was momentarily unable to see in the gloom. As his eyes adjusted he was able to see a short distance ahead. Sneijder stopped running and tried to listen. He held his breath.

The forest was silent and there was no movement visible. Koestler must have stopped somewhere ahead. In all probability he would now be waiting behind a tree, ready to take a shot at Sneijder as he passed. Sneijder crouched down and looked around him. Nothing. He raised the Walther in front of his eye and gently crept forward.

A gust of wind rippled through the woods, silently teasing the branches of the pine trees. A cone dropped to the ground behind Sneijder and he jumped. His heart pounded. When he had recovered a little he continued to move. There was still no sign of the German as Sneijder reached a small clearing.

There was a gunshot from somewhere and birds scattered away to the left. A second shot ricocheted off a tree trunk a metre to Sneijder's right and he threw himself down. A figure flashed through the woods just ahead. Sneijder rolled over and fired three shots quickly. Koestler let out a yell and crashed down through the undergrowth, then his cries were gone. Sneijder stood up and ran forward.

He came over a small rise and pushed the branches of the trees aside. About five metres ahead the ground dropped away; Koestler was lying at the bottom of the depression, obviously wounded. As Sneijder got closer he could see blood running from a large hole in his right thigh. He was breathing deeply, his head resting on the ground.

Koestler raised his head to look at Sneijder. He sighed as he approached, then gave a resigned smile. 'So, it has come to this.'

'It would appear so.' Sneijder stood over him, pointing his Walther at him.

Koestler laughed gently. He moved a hand slowly towards his pocket but stopped when Sneijder fingered the trigger. He opened his hand and continued, making sure Sneijder could watch every move. Out of his pocket came his hip flask. Koestler took a swig, then reached out and offered it to Sneijder.

Sneijder shook his head.

Koestler grinned weakly. 'It's good stuff.' He emptied the contents of the hip flask into his mouth and threw it aside. 'Right, you'd better get on with it, hadn't you?'

Sneijder did nothing. He stood completely still, the pistol trained on Koestler.

'Well are you going to do it or not?' Koestler challenged.

Sneijder frowned. 'She wouldn't want me to. You're her father.'

Koestler chuckled. 'Why do we do it, eh?'

'I know why I do...' Sneijder began.

Koestler's left hand flew up in the air clutching his revolver. Sneijder fired a single shot, the last in the clip, hitting the German in the heart and slamming him flat against the ground. As his arm hit the dirt the gun discharged, scattering a flock of pigeons in the tree beside them. Then it was silence.

When Sneijder returned to the farmhouse he found all of the Germans dead. A group of soldiers in green uniform were going round the bodies collecting tags. Before he could ask what was happening a grey-haired man who was standing in the corner of the sitting room turned around. 'Ah, there you are, Sneijder.'

Sneijder was astonished. The man he was looking at was Harry Wilkinson.

Later, with the farm secured and the bodies removed from the farmhouse, Sneijder and Wilkinson sat at the kitchen table drinking Lamming's strong home-made whisky and filling each other in on what had happened. Sneijder was surprised to hear that the paratroop drop in Arnhem was actually part of the biggest airborne operation ever mounted, with similar drops around Nijmegen and Eindhoven, and that ground troops were currently fighting their way northwards.

'All objectives have been achieved except the capture of the Rhine Bridge in Arnhem, but from what I hear the situation there is not good,' Wilkinson explained. 'The troops have been almost completely wiped out - you got out just in time. We're just hoping that some of the men can be salvaged.'

'For how long has this operation been planned? It all seemed so sudden; we never heard so much as a rumour.'

'As far as I know, it was only mooted at the start of this month. Since you left England the advance through France and Belgium has been extraordinary – the Germans have been retreating at a ridiculous pace. I'm not up to speed on all the details naturally, what with security and everything, but as I understand it Field Marshal Montgomery felt he had them on the run and that if he could get a bridgehead over the Rhine he could get into Germany.'

'It came as a shock, I can tell you.' Sneijder grimaced as he remembered the battle he had had to get through to escape. 'Some of the fighting I saw was brutal.'

Wilkinson sighed. 'Yes, that is the way of it, war. Just be grateful that you have not had to endure the horrors of battle.' He looked around the room, observing the bullet holes in the walls and added humorously, 'Although you have made a spirited effort.'

Sneijder said, 'You still haven't told me how you found me. I presume you received my message.'

'As soon as I found out about the assault on Arnhem I told the clerks at the wireless station to keep an eye out for messages from you,' Wilkinson went on. 'I was hoping we'd get a break and so it proved.'

'You expected a message from me?' Sneijder asked in surprise.

The Brigadier leant back in his chair and smiled. 'Well, you're a resourceful chap. I didn't think you'd be able to get out and in that case you'd have no choice but to signal for help.'

'I don't know what I thought would happen but I didn't expect you to come in person,' said the young agent.

'It was the only way I could be sure to get you out,' Wilkinson replied. 'Because of all the trouble we have had in Holland with double agents the armed forces are under orders not to liaise in any way with the Resistance. Nothing I said would get them to assist you, so I knew I had to come and take charge myself. One of our commando units dropped in with the paratroops but now Arnhem is a lost cause I pulled rank and took them back under SOE control. Those are the gentlemen outside.'

Sneijder sighed. 'Thank God you came. I was a dead man for sure.'

'It was the least I could do,' Wilkinson said. 'Tell me about Koestler.'

Sneijder gave the Brigadier a suitably abridged version of events relating to his attempt to assassinate Koestler. He omitted his self-doubt and guilt, and especially his relationship with Frauke, and stuck to the facts. He explained about the accident, Koestler's miraculous escape and the attempt to shoot him, and the confrontation at the farm. Then he brought up the issue of Guido de Beer's apparent collaboration with the Germans.

Wilkinson was visibly shocked. 'Are you absolutely sure? There is no way it could be a mistake?'

'I didn't believe it myself at first,' Sneijder replied, 'but I saw the evidence with my own eyes. His name appears several times on documents that were stolen from Koestler's office, one of which is a list of informants paid by the SS for their information. It seems that before he escaped to England, De Beer was given the sum of two hundred guilders for information which led to the arrest and execution of nineteen members of the Dutch Underground.'

'It couldn't be another man with the same name?'

Sneijder shook his head. 'There were photographs too, of the most prolific informants. A picture of him was amongst them.'

'My God,' Wilkinson blurted out.

'These were pretty obscure files,' Sneijder continued. 'I should think there was a good chance they could have remained undiscovered. But if Koestler had talked, whenever the war was to end, it could have come out. I think De Beer wanted to silence him.'

Wilkinson thought for a moment and then hissed angrily, 'The bastard. Using us both like that - and I believed him!'

'At the time you had no reason to doubt him, sir,' Sneijder reassured him. 'He has obviously fooled a lot of people, some of whom know him much better than you do. The question is, what should we do about it?'

Wilkinson's face was as hard as Sneijder had ever seen it as he said calmly, 'Mark my words - he will not get away with it. You can leave that to me.'

Sneijder gave a terrible grin. 'Yes, well perhaps we can discuss that.'

Wilkinson nodded slowly. For the next few seconds there was silence as the two men contemplated the situation, both thinking about the best way to deal with De Beer. After pondering for a moment Sneijder changed the subject and finally raised the question which he had dreaded to ask.

'Sir, did you find out anything about my family?' The words coming out of his mouth made him wince a little. 'I know there is not.....'

'Yes, I was coming to that,' Wilkinson said quietly and a little uncomfortably. He looked at Sneijder opposite intently. 'I'm terribly sorry, dear chap, I'm afraid it's not good news. When the Gestapo burned out your neighbourhood your family were sent to Westerbork - what I believe the Germans call a transit camp. From my various contacts and informants I gather that from there they were sent to another camp in the East. Nothing has been heard of them since mid-1943.'

Sneijder's head dropped, but there was no display of emotion. The truth was that he had accepted their deaths a long time ago, and while it was a hammer blow to hear such a depressing outlook, he was not shocked or surprised.

'I will continue to investigate it, of course, but it is not looking good. You should be prepared for the worst.' Wilkinson smiled a little. 'I do have one piece of news which is much better however. It's about your sister, Janna.'

Sneijder looked up. 'Yes?'

'We have found her, alive and well. Somehow she managed to escape like you to Switzerland.'

For a few seconds Sneijder did not react. In stunned disbelief he stared blankly, and then the emotion was too much for him and he broke down. His unbridled joy at hearing of Janna's survival was tempered by the despair of knowing he had lost everyone else; the conflicting feelings grasped his heart and squeezed so tight that he thought they would never let go. 'Alive? You are sure?'

Wilkinson took a roll of paper from his pocket and flattened it out. 'Here is the address. From what you have told us about your own circumstances, it seems she reached Nyon just a week after you left to come to England.'

'And is she well?' Sneijder asked anxiously. 'Please tell me she is okay.'

'I believe she is fine, but you can see for yourself,' said Wilkinson. 'I think you've earned a long rest after this. I'll see what I can do about getting you a ride to Switzerland.'

'Thank you, sir. Thank you very much.'

Sneijder sat back in his chair, breathed deeply and raised his eyes skyward. After all the waiting, the years of hurt and pain, the fear and the death, finally he had heard some positive news. The euphoria of knowing he would see one of them again numbed him to the devastation of losing everyone else, and for the moment he could not even begin to process the experiences of the past three months. His feelings about what happened would not become clear until much later but he was certain about one thing. The summer of 1944 would live with him forever.

CHAPTER TWENTY–SIX

It was a chilly October afternoon even though the sun was out, with a bitter north wind blowing across London. Dark clouds hovered in the distance, threatening rain in the next hour or so. Harry Wilkinson sat on a bench in St James' Park in a long overcoat, his head down and his face obscured by the hat pulled over his brow. He checked his watch as he waited, grunting irritably at the tardiness of the man he was to meet.

Sneijder stood hidden behind a group of trees about twenty-five metres from Wilkinson, near enough to be within earshot but well-concealed in a dark green jacket. He watched the short round figure of De Beer approach the park bench, a newspaper tucked under his arm, and sit down at the opposite end of the seat. He opened the paper wide in front of his face and then said, 'Okay, Harry, what is so important that it couldn't have waited until tomorrow?'

'I don't know, Guido,' Wilkinson replied cryptically. 'You tell me.'

'What is that supposed to mean?' De Beer asked.

Wilkinson ignored the question. 'I presume you heard about Koestler. We got him.'

'Yes, but your man very nearly blew the whole thing. I heard that you had to go and bail him out.'

'I hardly think you can blame him when half of the British Army suddenly descended upon him,' Wilkinson replied. 'That sort of thing does tend to make the Germans a little jumpy.'

'For God's sake, Harry, we put him in at the beginning of July,' De Beer said. 'How long did he need? We had already established that Koestler had virtually nothing in the way of security.'

'It's all academic now,' the Brigadier declared. 'Koestler is dead and the mission was a success. I should think you are particularly pleased about that.'

'Well, of course. To have Dutch citizens in the SS is morally unacceptable.'

Wilkinson continued to press him. 'But more so, it must be a huge weight off your shoulders, not to have that hanging over you.'

De Beer looked a little bewildered. 'I suppose.'

'I mean, with Koestler gone you're in the clear. It has all worked out perfectly.'

'What the hell are you talking about?' De Beer suddenly snapped. 'If you've got something to say then say it – I didn't come the whole way out here to play games.'

Sneijder could not suppress a smile. Wilkinson had De Beer rattled all right. It was a good feeling to watch him squirm.

'You know, Guido, I always wondered why you were so interested in eliminating this Koestler chap,' Wilkinson said, 'even to the point of defying the direct orders of Queen Wilhelmina. For all the explanations and patriotic ramblings, it still didn't really make any sense. However I figured that I was in your debt after that business with my agent in Rotterdam so I went along with it. I risked the life of one of my finest men. But it wasn't really anything to do with patriotism, was it? Well, nobody's but yours.'

De Beer put down the newspaper and turned to face Wilkinson. 'Are you trying to accuse me of something?'

'It seems that while Sneijder was over in Arnhem some interesting facts came to light,' Wilkinson continued. 'By chance he came into possession of some documents – files which were stolen from Koestler's office, files which detailed payments made to informants over several years, right back to mid-1941. Some of these informants were paid vast sums of money for information which led to the execution of Resistance fighters.'

'And?'

'There was an interesting name on the list. Someone who since getting out of Holland has projected himself as a man determined to serve his country, has condemned traitors at every turn, has sent other men to their deaths in pursuit of an ideal. It was very unfortunate that these files came out because with Koestler dead the whole dirty business could have disappeared.'

De Beer glowered and asked aggressively, 'What is it you think you know, Harry? If you want to question my integrity you'd better have some strong evidence.'

'You want to know what I think, Guido?' Wilkinson said. 'I think that while you were in Holland you were doing some pretty good business selling out your countrymen, taking cash from the Germans and sending real patriots to their deaths. You and Koestler had an excellent deal going but then something happened – things got too hot, perhaps you really did see the error of your ways. Either way you ended up over here, working for the government-in-exile. But with the Allied invasion being so successful the end of the war suddenly appeared imminent, and with that would come the capture and probable interrogation of high-ranking German officers - officers who were likely to want to talk in order to try to save their own lives.'

De Beer sneered, 'You don't know what you are talking about.'

Wilkinson went on. 'You decided that Koestler needed to be got rid of to stop him talking, in the knowledge that his files would probably remain hidden if he died. So you decided to use me, and so I became a pawn in using Sneijder.'

'Where's your evidence?' De Beer asked mockingly.

'You made me send that boy into the lion's den, almost to his death, to cover up your own treason!' Wilkinson exploded. 'You sat there and let me talk him into it, under the pretence that he would be serving his country. How dare you use me like that?'

'I suppose Sneijder told you all this?' said De Beer. 'You are relying on his word that these documents exist? It never crossed your mind that perhaps he was giving you an excuse for his failure to do his duty?'

'The evidence is there,' Wilkinson argued.

'But you haven't got it,' the Dutchman declared. 'Otherwise you would have brought a copy with you to prove to me that you have it. In fact, I'll bet that you haven't even seen it.'

Wilkinson's face was blank as he looked the other man in the eye, displaying no hint of emotion. 'Are you sure about that? Willing to put your life on it?'

De Beer stood up from the bench and turned to face Wilkinson. 'I am not prepared to listen to this. This is all nonsense, the idle fantasies of an agent with far less going for him than you might like to imagine.'

'Yet you have not denied it. Not once.'

'The thing is, Harry,' De Beer replied pointedly, 'if you have no evidence, I don't need to. This is all just the deluded speculation of a paranoid and overworked old man. Nobody will believe it. Now if you don't mind, I have important things to do.'

As De Beer turned and started to walk away, Wilkinson shouted after him. 'We have copies of the evidence. And I'll bet there are hundreds of documents sitting around in offices in Holland just waiting to be read by intelligence officers once the war is over. The thing is, Guido, now we know what to look for, you will be finished, forever branded a traitor. Even in a country like yours, which is so against the death penalty, I should think they will hang you out to dry. Well, hang you, anyway.'

'You don't have anything,' De Beer answered.

'Face it, Major, it's over. It's all just a matter of time before the truth comes out. You could save your country a lot of shame and embarrassment if you went straight back to your office and used that pistol you keep in the bottom drawer. Try to keep the little dignity you have left.'

'I'll take my chances,' De Beer insisted. He turned and began to walk away.

Sneijder moved out from behind the trees and glanced at Wilkinson. The Brigadier nodded. Once De Beer had got a little way ahead, Sneijder started to follow.

The Major left St James' Park at the southeast corner and headed east towards the river. Another of Wilkinson's agents was standing behind a newspaper stand on Parliament Square and he took over the duty of tailing him, replacing Sneijder who dropped off for a moment. De Beer continued beyond the Houses of Parliament and onto Westminster Bridge, crossing the Thames. Sneijder peeled off his overcoat and left it behind. Now wearing an entirely different colour of clothing he merged into the crowd and followed them across the bridge, keeping the other agent in view.

It began to rain as De Beer descended the steps onto the Albert Embankment which ran alongside the river. Watching from the bridge above, Sneijder saw him turn his collar up against the poor weather. A third agent moved out from the shadows and started to tail him.

It was now almost certain that De Beer was heading for his flat on Lambeth Road. Sneijder left the other agent to follow him and moved away from the river, around the back of the St Thomas Hospital. Having removed his own overcoat he was soaked thoroughly and he cursed his luck. He quickened his pace as he cut across the gardens of Lambeth Palace. At the end of the path Sneijder stepped behind a hedgerow and waited.

De Beer appeared around the corner a couple of minutes later, striding purposefully. The agent following him was now only a few steps behind and closing in. As De Beer dipped a hand into his pocket to find his keys he seemed to be suddenly aware of the man's presence. He looked over his shoulder quickly, an expression of panic on his face. Sneijder stepped out in front of him at the last moment. De Beer barrelled right into him and spun around, facing the other agent.

'Hey, wait a minute, what is this?' De Beer asked in alarm.

'You know exactly what this is,' the man in front of him replied in Dutch. 'Liquidation of a target.'

'No, hang on....' De Beer began.

Sneijder leaned in behind him and spoke in his ear. 'I think you should have thought about it a little earlier, Major.'

De Beer turned in astonishment. 'Sneijder, you...'

He never had the chance to complete the sentence. He was grabbed roughly from behind by the other agent, his arms pulled back, and propelled into the bushes. As he flew past, Sneijder already had the knife out of his pocket and the blade flicked open. He jabbed it into De Beer's body just below his ribs and gave it a twist. It was out again before he started to fall. The other agent moved in and plunged his knife into De Beer's back with terrific force, ramming the blade straight through his heart. The Major did not so much as cry out. His body shook and then he was still.

Sneijder felt no emotion as he wiped the blood from the end of the weapon. He hated himself for it.

Epilogue

Sneijder checked the address on the slip of paper in his hand as he walked slowly up the path. In front of him was a nondescript grey apartment block, the type of which could be found in any number of European cities. It was definitely the place; the large red letters emblazoned on the façade confirmed it. Sneijder moved to the front door of the building, pushed it open and carried on up the stairs inside.

At the top of the second flight of steps he turned into a narrow corridor which was cold and rather gloomy. There was a notice board on the right-hand side with messages in both French and German pinned on it. Sneijder reached the door he was searching for; flat number 2F. He knocked twice loudly. There was no answer. His heart sank.

For a few minutes he stood leaning against the wall, unsure what to do. Was she just out, as was more than possible, or was she not there at all? Wilkinson had been fairly certain that this was the correct address. Sneijder checked his watch. It was approaching six o'clock so if she had been working she would probably be on her way home now.

Sneijder went back downstairs and outside. Now that he knew which flat it was he was able to identify its windows on the front of the building. However there was a net curtain drawn across both of them and he could not see in. He sat himself down on a low stone wall which ran along the front of the garden. Out of the corner of his eye he saw a young couple walking arm-in-arm towards the row of shops across the street and he turned. The woman disappeared from view inside the bakery at the same moment, and the young man dressed in a dark suit removed his hat and followed. Sneijder looked away.

He did not notice them coming out again five minutes later. As they approached he was still looking in the opposite direction, but then the man said something and the woman laughed. Sneijder instantly recognised that laugh, one which he had heard so much during his child-hood. His head snapped around.

The woman noticed him instantly and stopped dead. Her hand caught her companion's elbow and she gasped. 'Johannes?'

Tears welled up in Sneijder's eyes as he was confronted with a face he had never expected to see again, with a pretty smile and big eyes. 'Yes, it's me, Janna. It's me.'

The man looked confused but Janna said something in French and his expression changed to shock and then amazement. Janna rushed forward and embraced Snei-jder and began to weep. 'Oh, Johannes, I don't believe you're alive!'

'Janna,' Sneijder said as he broke down. 'My beauti-ful sister.' He wrapped his arms around her and held her tight, squeezing her against his chest. For a minute he did not let her go and all the emotions he had kept inside flooded out. He had lost so many people over the past years but finally there was somebody he could hold on to. It felt good.

Printed in the United Kingdom by
Lightning Source UK Ltd., Milton Keynes
138396UK00001B/1/P